LEO CULLEN was born in County Tipperary and now lives in Monkstown, County Dublin. His collection of short stories, *Clocking Ninety on the Road to Cloughjordan and Other Stories*, was published by Blackstaff Press in 1994.

let's twist again

leo cullen

THE
BLACKSTAFF
PRESS

BELFAST

I would like to thank the following for their encouragement and direction: Ciaran Folan, Anthony Glavin, Oliver Marshall, David Marcus, John Kelly and cohorts.

Thanks also to family, both near and far.

Finally, I am grateful to the Arts Council/An Chomhairle Ealaíon for their financial help.

Extracts from *Let's Twist Again* have appeared in the following magazines, journals and books: *Force 10, Phoenix Book of Irish Short Stories '97* (Phoenix, 1997), *Wildeside Literary Magazine*, the *Sunday Independent, Writers Abú: Prizewinning Stories of Tipperary*, and *Exhibitions* (Arsenal Pulp Press, 2000). Excerpts have also been broadcast on the BBC World Service.

First published in 2001 by
The Blackstaff Press Limited
Wildflower Way, Apollo Road
Belfast BT12 6TA
with the assistance of
the Arts Council of Northern Ireland

ARTS
COUNCIL
of Northern Ireland

Typeset by Techniset Typesetters, Newton-le-Willows, Merseyside

Printed in Ireland by ColourBooks Limited

A CIP catalogue record for this book
is available from the British Library

ISBN 0-85640-695-3

www.blackstaffpress.com

For Carole, Emlyn, Lewis, Finn

To the memory of our young friends,
Graham Byrne and Robbie O'Neill

this train is bound for glory . . .
BOB MARLEY

PART 1

1

When I was eight and a half and a great judge of people out around the wide world of our street my father went away and did something. I did not know what it was. We had to leave our town. My father, the great horseman that I knew, had to take his horses and take everything. And me, rootin' shootin' cowboy who'd roamed all that town's OK Corrals, I had to leave all my six-gun pistols behind. After a long journey through the country we came to a house. Attached to it was an old castle. The castle had a crack in its side, where it bulged as if it might burst open. The house was named Ivyhall. This house, standing on its own, not another house or street anywhere, had a very forbidding look. We went inside. It was supposed to be our new home. But we found another family already sitting there. In the kitchen there was a smell of something slightly sour. Was it milk; milk for the making of bread? I did not know what it was.

What my father had done was to get married. It wasn't the sort of thing I would have expected him to do. What the sour smell turned out to be was the smell of kitchen tables scoured with caustic soda. She told me. The woman. 'Careful of that stuff, or it'll burn a hole in you,' she said. What the woman turned out to be was someone I was supposed to call my new mother.

Ten years I would live in that house of Ivyhall. I was eighteen and a half when I left. Ten years is short. Looking back on it now, ten years seems nothing. But I would think then that it was a lifetime. And in a way it was. With a beginning, and an end. What do you do in a lifetime? Learn things about what you do not know? I was supposed to know about caustic soda. What I did not know and could not understand about caustic soda was how stuff that looked white and harmless as salt, not as much as a flicker of a flame out if it, could burn holes in a young fellow. I was supposed to know the woman. And did not know her either. Mrs Connell was her name. Or used to be her name. Now what was it? Same name as my own? I could not make head nor tail of her. There was once upon a time a young fellow who walked the town with the widest main street in all of Ireland, who knew everybody in it, who had only to say hello to the people he passed and was already able to make judgement on whether or not they were willing to part with money so that he could buy himself ice-pops; and now he did not even know her, his new mother, from Adam. What was his world coming to at all? He knew nothing and had a long way to learn.

The day we drove into that place I had started upon a lifetime. That was the first day. The year was 1957. Here is the last day: it is ten years later. A lifetime has ended.

Now when you came down the stairs the doorway was a gaping hole. The men had removed the hall door because that was the only way to get out the big sideboards. When you went outside, the gravelled yard dazzled you with light. Furniture swayed out of the house and surfaces that had gleamed with indoor polish were hit by sunlight that stole their sheen away. It was like a procession, the May or Corpus Christi procession. Like streaming out of a church into the uncluttered light of day.

'Don't scrape the walls,' my father said. 'Mind the furniture.'

We made a hundred careful journeys down the stairs. We held our tongues between our lips in concentration; careful as could be with the furniture, careful not to hit one another. We worked earnestly, without pause, on our manoeuvres along the wide, shallow-stepped stairs. There were my brothers, my sisters, myself, our neighbours, who were named Fern and Thos. We were moving my family's furniture out of Ivyhall. 'Which belongs to Connells and which belongs to Connaughtons?' One lot went out the door; the other lot stayed put. I smelled the polish and I smelled the dust and I kept going.

But once I did pause. I stopped on the landing. I closed my eyes and tried to imagine what it would all look like from outside; from the position of someone looking down on it all. That was something I often did then: lifted myself from a situation and just looked as if from outside. A great trick if, say, you had fallen into a spot of bother or something like that. Calmed you down. Also, not that it would have been my intention, but when you saw things in such a way – from beyond rather than within – they stayed in your mind. In that very way has Ivyhall remained with me: that last day, I am full grown. I have not learned as much as I might have. I am high up on the hill, or even up in the sky, looking down.

Or maybe it was all some other time that Ivyhall became stuck in my mind. One of the times, maybe, when I really was up on that hill above the house. One day between my eighth and my eighteenth birthday. I used to stand up there and look at the chaos below. I would watch closely; I would listen for sounds from the kitchen and from the yard. I would gauge the mood of the moment.

Or maybe it didn't happen that way at all. And Ivyhall, simply, seeped into my veins.

Ivyhall: a big house, with an old Norman castle attached. Tufts of wild ivy grow out of the castle. The house and castle together sit

5

like a huge block on the level yard, the one level piece of land there is in all that country.

Yet, looking from my vantage point above, in the high sloping hills, in the cypress trees and tumbling heather, Ivyhall seems almost insignificant. There is a silence down there on this last day as we are packing up to leave. It gathers about the car and horsebox lorry parked in the centre of the yard. Figures of people stand in the silence, frozen by it. And figures of dogs – low slinking bodies with tails outstretched like branches of young fir trees. On the front wall of the house, three up three down, are six evenly spaced rectangles. Well, six normally but today only five. Five windows, like plates, they crackle in the sun's intensity. Where should be the door, the sixth plate, is today a broken hole plunging into the cavernous dark of the house. The door has been taken off its hinges and lies slumped against the castle wall. It is a white door, sunlight flakes off it, makes a halo round the ivy into which it has fallen. It has taken its opportunity to lie back, a first rest in a lifetime of scraping open and shut against the gravel beneath it.

There is a photo too, I should mention it just in case what I remember is only the imprint of the photo on my mind. This can happen: your memory can persuade you that black was white.

A little aeroplane flew over one day, right above all of us as we ran out on the yard, our hands to our eyes looking up. They did that, flew around and took aerial photographs of farms and then offered the photos for sale. That photo went with us to our new home. I do not know how it was not lost in the upheavals of our reconstructed lives. At some stage it became mine. It followed me around on my travels from place to place. Until it got left behind somewhere. We are all there in the photo. And the dogs are in it, and the car is in it. Mam is in it. Mam, impassive, broad-faced, as ever. She is standing in the very centre of the yard. She is looking up and she holds a tea-towel in her hand. She is not waving the tea-towel, just holding it, probably because she had been at the wash-up when the plane arrived. (It surprises me that, now I come to think of it, Mam doing the wash-up: Mam never did the wash-up. Or not that I can remember. Scrubbed the table with caustic soda all right; never did the wash-up. My sisters and stepsisters did the wash-up. Or Dancie did it, our housekeeper. It is interesting what the memory likes to discard, and what it likes to retain.)

We were younger then, when that airborne camera captured us and panned us out across our yard. We were younger and deeper in wonderment; woven, as we thought, into the heart of the country for all our lives. Not knowing that but a few years later we would pack up and leave it.

That photo: I can say about that photo that it might easily have marked the day we moved house. The differences being that the removal lorry – a large horsebox, big enough to carry six horses – also the pieces of furniture standing on the yard, these would have been absent from the photo. Whereas Mam, who was in the photo, Mam would have been absent on the day we moved house. On the day we left Ivyhall, Mam was dead. And the hall door of course – in the photo it was not lying, in apparent state of abandon against the castle wall, but was still holding its own in the doorway.

She died in the small cottage hospital, Clonmel. On one of those short days of mid-January. One of those twilight days, the light but an eggshell glimmer, quickly those days close in. And on a day of the following July, the sun standing in the middle of the sky as if stuck there for all eternity, we moved.

My aerial photo. Where is it now? I don't know. Lost.

There is one other photo; one other reminder of Ivyhall. A snapshot. I still have that one. It is faded now and tattered at the edges. A snapshot of a curly-headed boy, his eyes downcast in shyness; hesitancy, or is it a smile, or is it the crease of the photo, crossing his face. The boy's name is Christopher. When we lived in Ivyhall the photo of Christopher stood above the fridge in our kitchen. It jumped every time the fridge jumped into life but it never fell off. Dancie handed it to me once when I went on a trip to England. Christopher was her relation – nephew or son or what, it was hard to know – who had gone to England himself years earlier and had promptly disappeared.

'Ask around if anybody remembers him,' she said. 'Ask if they know is he dead or alive.'

'I certainly will,' I answered, never considering how the shy-eyed boy might have become unrecognisable in the young man.

The missing Christopher had been sacred to all of us when we were growing up in Ivyhall. He was not considered as having become a man. How could he have been? We hadn't seen him grow up. 'My little angel, Christopher,' Dancie would say.

The years would go by and Christopher would become a legend. From time to time he would find me. Searching in the folds of my wallet, I would flick across the photo and the image would become again the face and person I had built out of my childhood imagination and it would jump before me again and a feeling would take hold of me. Blue unsettling smoke; linking me with those days and with all of us who lived them. I would blow it away.

That feeling, how can I describe it? Awe, wonder? It had been an awesome world that had proclaimed itself in the taking away of Christopher. And we had been helpless in it. And we had accepted it. And that had been awesome too. We were only children, and we were looking into the eyes of the grown-ups and seeing there the shock, their shock. Not ours, ours was not reflected back upon us.

Fern measured across the width of the sideboard with his outspread hands. Five lengths. He measured the width of the hall door. Four and a half.

'That sideboard,' he said, 'is so big the house must have been built around it. Either that, or there was a wider front door once upon a time.'

'Take up thy bed and walk,' that was what he said to Thos most times they lifted a stick of furniture to carry downstairs. He got a laugh out of that. Another time, with a sort of reverence as they carried down the single bed from my father's room, he said: 'Go easy now and don't disturb the corpse.' Fern was a good laugh. He liked to joke about my father behind his back. Except that my father was no corpse. Not with the amount of work he did, even though he'd just had his second heart attack. Strain, Fern said, that was what had my father the way he was, one heart attack after the next. He should take it easy a bit more. This was a new way that Fern spoke about my father. It sounded as if he actually meant it. And this was strange coming out of Fern, whose comments about my father up until now never seemed to sense of anything other than derision. Was it because of all my father had been through?

It was Fern had the idea of removing the hall door from its hinges.

Early in the morning, while there was still a nip in the air, the door had been closed after each item of furniture that went through.

'Shut that door,' Dancie shouted. 'Keep out the draught.' Boxes were stacked everywhere, and loads of last minute loose things that hadn't gone into boxes: breadboards, caddies of tea and sugar, meat-mincer, grater. Then the children got up from breakfast and Dancie and her sister-in-law, Ettie, who had come round to help, began doing the wash-up. The last wash-up. 'Out, help yer father,' Dancie said. Then the children carried out all these loose things until after a while a jumble of stuff was piling up at the foot of the horse-box. And once Fern had taken down the door it piled up even higher. My father, who was packing it into the horsebox, couldn't keep ahead of it and I had to get in and help him. He was becoming impatient. It was stuffy in the horsebox. There was a smell of dry dusty hay. Children were handing up things, all kinds of things. My littlest sister, with great effort, managed to lift up a wooden box.

'What do you want that for?' my father said. 'I have no room for that.'

'It's the dolly's house,' she said, her face all puffed and red from the strain of lifting, little sobs bubbling out of her and tears not far behind.

'Ah, all right,' my father said. He opened the door of a wardrobe and wedged it inside. 'No more now, mind.' But I knew he would have put in more. He would have packed in anything they wanted. He could not refuse. And as I watched the urgent yet determined way he was packing the lorry, I knew the reasons why. There were two reasons, both of which gave me a shock. First reason: he wanted to be shut of Ivyhall; he would do anything now to quit the place as quickly as possible. Had things become that unbearable? Second reason: where little children were concerned he could never say no. Why had that shocked me? I had discovered, with a sudden collapse of my heart, that I had never played on his softness while I'd had the chance to, and now that I had grown too old to, I never could, ever again.

'Nothing left that belongs to the Connaughtons, boss' – Fern stuck his head out the window of my parents' bedroom – 'except, what about that double bed in here? You're sure you don't want to take it as well as the single?'

'I'm sure,' my father said. 'Leave it behind.'

Then he was ready to go. He, and all the children and Dancie, packed into the car. The horsebox was loaded with all our family's stuff, the Connaughtons' stuff. The Connells' stuff, the stuff of the family who had been there when we had arrived ten years earlier, was left behind. Once again isolated in Ivyhall. 'Left for the new boss,' as Fern had said. Connells and Connaughtons split down the middle, just as once upon a time they had been zippered together. There had been four young Connells and five young Connaughtons that first day. There were to be two subsequent additions to that union of my father and my stepmother. The Connell-Connaughtons, the two CCs, as we called them.

'Godspeed, boss.' Fern hit the roof of the car with the flat of his hand as they pulled off. My father, my Connaughton brothers and sisters, the two CCs and Dancie, packed tight, the windows open to let out elbows, Dancie blessing herself over and over again, 'Drive carefully now boss, drive carefully for the sake of the children.' She hated getting in the car with my speeding father but this time she had no choice. She clutched to her lap the little handbag that contained all her possessions. Dancie had two kinds of possessions: those that were for herself and those that were for the two CCs. Those things that were for the CCs were of more importance to her because since Mam died she had taken responsibility for the CCs as though they were her own. For the CCs there were the coins that would buy some sweets along the road, the spare hairclips to keep straight the hair of the little girl who had earlier cried for her doll's house, the bottle of milk, its teat turned inward to prevent seepage, that would comfort the little boy. For herself there were her cigarettes, her bottle of sleeping tablets, her compact of face powder and the photograph of the boy, Christopher. Small things, small important things, fitted neatly in her handbag, those were all that Dancie ever carried.

Out our driveway that car left a trail of fine powder. You could not see in the back windscreen, it was that loaded. Ettie, the men and me stood by the horsebox and watched them go. The dust was settling in the yard. The dogs were sitting down again, not knowing their days as excited escorts of young cowboys and

Indians were over and the next time they would stand would be for nothing more exciting than to relieve themselves.

Fern shook his head. 'We'll have a bit of peace at last,' he said.

'Too much of it,' Ettie said. 'What will we do without the noise of the children? What will I do when I look at an empty house? It will be like looking at a chopped down forest.'

Then the driver spat on his hands, roped down his horsebox and we too were ready to go. I sat in the cab; the driver, one side of me, Fern and Thos, the other, the gearbox beneath me. We pulled out of the yard. Ettie was standing alone, wearing Mam's wool-lined boots, proud to have been given something of Mam's, her thin legs sticking out of them like knitting needles. For a while I thought about the house we had left behind. It hadn't struck me until Ettie had said it, but yes there would be a silence across the countryside. The Connells had gone away for the day. It was the best solution to the parting. As to why, in the first place, the parting had to happen, too many things had been left unsaid. It was best they remained that way. When the Connells, brothers and sisters, would return in the evening to Ivyhall only deep repressed noises would come out of them, no more voices risen in the uncomplicated act of family warfare. They would sit at the table. Pass the butter, the boys would say. The girls would attempt to correct their table manners: Pass the butter, please. The boys, the young men now, would say Pass the butter, my arse, and that would be that. No more big family orchestrations. Ettie: she had wiped drops off her blue nose as she said goodbye. Suddenly into my ears came all the noise that for years we had been making.

After a while I settled down. There was a good view from my high perch in the cab. We wheeled around bends, ditches suddenly running at us; we straightened up again, the ditches running away from us now. We were coming out of the hills, County Tipperary sliding by us, a saucer of light in its hazy surround of mountains, and then we met a town. We pulled on to the main road; it was the town of Urlingford. Then we were humming along a flat highway, Fern singing, 'South of the border down Mexico way. That's where I fell in love when the stars above came out to play . . .' Oh, it was a great trip up to Dublin. Was I sad? Did I miss Ivyhall? No. Goodbye Ivyhall. Did I miss Mam? No. My life was singing out a song of its future. I hadn't time to think of things it had left behind. With every town we passed I felt like shouting yippee to the men. They too seemed to be enjoying the adventure. 'Up Kildare. Up the short grass county,' Thos yelped, looking over the Curragh. Four important men on a mission. Until, when we hit the first forest of television aerials, the others began looking at the traffic, helpless in its flow, saying, 'go easy', saying how they would be glad to get home. Then sitting sort of low and hunched in their seats, buried beneath the high houses of the quays. Fern and Thos and the driver and me, all squashed into the cab, all peering expectantly – all for our own separate reasons – for the sight of my father's new house.

Oh yeh. South of the border down Mexico way.

2

We were living in our hotel. On the corner of Main Street and Bank Street. Where I was born. Through whose corridors I had roamed since time without beginning. A town called Templemore. A sunny town. A mountain behind, called the Devil's Bit. I was eight and a bit years of age. Our Auntie Faith called us for a Sunday drive: 'Children, children, clean your hands and faces.' She told us it was to be a nice drive out the country with our Dada to see a house and to meet the children there. Their names were the Connells.

Dada didn't say anything, just looked on while Faith got us ready. His sister Faith, she did everything. We had another name for Faith. We called her Fay. It was a nicer name. Faith was a cold-sounding name and when you called our aunt by that name it made her seem cold too. And she could be that way, as though her face was turned away from you. But when you called her Fay it helped you see another side of her which was funny and giddy, so funny sometimes you thought she was coming down with a fever or something. For Fay was a mysterious sort of lady: full of mischievous laughter one minute, adult and serious the next.

Dada didn't say anything while Fay got us ready, but while we were driving to this place he was singing: 'Oh show me the way to go home. I'm tired and I wanna go to bed. I had a little drink about an hour ago. And it's gone right through my head.'

It didn't surprise me that he should be singing; he often sang when he was in good spirits. Or else when he was anxious about something. And today, for whatever reason, he was one or the other. What surprised me was that he should be singing one of my Mama's songs, and especially the way he was singing it, all out of key. I hadn't heard him sing one of Mama's songs since . . . oh I don't know . . . since she had been around. And that was how long ago now? It seemed ages. His own song was 'Down in Arizona where the wild men are and there's nothing there to guide you but the Evening Star and the roughest toughest man by far is Ragtime Cowboy Joe.' It was a more suitable song for him, that one. However, 'Show Me the Way to go Home' was not the worst of Mama's songs that he could be singing. It was a sort of funny one, and not one of those that could make him, make both of us, be reminded of Mama. To be reminded of Mama was the worst. It made you feel there was something wrong with you. Still, I was surprised. If I said, Dada, that's Mama's song you are singing, we would both have died with embarrassment. We just didn't talk of Mama. I did consider joining him in singing it; if it was all right for him to sing it, then it was all right for me. But in the end I couldn't bring myself around to it. I never sang Mama's songs now, not even to myself. That was a rule. And the records on the record player, those records of Mama singing, her voice jumping out at me and making me see her . . . Well, now I never played them either. That was another rule. Only once ever Dada talked of Mama. That was the day I said I hadn't seen her in a while and he told me that she had been taken to heaven, and that was why. He said that being such a good singer, she had been taken up there to sing with the choir of angels.

'Was she that good, Dada?' I said.

'Yes, your Mama was always an angel.'

Today Dada was telling us about places we passed. Pointing out landmarks. He liked to point out landmarks. We passed high walls.

'The man who owns that place keeps deer.'

'Deers, Dada?'

'Deer, not deers, dears,' he corrected us with a smile that was all patience and pleasure. Dada loved to correct our grammar.

I began to wonder what the trip was all about. It didn't seem to be the usual Sunday trip. We were a lot more than usually scrubbed and tidied.

'Surprise, surprise,' I could still hear Fay's voice, 'you'll meet new friends.' What was so special about meeting new friends? We were always meeting new friends. And then we never met them again and they became old friends. And we continued to remember them, even though there was no point in it.

We did a lot of Sunday driving. But today was the first day that Fay saw any need to give us special instructions. 'Show them your good manners,' says she. 'Lally, you are eight now. That's almost grown-up.' She laughed. Fay always laughed and expected me, being eight and the eldest in the family, to laugh too. I did. Even though I shouldn't have. Because I was a 'gummy-mouth'. So the hotel staff called me. 'He has his teeth rotted down from sucking ice-pops.'

'Moonshine', Dada was singing this time, another of Mama's not so serious songs. And then, to make it worse than anything, he starts off, in Mama's very own way, in the very baby-voice way she sang it: 'I know where I'm going. And I know whose going with me . . .'

Well, I don't know where I'm going, Dada. Oh please stop singing like that.

We went the back way instead of going through Thurles. That was a disappointment. Thurles was great. Whizzing through Thurles. All its shops, Woolworths, in whose glassy front you tried to make out your face in the car as its small reflection sped by. We were going for a long time. We came to a crossroads overlooked by a grotto. Our Lady, with piles of old rosary beads dangling from her joined hands. It was a famous landmark around these parts, Dada said. He got out to say a prayer. He had a special intention,

15

he said. They were the two important pastimes in Dada's life: pointing out landmarks to us and praying for special intentions. We watched from the car. Then the three little ones, Jamesy, Noeline and Martin, got out and knelt beside Dada. That left only Pam and me in the car. I watched a crow. He was perched on Our Lady and was looking down on them all kneeling together. Pam was a year younger than me and didn't class herself as one of the little ones any more, though sometimes she acted like it. She looked at herself in the mirror. She said she would be asking Dada to buy her a Walnut Whip. That surprised me. I never asked Dada to buy me anything except an apple. Why should she be able to make such big demands. I asked her where we were going and she said, why would she know, but that Fay said it was somewhere exciting. 'I know that already, stupid,' I said. Then she said, 'Stop being like that or I'll tell Dada on you.'

After that our drive took us further and further into the country, into a kind of countryside I didn't recognise; not like the fields around my town. Gently the fields around my town fold back from the road. These fields were bumpy, like bubbles rising out of the ground, wild and unshorn.

After the high walls and the grotto, the little houses started. Every now and then a little house, in its own small field with a few daffodils in it and a bank of turf. Nothing but little houses and banks of turf, until suddenly a tall house rose out of nowhere. A big woman came out and said hello to Dada. Her head was in a crown of black plaits, like those severe women from olden Greece in the *Pictorial Knowledge* book Fay showed me at nights. We were let out of the car. We saw children looking at us through a window, but they did not come out to say hello.

That was the first time we went there. It was not exciting. We went into a very large kitchen so brightly painted it hurt the eyes. We got hot milk. I smelled a sour smell. We saw two girls. On their heads stood stiff ribbons and they were holding the heads straight for fear of the ribbons wobbling sideways. They would not talk to us but sat very upright on kitchen chairs. One of them was pulling at the limp hank of hair her ribbon was tied to. There was nothing for it but to explore, so we climbed up a very wide staircase, whispering to one another in the cold air. Then one of the girls came out and told us that Mammy said we were to come down because we had to go home. 'Mammy' they called their mother, not 'Mama'. What a different word, 'Mammy', and what a difference in what it seemed to suggest. You felt in it none of the comfort that was in the word 'Mama'.

I met a boy who was a couple of years older than me. He wore long trousers, unlike my khaki shorts, which made him look really old. He had two enormous teeth; they were like saucers in the front of his mouth. How impossibly grown-up they made him look. And he wore oil in his hair, which made him look very serious. He told me we were not going home yet and he took me to a large yard and showed me all the outhouses. I wanted to see what was beyond the yard and so he showed me the wall. He said that from the wall I would have a good view. I saw the two girls again. They were at a higher window of the house now, looking down at me. Getting up on the wall I scraped the inside of my leg. The two girls didn't move their faces an inch from the window but kept looking and so I couldn't examine the cut. I couldn't mention it to the boy either, thinking to myself that if I had long trousers on me like his, scrapes like that wouldn't happen and so I would only be drawing attention to my short trousers. It was a bad scrape but I didn't want to wear long trousers; they looked ridiculous. I didn't want to wear a sports coat either, like he wore, with the two slits behind, making his bottom look large. What did he want the two slits for? Didn't he know that all the best dressed people, all the horse people, like Dada, wore only the one slit in their sports coat. A real little man he was. I didn't want to show the cut to the woman of that house; with those black plaits that crowned her head and with the plucked eyebrows, she looked like a statue. Fay would be there when I got home. Fay was just the ticket. No reprimand, no fuss either. Iodine swab: 'The sting will do it good, got to be cruel to be kind'. Clean job. Much better even than Mama, was Fay. Mama: she'd only have started kissing me and at the same time telling me where the fairies took naughty boys like me. And then there's me, boo-hooing my eyes out. Stop it Mama, don't be frightening the heart out of me. I don't believe in your old fairies.

A narrow road ran along outside the wall. There was nothing on it. But this boy with the big teeth looked down on it like it was the road to Wonderland. It seemed to me, used as I was to town traffic, that no traffic had ever run on it nor ever would. In town there were always cars, and always a few people. There was no time in our town when a few people were not standing about. Just standing. At the door of a shop, or between doors. Or beneath the town hall, the ones my Mama called corner-boys, scratching their legs. Were corner-boys waiting for other people to talk to or what were they doing? Some day of the week, sooner or later, Boland's breadman would come along, all the way from Dublin, in his brown coat, sliding trays of bread out of the van. He would have a word for them. They they would spit on their hands and shake their shoulders, an appetite for life suddenly revived. What did corner-boys do anyway? They kept the wall up, that was what Mama said they did. But that wasn't true. I watched corner-boys. I watched and watched to see were they keeping the wall up but they weren't. The thing about corner-boys, they never even leaned against the wall. Never touched it. They always stood six alert inches away from it. Always in a state of readiness, like soldiers, on their toes and ready to go. Oh they didn't like that wall. You got the impression from the corner-boy that if anybody stopped by in a car and asked him to get in, he would. He would be off. Corner-boys were always in a state of preparation, wellington boots rolled down, coat collar turned up. They would take to the road, any road. The wide road with the signpost pointing in the sunshine and saying, Limerick 49 miles. How silent stood the world out there beyond that signpost. I could touch it. A threshold, beyond which the ordinary world stopped and inklings of mystery began. I could hear noises out there, voices, faint and far in the forty-nine mile distance. Yet, with one bound, the corner-boys were ready to be gone. Whatever Mama might have said, I knew the corner-boys' least preferable location was the corner. But to pass away the time while they were waiting for that lift to Limerick they made brief talk and scratched legs and combed their hair and sometimes, if something broke the spell of concentration, one of them lapsed into song, 'Beside a garden wall . . . when stars are bright . . . you are in my arms . . .' He held his hands upright as he sang, as if collecting pennies falling from the skies. Then he stopped and reverently announced the snatch of song he had just sung: ' "Stardust": that's Nat

King Cole, boy.' He then relapsed into silence until something else happened, until the Odearest lorry pulled up or Roscrea Sausages and the driver said, 'How are ye gettin' on, men?', and then, very satisfied with that, he gave out a bar of another song, hands raised for more pennies from heaven. I would be sucking my ice-pop. Lost in my own state of preparedness. But here in this place . . . In this place nobody stood or sang or no cars passed or no signposts said Limerick or even Rathdowney.

A very interesting place to visit, Ivyhall, I thought. But not until we had left.

Dada sang all the way home: 'Moonshine, dear Moonshine, oh how I love thee . . .'

I broke my rule and joined in with him for a minute because, after all, I was a great singer. Everybody said it, even Mama, who said it was a gift from God and I shouldn't spurn it. It was a strange thing about me and the gift of singing. I got a pain inside me when I sang. But I got a worse pain when I didn't sing. It was better for me to sing than not to. It gave the pain some calming influence. Yet so often, when people asked me to, I would refuse them. 'Ah go on, give us an ould bar, Lally.' 'I can't.' Anyway, we were going home and I sang. And when Fay saw us she asked us didn't we absolutely love Ivyhall. Oh we did. And did you all have good manners, Lally? Oh we did.

3

'And if Moonshine don't kill me I'll live till I die,' Dada was still singing the second time we went. But I wasn't. This second trip was all different. Fay still hadn't told me what was happening, not even when I had requested that in return for going this one more time I would never have to go again. But why were we taking all our belongings? Why was I in the cab of the horsebox? Why was Paddy Barry driving behind us in the hearse with the belongings we couldn't fit into the horsebox? And Dada singing and singing. It had been excusable for Mama when she sang silly like that. Not for Dada. It had been all right for Mama to be silly. Dada was supposed to be an adult.

It was four Sundays after the first visit. All the scab on the inside of my leg had been picked off but now it was gone sore again from the sweatiness of the seat. When we got there the gates were wide open for the horsebox to go up the driveway. There were daffodils, bending on their stems now, and a little boy in the middle of them standing on a scooter. He dropped the scooter as soon as he saw the horsebox and he ran screaming to the house. Dada rolled down the window. 'Hello, Murt,' he called. 'I know that little boy,' he said to us then, laughing, not wanting us to get upset at the sight of a crying little boy. 'Come back, Murt,' he called, but Murt did not come back. Dada began nervously to hum again.

Did Murt know who we were? I wondered. The two girls, they were looking through the window at us as they had four weeks earlier. Did they know? Why were they laughing at us? Who dispatched all my luggage: my clothes, my marbles, and my cowboy figures? But what about all the other things that belonged to us in the hotel: the piano, the sideboard, the big racing pictures in the dining room: what was going to happen to them? There was no room here for them, not with all the sideboards and things that were here already.

I met the big boy again. 'Your new friend,' Fay had said before I left home. 'Be nice to him.'

Well I had to be nice to him. He was bigger than me. He was wearing the long trousers again. Another sports coat with two slits behind. His hair was oiled like before, a line of the whitest skin parting it along one side. He really was just like a man. And he was being nice to me. I didn't want to listen to all the things he was telling me but I was being nice to him too. On top of the wall again, he showed me fields up on a hill. 'Ours,' he said. Firmly seated on the clumping ivy on top of the wall, so that I would not fall and scrape my leg again, I wondered whose he meant by 'ours'.

He pointed: 'Moorpark, Rampark, Deerpark, Farpark.' Strange, new-sounding names.

'Deerpark, do you have deer too?'

'No, our grandfather did, though.'

It was the way he said it. It gave me the feeling that he knew this place. And not only did he know it now, he also knew it even going back into its olden days. It was his place. It was not mine. Richie, that was my new brother's name.

Oh I suppose I found what he was telling me very interesting. 'The hills are glacial,' he said. 'They were made by the Ice Age. See that river down there?' He pointed into a field down in a valley. I didn't see any river. Rivers around these parts, I decided, were a lot smaller than I knew rivers to be. 'That field is called Glen and the river is all that's left now of the glacier. See that other field with the small hills? They are not hills at all. They are man-made. The coal mines had workings down here one time many years ago. The place was crawling with people, miners. Those hills are from coal heaps. The Colliery, we call that field. There are still shafts there. Very dangerous. You have to keep away from them.' Richie was pointing out fields to me all over the place. I was so mesmerised by it all. And I really did want to keep up with him. Because I knew, oh yes I knew, I had to get the hang of the place.

And I was looking at this boy. So serious, did he ever play games? Did he know anything about adventure? What about that castle that was attached to the house? Empty black holes of windows gaped from it and so much ivy hung from its walls it was like a huge square tree trunk. A true adventure land.

I climbed on a gate, a big gate. I opened it and it swung me out on a lovely wide arc.

'Get off the gate,' he said. 'You'll ruin the hang.'

'Can people go in the castle?' I said.

'They can, but it's very dangerous. We had to knock some of it down because we were afraid of it falling on the house. We'll have to knock it all down some time, and fasten a lean-to against the house.'

He knew so much. Grown-up things. He kept showing me fields and telling me what he was going to sow in them. But I knew one thing. I would explore the inside of that castle. Surely I would.

Oh where was my town gone? Oh where was Georgey's shop? The high step up to Georgey's counter. Oh when are we going back home? Dada. We'll get in the horsebox and sing: 'Oh show me the way to go home.' But we never went home. We never went home again. Never again would it be just me and Pam and the three little ones, Jamesy, Noeline and Martin. Now there was Richie, there was crying little Murt, and those two girls at the window whose names were Marguerite and Breda.

Fay. What had our Auntie Faith been thinking at all? What has she been doing to us? Making up stories or what? At least she could have told me that the stern woman with the plaits like a crown over her forehead, like somebody at a funeral, was our new mother. Maybe Fay didn't want her to be our new mother either. Maybe Fay wanted to keep us for herself. That's what I had been wanting to think, but knowing it was not true. Fay, really, wanted to get back to America, from where she had come to mind us that time after our Mama died. That was the time when she had looked very cross, that first day she returned from her work in America to mind us. I didn't think then the job was going to suit her. But she got good at it. How long ago was that anyhow? It did seem ages. It was two years and a bit.

4

In the mornings in Ivyhall I woke up very early. Farmyard sounds made the windowpane jump: a dog barking down in a field, a gate clanging. It was very bright outside, brighter than in our town, where all the gables of the hotel shut out the light. With what a sharp glare did everything ring out in this new place.

But I wasn't really listening. I was thinking: it is Easter holiday. Easter Sunday is soon. If this is only a holiday, I was thinking, I don't mind. I can go home again to the hotel and play on the streets again. And then thoughts about this place can come back to my mind – the coarse linen on the beds and so on, all the unusual things about it. Once I am miles away from it, I can even enjoy thinking of it. Am I on holiday? I am not.

I heard voices somewhere outside, hup, hup, calling in the cows. Whistles. I wanted to go to the window and look – I was learning the noises of the old men who worked the farm – but I was afraid to get up for fear of waking the boy beside me in the bed. In the nights I couldn't sleep because of him. He always read a book; the light shone in my face so that no dreams could come in my head and then each morning I was awake before him. The tip of his black head poked above the sheet; and every morning the hair was dry and I wondered where all the hair oil he had plastered on it could have gone. Every morning early, in my new surroundings, I lay there in the bed. I was thinking: all sorts of thoughts: future fears and past happiness. Or had it been happiness? I was thinking about the last three months in the hotel. Before coming to this Ivyhall place. Those last three months were important; now I knew it. They were the doorsteps to this Ivyhall place and I had not seen them. For the last three months I had given up going to school. I had given it up as a bad job. Given it up altogether.

The end of my schooling: it all happened because I came home crying one day. When Fay asked what was wrong with me I only had to tell her I was scared of Brother Burley and that was it. She let me stay at home from school for three whole months. A lifetime.

And was I frightened on that day! Ever since I had gone into Burley's classroom I had been frightened. Burley's classroom, for third and fourth classes, was the middle room of the school. It had no gable-end windows, being the middle room, and only slits high up on the side windows, oh so high up above us boys, whose heads were always bent down. Brother Burley, with his sharp yellow teeth and green eyes, had you at his mercy in that room. You knew there was no escape. And for someone like me, who had recently acquired a taste for freedom, that was unbearable. For I was in the midst of the great days of my liberty, which had begun after my Mama died. I had been getting about the town. Mama had never let me out anywhere, unless it had been with her on visits to her friends in big houses. Now I roamed at will.

Here is how it happened. One afternoon – it was afternoon because that was the time the sun shone on my side of the street and I remember it shining into my eyes – I was in the thick of a carrot-throwing battle with some boys. Back and forth across Bank Street, we were throwing. Me against the three White boys. Dada would not have approved of me wasting hotel carrots, but Dada wasn't around much and wouldn't have seen. Brother Burley wouldn't have seen either, except that a carrot hit him on the side of the head and knocked him off his bicycle as he rode by and knocked his hat on the road. I had been firing from inside the doorway at the side of our hotel and because of the sun hadn't seen his arrival on Bank Street on his way down to the monastery. I had wondered all right why all the others had run away and why I was throwing into an empty door opposite, sweating from my exertions. And why all the hotel carrots were piling up over there, waiting for Mrs White to come out to her hall and gather them up for the dinner. But then I saw Burley toppling from his high bike and I bolted. I took only one look around. He was charging after me with short fast steps and his belly wobbling from side to side. I ran and ran, through the cattle-mart grounds at the back of our hotel, between the pens. I hid behind a sheet of galvanised iron standing against the wall. I hid there a long time until I began to think he had gone home. I hid in the silence but I jumped when I heard the shout alongside me.

'Come out wherever you are and face the music.' I peeped through a nail hole in the bottom of the galvanised iron and saw his sandals and the trousers tucked in the bicycle clips.

'I see you,' he kept saying, his trousers giving a little shudder every time he said it. The sandals and trousers were not moving in any particular direction but circling indefinitely at the other side of the galvanised iron. I figured, Either he knows I'm in here or he's lost the scent entirely. I waited and hoped for the best.

Then he said to himself, 'The little fecker has disappeared.'

If I hadn't heard him say that I might have come out to face the music.

Brother Burley was always talking about his leather, called Caruso. Brother Skehan, who we had in first and second class, was not as bothered with his. Jake, he called it. Brother Burley was always putting boys hands into his pockets to feel Caruso for him. He said there was a penny sewn into the tip of it. One slap of Caruso was a pennyworth, he said. Twelve slaps, a shillingworth. And God help a boy that someday was going to cause Caruso to dish out a pound's worth. A pound's worth would put a boy in hospital, and God guide him but some day he was going to do it because the boys in this town, some of them, were so deserving of a pound's worth. Caruso would sing, the Great Caruso, and by God he would teach boys a tune or two.

It was a frightful experience when Brother Burley asked you to pull his leather out of his pocket for him. You seemed suffocated by him as you did it, the smell of chalk dust off him, the musty smell off his soutane. Doing it for Brother Skehan, that was another matter. That was a joke. You put your hand into the pocket. It went down the front and you laughed when the leather wasn't there at all and instead you found his hand that he had put in the other pocket and it joined yours inside. Brother Skehan – this was the joke – had just one pocket. It went in one side and joined in the front and went out the other. Maybe that was the way all the Brothers' soutanes were made: so that the leather could be conjured out from either direction. You were too scared to explore that, though, in the case of Brother Burley.

So this was the morning after I had hidden down the cattle-mart, with Burley's crepe-soled sandals padding around outside my hiding place. Now he had the whole class lined up around the walls of the room, all except for twelve boys, me included, who had to remain seated.

'Twelve Bank Street boys, twelve Apostles, but among these boys there is a Judas,' he growled. 'This boy, Caruso shall make an example of.' He fondled the leather in his hands. 'In Bank Street there nests a viper,' he said.

Brother Skehan never said things like that about Bank Street. He only made jokes. He said that in Bank Street there lived the Brotherhood of Colours, because in Bank Street, as well as the three White boys, there also lived the Brown boys, five of them, the Greens, two of them, and Toddy Black. I was the odd one out. Usually that troubled me, who wanted always to be like everybody else, but not right now. Right now Brother Burley paced up and down the centre of the room, pausing over the squeaky floorboard each time for effect. He was saying things like, 'Own up, this boy, and the inquisition will be called off.' And the smells of the floorboards and of the desks and the chalk and everything were mingling

27

and making me faint with terror. I wondered was there the slightest chance he mightn't have known who 'this boy' was. Everybody on the way into school told me that I was going to be killed. The big boys in sixth had laughed their heads off, pointing at me. 'He knocked Burley of his bike with a carrot. Jesus, he's for it.' The word had travelled, everybody seemed to know. Yet, for a second or two, I wondered if it could be possible that while everybody else might have known, Burley did not, and all this prowling up and down the room was only to frighten a confession out of me. For one second I thought I might get away with it. Then Roddy White, the big fool, owned up. Roddy was my principal adversary among the boys throwing from Whites' doorway across the street. The others were only little squirts that didn't count. If he was going to own up, I would have to also, before he told on me. My head was down on the desk, I was sucking the wood. It had a waxy taste, like soap. One day Fay washed out Pam's mouth with soap. She had been telling lies, Fay said. That would stop her in future. I had tried out the soap on myself because anything Pam was getting, I wanted too. It made me sick. Could I tell a lie now? I wondered. A whopper? And I would lather up the soap as soon as I got home and give the mouth a thorough going over.

I never found out whether Roddy told on me or not: I went numb inside when I saw what Burley was up to. 'Caruso will scar you for life for this,' he said to poor Roddy and made him bend over and with Caruso held between his teeth he used both hands to pull down Roddy's trousers. All those standing looking on were stuck to the walls. I bolted. Without even asking permission.

I ran right through the Juniors. Brother Skehan made a joke as I passed. The Juniors were in the middle of choir. I saw all the white throats stretched up towards his tuning fork. 'Lally Connaughton is leaving the door open so that Brother Burley can hear how a song should be sung.' They were singing 'The Green Glens of Antrim': 'Far across yonder blue lies a true fairy land.' Brother Skehan, who was from Antrim was proudly showing off his Antrim tune for the benefit of Brother Burley, who had tried to teach us a tune once about whatever county it was he came from. But he had not been able to sing it and so we had not been able to learn it, and then he had brought it in on an old gramophone player, but we still hadn't been able to learn it. 'At least learn to hum it,' he said, 'if you can't learn the words.' 'The garden of Eden is banished they say. But I know the lie of it still', it started off. What county could that be, anyway? Burley, surely, could not have come out of such a beautiful place? It was called: 'Come back, Paddy Reilly, to Ballyjamesduff'. 'Hum it,' says he. He couldn't even hum it himself, his eyes closed and all, like a mad saint, every time he tried. The only tune he could hum was with Caruso and he was humming it now off Roddy White's bottom. And I was crying, tears like hot hailstones pelting out of me, down the street home.

Fay found me in the nursery room. She had to get me hot scones and milk. Then she told me I was a young man. 'Young men don't cry.' How awful it was to be told that and still not to be able to stop crying. Gasps would not stop coming out of me, enormous suckings, emptying the floor of my heart. And I could not tell her what had happened me. I could not tell her I had been flinging Dada's carrrots about the street. 'Brother Burley frightens me. I want to go back to Brother Skehan's class.' That was all I could say.

Going into the dining room for breakfast next morning, I overheard Dada and Fay in conversation. Dada and Fay enjoyed talking a lot together. They were brother and sister after all. They talked a lot about their past and the silliness of their parents and then collapsed in laughter. This time Fay was not laughing. 'Delayed reaction is the problem, and it is well known in psychiatry,' she was saying. Fay knew a lot about a certain sort of thing called 'psychiatry'. It was one of the many things she had studied in America before she had come home to look after us. But I don't think Fay's study of psychiatry would have been any use to her if I had told her that 'delayed reaction' had not been my problem. That there had been nothing 'delayed reaction' about my flight from Burley. With me next on the list for Caruso after Roddy White, my trousers next to be pulled down in full sight of third and fourth classes.

Fay probably did think she knew my problems – Mama's dying and all that. Yes I did have problems with that. The worst was the awful fear of Mama's continued presence. Dead, but still there. Wandering ghostily around the corridors of the hotel, waiting for her moment to appear. Detaching herself from the choir of angels.

And when would she make the appearance? Just as I would be turning into a corridor, or up on the high landing where the sun came in the window after teatime? A sudden apparition. Behind me, for example, as I came down the stairs. Boo! But was there ever anything there when I did look around, when I forced myself, because her presence had become so strong? Nothing, nothing but a window with the sunlight pouring through. Yet I could never breathe relief. Because, sooner or later, I knew it was going to happen. What was stopping her from doing it? And what was she going to look like? Would she show her disappointment at me? The thought of it terrified me. I would pray, and tell her, I love you, Mama, but please do not start appearing to me. A little voice within me would speak to my Mama: If you come back from heaven, Mama, and talk to me, I will not be able to talk back to you. I will not be able to cry or kick up tantrums or anything as before. I will have to be holy and silent. That won't suit us.

Yes, I had enough problems with that, but that was between me and Mama and was something I had to deal with myself. The thought of going back to Burley, the more immediate problem, that was more than I could handle. I stood behind the screen which cut off the area in the dining room where Dada and Fay sat for breakfast and I listened to them. I waved over at the guests so that they would not give me away – Miss Carroll, who was reading her paper, and Mr Scanlan, the commercial traveller, who was spreading marmalade on his toast. The dumbwaiter revolved between the dining room and kitchen. I gave the dumbwaiter a few quick spins, making the plates and saltcellars hop around on its shelves. I pretended to be knocking great fun out of that, watching the dumbwaiter fly around, seeing flashes of the kitchen and the maids within each time it opened – but I was listening.

'So what are you going to do about it?' Fay was saying. 'We can't let him stay at home from school. We cannot do what poor Mama did with him. He only had to cry and Mama let him stay at home from school. Too often she did, and that weakens a boy's will. So what are you going to do about it?' Fay was saying all this. I was wondering how staying at home from school weakened your will. It was Burley weakened your will. What was she talking about anyway? I couldn't remember Mama letting me stay at home from school because I cried. Or if I cried, I only cried a very little cry. It wasn't me who hadn't wanted to go to school; it was Mama who had wanted me to stay at home.

Dada said nothing to Fay, just kept eating his toast, so I was not to know what he did about it, but I didn't go to school that day. Nor the next day, nor the next. For three whole months.

5

Now here I was in this Ivyhall place. Waking up every morning to the sight of the black-headed boy alongside me, wondering would I have to go to school again, noticing the schoolbags
of the Connells under the sideboard in the hallway and getting a
pain in my tummy at the sight of them. And then, my mind
wandering away again, to the comforts of my previous life.

The best days of my life, I would say, were the two years after the
time of my Mama's death and up until the time when I went into
third class, Burley's class, and then had to leave school. Not the
three months, funnily enough, that I was off school, but the two
years that went before that. Why? I was a free citizen of the world.
Why? There was no Mama around to bother me. Fay was there all
right, but Fay only encouraged my spirit of adventure. And Dada,

he was far too busy. It was a time when I had the run of the town. I knew everybody; everybody knew me. I played with a gang up in Richmond: the Lamb Brothers' Gang. Catapults, lassoes, bows and arrows, and one pellet gun, which only the bigger boys could carry. Maybe play wasn't the word, especially if you were caught by the Parkmore Gang and they tied you to the tree where the pismire colony lived that crawled up your legs and bit you until you told the secret. What secret I don't know, we never had a secret. But I could walk home all on my own through that frontier town in the dark evenings, my lungs filled with the exciting air of gang warfare, my body tingling from the tumbles in the soft earth. I could stand as tall as anybody else. The only time there was a problem was once when Mrs Lamb called us all into her steamy hot kitchen because my mother was singing on the radio and she wanted me to listen. Mrs Lamb was boiling up dinner for her big husband Bob who worked in the bank. The song was 'Coortin' in the Kitchen'. A stupid song. Mama used to sing it in the nursery to Pam and me. Or play it on one of the records she had of herself and then laugh her head off after it was over.

Once, before Mama met Dada, she used to be a singer and she sang in concerts and her songs were famous. But not as famous as her sister Delia. 'That Delia Mooney one, she's a famous singer,' everybody said. Everybody in town had heard of Delia. Everybody said to me: 'Young lad, how is your Auntie Delia keeping?' I didn't know how she was keeping. 'Oh famous,' I said. But Dada said Mama had a sweeter voice. 'Hello Patsy Fagan', that was the best of them. She gave it all up to have me and my brothers and sisters and to run Dada's hotel and sometimes, by special request, to sing in the bar and bring happiness to all the whiskey-faced old boys at the counter. Now here she was on the radio. 'Ah your mother never died,' says Mrs Lamb. Indeed. And hearing that sort of thing, was it any wonder I still expected her to appear to me? The Lamb Brothers' Gang were all looking at me as Mama sang but I was not listening, concentrating instead on the bubbling of turnips going on in the pot up on the cooker. Trying to leap out of that pot, those turnips were.

That episode apart, I felt I could be as much a member of the gang as any of the others. I would deliver up my weaponry each evening; I would be given the password for the following day. I would walk home down the hill from Richmond, the smell of fallen leaves on the footpaths and on the lawns of silent gardens, the gurgle of the baby Suir, my mountain river, beneath Patrick Street bridge, our town in its last few frantic moments before shutting up for night. Then the shop lights were brightest, little girls and old women ran suddenly out of doors to get last messages, car doors banged simultaneously and cars drove out of town and the shopkeepers stood out on the street and looked up and down and then shut for the night. I could peer into the shadows of the big houses up in Richmond. I could hear sounds come through chinks of doors on Patrick Street. The silence descending, and every now and again the barking of dogs having to break it just because it was too much for them to bear. I could feel the heart of things. The smell of coal fires. A town beneath the dark but boundless sky. It was the time in my life when, without interruption from anybody, I could watch the whole world in its motion. Oh between the time of my mother's death and my leaving school . . . That time was the best time, and that town the best place on earth in which to be.

So those were the great times. Then Brother Burley took Roddy White's trousers down and sang with his leather, Caruso, and I gave up school. But why did times not become even better once I was rid of fearful Brother Burley and the tyranny of his classroom, and even greater lengths of day were available for roaming? A day would come, I was aware of that, when I would have to go back to school, something was going on in Dada's mind, I sensed it. But considerations of the future had never ruined the present for me before and certainly should not have distracted me from a present of blissful school-less days. Was it because Fay decided to take over my education, and because I had to help Dada with jobs? Were these the reasons why my days disimproved? How had my sense of citizenry of the free world gone and deserted me?

Education with Fay meant history, geography and more geography. That wasn't too bad. It was wizard, in fact. Fay didn't like the normal subjects; neither did I. We studied from a wonderful book of coloured maps called an atlas. We studied Munster. 'We'll start at our own front door,' Fay said. So Munster was my own front door.

But I didn't see my school friends any more. Somehow, not seeing them in school made it difficult to go out and meet them outside of school. Would I want to meet school friends who only remembered me as the fellow whose trousers should have come down in front of everybody? So that for evermore, when my name would be mentioned, a bottom, and not a face, would float before their eyes. And not seeing my school friends began to have an effect on me, to make me different. At least, according to the staff in the hotel, I was becoming different. 'Don't be pestering me, get out of the kitchen. Why can't you be normal like other boys, odd one.' Bid Cullen, the cook, shushed me away from the big table where she carved the beef roasts.

I was becoming an odd one. Bid Cullen was very definite in her opinions. If a diner didn't like the potatoes he was served up, Bid Cullen could always explain it to the kitchen staff: 'The poor dim creature, sure he can't tell mashed potato from mashed parsnip.' Because of her ability to hand down judgement on the character of her diners, she had come to be held as a general authority on everything. So I was an odd one. I began to notice it myself. I was seeking company among the hotel staff. Una, with her black hair, shiny as a blackbird. Why was I always getting on chairs, then jumping on her back? She didn't like it.

'Get off.'

'I'm only playing. Giddy up, Una.'

'I'll tell your aunt.'

But why did she like it when Grizzler from down the yard came up and winked at me as he stuck his hand up under her skirt and pulled at something inside that made a snap sound? The sound like a banjo going twang. That's what he said. 'I hear your banjo twang, Una.' Dropping the hand, he called it. Not lifting the hand, as it seemed more reasonable to call it. He loved dropping the hand, making dives at her, as she shrieked and ran between tables, knocking chairs. I could have told Dada on him. But then how could I when I began to do the same thing myself? The first time, I pulled my hand away as soon as I felt Una's skin. But once I had grown used to it, I let the hand rest there for as long as I was allowed, a dream of banjo twanging passing through me, even though I was making not a sound. Dada thought Grizzler was wonderful for a long time. He had sandy-grey hair. It curled tightly against his head. He had a wide forehead that went into creases of concentration whenever Dada was explaining jobs he wanted him to do: 'Right boss, right boss, as good as done boss.' As Dada said, 'He can put his hand to anything.' How could I tell Dada about Grizzler's adventures in the kitchen. He had put him in charge of all the other men in the yard.

The next thing, Grizzler was gone.

'He can grizzle his own wife now,' all the maids laughed.

'Where is he?' I asked.

'Oh, your father gave him the sack.'

The sack. What was the sack? The sack filled me with dread. Was it bottomless; was it dark; was it soggy, like the sack in the water barrel the five kittens were put in? Would I get the sack if I was found out? But what could I do? I was good when Dada was about, but I couldn't stop putting my hand up Una.

Rocky Dunne was another one that came into the kitchen. The maids didn't like Rocky at all. They just left out the buckets of slop for him to feed the pigs and then hunted him. Rocky took me down the yard. There was a shed he liked to take me into. He shut the door so that only a crack of light came through. I could barely make out the things in the shed, the handle of an old plough, a horse manger on the wall with strings hanging from it. In return for a penny, Rocky would ask me to sing for him. 'Three Lovely Lassies from Bannion', one of Auntie Delia's songs. I never sang except for money. In return for another penny, he would ask me to lean against him while he rubbed himself up and down against my tummy. The first time I was a bit curious at what was going on. But when I lost interest in proceedings, which was very quickly because it was boring, he grew even more interested. Then I hated it; I hated how he dribbled down on my hair, saying between dribbles, in an anxious voice, that it wouldn't take long. There was a smell of old potato skins off his clothes. The handle of the plough bore into my back, and I tried to make out the manger and the other things in the dark shed. 'I'll give you a penny, I'll give you another penny,' he pleaded, but when I struggled to break free of his clothes against my face he always let me go. At times other than during the 'Three Lovely Lassies' sessions in the shed I was happy to pal around with

Rocky. And for a while he was my only daytime companion.

Then he too got the sack from Dada. At least then I knew that the sack wasn't something you got for dropping the hand. But was it for rubbing me in the shed? So I had to go around for days, keeping out of Dada's sight, until I found out what it was you did get the sack for. Rocky got the sack for choking one of the pigs. A matchstick that Rocky should have seen in the slops and taken out had stuck in its throat. That must have been the day I saw the pig flat out beneath the gate of the pig pen, its head blue with the cold. Then I saw Rocky burying it under a cloud of flies in the dungheap. 'Don't tell your father,' he said, and I thought he was talking about the other thing. As if I could have told anybody about something as boring as that. When he was gone the maids said they'd miss him, bad and all as he was, because he was harmless. And they left out some milk for him each day, to take home to his mother. Though he had been my only company down the yard for a while, I grew used to his absence.

Miss Carroll had lived in the hotel for as long as I could remember. She'd always had the same room; a sunny room at the back and just above the kitchen. It was a cheerful room – certainly not lonely, being within hearing of the hub of everything that went on in the hotel – a cheerful room but very small and smelling slightly of the kitchen. It suited the size of Miss Carroll's pocket, I once heard Fay say. When my sister Pam and me were little we used to arrange all Miss Carroll's combs and brushes on her dressing table. She tied her hair in a grey bun at the back during the daytime but when she was in her room she let it down so that we could brush it out for her. It was thin and wispy but we liked to brush it. She had a huge bed, which took up most of the room, into which we used to climb. Miss Carroll at one side, a bolster down the middle, and my sister and me on the other side. Now I took again to visiting Miss Carroll. She didn't mind. She lay on one side of the bolster, I lay on the other and I told her about my geography lessons. She told me about her family from the County Offaly. I loved to lie there in her bed, the sun coming in the window and falling on my face and all down along the bed until it hit the mirror on her dressing table.

I had a game: Miss Carroll could hardly say a sentence without putting the words 'of course' into it: 'Of course, my father didn't approve of my becoming a hairdresser. Of course, he and my mother never stopped arguing about it. Of course, my mother believed in getting the girls out of the house: "Educate the girls, the boys will look after themselves." Of course, you had to go to Dublin to learn hairdressing in those days. And Dublin for young girls in those days was not of course . . .' I would count the number of of courses and tell Fay. For a while Fay was amused. Then one day she told me she was worried about the amount of time I spent with Miss Carroll because it was too much intrusion on Miss Carroll's privacy and she would have to speak to Dada about it. Fay knew that all she had to do to get me to do something was mention Dada's name.

'Promise me you will not see Miss Carroll in her bedroom any more.'

'I promise, Aunt Faith.'

'But promise you will continue to be nice to her.'

'Of course I promise.' As if I would let down Miss Carroll like that just because I was no longer going to bed with her!

My next bed-mate was Auntie Leg. She was Dada's aunt. Visits to her were not so satisfactory because she made me do what she wanted, not what I wanted, which was to lie on top of her big draughty double bed with its brass rails and imagine myself sailing across the seas on a tall ship.

I had to arrange all of Auntie Leg's shoes for her. She kept them under the bed, hundreds of them. I didn't mind the shoe arranging; in fact it was quite enjoyable finding the matching pairs. I didn't mind the smell either, which was of disinfectant – Aunt Leg was once a nurse and everything had to be disinfected. What I minded was the thought of the bed coming down on top of me. Auntie Leg was a very big woman and when you had to get out of her bed and go beneath it to do her shoes, or to find her hair-brooch which she was always losing, you heard the bedsprings rumbling above you like thunder in the skies. You wanted to ask her not to move about so much because she was going to bring the whole world down on top of you, but you couldn't draw Aunt Leg's size to her attention. I told Fay once that Aunt Leg was huge and she told me never to breathe a word to Aunt Leg about it. So here's me under the bed, the rumble above me, but at least happy in the one thought that

Aunt Leg would not die on me up there. Not like old Miss Corbett, who died in her bed on the top landing and Dada had to cart her off. Aunt Leg was a diehard and that was why she would not die. Dada said it: 'A diehard, green to the bitter end,' he said one day with an unhappy face. Here's me under the bed; above me, Aunt Leg's continuous chatter about politics, the great man de Valera, the mistaken ideas of the other side of our family . . . Other chatter she went on with: how it was going from bad to worse in the hotel. How since Mama died it was being poorly run. How she pitied Dada having to cope on his own . . . Uninteresting chatter.

Aunt Leg began to find too many jobs for my liking. I had to help her roll out her wool yarn and while she sat in the bed I stood on the floor until my arms nearly fell off from holding out the wool. I had to maintain a constant supply of toilet-papers by her bed for the receipt of parcels of catarrh silently expelled from beneath her tongue. But the day I had to empty her potty, I thought that was enough. On my under-bed crawlings I'd had always to avoid the potty, denying any notice even of its existence: 'Mind out for the potty, Lally,' the warning used to reach me through the bedsprings. 'I can't see it, Aunt Leg,' though its whiteness glimmered like pearl through the tangle of shoes. And now here it was, having to be hauled into the daylight, having to be held up and carried to the sink. There was no denying the existence of the potty after that. And so I gave up Auntie Leg. A diehard, with a heavy potty.

I began to visit Mr Scanlan. I visited in the early morning. Goodness me, all the people I was getting to know so intimately. And all because I had given up school. Was there any limit to the number of people a fellow might get to know if school didn't come in the way? The first time I visited Mr Scanlan was because I had taken on a new job. Denis, the waiter, polished the shoes of all the guests and then left them outside the doors. I liked Denis, who was getting very old, and I decided to do the shoe polishing for him. I polished all the shoes brown; even the black ones I polished brown. Dada's shoes were brown. If brown was good enough for Dada, it was good enough for everybody else. But then Denis told me I would have to give up the polishing. So I took to returning the shoes for him. Early every morning I rose, to return the shoes, and not just to leave them outside the doors but to take them into the rooms.

Mr Scanlan was the guest most pleased to see me returning the shoes. A sight for sore eyes, he said, and they did look sore, or at least very wrinkled. Like the wrinkled skin around the eyes of the old bullocks that skeetered the streets on fair days. His room was not so pleasant as Miss Carroll's; it was far up the corridor, which at that time of morning was very quiet. There was always a smell from his washhand basin. Stale soap, if such a thing is possible. And gobbling noises came from it every now and then as if it was about to spew up something ferocious. He did not do things to me as Rocky had done except for rubbing my face against the rough hairs of his. 'See how the fairies pull out my beardies at night,' he used to say and rasp me, laughing. He was a lonely soul and it was not until I developed the rash on my chin, for which I had to steal Fay's Nivea Creme to salve myself with, that I gave up going to him.

None of the other guests were permanent. I did not feel I knew them enough to visit, so that, bit by bit, I was finding myself more and more in the nursery room. My geography began to come on with great leaps.

Then I began to experiment with matches. It was Dada's cigarettes that started it. After Mama died I had to sleep with Dada to keep him company. I would be asleep when, after closing the bar and then cleaning all the glasses, he came to bed. The smell of the cigarette would waken me. He always smoked a cigarette before switching off the light. He must have thought that I turned into a sort of ball once I went to bed, because as soon as he lay down he bundled me up, kicking his legs all around me and I could feel all the moistness of him until I fell asleep, or he broke away from me, muttering loudly to himself. One night, after Fay had said goodnight and while the singing of the drunks went on in the bar beneath me, I lit up one of his cigarettes. I liked it. I liked the sudden rush of deadness into my head and then having to lie flat out from weakness while the bed seemed to float about the big room. But it was the lighting of the match that was best. And the little crackling and buzzing on the cigarette as it sucked in the flame. So I took to lighting matches in the nursery. And that was how, one evening after I'd had my bath, I lit the fire that had been set and my dressing gown caught flame and I burned myself. Fay congratulated me on my quick thinking, because I had pulled the dressing gown off and thrown it in the fire. But she asked me did I think Dada would be happy losing Mama and then me? She asked me to think about it.

I knew myself that it was Mama had saved me the night of the fire. An angel in the choir, she was more than that, she was a guardian angel – but then I began getting in other kinds of trouble that not only could she not save me from but I would have been ashamed for her even to have seen. I had stolen Fay's Nivea Creme to deal with the Scanlan rash. But the day I stole it, I saw money lying on her dressing table. Just a little money, enough to buy a fizz-bag or something. When I came back a few days later because of a sudden thirst that only a fizz-bag could quench – probably because of that fire and the drying effect it was after having on me that would not go away – there was all this extra money lying around, I didn't know how much. I didn't have time to pick and choose among the coins, so I took them all. When I went to Georgey's shop I was amazed at how much I had and so was Georgey, his long neck growing even longer as it stuck out of his collar and he looked down over the counter at me.

'Your birthday?' he said.

'Yeh,' I said. 'A fizz-bag, please.'

'And is that all?'

'How many can I buy?'

'Let me see, eight shillings and seven pence. Thrupence each. That's thirty-four fizz-bags and a penny-bar.'

I said penny-bars were bad for my teeth. Even though I ate them all the time, they got dropped from the menu once something better was on offer.

'Thirty-three fizz-bags and two sherbets then.'

I said, 'OK, thanks.'

'I like a lad with manners,' he said.

Georgey was a gentleman himself. That was why he liked boys with manners. There were not that many of them. Fellows came in from the country to Georgey's shop and bought ice creams so large they could hardly open their mouths wide enough to bite them and then the ice creams slipped through the wafers onto the high step outside his shop and they cursed, 'Feck ya anyway, Georgey, with your slippery feckin' ice cream.' Georgey didn't like that. Often I had to stop and admire Georgey's way of walking on the footpath: his walking stick, how dapperly he brandished it. How he could make it twirl! He passed by the hotel each evening on his way home to his house in Lacey Parade after locking up the shop for the night. Quick step, the hat on, the scarf around the neck, a twirl of the walking stick into the air, a flick of it, as if he was trying to dislodge a lump of dog's doings off its tip. King of the Templemore toffs.

On my way home to the hotel, my fizz-bags stuffed into my pockets, I gave over my mind to hard sums . . . I worked out that were I to consume eleven bags a day, then the fizz-bags would last me three days. Exactly. Wasn't it great to know your eleven and twelve times tables? I had got as far as big sums in school with Burley. I hardly knew myself now, I was so good at them. Even sums with answers bigger than a hundred. Sure I would never need to go back to school again. On my first and second day I ate a fizz-bag every waking hour and that was great, but on day three I opted for all my fizz-bags together because one at a time was becoming boring. The contents of eleven fizz-bags and two sherbets emptied into a glass and water poured over them. It was a tricky business. I accomplished it at the kitchen sink while nobody was looking. But the water had a problem getting into the glass; after the first few drops no more would go in because the fizz-bags exploded out of the glass as though they were a bomb and I got such a fright I didn't know where to go with the glass and ran through the kitchen, the glass spitting out all my fizz-bags and sherbets over the dinners sitting on the hot range ready to go into the dining room. Fizz-bags and sherbets don't go together, I'm afraid, I said to myself. But then Bid Cullen, whose attentions I was trying to avoid by smothering the glass against my jumper, shouted out that I was a rat belonging to a witch and got a sweeping brush after me and I dropped the bubbling glass and ran out in the yard.

Unfortunately, on a diet of eleven fizz-bags a day one develops a severe, to use Fay's word for her explanation for her ten cups of coffee a day, addiction. The next time I approached Fay's dressing table the idea was to return the hairclips that had been mixed in with the money and that I had in my haste taken along with it the first day. This time the money on the dressing table lay there all bare, no clips or hairs or strands of doubt in the way. Even before I mounted the high step to Georgey's, my mathematical abilities being now well advanced after the first day's exercise, I knew how many fizz-bags were within my reach.

'Let's see how much we have.' I could see Georgey's neck enlarging again at the sight of the money.

'Nine shillings and no pennies,' I said.

'Another birthday?'

'Yeh.'

'You'll be older than myself soon.'

'Yeh. I have two birthdays. One that I had with my mother and I still have it. One that I have with Fay since she found that the date on the birth certificate was three days after the date my mother said.' Which was true, by the way, confusing but true, except that my two birthdays were yet months away. 'Thirty-six fizz-bags, please, no sherbets.'

'Your mother God rest her.' Georgey's head sadly toppled from side to side on his long neck.

The next time I went into Georgey he didn't even ask me about my birthday, just handed over the thirty-six fizz-bags. That evening Fay told me that she and I were having a chat.

I don't think I will ever forgive Fay for her deception.

'How much bait would you say is required to rat out a thief?' Here was that word *rat* again. And a cold smile to go with it that was exceedingly threatening. It reminded me of cold meat on a bare dinner plate. 'Nine shillings, would you say, would that be enough to catch the little rat that has been visiting your aunt's quarters? Nine shillings might be a big hole in one's federal reserves, don't you think? And the poor exchange rate on the American dollar.'

'Is it poor at the moment?' I asked. Fay was always giving me bulletins about the exchange rate on her dollars that she was still getting from the diocese of San Francisco, where she had worked with the priests.

'If there is one thing I would wish, it is that you have an idea of the value of money.'

'Yes, Aunt Faith.'

She gave me an option. Either she told Dada or I was a big boy and received a tanning on the bottom.

I felt my face burn hot.

'Telling Dada is the worst,' I mumbled.

In the end she didn't give me the tanning on the bottom. But how could Fay have put me in such a predicament? I will never forgive her for that either. After all, only a few days previously I had complimented her on a shapely dress she had been wearing: 'I like that black dress on you, Auntie Fay.'

'Why do you like it?' She had been delighted, looking at herself in the mirror.

'I don't know.' And I didn't know how to say it either. 'Makes you sort of . . . something, I don't know.'

The truth was that I liked what it did to her, fattening her or something, making her somehow like Una. Not of course to the extent where somebody like Grizzler might want to drop the hand on her. That would be out of the question with Fay. Out of the question. But the black dress made her look pretty.

'You're growing up,' she said smiling, still looking at herself in the mirror, with her hands giving her titties a boosting. How could Fay have put a growing boy in such a predicament?

I didn't get the tanning on the bottom that time. But I got it shortly afterwards. I will not forget it, not to my dying day.

The tanning came another day, as a result of rudeness to Aunt Leg.

'Why didn't you keep an eye on Aunt Leg's ironing when she asked you?' said Fay.

'It was too nice outside.'

'What did you say to her when she came back from the toilet?'

'That it wasn't my fault what happened.'

'What else?'

'That she didn't have to iron vests and things, only skirts and blouses.'

'And?'

'She said vests and things had to be aired, that's why they had to be ironed.'

'What else did you say?'

'Nothing.'

'You did. You used shocking yard-boy language, which while it may not shock me, has greatly distressed your grand-aunt.'

It had been all Aunt Leg's own fault. I had told her I was not going to help her. Everybody thought that because I was not going to school I should be their slave. Especially Aunt Leg, wheezing beside her ironing board up on the landing every Tuesday with her sagging cheeks flapping around her neck like turkey wattles. And I having to rummage through her laundry for her and stack in piles, first her knickers, then her vests, then her hankies. And then stack them all again after the ironing.

'What's that smell?' says Aunt Leg when she comes back from the toilet and I had already told her I wasn't minding her stuff. She should have known what the smell was. She should have seen the big brown burn of the iron.

'The arse's burning out of your poor knickers, Aunt Leg,' says I.

It had been the first time I'd ever used that word. Having heard it in the yard, I'd only wanted to hear what it sounded like coming out of me, especially having found a use for it in an appropriate setting. And I'd only left the iron on her stack of knickers to see how far down the burn mark would get to. Aunt Leg was always making mistakes with burn marks, I had just wanted to see how long it took to make a mistake myself.

I think what I said next caused the real damage.

She said she thought she had only imagined I had used certain language and that maybe the word she'd heard was *arson* and she asked me what was she going to wear for mass now that all her knickers were ruined. Aunt always walked to daily mass at twelve o'clock. Her constitutional, she called it.

'Sure the priest is hardly going to notice your arson, let alone if it's a burnt arson,' says I. And I left her there, chuckling to myself about Aunt Leg walking to church, imagining herself the talk of the town, imagining everybody taking a look at her big brown burnt arson through her coat and skirt.

I actually don't know what overcame me, that I should have shot off like that, first one barrel, then the second barrel, of dirty language. But I paid for it.

'She is your grand-aunt,' said Fay. 'That makes her my aunt. Who I greatly respect and it is for that reason you are being punished.'

I heard Georgey out in the shop once talking to Fanning the butcher about the reason why the world was coming to what it was, and that was the lack of punishment that had a good effect on people. In Georgey's opinion what had a good effect on people was to take their trousers down and give them the cane. A great effect.

No Georgey. Never. It has a very bad effect, not a good effect, on people. Nobody should have their trousers taken down like that, because when the trousers comes down there is no protecting the little pure thing within. It's the window to the heart, is the arson. Which only wants to shrink away then and die of shame. Comfort, the heart needs then, not chastising. Chastising was what Fay did.

6

Geography with Fay, the company of the guests and the staff of the hotel, these were not enough for me. I had now gone ages without school, without so much as the smell of chalk dust, and I already knew everything. I had an appetite for the outside world. Dada could see that. I would have to learn to make a living, he said. He sent me out to work for him. That greatly relieved me because things were not going well for Dada. His various business ventures were failing. I heard it mentioned around the hotel. 'People are robbing the man; furniture is walking out of the hotel. Mama was the one who could run the show.' These were things I overheard. Well, now was my chance to help stop the rot.

Dada was the auctioneer in the cattle-mart and he posted me in the gap between the hotel yard and the cattle-mart yard. It was the first time I ever had to do anything for Dada, apart from riding the pony. Riding the pony, I was not good at; driving cattle, after a little instruction, I was. I always seemed to know which way the cattle would break. I was not afraid to stand before them and block them off. Dada did not have to shout too much at me when I drove cattle. Unlike when he had me on the pony's back. 'Are you heedless or what?' he would shout when the pony ran away with me. 'You must show who's boss or he'll make a proper fool of you.'

Cattle never went into much competition about who was boss. Indeed, I soon saw why that was the case. As soon as I had been installed at the gate between the hotel yard and the cattle-mart, and allowed to stand in line with Christy Horner and the other cattle-jobbers, they showed me. They showed me who was boss. All of them with sticks that had knobs on the ends, like golf sticks. 'Give him the knob of your wattle in the skull, young Connaughton,' Christy shouted to me. A crazy bullock, bellowing with fright, had burst past me, so that all I saw as he stampeded towards the hotel kitchen was his tail up and gushes of stuff coming out of his green hole underneath. Christy showed me how to do it. Crack crack, he swung at the bullock, crunching into its hollow dome. The bullock closed its eyes against Christy's whacks and went down on its knees before returning, beaten, to the yard. 'Lovely hurling, hold the gap.' That was the way all the other drovers did it also. Spitting on their hands and beating cattle from pen to pen and into the sales ring, where Dada sat high above the din, his hammer tapping for attention against the auctioneer's counter, announcing: 'Choice cattle. How much am I bid for this choice lot of cattle; cattle you could sell at any crossroads. Oh cattle sent to us from heaven.' Dada, who could calm the frantic sales ring, slow down the world, with his soothing voice.

And the cattle-drovers – they may not have been bosses of much else in the world, because for the rest of the week they stood at the town hall, being, as Mama used to call them, corner-boys. But each Thursday in the cattle yard, embattled and dung-spattered, they showed who was boss.

But Dada wanted me back in school. As soon as possible. I knew that. I knew it the day he gave me the lesson. On that day, he told me he would find me a new school even if it meant having to move house. The lesson took place a few weeks into my three-month holiday from Brother Burley. Only one lesson and in that lesson I learned to read. I learned so well that I could never forget how to read again. It was hard work, though. Tears for me: a sore throat from all the shouting for Dada – more shouting for him than on a day spent in his sales ring selling cattle. Only one lesson and it was enough. I didn't want any more lessons with Dada. And I knew he didn't want me hanging about not going to school. He didn't want a repeat of that lesson any more than I did. So you can imagine how I felt at my job in the cattle-mart. Knowing that while it was Dada had given me the job, there was the thought hovering over me at all times that Dada might give me the sack and send me back to school. It was enough to make a fellow lose heart in his work.

My lesson with Dada came about because of my big problem. My big problem was spelling. I hadn't known it was a problem. I knew where all the towns were on the map, all the capital cities, without having to know how to spell them.

I didn't know it was a problem when every day I went into the toilet and came out saying 'Armattack War' to myself, spraying imaginery bullets around the landing as I said it. That was what was written on the inside of the toilet bowl, and it was wonderful. I loved to say it. 'Armattack war.' It conjured the most ideal picture of armies, aeroplanes, at war.

'Armattack War,' I said whenever I got the chance. It was my favourite game.

'What are you saying?' Fay said. She was amused.

'Armattack War. Pyeuw, pyeuw.' (The sound of guns.)

'I see, anti-aircraft is it?' Fay was an expert on war as on everything but this time she had it wrong.

'No.'

'Aircraft carriers then?' Fay always liked to share my thoughts with me.

'No. Armattack War. It's written on the toilet.'

'I see.'

The next time Fay used the toilet she came out spluttering with laughter.

And shortly afterwards I overheard her telling Dada how she had evidence to suggest I was suffering from a thing called dyslexia and she told him about Armattack War. 'He's mispronouncing, can't you see? It's Armitage Ware.'

I couldn't make a connection between suffering from a disease and not being able to pronounce words written on a toilet bowl. But whatever the disease was, Dada cured it: *L.W. Connaughton and Company Limited. Undertakers, Auctioneers & Valuers, Victuallers.* We sat down at his high desk in the commercial room. He pulled out a page with those words written on it. Nothing else, just those words on the top, the rest of the page blank and waiting for Dada's fast slanty writing in the Biro that was able to travel much quicker than any pencil.

'Now, let us see.' Dada lit a cigarette, and he was smiling and gentle. 'Let me hear you pronounce that word' – he put his pen under *Valuers* – 'it is a simple one. You pronounce the sounds of the letters and that is how you get the word.'

'What word, Dada?' says I, hoping he would pronounce it for me.

But he only pointed to *Valuers* again with his Biro. 'That one.'

'Oh, that one.'

I got to work on *Valuers*. Real slow, I worked it out. 'Vee-ale-you-ears, Dada. Isn't that it, Dada? What does Vee-ale-you-ears mean?' It certainly did sound as if it meant something.

'Vee-ale-you-ears? Where in the name of God did you get Vee-ale-you-ears? What sort of word is that? The word is *valuers*. That's how you pronounce it. VALUERS.'

Oh God, we were only on our first word and Dada was already losing his patience. It was like when we schooled the pony over the fences, those enormous unavoidable fences that the pony didn't want to jump and I, on its back, certainly didn't want to jump. Only Dada wanted the pony to jump those fences. These big words were like the fences, huge, and I was out of control coming up to them. When Dada taught me to ride he carried a big branch for driving the pony. He dragged the branch along the ground at the pony's heels and that sent the pony hopping mad. 'Hold him up, hold him up, can't you? Have you any strength in your arms?'

That was the problem. I had no strength in my arms. As soon as the pony ducked away from the fence and bolted for home, all my strength left me. And all thought left my mind, until I found myself standing in the middle of the dark stable, the pony at a quivering halt, me miraculously trussed atop, arms pinned to my sides, feet tucked beneath me. Like a jockey, except that I wasn't one. And counting my arms and legs to see if they were still there and not shorn off by the door beams. A smell of damp pony droppings and fear. What could I do then but cry, and wait for Dada to return and tell me, with great disappointment in his voice, to get off the pony's back?

One time I did not cry. It was the time the pony ducked out at the right side of the fence instead of the left side and instead of galloping home to his stable, galloped into Tom Donnelly's yard. Tom Donnelly and my Dada had yards that ended in the same field. Into Tom Donnelly's he carried me. Dada shouting from behind. 'Turn him, turn him or you'll kill him.' We tore right through Donnelly's geese – I saw streaks of white in every direction – dashed through Donnelly's back door and ended bolt upright in Donnelly's kitchen, all the hens that roosted there leaping off the table and as many as could, flying out the door. The feathers floated all around me and settled in the sugar and the milk and that was the day the remarkable fact dawned on me that not all kitchens were as frantic as ours, that some kitchens could be so peaceful that the hens bunked on the table for hours on end.

Yes, hens were common guests in that kitchen. I could tell it because when the woman came through one of the low doors that led in from other rooms, Mrs Donnelly, she was not a bit surprised to see the hens who had stayed on, who hadn't bothered to fly out the door. Or to see the pony either. It was only me that surprised her. 'Glory be, is it little Connaughton in my kitchen?' she said. And she just shooed the hens off the bread bin in such a way that made me wonder what my Mama would have thought of a kitchen such as Mrs Donnelly's.

When you had riding lessons you could escape to the stable or to Tom Donnelly's, even though you might lose an arm or a leg. During a spelling lesson there was no escape. Riding the pony was one of the things I called 'Doing things Dada is good at'. And if he was good at it then, Jesus, what was wrong with me if I wasn't good at it too? I was useless. Spelling was another of the things big Dada was good at.

Valuers was the first word I ever learned to read. It was very late that night before Dada was finished with me. He didn't work in the bar that night. We could hear the din of last orders coming up the back stairs but he did not go down. I cried lots of times, I cried over *Auctioneers, Valuers, Undertakers, Company, Limited.*

'Pronounce that word. He pointed to *Limited.*'

'Elleye–emeye–ted. Big word, Dada.'

'Oh holy God, are you listening to what I say or are you heedless?'

Dada, please go down and help at the bar, I wanted to say. I'm worried about your business. It's going down the Swanee.

Then we got to *Victuallers.* Oh what a task of pronunciation that word set me. In getting my mouth around that word for my Dada there came out of me the most contorted, the most frightful sounds. I thought I was lost forever and seriously considered never opening my lips again. And it was then it happened. And everything became clear as day: for Dada explained to me that there were such things as exceptions: *Vitlars*, was how you pronounced it, he told me. 'Repeat that. Vitlars'. Just because you saw a C or a U or an A in a word didn't mean you had to pronounce the C or the U or the A. 'There are some words for which you have to use your ear.'

'Your ear, Dada, not your eye?'

'Yes, your ear.'

'Aren't exceptions great things, Dada. Are there lots of them?'

And that was it. I had cracked it. And after *Victuallers* I was able to read. Dada went down to clear the last drinkers and even before he returned I had it all. I could pronounce anything I liked. It was a simple matter of matching the words I saw on the page with the sounds I heard in my head. There I was, the sound of footsteps on the footpath outside, somebody singing 'The whistling gypsy came over the hill', doors banging, me reading the words on Dada's other letterheads: *L.W. Connaughton Wine & Spirits Merchants*, and so on. Because after *Victuallers*, normal words were a cakewalk: *Spade. Sand. The. Sea. Blue. Armitage. Ware.* A cakewalk.

I only had to find out then what the big words after Dada's name actually meant: *Undertakers, Auctioneers & Valuers, Victuallers.* And when I found out their meanings everything made sense. I had an ear for meanings too. And after that night, wherever I went around the town, new words kept appearing. Flocks of words. Falling into my eyes. Falling into my ears. Over at Dick Conroy's, the barber's, for example. On the racing calendars above his mirror: *The Cambridgeshire*; *The Cesarewitch*.

'There's a queer word I saw over at Dick Conroy's, Dada.' I spelled *Cesarewitch* out for him.

'Zaritch, Lally. Two miles plus handicap for three-year-olds and upwards at Newmarket.'

'Zaritch, Dada. Oh of course. That's a great word, Dada.'

I was receiving a rich education, and not a day spent in school.

7

Oh school days, school days . . . Were they the bane of my life or what?

There was a time – long before Burley and the Brothers – when I was not afraid of school. On the very first day, for example. At the nuns. When I was four.

On my very first day Mama held my hand all the way up to school. Other little boys and girls were having their hands held by their Mamas just the same as me and so I didn't feel too embarrassed. My Mama was walking very slowly, though, and holding my hand very tightly. I was not afraid. Other little children were very frightened. They were hiding in their Mamas' skirts. I saw Sausage Donnelly, the son of Tom, the man with the quiet kitchen on Main Street. It was the first time I'd ever seen him except from a window. He was hiding in his Mama's skirt. If I wanted to hide in skirts anyway, I couldn't. Mama didn't wear skirts like all the other Mamas. My Mama always wore her riding trousers. So there were all these children, getting lost inside their Mamas' skirts. And there was me and I could be seen plain as day between the legs of my Mama's jodhpurs. Then we got to the railings and we both looked in. I had never seen so many children. Running and bumping into one another. All the ones that were running looked very skinny to me; they pulled each other, shoved each other, with knobbly thin arms. Mama looked and said, no, you are too young to go to school. And walking home, she held my hand tighter than ever.

I was not afraid, either, on my second day. Dada said, 'Mama, you have to let him go.' We were halfway up our own wide street, before we even got near narrow Thomas McDonagh Terrace where the school was, when I said, 'We'll sing our song, Mama.' Mama always wanted me to sing along with her, so here I was, doing her a big favour. 'She wears red feathers and a huly huly skirt.' Once I got her a bit happy, I said, 'Bye bye now, Mama.' Then I let go. But I held hands with girls all day. They were the hugest girls I ever saw. The girls in sixth class. Their heads swam away up in the air, up to the tops of the doors nearly, above me, but not up as high as the nuns. The nuns were impossibly high, they bore their faces around on what I took to be skylights.

'Musha silly laddie,' says Mama when I had to describe the day's events to her at teatime. 'They are bonnets they wear that fit around their heads on a collar, and bibs. Not skylights.'

'Bibs, Mama?'

On my third day . . . On my third day I sat behind Sausage Donnelly. Sausage was sitting there, head on his arms, the quietest boy I ever saw, when all of a sudden he went to the toilet. I saw it. A visitor. It just slid down his trousers and sat on the bench with a twirl of itself beside him. She sniffed. Sister Annunciata was her name. She wore a wide belt. It tucked in her tummy and had a heavy rosary beads hanging from it with Jesus on his cross just about hitting the ground. The good thing for Sister Annunciata about having Jesus out like that instead of in a purse was that any-time of the day she desired she could rub him and say prayers. Now she didn't rub him but sniffed again. She removed Sausage

Donnelly but left young Sausage Donnelly on the seat. It sat there all day before me; richly brown it was at first but by the time we went home at lunch hour it looked licked and beaten.

I didn't tell Mama about any of this. Feeling already superior to at least one person, Sausage Donnelly, I thought I could handle the situation. But the fourth day I could not handle. On the fourth day Sister Annunciata came in with a bamboo stick. Sausage Donnelly's face went red. He licked the end of his long nose until I thought another young Sausage must be on the way. Suddenly, instead of performing his silent conjuring act, he jumped out of his seat and ran for the door. Sister Annunciata must have seen him, for she also made a swoop for the door. Sausage Donnelly got there first, though. If Sister Annunciata hadn't slowed herself up by grabbing the bamboo stick from beneath the table, she might have. There was consternation then. Because as soon as old Sausage saw Sister Annunciata grab the bamboo, he bawled and the tears leaped out of him. Instead of young Sausage landing on the bench as it normally should, it did not release itself from fleeing old Sausage until he was crossing the door threshold. Sister Annunciata, hot after him with her bamboo, slipped on young Sausage, so that we just got a quick glimpse of her as she went skating down the corridor, veils, rosary beads and windowpane headgear trailing in her slipstream.

Somebody took up a refrain: 'Sister Annunciata the big fat tomata.' I don't know where it came from, maybe the naughty big boys from Senior Infants had made it up, but I thought it was the funniest thing ever and before I knew it I had joined in. The next thing I noticed was the silence all around me and myself the only one singing 'Sister Annunciata the big fat tomata.' I had to look at myself to see if it was really me the voice was coming from, and only me. And there was Sister Annunciata, standing in the corridor just outside the door, about to bear down upon me. And oh what had she done to herself? Why had she discarded her bonnet? Its hinges were flapping at her chin like wings. And her plastic bib, a neat brown smudge upon it, was falling and rising like a yo-yo. Before I had seen only face, now I saw ears. And head, plucked like a chicken. Sister Annunciata, who has been getting at your hair? You looked a sight better with your bib and bonnet on.

I didn't know what sudden bravery overpowered me but I ran to the door and slammed it in her face. I held it there while she tried to push it in for I didn't know how long, all the class behind me joyfully singing 'Sister Annunciata the big fat tomata' again. Oh but it was desperation. Watching the door handle before my eyes, twisting, ratcheting. The door opening a little, the bamboo poking round the corner trying to get at my legs, like a snake. And I, so carried away by my strength, I slammed it out. In the end I could take no more. I let go and ran. But where was there to run to? I ran straight into the blackboard. Slam, I felt the huge lumps as they rose around my eyes and closed them. One of the big girls held my hand on the way home. I couldn't see her.

Mama couldn't understand why I had run into the blackboard. I thought the best thing was to say nothing; I thought that while school life with Sister Annunciata might continue to be frightening, at least now she would never attempt to touch me again. 'Oh children what will we do with this silly boy?' she had said as I had stood before her class, blind. Sister Annunciata: her tone of resignation said she had given up on me. But poor Mama, if she knew, she would only drown me with her tears and then blame Sister Annunciata and what good would that be? Especially knowing it was not true. That would only lead to a worse situation.

I should have told Mama, though. While I still had the chance of a person being around to take blame away from me and put it on somebody else I should have taken it. I should have told her.

And of course she was no longer around one day I did a sausage in my own trousers. A wet sausage in Brother Burley's class, and had to waddle home, juggling it from one slappy cheek of my bottom to the other.

Three months that period lasted, when all the boys were at school and I had an important job in the cattle-mart and in the mornings I studied geography and in the evenings I played a game called Armattack War.

I had done the six counties of Munster, the names of the capital cities of Europe and of the states of America, when my education with Fay came to an end. For every capital city and every state, Fay had a story. She hadn't stayed on the counties of Munster very long.

I think she found the place a bit limiting. But she could have stayed on capital cities forever. And so could I.

This day, Fay ticked off a spot on the map of Ireland with a quick correction mark of her pencil. She was back on Munster again and I was disappointed. She just very casually ticked off a spot.

'Where's that?' I said, bored at the sight of old Ireland. The tick was on the brown and green map, the one with only the mountains and rivers. No towns, no counties in their nice patchwork of colours, so I didn't know where the place at the tick was, except that it was up in the brown mountains.

Very thoughtfully she looked at it and then she said: 'Do you know what a watershed is?'

'No.'

'A watershed is a place on mountains where waters part company. Take the origins of the Three Sister rivers. They have their beginnings in little streams rising alongside each other. But then what way do they run? They run down either side of the watershed. They take totally different journeys until, becoming big rivers, they meet again at the sea. The mystery is this: from that spot I have ticked on your map, where do the waters take themselves? Down down the River Nore, down down the River Suir? Or even, maybe, down the River Barrow? It all depends on the tilt of the landscape.' Fay laughed. She loved mysteries.

'Oh,' I said.

And now here I was in that very watershed of the Three Sister rivers. It was early in the morning. I was in bed, where I did all my thinking. I was listening to the calls of a man hunting cows outside in a field somewhere in a place I only knew as a spot ticked off on a map. Beside me in the bed was my new brother. I was barely taking up any room; clinging on to the bed for life, for fear, every time my new brother turned or twisted, of falling out of it and toppling off in the direction of either the River Nore or the River Suir or even the Barrow. The great cattle-jobber, the one who got away from Burley, who slept with all sorts of people, who conversed with the commercial travellers of the world, there he lay, fearful of waking this new brother, fearful of having to talk to him. And then suddenly remembering something his Dada had said once when he told his Dada he preferred working to school, told him that helping stop his slide into financial ruin was preferable to a school desk: 'You won't have to go back to that school any more,' Dada had said. 'Even if it means we all have to move home, we'll find a new school for you.'

So was that why I had those long holidays? Three whole months. To give Dada plenty of time to look for this new home for me? Was that why Dada got married again? On my account? Oh no, oh please Dada no. Please. Tell me it was because of what Denis the waiter said. What I overheard him say once in the hotel kitchen. He said Dada's business interests were flopping. He said Dada needed 'a steady keel'. Please don't tell me it was on my account.

Morning after morning, in bed in my new house, I thought things over. Listening to the voices driving the cows in from the field, I soon recognised one of them. 'Hup, hup, get in you silly old lady!' Impatience, that was the normal tone of Dada's voice, but now what softer tone was there in addition? So Dada was up early to milk this woman's cows. He was out there, contented. I was lying in the bedroom, baked from the big heavy curtain that kept out the light but not the heat. And the woman was in the bedroom next door. I could hear the bedsprings groan underneath her just as they had underneath Aunt Leg. What else was there to do but think things over. Not the new things, not the woman lying among the snappings of bedsprings in the room next door, but the old things. The hotel. Only Dada went back there now, while we children had to stay in Ivyhall. There was talk he would have to sell it; furniture was still walking out the door. People with big pockets. Days in the hotel played over and over in my mind.

'Are you asleep?' Richie would say when at last he woke up.

He would ask a few times.

'No.'

'What are you doing?'

'Thinking.'

'Thinking what?'

'Nothing.'

8

B reakfast: it is always the first occasion by which you can tell the difference between places. In the hotel it used to be great.

Every morning in Ivyhall I was wide awake. Then when the big boy in the bed beside me woke up I pretended to be sound asleep. Until his questions became too insistent. Then he got up and after a while he said Mammy said I was to get up for breakfast. Mammy: that was a name that sat very awkwardly on my tongue. Mammy. And breakfast: could you call it that?

When I went down to the kitchen with the sour smell there was Richie seated before three slices of brown bread and he was slapping the butter on the bread. An inch thick he plastered it and his big teeth left marks like cliffs on the butter each time he took a bite. I looked around for the toast. In Ivyhall there was no toast for breakfast. No toast, not like in the hotel, only slices of brown bread. I didn't care; I told myself that. I ate whatever I got. Anyway, hadn't Sister Annunciata said there were children in Africa who didn't even know what bread looked like. I used to be choosy in the hotel, but not here. In the hotel I had known the foods that were good for me. That was due to Fay's education: salt is good for you but sugar is not. Marmalade is good for you but jam is not. 'We've got to be cruel to be kind.'

Once in the hotel, my sister Pam and me tackled the silver dishes of jam and marmalade laid out each morning on the tables in the dining room.

'I'll eat the marmalade,' I said. 'You eat the jam.'

In her innocence the poor girl agreed. 'I like jam,' says she, with an eager nod of her head.

'I know,' I said, 'and marmalade is horrible.' But I hadn't volunteered to eat the marmalade out of the goodness of my heart. I wanted to see how sick my sister became and conversely how healthy I became.

Down the stairs we went, to the kitchen. It was real early everywhere. The kitchen staff were quiet because they hadn't woken up properly. Bid Cullen saw us coming and asked us what mischief were we up to so early. We weren't up to mischief, just a lesson in healthy living.

Apart from Denis, there was nobody in the dining room. Each table had a full jug of water. The cutlery was all laid out, heavy and gleaming. Denis was going through all the tables, setting the knives and forks the proper distance apart and fluffing up the serviettes. Silently, waiterly, he made his round, pausing once to look benignly across at us. He placed a few spare plates on the dumbwaiter and revolved it so that it gave a little shimmering sound of delph. Then he went into the kitchen. Not a sign of a soul now, just the sound of Bid Cullen's voice coming through the dumbwaiter: 'Too precious those two are . . . if I had my way' – her usual complaining.

'Ready, steady, go,' I said to Pam.

We did the table under the phone. We did the tables beneath the racing pictures on the wall. It was enjoyable, eating and looking up at the long, stretched out horses and stretched out jockeys; seeing those jockeys that looked so confident with themselves in the picture of the start of the race and then following their progress in the pictures of them going over jumps and then in the picture of the finish. And concluding that those jockeys we couldn't see at the finish, and who we hadn't spotted falling into drains in the in-between pictures, must have fallen off at a jump that had no picture painted of it. No matter how confident they may have looked at the start. 'Just goes to show you,' I said to Pam. And it was lovely and quiet making these observations before the guests came down to breakfast with their noisy newspapers. We did the tables by the sideboard. Every now and then we stopped for conversations about how nice her jam tasted and how awful my marmalade was. 'A spoonful of sugar makes the medicine go down,' says I gleefully to Pam, and I hopping the salt off my marmalade to make me even healthier and hopping the sugar off her jam to hasten her demise. As we did the tables by the window I began to feel so healthy I thought I could afford to stop taking the marmalade altogether. I asked Pam did she feel sick but she said she didn't. So manfully I carried on, tackling the tables by the fireplace, the tables where Aunt Leg and Miss Carroll sat.

We had a few more conversations. I giggled a little to myself at the sight of Pam's jam-smeared face. That was another thing about marmalade and salt – your face stayed nice and clean. Then the only tables left were the table by the dumbwaiter and the table in the little dining room that was cut off from the rest, where Dada and Fay sat when they came to breakfast. Pam was getting despondent because the jam was nearly all gone. I was thinking that was the first sign of sickness: gluttony for more of what was bad for you; a person got that just before they died. God, she looked shocking, her mouth in a right mess. Then in pops Denis's head through the dumbwaiter. 'Refills,' he says and plonks two enormous jars, one of jam and one of marmalade, before us. 'Oh goodie,' Pam says. And that very same moment my healthy living failed me. All that goodness, it shot up from my tummy in a hot vomit like it was strung from a catapult. I had to stay in bed for days. The doctor said I was to have only toast until my tummy settled. 'Without marmalade,' said he. What sort of medicine was that for a doctor not to be ordering?

So no toast in Ivyhall, and no marmalade either. And Mammy.

Who was Mammy? She was the same person with the severe black hair, except that instead of dressing in black she had taken to wearing clothes with colours in them. Dresses, with flowers. Funny though, in my book they didn't make her any the less severe.

'Two slices of bread each. Down to the bathroom after breakfast,' she said. 'Queue up. First the boys and then the girls.'

As breakfast is the first event that gives you an idea of the rituals of any new house you move into, so the bathroom is the first room by which you may assess its character. That is because the bathroom is the only place in which you are on your own and have a chance to gather your thoughts. In Ivyhall the bathroom was shaped in the form of an L. You went along the first arm of the L, down cement steps, to where the toilet bowl stood. Beside it was an oil heater. The oil heater was turned on when you had a bath. I didn't know that then, though. When you went to the end of the other arm of the L, where the sink was, to wash your teeth, you were no longer within sight of the door. Then you got the panicky feeling. Strange that the phantoms whose appearance I was now in dread of were all new. All new dread beings I imagined hovering around the house of Ivyhall. Living silently in the garret at the top of the house, escaping every now and then for expeditions along the walls and the stairs. My Mama was not among these phantoms. They were a rougher lot, who had ousted my Mama from her prime position. She was drifting away, happier to be among her choir of angels. I found it difficult to go down that far arm of the L in the bathroom. Flushing the toilet was another problem. That too seemed to bring on the phantoms. And you couldn't get out quick enough either, after flushing the toilet or after washing your teeth, without feeling the wind of the whooshing phantom grab at your heels. In the end I had to give up flushing the toilet and washing teeth. Richie called me 'smelly'. He said the bathroom smelled of 'pure carrion' after me, whatever pure carrion was.

I can't tell at what stage I began to stop thinking over the things of the old days. Important and all as they had been. There had been my girlfriend, for instance. How could anyone forget Ann Morkan? She lived in a house on Patrick Street. I never spoke to her, but outside her house I lingered. She had a face narrow and wan as a crack of moonlight. The windowledges of her house had little ringed railings and one evening my finger got stuck in one of the rings. Hours I had to stand in the dark at those railings, wrenching and pulling at first and then giving up and pretending I was one of the corner-boys until, in the end, a woman came along and poured a saucepan of soapy water over me and the finger slid out. It was bruised and so knobbly sore. Just like the way my heart was for Ann Morkan, to whom I had never spoken. I can't tell either when the songs I learned in the hotel began to go out of my head:

> Hey round the corner, yuhoo.
> Beneath the berry tree.
> Hey round the corner, behind the bush,
> Looking for Henry Lee.

Who was that fellow, Henry Lee? What was going on down around the corner behind the bush? Was Henry scaring the girls? If he was, why then did they go down there? Mama and me used to sing that song, daring ourselves not to be scared as we sang it. Who, in the name of all the saints, is Henry Lee anyway, Mama? A right boyo he was, according to Mama. He'd break a girl's heart. What do you mean by that, Mama?

Oh God, my understanding of all those things that sent my own heart into a dither . . . In those regards the sudden shift to Ivyhall had left me uneducated.

And now the old conundrums had to go. Now there were new things to be puzzled out: the height of the dunghills in the cattle-houses of Ivyhall. What was the idea at all? There was the puzzle: build the dunghills any higher and the cattle would have to shrink to get in or out. The hens in the yard could not walk into the houses to do their foraging but had to take to their wings for the high flight up. On my very first day in Ivyhall I worked like a Trojan. The fork that Richie held was called a sprong. A sprong, he said, was a fork with four prongs coming out of it. And the prongs were called grains.

'Here, take this one, a sprong is too heavy for you.' He handed me a fork that had only two grains. It was called a pike. I liked all the terminology of sprong, grain and pike, but it was impossible to get a grip on the dung you had to shift when you had a fork with only two grains.

'Why is the litter allowed to go so high?' I said to Richie. The two calves in the corner of the house, which had not been let out with the others because of coughing, were scratching their backs on the rafters.

Richie had his sleeves up and he was shifting layers of dung with his sprong. 'You throw on dry straw every day,' he said, 'on top of the wet stuff underneath. That saves you work. And keeps them warm.' He was clearing a little space by the gate. He pointed at the two calves, now high above us. What were they thinking of us funny creatures, as, with each moment, we grew smaller?

'Oh,' I said. 'I understand.'

At this stage of our relationship everything Richie said made the utmost sense. Everything Richie said was fine, though I couldn't help wondering how many years of litter had been allowed accumulate. Was I the slave, I wondered, who had been delivered to bring the litter down to size? And were the calves going to be freezing when they were brought to ground level?

Richie continued to throw sprongfuls. They came down on the floor of the yard with a thump. A sharp smell pinched inside my nose and brought water in my eyes. I teased and tossed the dung with my little pike. The dung was dense and matted. Every time I thought I had a grip of something substantial I tugged at my pike, only for it to slide upward through the dung and lunge forward as if it had a life of its own.

'Mind where you go with that pike,' Richie said.

'I'm minding,' I said. And that was the very first seed of the breakdown in our relationship.

'You'll stick me,' he said, one time my pike flew past his face.

'I won't.'

My problem was balance. I was wearing a pair of wellingtons that belonged to Richie. Far too big for me. (That was the problem, everything was too big, but that was not something to be admitted.) I could get no grip in the wellingtons and the dunghill had turned into a treacherous slippery slope.

'You're doing it wrong,' Richie said. 'You have to take it in layers.' So apparently the slope was my fault. The dunghill would have stayed level if I had taken it in layers.

'I'm doing it right,' I said.

'Here, let me show you.'

He showed me. And I must admit it. On only my first day in my new life of forking and shovelling I learned how it was done. It was done with a simple leverage of the knee against the handle.

'Saves mullocking,' Richie said. *Mullocking.* What sort of a word was that?

'Look at this,' I said to Richie. I wanted to show him how I had mastered the layer method of dung removal. On my fork this time, I had captured a layer so vast that I had the whole width of the floor on the move. I was proud of myself. But when I went to lift, using the knee as Richie had demonstrated, my forkload was so heavy I could not budge it. Time seemed to stand still as I continued to attempt it. Grunt. Pant. A robin that had been hopping around in the straw came over to have a look. Its eye cocked up at me.

'Your knee, use your knee,' said Richie.

'I can't.'

'Why can't you?'

'Too, uhhh, heavy.'

God it was easy to fall out with Richie. I could have stuck him. Couldn't he see my problem?

'You try it,' I said and walked away leaving my pike in the dung, quivering like a tuning fork.

Richie had a virtue. It was that when a situation became ruffled his mind could turn towards something practical instead of further ruffling it. A virtue which many times in the future would annoy me but here was the first time I watched it in action.

'We'll lift together,' he said. And here was another thing about him. He always wanted people to do things together. Not me. I was the Lone Star.

'Heave.' He was actually laughing. I laughed too, and the same fellow, only a second earlier, I had felt like sticking him.

We heaved. The dung beneath our feet moved. The ripple of its movement went across the shed like an earthquake. But we could not lift it.

'Jaysus,' he said.

'What?'

'Nothing, heave again.'

We heaved again.

I felt something slowly move. Somewhere in the depth of the dung I was grappling with something big. I felt it bite on the teeth of my pike. It seemed to stretch towards me, like elastic. I tugged. Then it sprang away and my pike came free in the air and I was thrown backwards across the shed, falling against the wall.

'Hey, Jaysus,' Richie said. 'Stop a minute.'

I was very keen to get on with my fishing beneath the dung. But I stopped.

He scraped away the top layer.

'Jaysus,' he said, replacing the top layer again. 'I'll be back in a minute.'

I waited until Richie had gone before clearing away the top layer to see for myself what was beneath. Then I saw the head. The mouth was open, yellow, dung-stained teeth stuck out of the lower jaw and the tongue stretched forward along the ground as if it had been pulled. Maggots were falling around on the tongue. The smell was bad, dull and deathly, not like the zingy smell from the dung. I hadn't much time to think about how the dead calf had got there, assuming that however it had, it must have been Richie's fault. Because I heard the tractor. I heard the chain opening on the yard gate and the tractor drive in. I hadn't got time to uncover the body for further discoveries. Concluding that it must have been the calf's hide that my fork had caught in, I threw some dung across the head.

My stepmother was driving the tractor. Where was Dada? No Dada. Dada was away in the hotel, of course. He would be doing that every day; leaving us behind in this strange place, at the mercy of winds, colliery hills and dunghills. She wore wellingtons. But her coat came down only to her knees. Is she cold? I thought. The knees, they were white and bare as marble. Do you get cold up on a tractor? She looked cold, and even more stern than ever. She backed the tractor towards the shed, straining her neck with stiff backward glances. She settled her jaw in a grip when the tractor wheels were locked tight against the cliffside of dung. Then she got off and tied a rope around something in the dung. The neck of the calf, I supposed, not looking too closely to find out. The rope went taut and made cracking sounds when she revved up the tractor. Tractor wheels skidded and kicked up muddy gravel in my face. 'Outa the way,' Richie motioned to me. Dear Jesus, I prayed, I hope the head doesn't tear off on its own. Then a chunk of the dung came unstuck. She drove away with it and I saw it rattle along the ground behind the tractor and the straw come tumbling off, until I could make out the long length of the calf. Its tail trailed along the ground. She drove up the lane to the hills. Where was she going to hide it this time? What else lay buried in this place? So much hidden, so much unmentioned. So much burned away with a scrubbing brush and caustic soda. Richie's father, there was never a mention of him. My own mother too would have to get the same treatment. Control over what you said was going to be important.

From all of this one thing became clear. The death of that calf and its disappearance in the dung had not been Richie's fault. And even if it had, he still had not kept it from his mother. Richie and his mother worked as a close team. And the roping of the dead calf gave Richie an idea. When Mam returned from the hills with the tractor he showed me how his idea worked. I had to dig trenches in the dung. Then he tied the rope around the trenches and pulled with the tractor. Bit by bit the shed was cleared. The two calves standing in the corner looked like dwarfs when it was all over. And the state of the yard outside was worse than the shed had ever been. That was the day I found out how much Richie loved the tractor. Richie would yoke up the tractor to do anything. If he could have yoked it up to blow his nose, I swear he would have.

All of which was to me rather a pity. I was just getting into the swing of the work. And it was the sort of work I knew I could be good at. Forking, forking, thinking my thoughts. The hidden things in Ivyhall. But that tractor, Richie's tractor: I could already see it loom on my horizon with the same threat that Dada's pony's had once posed. It too would hold mastery over me.

9

What else was there in Ivyhall at which one might work like a Trojan? Because I had to work like a Trojan. There were lots of things to work at like a Trojan in Ivyhall. Working like a Trojan was the way to be noticed by Dada. Except, unfortunately, that Dada was not around to notice. Each day except Sunday Dada had to return to work at the hotel. The hotel, the butcher's shop, the undertaker's and selling wool and the horses and other business. I no longer knew what went on there. I had no way of knowing how life in the world of business was faring. In Ivyhall only Mam was around to see who was working. And it was only Dada I wanted to impress. What did she mean to me anyway, that I should wish to impress her? Mam. That was the name that came about in the end. I wouldn't call her Mammy. Her own family, the Connells, called her that. But our mother had been called Mama. And why should it be we that had to change? I wouldn't call her Mammy. For a long time I wouldn't call her anything.

It went like this, and it was on Easter Sunday it happened, because it was a few Sundays before Easter that we moved to Ivyhall.

'Can I have another Easter egg?' (They were the tiniest Easter eggs, nothing like the Easter eggs in the hotel. I didn't really care to have another one; it was my way of letting it be known they were too small.)

'You can if you may.' This was Dada speaking. Dada was very good at grammar. It pained him to hear bad grammar. I was worse at grammar than anything in the world.

'May I have another Easter egg?'

'May I have another Easter egg what?' Now it was her speaking.

'May I have another Easter egg, please?'

'May I have another Easter egg, please, what?'

'May I have another Easter egg, please nothing.'

'May I have another Easter egg, please, who? Have I a name? Or am I the dog?'

Now I knew what she was getting at all right. Except that now I'd lost my appetite for another Easter egg.

'It's all right, thanks. I've had enough.'

I knew what she was getting at. But I was not going to get involved. She knew I knew what she was getting at and she gave me a look to show it.

Dada's face was sunken with disappointment when he got me on my own afterwards.

'Your Mammy is disappointed with you.'

What could I say after that? So the next time there was a situation I tried a new word: 'Is it all right if I have another slice of bread, *Mam*?' My heart was in my mouth. Waiting for the thunder to fall about me.

'Yes, Lally.' That's all she said. But there was a flicker, just a little flicker, that passed through her eyes, and burned me.

And after that she was Mam.

The other christening was for Dada.

It was a few weeks, I don't know how many, after we moved to Ivyhall. We were sitting like mice at the kitchen because we didn't know what else to do. The young Connells were getting out the breakfast things. Dada was not there because every morning Dada drove off to mass. He was just returning because we could hear the car drive up outside. Richie looked out the window.

'He's a bad driver,' he said.

'Who is?' says Mam. Impatient, in that tone of hers I didn't like.

'Their father.' He points at me. 'He crashed the car coming home from mass and now the driver seat won't open.'

Mam was pouring tea but she stopped and went over to the window. 'Thank God,' she said. 'He's all right.' Then she turned on Richie. '"Their father". Is that what you call him? Has he no name?'

It was Richie's little brother, the little fellow who had dropped the scooter and ran for his life the first time he saw us, who came up with it.

'He has a name and it's Connaughton.'

Mam could not help laughing. She burst out, 'Connaughton, that's a howl!'

And it was. Whatever way he had said it, every single one of us laughed. And finding ourselves all laughing together for the very first time, we laughed even more.

'Tell Daddy Connaughton to come in and not to be looking at the car like an unhappy dog,' Mam said.

We all laughed again. And by the time Dada reached the kitchen he was no longer Dada. He was Daddy Connaughton.

I was the only one who persisted in calling him Dada, but after a while the word began to sound foolish on my tongue and I stopped.

Daddy, I tried it to myself, Daddy.

'Daddy.' I said it aloud to him one day.

'What is it?' He never noticed the difference.

There were to be further rechristenings. In the beginning my father and me had the same Christian name: Lally.

Out of the blue, one day at the table, Mam says to me: 'From now on you are JJ Connaughton, and your father is Lally Connaughton. It will prevent a lot of confusion.'

JJ. Where did she get JJ?

'Second and third initials,' she explained without my even asking. 'Lally John James.'

JJ. I didn't much like Lally anyway, being a person who would have preferred the sort of name that most people had, like Michael or Tom. But JJ. That was like something you were called if you were a pony. I refused to be enthusiastic about JJ. It had to be repeated three or four times before I would answer to it: JJ JJ JJ JJ. It was like the sound of a train. After a while I got back my own name again and Mam found another way of preventing confusion. My father became Connaughton. Eventually that was the name he came to be known by generally. Even we children would call him Connaughton. Dada, in the end, was well buried.

Lally, my own name; I did not get my own name back for long: I don't know how it happened but no sooner had I taken up residence in Ivyhall than something happened my eyes. They got tired and anxious. I had to blink them to get any comfort. I found it very pleasurable to slide my soft eyelids down over my eyes. I don't think I had noticed myself that I was doing this thing, until one day Richie pointed it out to me. He called me a name. That was how he pointed it out. I hated the name. And the more he called it, the less control I had over my eyelids. He called me Blinky.

Every night in bed, Richie, lumped up in a mountain of bedclothes, turning the pages:

'Turn off the light, Richie, my eyes are burning.'

'I'm reading.'

'But I can't sleep.'

'Close your eyes, Blinky.'

'I can't.'

'Do you want blinkers?'

'No.'

As the nights went by Richie became more exasperated with me. I didn't want him being exasperated. I just wanted to sleep. In the end he bought a little flashlamp in Woolworths and he was delighted with it.

'Are you satisfied now?'

But I wasn't satisfied. I would lie there. Richie's pages would turn. Then the girls in the room next door would start talking. They always had a loud talking after their light went out. I think the girls were making a better fist of being sisters than Richie and me of being brothers. This bout of excited talking went on every night and I wished I was in there with them.

'Shut up in there,' Richie shouted then and our bed bucked with his exertions.

A silence for a minute. 'Why should we shut up?' It would be Marguerite, Richie's sister.

'Because I can't read, you bloody nuisance.'

'Do you hear what he called me?' Marguerite's voice drops as she talks to my sisters, Pam and Noeline, and her own sister Breda. 'He called me, bloody.' Then the voice rises again. 'I'm going straight down to Mammy to tell what you called me.'

'Go down so, straight down, through the wall. Or crooked down, I don't care what way you go.'

'I will.'

'I'm not stoppin' you. Just shut your trap.'

'Do you hear what he said? Will I tell Mammy?' The powwow would go on for a while in the girls' room but in the end they always went silent.

I didn't like the row to come to an end. I liked to see Richie fight with his sisters. It weakened the opposition. But Richie only wanted peace so that he could read. So that he could tuck his mountain of bedclothes around him once more, give one last mutter to himself about the fuckin' nuisances next door and begin again the turning of the pages. Page after page and the light of the flashlamp jumping over and back across the wall.

Then the flashlamp broke one night; he cursed and tried to mend it but couldn't and the big light came on again.

A night came when I thought I had found a solution to Richie's late night reading. It was a night he was a good way through *Lorna Doone* and I was afraid he would go on to the end. Then I heard him leaf forward through the pages to see how much further he had to go. He decided to stop and with a heave he threw the book on the floor and said to me, as he always did: 'Turn out the light.'

'Why should I?' I said. If he had to turn out the light himself, he might not be so anxious to read in future. That was my strategy.

'Suit yourself, Blinky,' he said.

The light stayed on all night.

I sweated the hours away in the bed, the light danced before the thin veil of my eyelids and I wondered were his made of leather. I sulked. I hated him then. He had so much power over me. He could even leave the light on all night and not be bothered by it. That was the night I realised something had to be done.

And so I joined him. All I had been able to do for weeks was look at the covers of Richie's books and watch him turn the pages. *Black Beauty*. That had been the first of many. And in the middle of the night, when he had read it and put it away he said, 'Hey, that's a great book,' and told me about all the men, kind and cruel, one after another, that had owned Black Beauty. Then he started on *Treasure Island*. Then *Kidnapped* . . . Me looking at the book covers, into a world where vicious-faced pirates in three-cornered hats slashed one another with swords. So I joined him. Wasn't it a good thing I had learned so thoroughly how to read? On the landing outside Richie's room stood a big bookcase. If there was a treasury any-where in Ivyhall, it was there. Nine big red volumes: *Newnes Pictorial Knowledge*. The very same as the volumes we had been shown by Fay back in the hotel. Except Fay had only two volumes, Mam had nine. She had bought them for her children. That must have been after her first husband had died. I heard her once say to Connaughton that her children had needed an investment in their future and this had been it. All you wanted to know about the royal family in England was in there, and the sporting heroes, and war-riors of Rome and Greece. Oh the odysseys they travelled! So while Richie read the books that Mam called the Blackie Classics, I read all about the world. We went into competition. We didn't state it, but it happened. We read all night. In the mornings there was no longer a problem of early awakening. When the shouts to get up eventually penetrated my ears they had to do so through dust kicked up by Greek or Roman heroes who stood on bridges or on narrow mountain passes against the vastly overwhelming enemy. And I went through all my early Ivyhall journeyings in a daze.

Then one morning I didn't get up. I didn't know why, except that it seemed like a great idea to be staying in bed, reading about ancient rebellions. Maybe I was having my own rebellious urges.

I could hear the others downstairs. I heard Mam shout to Marguerite, 'Tell him get up.'

In the end she came up herself.

'Get up. You're not in a hotel, you know.'

'But I was before,' I said.

She looked at me.

It was a look that said, pull in your horns.

I did.

Daggers had been drawn but I had not been able to outstare her. I called off my rebellion. Yes. I became a farm boy. The only contacts with the boys of my old town of Templemore – we were now living near a place called Wolfdyke – would be if someone from my old town wandered out in our direction. Or sometimes I would see them at hurling matches, squinting their eyes like the grown-ups they were becoming, but I would recognise them. And the Templemore corner-boys, I would recognise them standing by walls in many of the towns I would visit for matches. Yes, corner-boys did travel, as I had always suspected. I didn't know it then but as the years would go by I would continue to catch sight of people from my town. I would always recognise them. I was always on the watch, I suppose. They never recognised me.

PART 2

1

I called off my rebellion. Or I called a truce. But it was only an outward truce. Inside my head I still knew who my enemies were. I was the eldest of the Connaughtons. Richie was the eldest of the Connells. In my mind I would always be protector of my family. Pam needed me now; so too, the little ones. If Connaughton couldn't, or wouldn't protect us, I would. Richie and his Mam were my enemies.

My truce did allow me to travel in the car with them: Clonmel. I remember the first time I went there. Like most places I have been to, it turned out to be totally different to what I had imagined. The sounds of town names got rolled around inside my head, ever since the day of geography with Fay, until they became landmarks in there, anchored by imaginings. That is what had happened with Clonmel: Caramel it had become. Toffee. Sweetness of sunshine pouring over quiet streets. It turned out not to be like that at all.

We had a long drive of it through the county that day we went to buy the Mercedes in Clonmel. It was during my first summer in Ivyhall. We drove, Connaughton, my new Mam, my new brother Richie and me, in the big green Consul that – according to Mam – was beginning to give trouble. The drive was unhappy; Connaughton was complaining about the car and about time-wasting when he should be at some other work and Mam was saying, When we drive home we'll all be happy in our new Mercedes. That is precisely the trouble, Connaughton was saying, how can a change of car suddenly make somebody happy? His forehead furrowed and he looked out the windscreen, the question of how a new car can suddenly make somebody happy sitting worriedly on his shoulders. Mam said she would give up on him. Could he not be less complicated? Be a bit jolly, sometimes. Ah leave me alone, he said. And I felt very sorry for him and Richie didn't care one bit. All Richie was thinking was how bad a driver Connaughton was and how it was no wonder the Consul was wrecked with the way he drove it on its clutch. I didn't think much of those Connells, Mam and Richie, because of the way they tortured my father. In fact I hated them. Connaughton and me, we were alone against the whole world.

It was raining in Clonmel and we didn't park on a quiet sunny street as I had imagined but up a timber merchant's yard. The black Mercedes was there, looking very shiny beneath the glinty dark sky. Connaughton got out of the Consul and went into a timber hut with a wide window in it. Richie got out and looked at the Mercedes and in its window at the dashboard and then underneath it. Richie, who only had a mind for things that went on four wheels. That left Mam and me in the Consul. A man came out of the shed with Connaughton. He wore a hat with a feather in it. He wore a knee-length coat of yellow suede. Like a man from the forests of Switzerland. Aha, a timber merchant, I said to myself. Typically dressed for the job. Then Connaughton was scowling at the Mercedes. All the tall planks and upright piles of poles crowded around us and made his scowl even darker. The man was pointing out things about the car in a very brusque manner. Mam let down the window to hear what he was saying and he was saying that the bumps on it were only very minor and that the car had not been abused in any way and not to pay any attention to the hitch because it was never used to pull any more than his little caravan to Tramore and that but once a year. And Connaughton was saying that, of course a car in a business such as the man was in must be abused. The man said very gently that he had lorries for that kind of work. Would you, my good man, he said to Connaughton, plough your farm with that Consul there? No you wouldn't, you'd use a tractor. Mam laughed at that. Yes, he would, she said to me. He would plough with the Consul. Then she turned round to me until she was facing me completely and she said, Wouldn't we look style in that Mercedes? And I agreed with her because I thought we certainly would. We'll smile out at your father, she said. Jolly him up and maybe he'll buy. Then she asked me to get out and tell him I liked the Mercedes and I did just that, feeling that in relations between Mam and me a little alliance had arrived out of nowhere and that it had brought a sudden shot of warmth between us.

It's funny I should think of Mam now like that. As though she and I were accomplices in a conspiracy against my father. Indeed the memories of Mam come back to me differently now. Not harsh as they might be. There was a time I certainly would not have felt about Mam in such a gentle way. My feelings about her went through me so hard that it hurt. So hard that I wished they could be outside me, passing over me as if they had nothing to do with me. If only I could have been someone in a dream, looking at my feelings pass over my head.

We bought that Mercedes that day, and going home, Connaughton went out of our way so as to race it along the new road, saying what a great road it was indeed for all the new fast traffic. That's the ton he's getting, Richie whispered to me. Mam was laughing in little titters. Go easier now, she said. Because of his having bought the car, she was being a bit indulgent with him. Then suddenly he stopped and got out. We had just come off the main road at a small town and had turned onto the side road that led to Ivyhall. I had travelled this road before. I knew it well. The town was the one with the Protestant church on the end of it. It was called Littleton, the sun had come out, the sky had gone blue and a long scar of white was halfway across it. Look, he said. He pointed up. I was racing that to Littleton. That's a jet.

When he shut off the diesel engine of the Mercedes alongside the old Protestant church it went so quiet in the world that we could hear the sound of the jet. A drone of dreamy thoughtlessness up there. And then we all stood out on the road and looked very closely and discovered that at the beginning of the white gash in the sky, where it was moving forward, before it began to spread out, there was a little gap and just before the little gap there was a little silver needle . . . It was moving too, ever so slowly. That's the jet aircraft now, Connaughton said. I had never seen a jet before. It was as if, all of a sudden, the world was unzipping. But yet, too remote from me to be of any consequence. Then Richie told us to look at the distance between the two white lines behind the jet. That is a distance of ten thousand miles, he said. He had been told this interesting fact by a neighbour who knew all about jets. Around these new parts I was living in, there was, it seemed, an expert to be found on everything. I put my hands on the roof of the car and let the breeze go inside my shirt. Mam leaned against the bonnet, and we all looked up.

Ten thousand miles. To me it could have been anything. It could have been the distance of time itself. And now I think back on it and it was. That wide blue sky across the roof of the world and the white line chalking slowly across it was the distance of time itself, and of all my life within it that seemed to have had no beginning and to have stood still forever since. But that sort of stillness and the thoughts that went with it came only in certain moments. In moments when Connaughton stopped the car that was doing a ton and looked at a jet that it seemed wasn't doing anything at all. And Mam, with the light breeze blowing on her white arms, looked up also. And you were parked outside Littleton by that derelict Protestant church you had always before passed without as much as noticing. That had become a place not outside Littleton or not outside anywhere at all but a place in the silence of the mind, a place of nothing happening. A monument to forgetfulness. Before all starting up again when Connaughton got back in the car and turned on the ignition for the final leg of the journey home to Ivyhall.

To the battleground.

2

Yes, there were lots of jobs in Ivyhall. There were lots of other jobs, besides cleaning out dung houses, at which one might work like a Trojan. At which one might work just as hard as Connaughton and so be just as good as him. And so be noticed by him. Why did he have to work so hard anyway? He would work like a slave in Ivyhall before heading off for the hotel and his other jobs; it was not easy to keep up with him.

Connaughton worked too hard. Everybody said it. 'He'll kill himself working, that man. Does he never take a break?' Mam's sister in Thurles was the one who kept the closest eye on Connaughton's work rate. She whizzed out to Ivyhall every day, thirteen miles, for a chat with Mam. When she got to the yard gate she stopped and blew her horn. She blew and blew until somebody went out and opened the gate for her to drive through. It was her husband's car, a long green car. Uncle Gregory, he was called. He never drove it because he was the manager in the oil company and stayed at his office all day – in fact we never saw him – but we had to be very careful to hold back the gate as she drove through. 'I'll be killed if he sees a scratch on it,' she said. Her name was Aunt Tessa.

She was always saying Uncle Gregory was going to kill her. She sat with Mam for hours at the kitchen table; smoking cigarettes or cracking monkey nuts and chewing them at rapid speed. 'He'll kill me if I don't go home. He'll kill me if I put on any weight. I have a mountain of work waiting for me at home. Oh he'll kill me.' Then she applied her lipstick, poking it into the corners of her lips, and looked at herself in her little mirror and pressed her lips against one another until she was happy that she looked perfect. 'Another Mae West,' Connaughton said to Mam about her one day after she had left. Aunt Tessa was modelling herself on the film stars and on the perfectly happy lives they led. And Mam said she would never have thought her own sister would have turned out like that. 'A mountain of work waiting for her indeed. Oh all the children she has to care for.' Aunt Tessa had no children.

I was living in Ivyhall for a few weeks when Aunt Tessa began to turn up. Or maybe she came at the start, I'm not sure of that. She came for Frank Sinatra. There was this programme on the radio that played the songs of the singer Frank Sinatra. She would rush up the lane, jump out of the car, grabbing her cigarettes, saying, 'Don't say I've missed Frank.' Then she and Mam would listen to him, only half listen really, between talking and smoking cigarettes. I think Frank meant more to Mam that to Tessa. I heard her once say to Tessa that one had only to hear the first few words of a song of Frank's to be in the mood.

Maybe I didn't notice Aunt Tessa on her first few visits – there being so much else to become accustomed to. But it would not have been long before I would have had to put a name on her and to place her in relation to everybody else. Most mornings Connaughton went to his work at the hotel and the stall and the undertaking, but sometimes he stayed in Ivyhall. These were the days she seemed to favour for her visits. Frank Sinatra didn't even have to be on the radio. As soon as Connaughton would walk into the kitchen, with a feed bucket or something, she would go very quiet and take long looks at him. 'You can never get a giggle out of him,' she'd say when he left. 'He'd frighten you.' She never cared what we children overheard. 'He'll kill himself working, that man.'

As I said, there were lots of jobs in Ivyhall. I worked too hard also, but nobody said that work was killing me. I fed the calves. I worked with the sheep, the cows, the cattle. I had changed. I didn't play games all the time like I used to in the hotel. Games were something only children indulged in. It was work and more work. It was the way of the country. I was a quiet boy now. My decision or the decision of Ivyhall, I don't know, but I had become a quiet boy. The only problem was, I didn't know whether to act old or to act young. It was a difficult age.

This morning I was waiting at the gate of the Rampark. I had all the buckets lined up. And the two sticks for beating the calves back. The calves were waiting too, squelching in the mud, licking the bars of the gate, scrumming with one another in their attempts to hold on to the best feeding positions as they waited for Connaughton to arrive with the skimmed milk from the creamery. I knew all the calves by heart. I had my own private names for them. Those that bullied during feeding got clips on the ears from me. Not too hard, just sufficient for them to shake their ears and move away to give room to the others. Dribbly babies they were really, the smell of milk off them.

Connaughton drove up the laneway. He got out of the car; cheery after morning mass, hungry after fasting for his holy communion.

I helped him lift the heavy churns from the boot. Then he saw the green car in the yard. He clicked with his tongue. I knew it was the sound of disappointment. 'Aunt Tessa,' I said. I just said, Aunt Tessa. Not fuckin' Aunt Tessa, isn't she a nuisance? Or Aunt Tessa, isn't she a fuckin' nuisance? No, I could not be sure of what to say to Connaughton.

'Yes, Aunt Tessa,' he said. 'You'll find a bag of Brown & Polson in the back seat. The big calves are old enough for it now. Try them with a fistful each.' That's all he said. Brown & Polson. Nothing about Aunt Tessa. Nothing about how she talked until her neck went pink, about how she blew into her low-cut dress to cool inside. Nothing about her sunglasses. Nothing of all the things he should have been able to say to me.

Then he went in. I fed the calves and then read the newspaper. Every morning I did that: read the story of Jack Dempsey the boxer that was on every day, and this day as well there was the report of the build-up to the big hurling match. Jack Dempsey the boxer used to be a hobo. A bum, he called himself. He bummed lifts from one city to another, looking for work. On the roofs of trains. Eating bread and throwing the crusts at the passing country. He was an old man now and he was writing his memoirs. What a great life. I knew all about Jack Dempsey and me knew every player on the county hurling team.

If Connaughton went into the kitchen when Aunt Tessa was there, you could say goodbye to him. He would have to stay there for ages. A lot more talking seemed to have to be done when Aunt Tessa was there than when Mam was there on her own. Aunt Tessa told lots of stories about how the marriage of Connaughton and Mam was being talked about by the people in the town. And they had to listen. It would not have taken Connaughton that long just to eat his toast and read his post and give the orders for the day and then get out again to work. But he had to stay. He was a gentleman, that was said by Aunt Tessa herself. And that was why he stayed. He didn't want to hear about what people thought of his marriage. He was having enough trouble. He had already given the sack to some of the men that worked for Mam. That did not go down well with people. Mickey Byrne and Bob Stakelum were nice old fellows. I thought so myself. These were the men whose voices I had heard those first mornings as I had lain on the bed. But I was beginning to have a feeling for Connaughton's disposition for sacking people. People who talked instead of worked got the sack. People who went to the creamery and didn't come home until the calves were weak from waiting for milk got the sack. People who thought their ways were best, because after all they knew Ivyhall and Connaughton didn't, they got the sack.

Connaughton may not have wanted to hear about what was going on but I did. I think it was for that reason – to learn things – that I developed a relationship with Aunt Tessa. It became somewhat like the bedroom relationships I used to have in the hotel. And it happened like this. Not only did Aunt Tessa hate getting out of the car to open the gate into the yard but she also hated getting out to open the gate down on the end of the lane. She would open it coming in because she had to or else she would not be able to drive up to the yard, but she never closed it on her way out. That drove Connaughton mad. Because the cattle wandered off on the road and got lost. So she said to me one day, 'Come down with me and close the gate or your father will blow a fuse.'

'Blow a fuse is right,' said I.

'Your father is making big changes around here,' she said, driving her aeroplane of a car down to the gate as if it was on a runway and not a bumpy lane. 'And about time changes were made. About time people drove cars instead of carts to the creamery. That lazy old Stakelum. Takes the horse and cart to the creamery in the mornings and the horse has to take him home.' Aunt Tessa talked along like this and sometimes we kept going at our gate and drove on about three miles and up the long hill into the village called Wolfdyke. There I would run her errands, run into the shops, get her monkey nuts or cigarettes. Then she would drive by the men who stood on the street corner, sometimes drive by them twice, studying them, to see if they were healthy and well built. And all the time she talked, never about the men on the corner, but about the workmen, about Stakelum: 'That old horse knows his way from all the times old Stakelum lays drunk on the cart. A breath of fresh air around here, your father is. Some of the lazybones around these parts haven't a good word for him. No harm to have people talking about a good man.'

'That's right, Aunt Tessa,' says I.

But that was a lie: I hated people talking about my father. And the most wonderful thing, the only good thing that had happened me since my arrival at Ivyhall, had been the Saturday coming home from the creamery in Wolfdyke with old Stakelum. That had been the best. I bought five small apples and ate them. I passed beneath a pine forest, a million starling birds swirled overhead while the rubber wheels of the cart floated softly over the pine needles on the road. I talked to the horse while Stakelum slept. 'Woah, the fellow.' I thought of composing a composition: 'A Day at the Creamery'. A composition that had no mention of fathers who were talked about or of a place called Ivyhall.

Connaughton was the first person to take the milk to the creamery by car. People said he would destroy the chassis of the car with the weight of all the churns in the boot. But he went anyway. After a while other creamery-goers took their churns in their car boots. Aunt Tessa said Connaughton was a pioneering spirit. Then Connaughton allowed Richie take the car to the creamery. You could hardly see his oily head of hair above the side of the door. That changed Aunt Tessa's tune.

'Your father is a reckless man letting a fellow that age drive to the creamery,' she said. 'A softy, he is. Just to keep your mother happy, he lets little Lord Almighty do what he wants. He should put his foot down.' Aunt Tessa didn't like Richie and for that I couldn't but like her.

'I wouldn't have any particular desire to drive myself,' I told her.

'You're right. Now like a good young lad get out and close the gate after me.'

'Or my father will blow a fuse.'

So here I was, standing at the Rampark gate, reading about Jack Dempsey the boxer. The calves, fed now, milky mouthed and getting hungry again, were sucking the bar of the gate in the delusion that milk was oozing out of it. Suddenly a big car, a horse trailer in tow, sprang up the laneway. Kimberley Hunt, you could hardly see him, was behind the steering wheel. A little man with a hump on his back from riding horses, Hunt was a neighbour from somewhere around Fethard, horse country, but I think Connaughton had known him before Ivyhall. Connaughton knew all the horse people across the whole country. I think I myself may have gone to his house once with Mama. Mama used to be a great visitor to those big houses with the tiny box hedges around them. I had a memory of moss and of dampness. And I had a memory of a woman called Ducksy, who, like Mama, wore jodphurs. Unlike my Mama, though, Ducksy looked like a man. She did paintings of horses all the time; flat-looking horses that, it seemed to me, would be too stiff to move, let alone gallop. Horses whose feet were too firmly planted on the ground, because in real life a horse never stood four square but with a slight sag on one quarter, so that it seemed always on the point of going lame or of losing balance.

It was now getting on to mid-morning; the calves licking up wavy slicks on their sun-struck coats. I was waiting for Connaughton to come and help me carry the buckets and churns back to the dairy for washing. As the car drew up to me I stood away from a puddle so that I wouldn't be splashed. The car turned in a circle until it was facing down the lane again. It halted by the puddle's edge. The puddle shuddered slightly, like jelly, without being disturbed. Then Kimberley Hunt got out of his car and jumped into it, splashing muck on my face and up his trousers. He unhitched his horse trailer and returned to the car. He stood as straight as the hump on his back would allow but his head still only reached to the hood of the car.

'Your father rang,' he shouted. 'He wants the loan of a horse-box.' He slid back into the wide front seat of his car again. 'He can have it. Remind him of the hole in the arse end of it before he puts anything into it. I told him about it, but he'll forget.'

He said something else but I couldn't hear because he had shut the door and I could only see the mouth moving. He changed gears, swinging out of the gear-handle that branched from the steering column. Like a tiny monkey he was. Strange, I thought, that such a small man should be constantly dragging such big cars and horse trailers and machinery over these hills, and using such bad language. He didn't seem the sort of husband for a wife like Ducksy, who painted horses and did nothing else. Didn't have time even, according to Aunt Tessa, for making the teas for the men at her church, the Protestant church. She just talked at the top of her voice about how she could only tolerate males once they wore pink coats and riding caps and sat fifteen hands off the ground; Kimberley, according to Tessa, being, since his riding accident, too much on the ground for her liking.

Our departure from the yard was hurried as usual but now I was beginning to relax. Both of us were. All Connaughton's jobs done, all his talking done, he was on the road. Where he liked to be. Where I liked to be. With him, alone.

We crossed flat land. Quietly, steadily. After a while, high ground rose again before us. We were off to collect a mare who was with a stallion and she was at the other side of that high ground. I was picturing her out in her field. She was a mare we had brought from the hotel. She had a foal at foot, her first, and I was picturing her nudging its neck and then pushing it out of her way so that she could eat the nice bit of grass beneath it.

Connaughton didn't say much. 'I hope they got her in foal,' he said once. 'If we get a foal out of this stallion, we'll celebrate. It will be a lot more valuable than the foal she has at foot.' Another time he said: 'She's a complicated one when she's in season; a hard one to get in foal. You should have seen her first sire. He was strong but he was no beauty. Head plain as a bullock's but he was the only one she would take to.' The stallion must indeed have been no beauty, judging by the way Connaughton winced when he talked of him. I didn't say much. It wasn't my sort of conversation. Connaughton said, 'This year we shall hope for better things.'

Then the car was zigzagging its way up a mountainside.

'The top,' says I.

'No,' Connaughton smiles, cutting to a lower gear.

I was taking a chance; but I sensed in his smile an invitation.

As we neared the next ridge I crowed again: 'The top.' It was an old game. It was about time it was revived. Not since hotel days had we been alone on the road together. 'The top,' I crowed.

'No,' he said.

'Well this is it,' I proclaimed as we climbed the next ridge.

'No it's not.'

'This must be the top this time.' I was pretending to be exasperated.

'Are you sure? We'll see.'

We were cresting all these humps. It was great fun: 'This is it.' 'No it's not.' The clouds were gone. The sun glanced across the mountain ridges.

Then Connaughton lost interest. And I knew why: his mind was wandering: mares and valuable foals were again parading across it.

And I felt a foolishness creep all over me. My responses began to lack all conviction. I began to curse my age. I was ten and a half, too old for acting silly baby games. I wondered how I might drop the game. But then something just swam into my eyes and I was able to change the subject. 'Look Daddy, look,' I said. 'It's snow.'

'Well I declare,' says Connaughton, 'snow still on the mountain. And already the month of May.'

It lay on a bank above us. I wanted to stop and have a look. Dearly I wanted to stop and climb up but I couldn't ask. I never asked for anything nowadays. Afraid of being refused, I suppose, and then seeing the sight of Connaughton's hurt face for having to refuse me. Not since I didn't know when, since I had been a baby or something, had I asked him for anything. And it was even worse nowadays, since the Connells joined up. In seeking his favour I would be placing myself ahead of the Connells. It would be putting him to a test. I wouldn't put him in that position.

You can imagine my surprise when he drives right up to the top of the road and the next thing, he is leaning across and opening my door for me. 'Now, like a good lad. You can go and run down to the snow. Isn't that good, instead of having to climb to it?'

The air at the top. It was cool as ice cream. And the song of sky-larks; it was sudden and everywhere. It hung in the blue sky, inviting relaxation. But not for me. I raced down a sheep path to the snow. No sooner had I got there than I had to show him what I had found. 'It's not like snow, Daddy.' I hared back up again.

He was standing on the top when, all out of breath, I reached him. He was looking across the plain below. 'Immense,' he was saying in a whisper. Then he said something unusual: 'Do you know what age I am?'

'No, Daddy.'

'Well, I'm thirty-five.' He paused. 'I can't help feeling I'm standing at the peak of my life. And yet it would only take the smallest thing to happen and I would be toppled from it.' He was looking away into the distance. His eyes had become watery with the tug of the breeze. He was looking in the distance yet it seemed his gaze was turned in on himself. 'The smallest thing is all it takes to topple a man. And after that it is downhill all the way.' He looked at me. 'And I can't help feeling it.'

I didn't know what he was feeling, I only knew it was something wondrous. I wasn't sure if it was fair that he should have to be burdened with such big thoughts. Was he gladdened or was he afraid? Was he saying yes or no? Then he gave a shiver. 'Lost in my dreams, excuse me,' he smiled at me. 'That is a biting breeze across that mountain.'

'It's not like snow, Daddy,' I was yapping at him.

'What's not?' he said mildly.

'The snow, it's not like snow. Look.' I handed him a lump of it. I had kicked it out of the snow hollow. 'It's not white.'

It looked waxy, like candle grease.

'Melt snow,' he said. 'Soon it will be gone.'

Then we began the descent. The horse trailer nudging us downward.

I called it a town. So seldom I saw towns nowadays. But it was no more than a ribbon of houses at the side of shimmering tarmacadam. A ribbon of bungalows on a fast stretch of road in Wexford, all brightly painted, some of them made into shops.

'I'll only be a minute.' Connaughton got out of the car. 'This man has a pub and business as well as the stud.'

After half an hour a woman came out. 'Come in,' she said, 'and have your dinner. What kind of father have you he wouldn't tell us he had a child in the car? Aren't you hungry?'

'I am, please.'

I followed her through a wide door above which was written the word 'supermarket'. The sun shone on two counters. The smell of fresh white bread was everywhere, but the counters were empty. A shop with more than one counter, now that was what was called a supermarket. How modern it is, I thought, on this side of the mountain. The house was low and flat, made up, endlessly, of long corridors and small rooms. It was like . . . this is what it was like – a house a fellow would build out of playing cards. When I built my own playing card houses they had rooms that went on forever on ground floor level; never an upper level, for fear of the lot crashing down.

We reached a room which had more than bare walls to it. This room was cluttered, slightly foggy with a smell of dinner. Something burnt, mutton chops. A good smell. It was the only room that seemed to be lived in, an older room. It had a wide plate-glass window. Because of the rough cement around it, I knew the window had only recently been knocked into the wall. Now I was able to look on to the back of the house but I was disappointed at what I could see. I had entered the house from what I had taken to be a street and now expected to see more streets behind, but there was only a field with a broken-down child's swing and a rusted child's car. I didn't see any child. There was something lonely about it all and I felt I might as well be back in the middle of the country.

By a table at the window sat my father and the publican. The publican, a small man, had eyelashes so short it seemed they had been snipped by a nail-scissors. It was unfortunate, because he was the sort of man who needed to be hidden behind something and here were these eyes, unwillingly exposed to the world. I thought to myself how his face was like the countryside around these parts – bald fields, fences all tightly shorn. Having nothing to hide behind, he kept his eyelids half-closed and only came out from behind them when either spoken to by Connaughton or prodded by his wife.

'I have my doubts,' he was repeating it over and over. 'I have my doubts, but there's no harm in giving her another try.' He scraped his dinner plate with his knife. All that remained on it was a streak of mustard. Connaughton sat at an angle to the table and clasped a cup of tea to his hands as though his salvation depended on it.

'What's the matter with your father he won't eat?' the woman said. She looked at the bare spot on the table before Connaughton as if accusing it for not being stacked with grub. 'So you don't like dinner till teatime, you tell me, Mister Connaughton. That's a strange way you have. My man here likes it early.'

I saw the publican's eyelashes quill, like a hedgehog retreating into itself. The publican's wife wore thick spectacles. An impression of a jelly-blue light came from behind the glass, but it was by way of her mouth that she made contact. Quick jerks of her mouth, at me, at Connaughton, at her husband.

'You'll have some dinner if your father won't.' She made me sit down.

'Thank you.'

'The boy is not hungry,' Connaughton said. 'A cup of tea will be fine for him.'

Why was it my father would never be beholden? He was afraid a dinner might be considered as part fee for the sire's services – was that why? A dinner in my tummy as part bargain for a mare in foal. · In any case, the woman cut some bread for me, and while the men talked I ate six slices, light with the hunger and loving the bread's uneven buttering and thick slicing.

'So you are not too hopeful,' Connaughton repeated for about the tenth time.

The publican rolled his head from side to side, managing at the same time not to look at anybody. 'I think she may be still in season,' he said. 'But she is not showing any interest. However, as you say, sir, you are after coming a long way. We'll try once more.'

The publican stood up in his stockinged feet. He padded soundlessly across the linoleum floor to where his wellington boots stood.

'Should you change the trousers, Martin,' his wife's mouth reached at him.

He gave a helpless look at her but at the same time plunged his feet into the wellingtons.

'Suit yourself so,' she said, 'but that's your trousers for the horse show this evening remember. He's judging horses at 'Clody show this year,' she explained to Connaughton.

'Spacious house you have,' Connaughton said, making conversation, as we walked to the car.

'I wanted to fill it with kids,' the publican said. For the first time he looked directly at Connaughton, then he looked behind to see was his wife following, but she was not.

I was sorry to be leaving her. She had a grizzled face, but she was kind.

In a paddock, dark green with dock-leaf and nettle, stood our mare and foal. It had only been a short journey in the car but already we were hot. The publican sponged pinheads of sweat from his forehead with a large handkerchief. 'Hottest day of the year so far,' he said. The sun was behind a cloud but it was baking. 'We'll let my lad out to her and see what he does,' he said. 'See what Father Murphy does. Is he going to give his blessing, hah? Is he going to give out communion?' He laughed. He seemed to have turned into someone a lot funnier since getting away from the house. And Connaughton looked anxious and I knew why. He didn't like jokes about religious things.

I didn't wait around to see what the stallion would do. While the publican walked across a yard and unbolted the halfdoors of his stable, I took off for a walk. I heard the men talk and then shout and then I heard the foal squeal. It was high-pitched and terrifying, the sound of a wild animal. Why the foal, and not her mother? I wondered. It was enough to make a fellow walk away forever. But when the silence returned I walked back. We loaded up and took our horses home. I said nothing, I asked nothing, about whether our mare was in foal. It was not my kind of talk.

3

That mare of ours never went in foal. And shortly after our trip to Wexford she suffered a leg injury. But Connaughton would not have her put down. He loved her too much. We did go back to that place over the mountains again. And we took the horse trailer. This time we did not go alone. Mam came, and some of my brothers and sisters. This time there was no game. No this-must-be-the-top-this-time game. There was no snow on the mountains. There was no mare in the horse trailer. No talking at all in the car, because something was up.

In the car on our return this time we carried the woman of that bungalow by the tarmacadam road. In the horse trailer we carried her bicycle – her lady's bicycle – and a chest of drawers. That was all she had gone there with, she said, that was all she was leaving with. The man of that house, Martin, owed her nothing. She had given her life to him but did that mean he owed her anything? It didn't. He had not been a bad man, she said. She hoped he would manage. He was not good at looking after himself.

She blessed herself with the crucifix of a glass-coloured rosary beads at every dangerous bend of the road home. That fellow, she said, nodding towards Connaughton, he is a dangerous driver and when I get out of the car I won't never get back in with him again. Dangerous driver. Never, never sitting in the car with that fellow again. Mam said, Go easy, Daddy, but then laughed. From the very start Mam found her funny. I think that puzzled her a bit. Her blue eyes, magnified behind spectacles with rims the same glassy colour as her rosary, looked hugely baffled. It gave you the effect that you were looking into her. And every time she saw small children on the road, or even a pram, her eyes worried over, ever more blue and more translucent, as she called out to Connaughton to slow down in the interest of the children's safety. She liked small children. I could see already that Mam wanted her for Ivyhall.

She was given a room at the back of the house that I hadn't known existed until then. The chest of drawers went in there. The room was damp; an oil heater had to be installed. The big black bike went into the coal house. The cats made a nest beneath it. She took it out on Sundays. She was short and couldn't sit on the saddle but had to stand on the pedals. She would pedal for a length of the road and then stand on the pedals for a rest. I don't know what age she was. Old, but able to wobble along on her bicycle. Every Sunday she rode out of Ivyhall on the high bike. Off she would go after the dinner, but she would always get back to make the tea. Then she would take off her coat and wrap the pinafore around her again. She would become a bundle of strings and safety pins when that pinafore was wrapped round her, tightly enclosing her like a present that was not to be opened. She would wash windows, then, saying it was a wonder we ever saw the outside world. And Mam would laugh, telling her to go easy as it was Sunday. She was good for Mam, and that was a good thing for everybody.

Where did she go to on Sundays? We didn't know. My eldest stepsister, Marguerite, asked, but Mam told her not to be so inquisitive. That shut up Marguerite. Marguerite got it hot and heavy from Mam. Did she not like her own daughter, or what? It was strange. Into our local village of Wolfdyke the woman went, or so we had to suppose. I would picture her riding to Wolfdyke. Over the hills and down the hollows, her thick spectacles like a windscreen, arriving in Wolfdyke when it would be at its very quietest. Sunday afternoon, all the mass crowd gone home or locked into the pubs. Wolfdyke was not a friendly place, not like my old town. She would not feel at home there. I could picture her cycling beneath those low telegraph poles that never stopped humming in that town where nobody said hello. Nothing there to amuse her but count, one two three, the telegraph poles. Unable even to take a rest on the saddle, it being too high, but having to push on her pedals. After riding through a countryside, which has nothing but fields and more fields to show for itself, a person should at least be able to rest on the saddle on arriving in a town. A cyclist from the country should at least be allowed the opportunity of looking at the townspeople rather than scurrying through like a hare on the run. Especially if the town is Wolfdyke, which is no sanctuary for anything, hare or woman. What did she do there? It was a mystery.

Her name was Dancie. I had a slow business of it getting information about her. One of the grown-ups would let something slip every now and then. Everything I had learned in the hotel on the art of overhearing, I now had to bring to bear. In Ivyhall, where conversation was guarded except when Aunt Tessa was around, I had almost lost my knack. Where once upon a time grown-ups would have talked all sorts of grown-up things above my head and I would have feasted to my heart's content, now I had become deprived.

In the end I learned only what I was allowed learn: she was not the publican's wife. She had never even been his wife. Many years earlier, on the afternoon of a gymkhana in Wolfdyke, she and her sister and her friend Ettie had taken a lift from that publican. He was a long way from home. There had been an accident. She and her sister were injured; Ettie and the publican escaped. People said Dancie had been very beautiful but after that accident her looks had been impaired. But she had recovered. At least she had recovered; her sister had not and died a few weeks or so later. Some time after the accident a little baby had appeared on the scene. A little brother for Dancie. A gift to soften her troubles. Her mother, who was quite old now, had had a baby. Dancie had taken charge of it.

I would hear these stories while Mam and Aunt Tessa drank tea at the kitchen table. Dancie herself, if she was in the kitchen, would sometimes talk. When she could be persuaded by Mam, she would slow down and take tea. She talked one day about the time she had made the decision to bring up the baby. I was walking through the kitchen with a bucket of milk, to which I had to add hot water – calves who were sick needed it that way – and I made myself invisible over by the tap. It was painful listening to grown-ups; you felt the weight of your imminent discovery bear down upon you, you felt your ears burst with the strain of listening, but what else could you do? You had to know. You vanished into thin air. Here is what I heard.

When Dancie heard that the baby was about to be taken away to an orphanage she declared that over her dead body would such a thing ever happen. The people in charge of adopting babies had said that Dancie's parents were old and could not bring up the child. The parish priest agreed with them. Dancie then said that she herself would adopt and bring up the baby, whose name was Christopher. He would be her brother and also her adopted son. The publican had been good to her after her accident – he came every day to see her and her sister when they were in hospital – and now a priest drove her to the publican's house near Bunclody. The publican said she could work for him and in return she would bring up the boy in his house. He wanted to be the baby's adopted father. He wanted her to be his wife, but she had said, no thank you. After six years she sent the young boy Christopher to live in her old home outside Wolfdyke with her parents and with her brother who had got married to her friend Ettie and they now had other little children. She said a public house was no place to bring up a young boy. The boy would have company in her old home and would grow up happily there. When Mam and Aunt Tessa heard all this they were very sympathetic to Dancie, making clicking noises with their tongues and nodding to one another over her head while she was not looking and saying how she must have missed Christopher. I was remembering the broken playthings I had seen in the publican's back garden that day I had sat in his kitchen.

Now Dancie too had returned. Her parents were long dead. Her brother lived on the far side of Wolfdyke with Ettie and their large family. It was where she made her Sunday cycle trips. Christopher no longer lived there. He was lost in England.

Dancie had been the publican's housekeeper and from now on she was going to be ours. On her big black bike I learned to cycle. I pushed it to the top of the grassy hill one day. I made sure Richie wasn't watching. I steadied myself on the pedals, took off and, bumpety-bump, a tree was rushing up to meet me. I pulled the brakes but that made me go faster and, crash, I landed on the tree. I had a green scar all down my side. I buckled the front wheel and did not tell Dancie but wheeled the bike into the coal house and left it there. Then when she rode the bike it was buckled as well as being too big for her and it headed towards the ditch all the time. That was the way with Dancie. Things of hers were broken; her cigarettes were stolen. She complained and said sharp words. Mam then became very angry, saying she would skelp whoever the culprit was, but at that stage Dancie would say it was all right, she was not worth a child getting a skelping for. And besides, she would say, she was a stupid old woman. She would exaggerate, and sound more like a child than a woman. Mam would laugh at that but remain intent on hunting down the culprit, until in the end Dancie would have to tell her to sit down with her for a cigarette. A few moments seated with Dancie and Mam would be soothed and the culprit would be overlooked. Dancie had that effect on Mam.

I laughed at Dancie also, pretending I too could humour her as though she were a child, thinking that was the way she liked to be regarded. Mam regarded her that way. But from the very beginning I knew she was no child and felt foolish for pretending she was.

4

Walking the land; it was the thing you did when you bought a farm. Connaughton had left it late to walk the land; that was because it took a long time before a day could be found when Father Glee, the parish priest, was available. At last a day suitable to all was selected. It turned out very foggy. The priest's big car loomed up our lane. We were all lined up waiting and we became very quiet as he approached. He was to walk with us and bless every field and all the cattle, but because of the fog and because it was hard to see anything, he just stayed in the yard and blessed the land from there. He tried his best, with a shaker that had a knob on the end of it, to spray his holy water as far as possible over the land. Then he saw Our Lady. 'The fourth Glorious Mystery, the Assumption of Our Lady into Heaven,' he said. He pointed into the fog, in the direction of the clothesline. 'Do you see her assuming into heaven?'

he said, his face as serene as the face of a statue. My new mother shook her head and said, Thank you for coming Father Glee. Thank you for blessing the land. But he continued to point out to us where Our Lady was headed for. Visibility was not great, he was saying. Our Lady would be our guide.

We put on the wellington boots and left Father Glee swirling his arms in the drizzly air until he and my little brothers and sisters, who remained listening to him, were lost in it. The last I heard was Dancie calling them into the house and not to be listening to a madman. Then even the castle was lost to sight. It was my first stepping out over all of Ivyhall, with its hills, marshes and hidden streams. I felt like I was Vasco Da Gama. I did not see the Blessed Virgin, yet in some hazy way I did have a glimpse of the future. And I saw the Three Wise Men.

Mam was the first woman I ever saw in wellingtons. No, that is not true. I had seen women in wellingtons before. One stood in every yard that Connaughton and me drove into on our journeys out of the hotel. This woman was different. She was not stringy-haired and mournfully thin like those others. The bulges of her legs broke out attractively through her wellingtons. Connaughton was whistling to himself that day as we were headed out on the farm, happily released from Father Glee. Then another car pulled up the laneway, slosh splash, as was the condition of our lane before Connaughton later mended it, full of rut holes. Three giants in black coats got out. Who were they? I didn't know. They linked up with the posse.

So what did we all look like as we walked up the hills: the three giants, Richie, me, Mam and Connaughton? The giants looked as though they were part of the land, growing out of it. Connaughton looked like a lath against the bumpy skyline and I was wondering why Mam had not married one of the giants instead of marrying him, because any one of them would have been a more suitable size for her. They were nodding their heads very seriously, looking in notebooks and then staring into the fog, the water gathering on the tips of their noses. They were stooping like protective trees around Mam, saying to Connaughton: 'No, that field can't graze any more than twenty cattle, and those fields won't grow corn, and no place in the whole farm will grow potatoes because it's too wet. And, of course, you are not authorised to buy cattle; we will do that for you.'

Were they giving out to him, or what? How could anybody have reason for giving out to my father?

Bullocks crossed the fields before us, loomed out of the mist. Sad old lads, shaking their heads at us, telling us that of all the creatures in the fields a bullock's was the most humble station.

Yes, the men were laying down the law and Connaughton was whistling away to himself, lowering or raising the barbed wire for Mam every time we went over a fence. And Mam was saying, No, it's all right, I can get over the fence for myself, but letting the wire twang before the faces of the giants when she got through and then smirking at Connaughton. Richie and me struggled along behind this procession of black coats and notebooks.

I never saw three men as perplexed. Every time Connaughton asked something like, 'Has that field ever once been limed?', they went into a huddle that seemed to continue to exist even when they came out of it, their talk continuing as if they were still in the huddle, rather than one person speaking at a time. 'Oh, we as Executors of the assets of the Will . . . and the farm thereof . . . in a court of law . . . liming this field would be throwing good money away.' What were they talking of . . . Executors . . . Will?

Once we came to a river which was hidden under deep grassy banks. The giants stepped across it. Connaughton jumped. Mam had to lift her coat and make a leap. When she fell at the far side of the bank she laughed and pulled her coat down over her legs and the giants looked away up in the sky until Connaughton had hauled her up. Richie leaped across too, but I couldn't. 'Daddy, I can't jump it.' I said. Then the giants looked down at me with their perplexed faces. I think they would have helped me. They may have had suspicions that Connaughton was from another planet but I felt they didn't think the same about me. Their arms may slowly have been winding up like clockwork to help me when Connaughton said, 'Why can't you jump?'

'I'm afraid to.'

'What are you afraid of?'

What did he think I was afraid of? Falling in, of course. What did he do? Jumped across the ditch again, caught me, 'Ahup, two, three.' I can still remember how he swung me. Buck up, boy, his sharp grip was saying. He threw me across as if I was a football and I came down with a thump of guts on the far side. I went into a fit of the whimpers then, I'm afraid. Which, of course, is mainly why I will always remember walking the farm. Not the giants I remember most, but my shameful snivelling before them. Connaughton thinking I should be more grown up.

The next time the giants called, Connaughton and Mam had a name for them: the Three Wise Men. Oh they laughed when they thought up that christening. The visits of the Three Wise Men: I swear to God, Mam and Connaughton got on like tops whenever the Three Wise Men turned up. It gave them a common enemy.

More walks around the farm, the giant men, Mam and Connaughton sniggering at them, the bullocks of the farm chasing after us. And what would have got into those funny bullocks anyway? They would gallop up and down the ditch in our wake. What excitement goes on in the heads of bullocks? I would wonder to myself. Did they think they were racehorses? Well, if they did, they had missed their vocation. Same, it seemed, as had those Three Wise Men. They leaned carefully around Mam, as if erecting a shelter about her. I liked that about them. I felt sorry for them. She walked away from them.

More walks around the farm, more questions from the Three Wise Men: 'We hear you gave Ted Ruttle the sack. Are you authorised to give Ted Ruttle the sack? Who are these new workmen you've hired?' That was not their main worry, though.

It was now the end of our first summer in Ivyhall. Connaughton had grown corn, acres and acres of corn. In those moor fields, those hills, that before had looked coldly down on the countryside, he had grown waving acres of yellow corn. And everybody looking up said, 'It looks great. But will he be lucky?' He wasn't lucky. Because in September there was a storm. A storm on those exposed places. Then it rained and rained. All the corn lodged, stuck to the soft ground. The combine harvester lumbered up over the hills, a place where no combine harvester had ever before been. But its cutter couldn't get beneath the flattened corn. And down it lumbered again, beaten. Then the corn grew musty and mildewy. I didn't know much about farming, but I could see for myself: straw which should have been dry and yellow was going blacker day by day.

It was then the Three Wise Men turned up again and shook their heads darkly beneath their caps and took huge handkerchiefs out of the pockets of their topcoats and spoke into them as if they were telephones. 'We told him not to, but would he listen? No. Now he's ruined the place on us. We, as Executors . . . he's ruined us.'

Then Connaughton came up with the idea of the threshing machine. The good old Ransome threshing machine. He was always talking about threshing machines anyway. I loved to listen. They were his good old days. Listening to him talking about threshing machines made me so happy for all his rosy chaff-clouded Septembers of old. And yet he would say you should never return to the past. He would say he had made so many mistakes in his past that it was not worth returning to. This time he did and it turned his fortunes for the better.

He walked into the kitchen with a handful of musty straw one night. 'Only one thing for it,' he said. He scoured the country then until he found a threshing machine in working order. Connaughton was full of all sorts of old phrases once he got started on the idea of the threshing machine. 'Opening the headlands,' he called it when he cut all round the outside of the cornfields with a scythe. He walked off in the morning, around the outside of the fields with his scythe, cutting the headland, and didn't turn up again until dark. All day you only had an idea where he was by the sound of him sharpening the scythe somewhere.

We cut the corn in sheaves and stooked it and stacked it to dry. I was off school for days. I never saw Connaughton as happy before or since. Stories of old threshing days spooled out of him: one about when he had been a boy and his own father was worried about cutting the corn, but on the same day he himself had gone off to a neighbour's house. His father had hit him on the face with his open hand when he returned.

'Where did you disappear to when I wanted you?' his father said.
'Did it hurt you, Daddy?' I said. We were getting on so well

cutting the corn I was able to ask him that.

'My feelings were hurt more than my face,' he said. Connaughton's feelings. I was grateful I had no more than rippled them. Nor would I ever; waves – swelling so deep down – they could easily drown me.

Men turned up at our gate the night before the threshing. They were curious: it was the most important event that had hit the countryside in years. 'This new man in Ivyhall is taking us back to the old days.' They were excited. Then we heard the puff-puff in the distance. 'Whisht lads, I hear it coming,' they shouted. 'Listen, that's Lahart's Hill it's coming over.' 'Now lads, it's coming up by Mardyke Cross.' There they were, all forecasting the whereabouts of the threshing machine by the loudness of its puffing spates. Then the first signal of its arrival: the showers of sparks chimneying into the darkness of the night. Connaughton was full of business. The gateway was not wide enough to let in the engine and mill. It had come in two parts, what a contraption; engine pulling mill. He knocked down the pier with a sledge. 'He's knocking the place down,' the local men were whooping with joy. It delighted me when some of them turned to help him. I had hated how apart my father had been from the people who lived around Ivyhall, and this was good. They turned up next day also to help, breaking down piers and ditches, breaking down barriers, making it the beginning of Connaughton's contacts, real working contacts, with men I too would get to know, men such as Fern and Thos, old Gananny, old Meagher.

Next day was the threshing. I went around eating little apples and bringing drinks of barley water to the black-faced man on the engine – the 'injun-man', Connaughton said he was called – and bringing twine and bags for the man who stood at the chutes letting out the river of corn. Every now and again Connaughton rushed by, helping here, helping there, as well as doing his own job of feeding the sheaves into the straw beater, a specialist job, as he said himself.

'He's a hard hoor of a worker,' I heard men say. 'Or a madman; you'd have to respect him though.'

That morning a huge stack of straw had stood in one spot. By late that night it stood in another, hulled of its harvest: a mountain of bags of corn. Everybody was happy, my daddy was happy and that made me happiest of all.

Weren't you just great, Daddy, I was saying to myself, weren't you great to have thought of all that: the thresher, the injun, the injun-man?

And then the fields were all cleaned up and for the following year he bought three hundred sheep from Slievenamon. They could never be fenced in, but it gave the Three Wise Men great exercise having to keep an eye on them.

Out of the sale of the corn, Connaughton had money for the court case. I knew nothing about the court case. I heard words mentioned all right. 'Appeal' was the main word. Mam and Aunt Tessa, sitting at the kitchen table, throwing their eyes to heaven. 'Please God now . . . the appeal will go right.' After the rosary every night we said three Hail Marys for a special intention. Then the Three Wise Men came around no more. I asked Marguerite was it because of the court case they no longer came. Yes, she said. Mam and Connaughton won in the High Court.

'Is that the special intention we say the three Hail Marys for?'

'No.' Marguerite knew everything and I knew nothing. 'The Hail Marys are for Mam, having the baby. Are you blind or something?'

'A baby?'

'Yes. And Dancie says it's going to be a girl and Mam is going to put her in charge of it.'

And a while after that we had the new baby. It was a girl. And Connaughton bought a bull. It was to celebrate he and Mam getting control of the farm from the High Court. They would remain in charge until all the Connell children had come to a certain age, and even after that they could continue to live in Ivyhall if they wished to. That was the High Court ruling. Only if Mam died could control revert to the Three Wise Men, who were called the Executors of the Will. 'Please God you will have a long life and spite them,' said Dancie to Mam.

Yes, there was great spending for a while. Connaughton sold the hotel. And said the money would go to upgrading Ivyhall. The first he would build would be a new cow-house and then a dairy and silage pit. There would be no stopping progress now.

Only one thing I was uneasy about: Mam, it now seemed, preferred that Connaughton, and not the Three Wise Men, should be her protector. Would he be able for that? Would all of his life be taken up by it? Why was she worth it?

5

We were in the car another day, Connaughton, Richie and myself. On the way home from a dark and lake-potted part of the country, very far away. We had been returning a dog. 'An unfortunate creature,' Connaughton said he was. Two weeks earlier Connaughton had bought him. A sheepdog called Juice, for rounding up all the wild sheep that Connaughton had bought off Slievenamon to graze the high fields of Ivyhall. The dog had been part of the spending spree. It was after the harvest time, coming into our first winter, and the farm was in danger of being overrun by the sheep if something wasn't done about them. We had collected Juice off the train. We had carried him home in the car boot, and the moment he was released he had slunk into the coal house to lie on a jute bag, shivering.

That day Connaughton dragged him out to round up the sheep,

he was terrified. He drove the sheep across fields, through ditches, into the neighbours', so that I couldn't tell which, dog or sheep, ended up the craziest. I don't think Juice knew what ditches were, coming from a place where only ribbons of stone and sod divided the fields. Then Connaughton gave him a cuff of his stick on the head and he somersaulted on the grass a few times and headed for the hills. It was that day that started the sad howling. He never let up the howling, never again touched his food. And never let up his shivering, so that here we were, having to return him. 'No good throwing good money after bad on that mutt,' Connaughton said. 'We'll take him back in the car; it'll cost less.' I could see he was thinking of retrieving his money.

The journey seemed further than any I had ever been on. We stopped only once. Connaughton went into a shop to get cigarettes and while he was gone Richie and me had an argument.

'See that tractor with the bucket on the front?' Richie said. There was a tractor outside the shop. The bucket of it was cocked in the air, with bags of cement inside it. 'Guess how much weight that tractor needs on the back to balance those ten bags of cement in the front.'

'I haven't a clue,' I said. This was dangerous territory. No matter what I answered I knew it would be wrong. He was the expert; I knew nothing.

'Guess.'

'You're only trying to catch me out.'

'I'm not.' He wasn't either. Richie didn't ask you things to catch you out. He asked you things because for some reason that was desperately important to him he wanted you to know them.

'I can't guess.'

'Why can't you guess, Blinky? Stop blinking and start guessing.'

'I don't want to guess.'

'You never want to do anything.'

Richie was right. I never did want to do anything.

'Ten tons so.'

'Jesus.' He threw up his head to heaven. 'Did you never hear of the Law of the Lever?'

'Don't call me Blinky again.'

That was the end of conversation between Richie and me. It suited me. I liked to be able to enjoy a journey.

The road on this long long journey was so dark and damp it made the car leather go clammy. The place we returned poor Juice to was up a mountain, and most forlorn. The children of the house stood in wide wellingtons and stared at Richie and me as though they had thought themselves the only children in creation. We stood above a lake, black figures, looking at one another, and when one of them spoke I was so taken by surprise I jumped.

'Get into the house, get in, be damned,' the boy said, and it was skulking Juice he was speaking to, not us. Then he looked at his brothers as though he had done an important deed. And his brothers looked back at him, on the alert for any other deed which required doing. Alert, yet still.

'Do I need that useless creature dangling around my neck?' Connaughton said when the farmer told him to take the dog home again because he wasn't going to give him his money back.

'Have you ruined him?' the farmer said, and began straightening a paling post by his gate. Vigorously he pulled it out of the ground, waved it in our direction, and stuck it back in again. His children watched, as if keen to help him. 'Get that dog back out here and put him in that car,' he said to them.

'Leave him where he is,' Connaughton said.

The farmer's sons fidgeted; balls of thread danced in agitation from their torn cardigans but none of them moved. Richie and me stood behind Connaughton. I wondered how long we were all going to have to stand there. I looked away from the children with their squelchy wellingtons and flapping clothes. I began to count below us all the little lakes glinting up at the sky with its rain cloud that hung up there as if about to come spiralling down and send us all toppling. Then there was a sudden commotion. A hen flew, squawking from a door, a dog after her. A mostly white dog, but with brown patches over its eyes which made it look mad.

'Get down, get down,' the man roared.

The man's children roared too. 'Get down, Sam, get down be Jeez, and quick.'

Sam did get down quick, his eardrums paralysed probably.

'A gundog,' Connaughton said. The dog had dropped to a crouch position. 'Trained, is he?'

And that was how, on the home journey, instead of a sheepdog called Juice we had in the car boot a gundog, who smelled of jute sacks, called Sam. Just to show there was no hard feelings, said Connaughton, just to show he was a reasonable man. And just to show he too was a reasonable man, said the farmer, for this dog, who could set a snipe in a storm, he would swap the sheepdog.

We were on our return journey now. We were well away from the hills and lakes, driving across flat land, big fields all around us, big and black in the dusk. I could see Connaughton was in a good mood, having recovered his dignity. And suddenly we stopped.

'See that tree?' he pointed.

'What tree, what tree, Daddy?'

An enormous shadow mushroomed out of the centre of the field.

'That tree,' he said. 'I've been looking out for that tree for the past few miles. That tree marks the dead centre of Ireland.'

'The dead centre of Ireland, Daddy?'

Sometimes, if he was in good form, Connaughton said great things like that. I looked again at this most important landmark. History, I was saying to myself, geography, thinking of far sea-coasts all around me. What could I see? A few shadowy cattle stomping beneath a tree. Already we were whizzing away. Connaughton never delayed anywhere. And what I saw was what I always saw when Connaughton showed me things: a place lasting long and lingering in my mind. A mystery.

Then Connaughton stretched himself out a bit because of the wider road we had got on to. And I knew what was about to happen next. He stuck his hand in his pocket, dug out the rosary pouch. That time of night had arrived: 'Richie, like a good lad get out my beads. With the help of God we'll say the rosary. In the name of the Father and of the Son and of the Holy Ghost.'

The Holy Ghost, where was he? Beneath the tree in the middle of Ireland? Here was shadow-land indeed.

Then a real ghost loomed up before us, hand outstretched.

We were speeding. But Connaughton put on the brakes. And after about a hundred yards the car stopped.

'Damp night. Are you going far, boss?'

'A bit. Down the country.'

'I'll get in with you so.'

Connaughton always picked up hitchhikers. He liked the company. Kept him awake, he said. So did I, usually, but a hitchhiker in the car during rosary time, I didn't like that.

He climbed in the back alongside me, wheezing because of having to run to catch up with the car. I smelled his coat, oily, a smell like sheep's wool. He wore a cap. In the dim light of the dashboard I made out a long nose and big eyebrows. His arrival delayed the rosary because Connaughton had to talk to him a few minutes.

'Are you from these parts?'

'Indeed I'm not, these parts are the middle of nowhere.'

Connaughton could not think up anything that would make the man more cheerful about the parts we were travelling through.

I said to him, 'We're near the dead centre of Ireland, you know. We saw the tree.'

A minute passed. I thought he had nothing more to say, like some of the hitchhikers we picked up, either too timid or too hostile to say a word. The sort who caused a strain in the car. I was relieved when he spoke.

'You're right, young fella, dead centre.' He spat, making up for his minute's silence. It landed in the dark at his feet with a thud soft enough to give me hope that Connaughton mightn't have heard. Was he a spitter? I wondered. If he was, the back of Richie's seat was going to be in a bad state. 'You're not from these parts, young fella?'

'No,' I said. He seemed pleased when I told him where I came from.

'I've been there,' he said. 'Worked a circus there once. Considering places I've been, not a bad spot.'

For one moment I thought there was a chance that Connaughton would not begin the rosary. Not even Connaughton, surely, expected a circus-man to know the rosary. I dreaded a hitchhiker in the car during the rosary. Why? Because sometimes he didn't know a word of it. Then Connaughton had to recite both his

113

own and the hitchhiker's parts, his voice heavy with disappointment. Connaughton expected people to know their rosaries.

Sometimes we passed a light on the road and as it flashed through the car I got a look at him. He wore a scarf. A car came against us. Its headlights filled our car for a while. The shadow of Connaughton's head swarmed around the back of the car. Richie's low shadow barely jumped beyond his seat. The shadows beneath the hitchhiker's eyebrows flew sideways. And I saw staring watery eyes.

Richie had been holding Connaughton's beads all the time. As the headlights swooned away out of our car Connaughton took them from him. 'The First Sorrowful Mystery: The Agony in the Garden.'

The mysteries of the rosary, of the slow, sleepy rosary. For once I found myself wide awake for it. I think the man knew when it came to his turn. But he said nothing. Connaughton started it for him: 'The Fourth Sorrowful Mystery: The Carrying of the Cross.' As Richie and me began to mumble the response, the hitchhiker called out: 'Wait a minute.' He told us he couldn't believe in rosaries any more. And we shouldn't either. Connaughton said we did. He said a rosary could change a man's life. If we could only hear ourselves, the hitchhiker said. We sounded like the savages.

'Like who?' Connaughton said.

'Like the savages, like backward people I've seen. Casting spells on themselves, codding themselves. There's no escaping what's laid out for you.'

'Well I'm not codding myself,' Connaughton said. He continued then with the rosary. He finished off with the litany, slowing down only at the very last word and then he turned around to the hitchhiker.

'So you've travelled,' he said, with not the slightest annoyance but with real interest showing in his voice. Peaceful after the recitation of the rosary, even without the hitchhiker joining in.

The hitchhiker told us of his travels. He was a sailor. I wondered was he still one, and why was he so far from the sea if he was. But I was impressed with all the places he had been. I could see Connaughton too was impressed. 'Amazing world,' he kept saying, as he asked the hitchhiker for more details of his travels.

'Tierra del Fuego,' the hitchiker said. 'The Land of Fire.'

Connaughton asked him why it was so called.

'Ice on fire,' he said. 'Frozen solid wall of fog and ocean on the edge of the world. Lit by the sun's flames. Only if a fellow was driven by something did he go through that.'

'What drove yourself?' Connaughton asked. There was a laugh in his voice, he was enjoying the story.

'Oh a woman,' the hitchhiker said. 'What else, only a woman, could drive a fellow around Cape Horn.'

That seemed to stop Connaughton. I wanted to hear more about Tierra del Fuego. After a long time he asked: 'Are you married now?'

'No sir, no thank you,' the hitchhiker said, so definitely that I thought the conversation was over for good. But he himself started it up again, asking Connaughton where he was coming from. When Connaughton told him the story of the sheepdog and the gundog he laughed. 'So now you're without a sheepdog,' he said. 'Are you looking for a sheepdog?'

And that was how, when Connaughton heard about the time the hitchhiker had settled among the Indians of Tierra del Fuego – the people whose incantations had sounded like our rosary – and heard he had kept sheep there, had managed them without any sheepdog other than himself, that was how Connaughton hired him. 'Take me out of this godforsaken hole of the country,' the hitchhiker said. 'I worked a circus once in Tipperary, take me back.'

That was how our journey to that faraway place found us a gun-dog and a sheepdog. And how along the way home an image arr-ranged and rearranged itself in my mind: a place of ice and fire. The hitchhiker's Tierra del Fuego. But fading, no longer the streaks of sea and sky as when he had described it. Shadows getting in the way: a lone tree, ragged children. Then the hitchhiker began to snore, his head lolling and banging into mine, and Connaughton asked Richie to get out his beads for him once again, like a good lad, so that we could start on the Glorious Mysteries because they would lighten the journey home.

And then once, when the hitchhiker looked up with a start, we were passing a high dark hill and there, at its summit, was a light.

'Can you see the cross on Knocksheegowna?' Connaughton said.

'What's that?' the hitchhiker said.

'That's Knocksheegowna, the mountain,' Connaughton said mildly, slowing the car so we could all see. 'They brought electricity to the cross to honour the Marian year.'

'I thought it was the fairies for a minute,' said the hitchhiker. 'But it's only more religion. Drive on.'

And I thought to myself that here was a queer fellow we were taking home with us to Ivyhall. And what was Mam going to say of it. Was she going to ruin this welcome development?

6

We were sitting at the kitchen table. Mam looked out the window while Dancie gave us breakfast. 'Would you look at the sheepdog the boss brought home last night?' She made Dancie look out the window. 'A bit decrepid for chasing sheep, wouldn't you think?'

'I don't see any dog, ma'am,' Dancie said.

Mam laughed and laughed until she nearly fell. 'Would you fancy him, Dancie?'

Dancie, who was holding the new baby in her arms said, 'I have my hands full, thank you.'

And I sat at the table, trying to bring to mind again the perfect encounter I'd had with the hitchhiker and the image I'd had of Tierra del Fuego, the land of fire, before Mam had got in the way.

But the only place that came to my head was the place outside our window. A frozen, boiling place. The cold sun flaming between the bars of our old yard gates. The fire off the rims of my wellington boots burning my legs. The hill in front of our house, the cutting wind from it that sliced the mind in two. Frozen and boiling at the same time.

The hitchhiker. What does he look like by day? I wondered. The man from Tierra del Fuego.

To find out what the hitchhiker looked like, I didn't have long to wait. As we were about to go off in the car to school and everybody was fighting for coats and schoolbags under the sideboard in the hall he came in the door with the bucket of milk for the house.

Connaughton might have hired him as sheepman but he hadn't taken long to make him cowman as well. He stood in the hallway a second, not knowing where to go and then went into the kitchen and lifted the bucket of milk onto the table. His head was stooped and Mam said good morning to him and then he raised the head and we saw the big red mark down the side of his face. All one side of his face, from eyelash to lips. It gave me a fright because I hadn't seen it in the dark of the night before. There he stood, his tongue sticking out, not knowing what to do next, muscles quivering beneath his shirt. He was not half as certain of himself as he had been the previous night. The red stain was the first thing I noticed about him, even though I pretended I wasn't noticing; his tongue was the second, the length of it, because he had stuck it out and with it he was touching the tip of his nose. (When I tried to do the same thing going in the car to school I could not do it.) The third thing I noticed was the way Dancie looked him up and down and then looked into the bucket of milk, sniffing at it as if it was from the sheepdip tank. He was in a pair of ragged trousers, a shirt whose sleeves were torn up to the elbows. His thin arms dangled uselessly and as Dancie continued to look at him his hands began to twitch. They would have stayed twitching like that had Mam not told him to sit down: 'When did you eat last? Dancie will get you breakfast.'

Connaughton drove us to school because he had to go on to business in Templemore. Mam went too because she had to bring the car back. That was often the way of it – it meant that we were all bundled into the back seat and squirming and scraping like cats.

'And now that you've hired him, where do you propose to put him up?' she asked Connaughton as we came up to Ballynonty Cross.

'I don't know. I thought that you might have an idea, dear.'

'It will have to be the luxury suite, I suppose.'

That evening when we got home we had, as well as our normal jobs, an additional task: the cleaning out of the feeding house for the hitchhiker.

I suppose the feeding house was chosen because of having a cement floor and an electric light. It was dry too, and warm, being next door to the pig-house.

The boys' job was to bucket away all the feed grain, the rolled oats, the crushed barley, the dried beet pulp. These were in three separate piles and were mixed each evening in varying amounts, depending on whether for calves, cows, pigs or horses. That was a nice job, one of the nicest in Ivyhall. The textures were pleasant, you could chew bits as you did it. It was good for you. Good, like the marmalade in the hotel. In any case, the feeding house was now being given over to the hitchhiker and all the grain had to go. The girls' job was to sweep the cobwebs down off the stone walls, to wash the window, to get a table from the house and put an oilcloth on it. Mam's job was to whitewash the walls. Such a rush of spiders trying to escape. There was something good about us all working like that, with Mam in charge. As long as Mam was working on something she was in a great mood. When she was working she complimented everyone on how well they too were working. The last thing to be done was the balancing of the oil heater. The oil heater had been brought from our bathroom, where it was lit on Saturdays so that we could have our baths. Richie was the balance man. He got out a level and plum. Nobody else was allowed do that job. 'If it's not balanced the whole place can go up in yellow flames,' Richie warned.

The feeding house looked very inviting when we had finished. I envied the hitchhiker the peace he would have down there. Mam took a last look, she was pleased with herself, then she set a rat trap, placed it under the narrow bunk we had installed for the hitchhiker and closed the door.

It was going to be strange to think that down in our yard, behind that door where once there had been mounds of grain, there was to be a man. It pleased me. I think that the isolation of Ivyhall had reached into me without my noticing. Where once upon a time I would walk through the streets of my old town and be noticed by all its citizens, where once I would collect a pocketful of money before heading to Georgey's and spending it on ice-pops, now the only contacts with the outside world, or rather the only visitors to Ivyhall, were the vet, the AI man, the lime delivery man. And all of these were treated with wonder rather than with the indifference with which I once used to treat people. Now there was also a neighbour to wonder at.

How does a man who has been to Tierra del Fuego settle in a feeding house in a yard in Tipperary? Does he be satisfied with his lot? What changes does he make to his place of accommodation? Well, the first thing I noticed of change about the feeding house were the rats in the bucket outside the door. I didn't notice them for a while; not until one morning after a night of rain. Passing to the grumbling pigs next door with two buckets of separated milk from the dairy, I noticed the brown bodies afloat in the bucket which had been left beneath the gutter pipe. They gave me a terrible fright. Floating like that with their mouths opened back to their teeth. As if sucking for air. And only waiting for the bucket to be tipped over and then away with them. I didn't trust them. I had never seen one rat before, not to mention a floating family of them. When I told Connaughton about them he laughed and said that as well as being a sheepman, the hitchhiker must also be a rat-catcher. 'A useful man.'

Mam was not amused by the rats.

That rain lasted for ages. The yards and fields were flooded. One morning the hitchhiker was having breakfast and he had to take off a sack he had been wearing over his shoulders before sitting at the table. He looked miserable. Mam picked up the sack with a pinch of her fingers and put it outside the door. Without saying a word she went upstairs and came down with a Crombie coat of Connaughton's. 'Here, have that. By the way, I see the rats are deserting ship.'

'Yes ma'am.'

'But you're not sinking, sir.'

'It's nice to be told that, ma'am.'

'Bury those rats.'

'Yes, ma'am.'

That was the way Mam spoke. Short and sweet. I didn't like it; I found it too abrupt. But the hitchhiker didn't mind. He buried the rats. There was never another rat seen in the bucket, so we didn't know if the rats finally worked out that the feeding house was out of bounds or if they still continued to be caught in the rat trap but the hitchhiker was rising early in the morning to bury them. The funny thing was that his face with the red stain had the look of a rat about it. I got the impression that he knew all about rats.

I took a look inside the feeding house one day. The door had been left open a little. Nothing had changed about it since the time we had cleaned it. The bed was in the same corner, the little table with its oilcloth, the oil heater and the chair. It was silent as the grave in there. If the man who lived there had stories to tell, he seemed to have buried them all. But then, without my knowing where she had come from, Mam was standing alongside me. 'Shut that door,' she said. 'Don't let the dogs in.' She was holding a vase of flowers in her arm. She took the fresh flowers to the hitchhiker's table beside his bed and looked around the room. She straightened the bed and straightened the tiny picture on the nail above it. She straightened the shoes beneath the bed. She straightened everything that needed straightening. Such straightening. It made you feel she was attempting to straighten the man that lived there. It made me feel what I had known all along: that she was a straightener. I could even feel her straightening me, she'd been doing it since I'd met her. But I wanted to be crooked.

Dancie never touched milk again from the day the hitchhiker came. 'God bless the mark, the poor man,' she said of his red half-face. Instead she went over to the sink to cool her tea with cold water. 'A port-wine stain,' Mam called it. 'It's not contagious.' We got used to it.

His name was Harry Crowe.

On nights when Connaughton worked late at his business in Templemore, Mam helped the hitchhiker with the milking. It was on one of those nights she caught the kick from the cow. The hitch-hiker linked her by the arm across the length of the yard. 'Ooh, Harry,' she said. 'Go slow.' He was helping her get up to the house. I was standing by the wicket gate. I caught sight of her face in the moonlight. She was trembling.

7

This Sunday I was up at the Rampark gate feeding the calves as usual. By now I could handle four calves at a time – a half bucket or so of milk to each, depending on its size. I could do this while, at the same time, opening and shutting the gate. And during each lot of four I could read the sports in the *Sunday Independent*. This Sunday was different, though; I got so absorbed in the paper I forgot about the calves and the smell of the hot churns and even of where I was. Until I looked down and saw the bigger calves muscling the smaller ones away from their buckets and swelling themselves with milk and wind. The muck beneath their feet was coloured with all the milk they were spilling. I had to attack them with the stick. I hit them along their whiskery pusses; the quickest way to get results. It was the day of the Munster final and I wanted to get back to reading the newspaper predictions:

'MATT DONOVAN TO DECIDE OUTCOME', said the headline. Reading good reports about my heroes was the spice of my life.

Fern was an hour waiting on the crossroads when we stopped for him. 'Yipee,' he said. 'Donovan needs us. Move over there.' He got into the back seat alongside me. A cheeerful fellow, Fern. He had a farm that grew only fern and furze and that's what gave him his nickname.

Thos was not as happy when we pulled up at his house. Thos was not the happy sort. 'I'm going to miss the minor game,' he scowled. He didn't say, 'Donovan needs us.' Thos, like me, needed Donovan. Thos and me were big fans. However, within moments, he too was settled in the back of the car. Carefully folding his coat, placing it at the back windscreen, rolling his shirtsleeves, he nestled like a hen in alongside us.

'All right there?' Mam looked around from her front seat.

'Snug as a bug in a rug, ma'am,' Fern sang out in reply.

Mam was not all right herself, but you would never have known it from the way she greeted the men. 'Awful speed,' she had been saying to Connaughton, 'leaving it this late to get off is asking for trouble.' The arrival of the two men seemed to revive her spirits. She knew they both liked her. The truth was, something I was discovering as time went on, all the men around Ivyhall liked Mam and she played along with that. Fern, 'the harmless fool', as I had heard her once say of him to Aunt Tessa, had even proposed marriage to her before Connaughton arrived on the scene.

'Awful speed.' Mam said it once more. 'Eighty on a bumpy road.' But now, because of the men in the back, she didn't say it as loudly.

'Can I put on the radio and get the minor game for Thos?' Richie asked. He was wedged in the front between Mam and Connaughton.

Mam looked at Connaughton. I waited for an argument. He hated the radio. 'Turn off that bloody thing,' he always whined whenever the radio was on. 'That screechy bloody thing.' He and Mam had an argument over it once. Frank Sinatra was on and Mam said he would stay on until his song was finished, thank you. Connaughton said that if she had to listen to somebody, it beat him why it couldn't be Bing Crosby, and then when the song ended she snapped off the radio until the silence was so bad I could feel Connaughton being hurt by it. There was no argument this time, though. Connaughton was already in Mam's bad books, so he had to keep quiet.

Connaughton was in the bad books because earlier in the morning Miss Turner, the Chief Whip of the Tipperary Foxhound Hunt, had come to inoculate two foxhound cubs which we were rearing for the hunt. And Mam was in a hurry to get to the match.

'Coming on a Sunday morning like this,' Mam said, 'she's nothing but an atheist.'

Connaughton went out to Miss Turner in the yard and stayed with her for ages and when he returned he was in great form.

'You're in great form now,' Mam said. 'Meeting the trollop, is it? Law dee daw talk and gold tooth, is it? Why couldn't you be like that with me?'

'You know I am like that with you,' said Connaughton.

'No, you are not. You walk around me like misery.'

Connaughton ran for the yard with two buckets of gruel he was making up and it splashed on the hall floor as he headed out. 'Now look what you've made me do,' he said.

The next time he came into the kitchen he said that Miss Turner was not an atheist but an agnostic. It was an important distinction, he said. Mam said she didn't give a damn, she was a horse Protestant one way or the other and she would have no more of it.

Connaughton had a hard job of it with Mam sometimes when he defended his old friends. Kimberley Hunt's wife, Ducksy, for example. Who drew horses all day. Mam said she was nothing but a horse Protestant either. One of Ducksy Hunt's paintings hung in our hallway. The specimen of horse in that painting, Mam said, should have been carted away to the knacker's yard. Connaughton said Ducksy Hunt was an artist. It was a lot harder to draw horses than ride them. He gave out a sigh when he said this. A lot harder. And Mam said he was very touchy about his friends.

But today he'd had enough argument for one day and that was why he just nodded 'All right', in mournful resignation when Richie asked to put on the radio. So Richie fiddled with the radio until the commentary from Limerick leaped into the car. It roared and faded then, depending on whether we were rounding a corner or climbing a hill. But when we got over that hill where Connaughton always declared, 'Look, there's the Golden Vale', the commentator's voice bounced around in the car so urgently it sounded like the senior game was on and not just the minor. It made me very nervous about the outcome of the match.

I tried to settle down. I drew Matt Donovan's head with its funny-shaped nose on the fogged-up window.

'That man's nose is broken from hurling,' Connaughton told me once. 'Brave man, puts his head where another won't put his hurley.' I drew Donovan's squashed nose, wondering why Connaughton never got excited about him like I did. Why he said things like 'lion-hearted', and 'finest hurler of his generation', about Donovan, yet didn't truly love him, not as did Thos and me. We would die for Donovan. I liked the name Connaughton gave him, though: Matt the Thresher. After a character with the same name in a book he had read as a young man. '*Knocknagow*. Best book I ever read,' he would say, his eyes going all soft and wistful as he thought back about it, and about those days when he was young.

I knew Matt Donovan well. I knew his nose. I'd seen it close up. He pulled up to Ivyhall on the oil lorry. He drove the oil company lorry in town. He came up to us twice a year. One time, I knew he was coming. I was out pucking the ball against the wall. Smack, smack, the sponge ball against the butt of the wall.

He was a sprightly operator. He jumped from the lorry, rolled the hose pipe off the drum, stuck the gun into the diesel tank and kicked the pump start. The pipe swelled up and writhed and he jumped out of the way. 'Give us a look at your hurley, young fella,' he said. My little hurley was like a wand in his hand. With the pump roaring loudly and the lorry vibrating, the sound of the hurley hitting the ball was like scarcely heard pants of breath. 'Watch how you put a slither on a ball.' He showed me his wrist movement. Each shot scudded the ground a few feet from the wall and then slithered into the wall at a sharp angle. 'Do that, young fella, and you'll break the hearts of goalkeepers.' Then he shut off the engine and with the three dockets in his mouth went into the kitchen, shaking the oil from his hands.

Fern looked at my drawings on the window. 'Do you want a game of noughts and crosses?' he said.

'Whisht can't you,' Thos said, 'and let me listen to the match.'

'No, I'm no good at noughts and crosses,' I said. I was thinking of Donovan: 'Lion-hearted'.

When I told Donovan what the Master in school said to me – 'Connaughton, you'll never be any good of a hurler because you're only a coward' – this was what Donovan said: 'It's easy for some of us to be brave, when we're too fuckin' thick and ignorant to be any other way. You need imagination to be a coward.'

A bend came up ahead of us and Connaughton took the car around at such a speed that Fern fell into Thos's lap.

'Jaykies you'll kill me, Fern,' Thos squawked. The breath was knocked out of him. 'You hit me on the laddie-boy,' he said in a lower voice so that they couldn't be heard in the front seat.

'You were giving your laddie-boy too much comfort,' Fern laughed and gave him a puck, an intentional one this time, in the same place. I nearly died laughing at the two of them.

Then Mam got into the laughing act but it was something else, thank goodness, that she was laughing at.

'He'll kill us all if he keeps driving like this,' she said. 'And then none of us will see the match. And that'd be no harm.' She winked at Fern, who always enjoyed winking back to her. 'Because you're going to lose anyway.'

Winding us up, that's what she was doing. Me and Thos, but me mainly. 'They'll beat the socks off you,' she said. 'You'd need to put some more pan loaves into you, because you're too weak.'

I just bit my tongue and kept my mouth shut and hoped Connaughton would say something for me.

'The city slickers, they'll teach the country goms,' she kept at it.

Shut up, I felt like saying. What do you know about hurling anyway? I was furious. But that was exactly what she wanted: me to lose my head so that they could all laugh at me. And then, with me to focus upon, the row that had been going on between Connaughton and herself could be abandoned. I was not a good person, I knew that. Something was definitely the matter with me and it was me, not things like Miss Turner the horse Protestant, which was the cause of rows between Mam and Connaughton. But Mam was not good either. Why couldn't she just say I was bad and that my badness was the cause of all the unhappiness between them. And then I could say, yes I know, the fault is mine. In that way I would have it all over and done with, then the path of my life would be a lot clearer. But oh God, what kind of hurling supporter was my father. The hardest pill of all to take, that was: why he couldn't back me up. And the time flying by, half-time in the minor match and we miles away from Limerick.

We were on a straight stretch of road. Cars flashing by one another all along it, overtaking one another until there were no longer spaces between them. Poking their noses out, then tailing in again.

'This is a bugger,' Connaughton said. We were at the end of the procession. He spotted a gap at the top of the line. He pulled out. Down went the foot on the accelerator. He passed one car, two, three.

'Pull in,' Mam shouted. He passed, four cars, five. We all saw the bend up ahead, and he was not going to make it.

'Pull in!' Mam shouted.

'I can't, nobody is pulling over to let me in.' He really let the foot down. The car shot along the line, past big cars, small cars, full cars, one-man cars. But the bend was just ahead.

'Get back!' Mam shouted.

Connaughton blew his horn. 'Move over!' he shouted at the car to his left. 'Give me a gap.' It was a long black Zephyr driven by a man in a hat. Connaughton waved at him.

'He'll think you're mad,' Mam said. 'He'll stare in at you.' The man in the hat did not budge. He didn't have a moment to spare for staring in at Connaughton.

Connaughton's hand came down on the horn. 'Bugger driver, sound asleep.' He held the horn down. But the Zephyr gave him no gap. The corner was coming up. Even I was worried now; we might be getting to Limerick faster, but even I was worried. What was coming around that corner at us?

'Now look what you've done, you've killed us all,' Mam said, her voice had become fragile.

Thos called out 'By Jaykies, sir,' and held himself.

'Pull her over to the right, boss,' Fern gave rapid instructions. 'Into the ditch on the right, boss. Park her on the right.' Fern gave driving lessons at home on the crossroads. He was now dishing out the sort of instructions he gave, in those more sedate surroundings, to his learner drivers.

'Are you mad?' Connaughton asked him in amazement and plunged down on the horn again. 'Bloody bugger,' he shouted at the Zephyr, 'does he know he's trying to kill us?'

Behind the wheel of a small Anglia in front of the Zephyr sat a man who was also in a hat. Suddenly everybody seemed to be wearing hats. Instead of pulling back, Connaughton drew up to him. Imploringly, he looked in at him. We all did. But it was no good. The man's neck was locked in forward position. Dead silence in our car now. We were on the corner. Why was time going so slowly?

'Hail Mary,' Mam said.

Connaughton pulled alongside the Anglia until the doors almost touched. Still staring ahead, the other driver pulled in. The ash saplings in the hedge crashed and broke against his bonnet. I could hear the sound of them. Then the two cars, as one weld of metal, rounded the bend on the correct side of the road.

'I thought we said our last prayers then,' Fern said in a way that sounded as if he was still praying.

Connaughton checked for traffic coming against us. There wasn't any, so he pulled out on the road's centre again.

'You got lucky once more. Some day you won't,' Mam said. 'You can stop blowing the horn now, they all think you're mad anyway.' She set her face against her window then, as if she would never talk to him again. But she had to. A horn pinged behind us. Now there were two horns at it. 'Why are you still blowing?' Mam asked, as the other car passed, and left us behind as though we were standing.

'I wonder what speed that fellow is doing?' Connaughton whispered in awe.

'He's a dangerous bloody driver, boss, whatever speed,' Fern said.

'Why is your horn still blowing?' Mam asked once again.

'Because it's stuck.' The answer came from Richie. Of course it was simple to him. Richie, the mechanic.

'You're right, it's stuck.' Suddenly it was also simple to Connaughton.

'Well stop the car and unstick it,' said Mam.

'What, and have them all pass me out again. Led by Slowcoach in the arse-up Anglia.'

This seemed to be a signal for the men in the back to collapse in laughter. The air came out of Thos like air being let out of a tyre. 'Slowcoach in the arse-up Anglia,' they repeated it. Laughing their heads off. 'That's choice.' I must say I was surprised a bit myself: Connaughton never used bad language, apart from 'bugger'. An eloquent man with words, Auntie Tessa said of him.

But then Fern whispered to me, suddenly serious: 'Dangerous man, your father. Kill us all to get there, and he having no interest in going himself.'

I didn't think Fern was being very grateful. I wanted to say to him, You're not interested either, Fern. Why do you go, but to drink and to laugh? But at least Fern did go for something – to laugh and drink. What did Connaughton go for?

I didn't care, right then, what he went for: I was excited again; it seemed we might make the match in time.

Into the streets: the tall houses trapped the blare of our car horn and it deafened us. Mam clasped her ears: 'Stop the car, Jesus, let me out.'

'Why?' Connaughton asked.

'I'm deaf from that horn. I'm going to a hotel.'

'It's a long way. I'll drive you.'

'Let me out.'

The first traffic lights into the city came up. On the amber. Connaughton put his foot on the accelerator to beat them but the car in front of ours slowed and stopped.

'Bloody bugger,' Connaughton moaned, our horn blasting the car ahead of us. The driver looked around.

'I'm getting out,' Mam said. 'Goodbye.'

'Ah don't worry, ma'am,' Fern called. 'As soon as we switch off the engine our horn'll conk out.'

As Mam leaped from the car the lights turned green. Connaughton grabbed at her to pull her back in but the car behind was blowing now as well. We had to go on. 'You can read the papers, dear,' he called after her. 'Go to Cruise's Hotel. Have you money?'

But she was gone. We saw her limping along the footpath, as fast as she could get away from us.

'Why is she walking lame like that?' Connaughton looked after her.

'Stiff from sitting in the car, boss,' Fern said, looking ahead. 'Watch out. There's dangerous drivers in front of you.'

We pulled into the wide quay where the river flowed. Cars were parked everywhere. People standing by them finished sandwiches and flicked tea dregs into the river. They jumped out of the way in pretended alarm at the sound of our horn.

'See that bridge, son?' Thos said to me. He must have forgotten his fright for a moment. 'It's half a mile across; it'll be solid bedlam up there.'

'Better mind the crush across the bridge, boss. With all the late crowd crossing it at the one time, it could be dangerous for the young lads.' Fern was all talk now as well.

'Hats, dolls or colours.' I heard the fellow with the colours before I saw him: swivelling between cars – blue and gold or red and white. Connaughton leaned out his window and bought two paper hats, one each for Richie and me. The good old blue and gold. Onto the rim of my hat I stuck the label on which I had earlier printed the words: MATT THE THRESHER. Richie looked at me with a scornful smirk. 'Blinky,' he said. I couldn't help it if he hadn't the slightest interest in the blue and gold, and preferred cars.

Everywhere our honking car went people looked in. I wished they wouldn't. I was fed up with the horn now too. Only the fellows selling fruit and chocolate carried on regardless.

'I don't know why they are all lookin' in at us anyway,' Fern said. 'Bet you all the horns are blowin' on the other crowd's road into the city.'

Thos was only too willing to agree with him: 'Of course they are, Jaykies 'tis like a wedding among the other lot. A dour old crowd our lot are.'

'We are a reserved people, we like to wait until we have something to shout about before we express ourselves,' Connaughton said.

'Be Jaykies, I hope we won't be waiting for him to shout,' Thos whispered, and Fern sniggered.

There was singing going on somewhere. But our horn drowned it out. It was the song of the other county. Why did they always have to be loud and frightening like this before matches. They were upon the bridge, all the red hats.

'We'll see you inside, boss,' Fern suddenly shouted and opened his door. 'Don't worry, your horn'll knock off once you switch off your engine.'

With the sniggers escaping out of them, Thos and he ran away then, in as much hurry as if they were running from an explosion. One minute I saw them knocking at the back door of a tall house with a drink sign above it. The next they had disappeared within. Connaughton shut off the engine, but the sound of the horn didn't stop.

'Bloody bugger,' he said and stood looking up at the clouds as if the sound was coming from there. It gave Richie his chance. He jumped out, cocked up the hood and stuck his head beneath. Connaughton looked into the river. So did I. A big tree trunk, all rags and weeds on its dead branches, was floating by. 'We can forget the match now,' he said.

'You go on, I'll stay here and fix it,' Richie said. He rubbed his dirtied hands on the blue and gold.

'Are you sure?' said Connaughton. 'Look, you hang on to the sandwiches.'

Of course Richie was sure. He was far happier larking beneath the bonnet of a car than watching a hurling match. Connaughton didn't have to feel sorry for him. Or leave him all the sandwiches.

So that was it; only my father and me left together in the end. We rolled our plastic raincoats, clenched them under our armpits and hit off. It was nice, in one way, having him all to myself. But not in another way. When you were on your own with Connaughton he told you not to be getting excited. Once, at a match, I cursed at a player who hit Matt Donovan out on the sideline. Poor Matt, his legs were sticking in the air and the fellow belting him. 'For two pins, I'd report you to the guards for cursing,' Connaughton told me.

We had to climb through a tunnel cut out of rock to get up on the bridge. It was dark and dripping with water. A blind musician huddled there. His head, following the sound of people's movement, was going from side to side. As soon as we stepped from the tunnel onto the bridge the sound of our car horn was no more. There was a sudden light that blinded me. The crowd swayed and shuffled. And the roar; so loud I got a fright: '...Where I sported and played, 'neath the green grassy glade. On the banks of my own lovely Lee...' All the red hats, singing it. They were invading the bridge from the steps on the opposite side. Clenching bottles in their hands. Far noisier than our crowd, who had climbed up from our side of the bridge. Their crowd, all small men and women, dark-haired and sharp-eyed, walked with quick giddy steps. While our crowd wore the methodical faces of giants and walked as if on slow springs.

'That's the difference between city people and country people,' Connaughton said with a laugh when I pointed out my observations to him. 'They mean business.' It was on that instant I knew, with a drop of my heart, we were going to lose the match.

A squad of them advanced. 'The meeting of the Tribes,' that's what Connaughton said. 'That's what a Munster final is all about.'

Well this Tribe crashed straight into us. One of them spotted my hat and bawled out: 'Who the fuck is Matt the Thresher?' and speared his flag up to heaven. Somehow I was pushed into a siding in the railings. I saw Connaughton twisting like a top, as if he was in a stormy river. 'Who the fuck is Matt the Thresher?' All of them were chanting it now. It was like a battle cry.

'Savages,' Connaughton said to me. 'Hold on to those railings.' Now he was not laughing.

He was deep in concentration, his feet braced against the ground, his back hunched. A banner fell across his head. They pushed him. He didn't budge. 'I'll tell you who is Matt the Thresher.' I could hear him say it. I think he must have forgotten me. A current was bashing him. From side to side they shouldered him but he wouldn't move.

'Daddy,' I said, that's all I could do.

He began to stumble then. And I heard the shouts coming out of him: 'You want to know who Matt the Thresher is . . . Blast you, have manners and listen.' They pushed him until his knees met the ground.

The worst was to see the crowd laugh at him. They laughed at him because he was raging, spit on his lips, shouting at them: 'The great Matty Donovan, that's who Matt the Thresher is. Now do you know?'

They jeered: 'Look at the madman.'

But I didn't look. Matt the Thresher was the hero in Connaughton's book which he had read a long time ago when he was sick in bed after shooting off his finger by accident with a gun. I didn't look. I felt my grip on the railings loosen. And I wanted it to loosen. Because I couldn't hold on any longer. When I let go I was carried away. Away with the Meeting of the Tribes I was carried, across the bridge. Then I was on the far side, among the crowd fanning out. Horse-drawn jarveys were wheeling away, loaded with people for the sports field. Then Connaughton was at my side again. We were rushing forward, rushing for the start of the match: 'Apples, oranges, pears and ripe bananas. Get your colours; hats, dolls or colours.'

'Will we win, Daddy?'

It was a sad procession we joined going home that evening. 'They tried their best but it wasn't good enough,' Connaughton said. 'The best team won.'

'The best team did not win,' Thos said.

'Not enough pan loaves in you.' Mam was at it again. 'How could you win anything when you're too weak?'

Connaughton laughed. 'How right you are.'

Nobody spoke then for ages. Images of dejected hurlers in blue and gold would not leave my mind: Matt Donovan, as he shook hands with Christy Ring and then lay on the ground. We couldn't even blow the horn to tell traffic to get out of our way because whatever Richie had done to mend it not a beep could now be got from it.

'Are you all right, dear?' I heard Connaughton say once to Mam. 'I thought I saw you a bit lame earlier.'

'You must have been seeing things,' Mam said.

I kept my mouth shut the whole way home. I just kept looking at the mild expressions my father was making towards Mam. How could he be so meek and mild. Could he not speak up? I kept thinking of him on the bridge. Had that really been him?

It was only coming back to me now. I had been crushed. And somebody, a man, had lifted me above the throng and I had been freed. Then the man had put me down. I don't know how long I had stood there in a little island all my own outside the stream of match-goers before I noticed the silence. It had been all around me. And within it I had heard my own whimper. The same whimper had been coming out of me since I had stood on the bridge. But only now I had heard it: 'I can't breathe, I can't breathe. Daddy, I'm here . . . I can't breathe . . .' Even when I had seen him, struggling towards me out of the crowd, relief on his face at finding me, I still could not get my breath. It had taken ages before my breath returned. It had been even worse than on previous times when I had cried. There had been nothing I had been able to do about it but continue to gasp.

'Are you all right?' he had said. 'Don't cry.'

'I won't,' I had said. A million other things had been whirling in my head to say to him: Daddy, you are brave to stand up to those men. It's all right, you can leave me, you can leave me on my own whenever you wish. And at the same time my mind was screaming to say: Why did you abandon me? Why have you abandoned me for all of my life? I'm crushed when you are gone and I'm crushed when you are there. I'm crushed between you and Mam and it's all my fault, I shouldn't be in your lives. My wits had been so squashed out of me I had wanted to say all that. But I hadn't said it. He would not have understood. And then, caught up again in the welter of men shouting 'hurry hurry' to one another because the match was about to start, wouldn't I have looked a proper cry-baby?

And had that really been him? I looked at him; he drove carefully now in the evening sunlight, every so often stole a glance at Mam, asked her again what had been the matter with her leg and if it was better now.

'There is nothing wrong with my leg. You were seeing things,' she said again.

Had I been seeing things too?

Connaughton's stand on the bridge: looking back on it now something else occurs to me about that day. That day may have been the first indication of the trouble with Mam's leg. None of us saw that.

Or did my father? He had only gone to that Munster final to please my mother. She had only gone to please him, to have some banter with us children. He had not gone to prove himself a Tipperary hero, nor had she gone to shout for the opposition. But had something unbidden arisen in him on the bridge? Had he been visited by an intimation of future troubles? Attempting to withstand the immediate forces he saw gathering against him, had he stood his back against them, mulish and hopeless?

8

First we went to school in Thurles. We went there for the first
year of our Ivyhall days. In Thurles you were shifted from one
classroom to another and you never knew where you were. The
daily dose of dread at not knowing, from one day to the next, what
Brother you would be faced with kept you on your toes. 'Will we
put this boy in second class, in third or in fourth?' Dropping out of
Burley's class without finishing the year had made me into an educational enigma in their eyes. They never knew where to put me
and I was tried out with Brothers of all hues and sizes. The very first
day I was sent to Thurles school I told myself that I was now a big
boy and was not going to be frightened any more by the likes of
Brother Burley. It didn't work out like that, though. Terror was
always somewhere close at hand, lurking in the next corridor, in
the hands of the next Brother, in whose classroom I would find

myself. For someone as mad as Burley, making your heart jump, would be sure to pop up sooner or later.

Then one day Mam said she was sick of sending us to the posh of Thurles. What, after all, was wrong with the locals schools, she said? Auntie Tessa said there was plenty wrong with them. Mam told her she was a snob and said she was sending us to Wolfdyke and she did. The girls to the convent, the boys to the national school.

Now, instead of the Brothers with their soutanes and deep pockets, I had a teacher who wore a shirt and tie and who was called the Master. One teacher only. One classroom only. No more Brother Burleys on my horizon. And slowly, the surprise began to drop out of my school-going days. When surprise goes, life become uneventful. The Master, Mr Flynn, created terror too, but in a daily, grinding way, which caused your heart not so much to jump, as to barely tick. He was a little man who wore a narrow moustache, no wider than a thin line, and a platform on one shoe which made him slightly gimpy. He measured his moustache with a ruler by the mirror. He liked to call himself Errol. Errol Flynn. So the Wolfdyke crowd called him Gimp. Gimp Flynn.

I had to fight my way in order to be accepted at Wolfdyke school. On my first few days there I was alarmed at how old and run down the place was. I sat at a desk on my own. My strategy was to keep quiet, not to be noticed. But I had to look up from time to time and each time I did so, I found something new to be alarmed at. The windows were so high that there was no point in looking out of them in hope of distraction, because all one could see out there was sky. And the light that flowed down into the classroom made the place dance in a perpetual fog of pencil shavings and chalk dust. Most of the other boys seemed already to be men. They had droopy Adam's apples and sores on their faces, like they were shop assistants or at some such job. They had croaky voices and pencils behind their ears. I was so lonely; wishing for pipey cheerful voices, like those with whom I had mingled back in the days of Brother Skehan and 'The Green Glens of Antrim', even of Brother Burley. Most alarming of all, was to find that my classmates wore long trousers. After a few days I discovered that the classroom housed the four Senior classes and the part I had been put in was where seventh class sat. I had never heard of a seventh class before. It was for fellows who were not going to secondary school but had to wait at primary until they were fourteen. Then they could go and work in the mines, or get permission from the priest to go England, or get jobs in shops in Thurles. Meagher and Gananny were in seventh. They were my neighbours, though this was my first time meeting them. They were sons of the men who had helped Connaughton the day of the threshing. A fellow called Bunny Witheroe was in seventh. He was someone I would get to know more closely.

Lawlor and Considine were also in seventh. I noticed Lawlor and Considine from the start because they were the biggest boys of all and they terrorised everybody else. Lawlor was always talking about how he would soon be going to work in England. You'd think he was there already the way he carried on. I felt very much apart from everybody and I decided that the way for me to mingle was to pick a fight with Lawlor and Considine. I did that. 'Put 'em up,' I said to Lawlor, raising my fists. Wasn't that the way you did it? Well, first Lawlor, and then Considine, beat the stuffing out of me. I couldn't believe I could suffer such hard wallops. I couldn't believe I could see stars. I thought that only happened in comics – where fellows saw stars from bonks they received on the head. Now I saw them. Now, like everybody else, I was being terrorised by the bullies. But I was still different. Even were I to fight with Lawlor and Considine every day of school, to get beaten black and blue every day, I would not have been accepted. Ivyhall kids were different. And that was not my fault: my brothers and me were given different lunches to everybody else – ours came in lunch boxes not tobacco boxes; we carried leather, not canvas schoolbags; for lighting the school fire we brought in real pieces of timber instead of twigs; and most important, we were driven to school by car. We just were different, what a pity. But I got used to this state of affairs and made the best of it.

Simply reading the essays from our book *Forty Specimen Essays* was no longer good enough for Gimp Flynn. That was too easy, he said, puffing into his hands. There were some boys, and I was one of them – because Gimp Flynn had one day decided I was a scholarship boy – there were some boys who would have to learn off the essays. That was not easy. That turned me against essays. Only one among the entire *Forty Specimen Essays*, and only a solitary phrase within that one essay, continued to have any appeal after that. The essay was called 'Summer'. It depicted the long days, the hay and turf saved, the sounds of cuckoo and corncrake and so on, and then it came to a part which said: 'the sounds of lusty-voiced boys bathing in the depths of a shady river'. That was the phrase. I was very envious of those lusty-voiced boys. I saw them swallow-diving in that deep pool. I saw them running along the bank, slapping in and out of the shade beneath the trees. Maybe it was because of them that one June day I dammed our little river down at Glen, and got into the terrible trouble.

Why was it always down in Glen the trouble began? The small river was banked on either side by a hazel grove. Was it all those hazel trees that made the mischief? Or was it the slag heap from the mines, riddled with old mine shafts burrowing into the depths of the earth? There were stories of fairies about Glen. And stories of the ghosts of miners from olden days. It was said the mines burrowed far and deep beyond the mouth of the colliery. Once upon a time miners hunted after seams of coal lying beneath the course of Glen river, light dripping from the lamps on their helmets.

The other fields of our farm at Ivyhall were up the hills above our house. Far up in the wide open. Up there were the horse-gallops, and all the action. A wind blew through those fields. Glen was warmer, nearer the house – it was possible to make out the windows at the back of the house from Glen – and yet it was the forgotten field of the farm.

In Glen you could hide. In Glen the straight long hazel rods grew, out of which you made bows and arrows. During the summer the cows lay hidden in the tall grass of Glen and we went hunting them, skimming arrows off their bony backs. The buffalo cows. 'Strange field is Glen,' my father said. 'A late field for grass, but once it starts to grow, the cows have to be left there full time to keep it down.' Other things also grew in Glen during the summer. Lots of wildflowers along the river bank, and the thick stalky flaggers in the parts where water had lain on the ground during the winter. A sort of Iris, Mam said the flagger was. It bore a yellow-headed flower; it always amazed me, the delicate petals that came out of those coarse stalks. Sometimes we took them up to decorate the house and then the slightly rank smell of Glen was in all the rooms. The cows loved to lie on the flaggers. Instead of eating grass to make milk, they lay all day in the coolness of the flaggers. Then we hunted them out. But not because we thought they should be making milk, rather because we enjoyed looking into the flagger beds: those flattened out circles, shining like nylon in the sun. And then we lay in their silence ourselves. The cow nests, we called them.

Meagher and Gananny: they were not exactly the lusty-voiced boys one might imagine bathing in the river of my *Forty Specimen Essays*. Their bodies didn't have the correct shapes for it. Meagher's was a shape the same as a bagful of bags; so many clothes on him you couldn't see any lumps. Gananny's was the opposite – bony and long, the thin clothes stretched beyond their limits.

Meagher and Gananny were the boys I knew from school. I also knew them from sometimes coming across them on their wanderings about our farm in Ivyhall. They rarely went to school. They went badger-hunting. They travelled with a little posse of terriers. In all truth they behaved less like boys than men. However, for swimming in Glen, I decided they would do just as good as any lusty-voiced boys and this day that we bumped into one another at the ford of our little river I persuaded them to help me build a dam so that we could go for a swim.

They didn't think a swim was a good idea at first, and began talking of other things. Meagher knew all about the mines. He said there was still plenty of coal, seams of good anthracite, in there. But it was down too deep and much too hard work to get it out. And much too dangerous.

'A swim is a great idea,' I said. 'It's too hot. We'll cool ourselves.'

I don't think they had noticed that it was a hot day. Or known that what you did on hot days was swim beneath shady trees. The only thing they seemed to know about hot weather was that it was not suitable for badger-hunting. The terriers were in the shed at home, they said. They were not allowed out except when they were hunting because it took the edge off them. Meagher told me about the cracking sound a man's leg made when a badger broke it. A badger never let go once it had you by the leg, never let go until it heard the bone crack. In the end they ran out of things to talk about and the idea of the dam began to appeal to them.

'Sods and rocks, lads,' I said. Gananny and me got down to the job in our bare feet, our trousers rolled up, walling in the water with sods and rocks. Meagher would not take off anything; he sloughed around the river in his wellingtons. I was already wondering how, if he would not take any clothes off, I would get him to swim. When the water reached up to the top of his wellingtons I told him he had better get out. I could see that the pressure of the river was buckling the boots in against his legs. He just sniggered at me and let the water flow into his feet. When Meagher sniggered, his face always twisted in a sort of sly malice. He probably had no malice in him, or slyness, it was just the way he looked when he found something funny. Then Gananny laughed. They were both laughing; it seemed somehow hilarious to them to see the water flowing into Meagher's wellingtons. I started laughing too. Then a cow which had been lying in the flaggers jumped up with a creaky sound and ran away with her tail in the air and that made us laugh even more. Meagher jumped out of the river in an attempt to chase the cow.

'You ould bitch, come back and I'll ride you,' he shouted, grabbing at the front of his trousers. It looked as if he wanted to leap up on the poor cow but he fell over with the weight of water in his boots. Startled cows wheeled out of the flaggers and ran from us in a wide arc.

'Your socks are wet,' I said.

'I don't give a shit,' he said. He pulled off his wellingtons and upended them so that the water came glugging out of them. Now we couldn't stop laughing if we tried. Gananny threw his long arms around us and we ended up all falling into the cow nest.

I didn't know how long we had lain there. Meagher had begun telling stories about women in their buffs and about the antics of Paddy the Irishman. We were still laughing but now the laughter had become more serious. The sun was burning down on us. I was sweating and uncomfortable with the dirty water drying on my legs. I could smell the mud. It was then my mind returned to the *Forty Specimen Essays*: to my invigorating idea of earlier.

'Come on, we'll go for a swim,' I said, and I stood up.

I could immediately see that the others did not share my

142

enthusiasm. The river was now brimming over the dam, knocking out a little channel in the top sods, and the water was running clean. I was standing over the river, wondering was it deep enough to cover me if I lay flat out, when they began pelting it with stones. All the laughing seemed to have got them into a stone-pelting mood. Big lumps of stones; they were crashing them into the river as if it had suddenly become their worst enemy. Then they fell back in the cow nest, worn out.

'Ah come on, lads.' I still thought the swim was a great idea. I took off my shirt. I could swim in my underpants. Did they wear underpants? I wondered. I knew some boys didn't. Mam said it was a bad habit not to. If a fellow didn't wear underpants, it would be difficult to get him to swim. 'Ah lads, come on.'

'It's too dangerous,' Meagher said.

'Too dangerous,' Gananny agreed, his voice gone all idle.

I was unhappy. All of a sudden the urgency seemed to have dropped out of the day, the sun to have sapped all the energy from it. Everything had become sleepy; the grass had become flat and listless. Nobody talked. We could hear the popping sound of seed pods. Cows had begun to graze close by, no longer frightened of us. Then a cow gave a belch and Meagher laughed, throwing a root of flagger at Gananny.

Gananny stirred himself and stood up. 'Ah feck it all,' he said and gave Meagher a lazy look, 'I feel like getting out the Lone Ranger.'

I didn't know what he was talking about.

Meagher gave one of his sly laughs: 'Do so.'

'The Lone Ranger?' I said. 'What's he, one of the dogs?'

'He's not for huntin' badgers anyway, I'd say.' Meagher sniggered again. 'What's the Lone Ranger, Gananny?'

Whatever Gananny's Lone Ranger was, he seemed suddenly very keen to show us. But he had to make a big backward bend of himself, his tail end poking into the flaggers, his hands fumbling with his trousers front, in order for us to see it. 'Me trousers is all hitched up by him,' he said. Suddenly the trousers flew downwards. I knew then Gananny did not wear underpants. I knew that whatever else he would do he would not be going for a swim. And I knew what the Lone Ranger was.

'Woops,' he said. 'Don't run away on me.' The Lone Ranger

stood there before him, yet apart from him, so that it seemed to be leading a lonely life of its own.

Meagher laughed. 'Ha ha, Gananny, another leg. Wouldn't you think two long legs would have been enough for you?'

'Show us yours so,' Gananny said.

'Yours is enough.'

'Ah go on. I see the lump of him up your jumper.'

'Up me jumper?' Meagher looked down at himself in dismay.

'Yeh, go on.'

'Ah it's too cold.' Meagher lay down on the flaggers.

'Show us yours, Connaughton.' Gananny swung around to me and his Lone Ranger swung around too and nodded as if it and not he were doing the talking.

'Mine?'

'Yours.'

'ok.'

'Young Connaughton is letting his beast out,' Meagher said with his snigger. 'Fence your ditches, lads.'

I didn't know what had overtaken me. I'm not sure if I had ever even noticed my own Lone Ranger before – maybe it was because I had been watching Gananny's and now mine too was suddenly demanding attention, or maybe I thought Gananny's needed company – but once the first outdoor breeze crossed mine I felt it belonged out.

'Tell your little lad to say hello to spare-leg.' Meagher looked down at me.

It was true, it was smaller than Gananny's but now it was out it was staying out.

'Hi ho, Silver, away,' Gananny said. He swung his right leg around as if he was getting on a wild horse and he grabbed himself for fear of toppling off.

'Giddy up,' said Meagher.

'Do that,' Gananny said to me.

'What?'

'Rub it like me.'

He was rubbing the Lone Ranger. I rubbed mine once. What was there to lose? I rubbed it a few more times.

'Go on.'

'It hurts.'

But I did it. And soon Gananny, now switching his attention solely upon himself, began to sway. Or the hazel bushes down at the
river began to sway. Or the ground, or something. Or everything.
And inside me, welling, welling, trying to get out, was a deep pain.

'I can't do it. Auh. My ears are sore.'

The pain was growing deeper. I was paralysed by the rubbing,
paralysis going through my whole body, even into my head.

'Why can't you do it?'

'It's sore.'

'You're doin' it wrong.'

'I'm not. It's sore.'

'Look, watch me. Now do it like that.'

'Ow. That's worse.'

'It's not worse. It's nice.'

'How could it be nice?'

'Because you're not doin' it right. Here, let me do it for you.'

'No, get lost.'

He shuffled towards me, hobbled by the trousers tightening
around his ankles, and he reached out the hand he was not using. I
turned away and nearly fell on the ground because of the weakness
and because of nearly tripping over my own trousers. Suddenly he
withdrew his hand and used it on himself along with the other one.
And then with the two hands going together his twanging got
louder than elastic, and for a while he forgot about me entirely but
began looking in the distance.

'Watch,' Gananny said. 'The train is coming. Now, watch,
watch, watch, watch.'

'Giddy up,' said Meagher.

Then there was a spurt. It frog-leaped across the flaggers. Quick
as silver. Then another one. This one took longer, like washing
water being slung from a basin.

'That's what you're supposed to do,' Gananny said.

I didn't know if I should feel sorry for him; his face looked
painful.

'Fire away, yourself,' Meagher said.

'No,' I said. 'My ears.'

'Don't mind your ears.'

My ears had filled with a boiling waterfall. And down there, and my whole spine, all the way up to my brain, was paralysed as concrete. I knew I would have to stop this thing that I was doing, even though I was in the grip of some force making me continue and Meagher was saying, 'Fire away, young Connaughton.' I knew something inside me was not ready. Something that was too raw, that was not yet ripe, and if I persisted I would only break it. I might be damaged inside forever.

I stopped. And after ages I managed to lift my trousers over myself.

'Hi ho, Silver, away,' Meagher said. 'A pity he ran out of ammo.'

When I got back to Ivyhall the shadow and coolness of the hallway surprised me. I looked up at the landing window because there was dark up there where there should have been light. Then I saw the shadow. It was Mam. And I got the goose pimples out through my skin. Mam was looking down at me. She had Connaughton's binoculars hanging around her neck.

'Come up here until I show you something,' she said.

The stairs in Ivyhall were wide, with shallow steps that you normally flew up but this time I was in no hurry. Mam was energetically flicking through the bundle of reserved enclosure tabs that Connaughton had tagged on to his binoculars from his racing days before she had come along and spoiled everything, so that now he couldn't go any more.

'Ooh,' she was saying. She made her voice sound sweet. 'Chepstow, Cheltenham, Punchestown, Sandown. These must be very strong binoculars indeed to have been to all these places. Now let's see how far they can see in Ivyhall. Hey, have a look. You'll be impressed.'

Standing at the windowledge, my head reached just to the level of her necklace. I could not look up at her face. The beads of the necklace swung viciously before my eyes. I looked in the binoculars to get away from them.

Impressed was not the word for what I could see. The river had jumped up to meet my eyes. The dam had burst and the water lay smooth and glassy in the afternoon light. I had not realised how exposed it had been at that spot, how far from the hazel grove. A spotlight might as well have been shining on it. Sweat broke out on my face and neck. It was as if inside myself the dam had burst. It trickled all the way down the back of my trousers. The sunlight coming up the barrels of the binoculars was dazzling me.

'Nice friends you were with.' Her voice had become even sweeter.

'Yeh.'

'Was that Gananny?'

'I don't know. It was you had the binoculars.'

She went very silent then. I didn't look at her but prepared myself for the blow, hoping I might get the whole business over and done with quickly. But the blow didn't come. The sweet voice returned.

'Did you enjoy your swim?'

'No.'

'Did Gananny?'

''Twasn't deep enough for him.'

'Funny. I thought I saw him making great strokes.'

'He can't swim.'

'I suppose we can't expect a stork to be able to swim. And what else were you doing?'

'Only talking.'

'What about?'

'The coal mines.'

'Ah. What about them?'

'That the work is dangerous.'

'Ah. And the other genius Meagher. He was only talking too?'

'Who?'

'Oh it wasn't Meagher? Maybe these binoculars of your father's are not that strong after all. We'll have to ask him to test them whenever he gets home. Good thing we'll have the light of the long evening.'

'Yeh.'

'Have you any homework to do?'

'Yeh.'

'Better get cracking then. Do you need any help from me because I'll be asking your father to examine your homework when he gets home?'

'No.'

'Why? What is the homework?'

I was about to mumble something but I stopped. I was about to mumble that the homework was simply learning off one of the *Forty Specimen Essays*, that it was really easy. But I couldn't say it. Suddenly not another word could I dig out of myself. And I just stood there for ages, Mam's necklace, immovable now as heavy marble, before my eyeballs. And to pass the time I began doing calculations. I was calculating depth: how many miles deep those seams of coal travelled into the ground, those glinting seams of buried anthracite.

9

Mam had one saving grace. She never told Connaughton anything. She did not tell him about the Lone Ranger. Why
was that? This is the story of the Little Yank. It concerns another
occasion when Mam kept something from Connaughton. Or
would have, if somebody else hadn't told him. It all came about as
a result of that swim in Glen, so maybe it was all my fault.

Jamesy was my younger brother. He was not figuring in my life
nowadays; my being preoccupied with Richie and all that. But
back in the hotel days I had seen quite a bit of him.

After our Mama died a lot of offers came flooding in from relatives all over the place to take us children off Dada's hands and to
rear us for him. Dada fought them all off. He recalled Fay from
California and that helped repulse them. But the most insistent
offers kept coming from my aunt and uncle in New York. And it

was Jamesy they wanted. The problem was they had no children themselves and they saw in Jamesy a little dote, with his curly brown hair and brown eyes. Fay herself said it was not a bad idea to let Jamesy go. America was a land of great opportunity. She knew; she had just come back from there. Uncle Mike and Aunt Ita, she said, lived in a tidy apartment in Manhattan – Stuyvesant Town was the address, I read it on their letters – and Jamesy would be cherished like he was their own. But Dada said such a course would break his heart. Dada loved Jamesy dearly, and Jamesy stayed.

Why did I protect Jamesy? Why was Jamesy the one the Connells picked on? Why, in all probability, would I have picked on him had we continued to live in the hotel and did not have Ivyhall to contend with? Why was he picked on? I don't know. He was a sunny fellow. He had this smile, though, that was almost too much. A smile almost painful to look at because it was so open. People seemed to want to close down whatever it was they saw in Jamesy. I know I did sometimes. One way was to clobber him until his lips went blue with crying. But now I had to protect him. Now it hurt me to see him hurt. It was ridiculous really. The way to get at me was to get at him. And the way to get at him – when it was not possible to hit him – was to get at the ponies. He loved the ponies. The way to have him in tears was to throw stones at the ponies. The Connells threw stones at the ponies. Gananny, Meagher, they too threw stones at the ponies. To see a sharp shard of stone bounced off the flanks of a pony and watch it wheel away in distress was not a pretty sight. Which all ended up with me defending the ponies. When it came to Jamesy, I became grown-up.

In any case, on this particular night Jamesy and me are having our bath. Bathtime in Ivyhall is quite an affair. There are ten of us now, counting the new baby.

Bathtime: first the girls, starting with the youngest, two at a time. Then a top-up of hot water and it is the boys' turn. When it gets to the two eldest boys – Richie and me – the water is changed. Why do Richie and me get the specially clean water? I don't know. Not fair, the girls say. Hard cheese, Richie says. I get in the warm water with Richie. What can I do about unfairness?

After a time it was decided that the bath wasn't large enough to hold Richie and me together. Thereafter, Richie had his bath last, on his own, the king. And I, though I still got the clean water, shared with one of the younger ones. Yes, it was because Richie and me were the eldest we got the special treatment. Also, more importantly, because we were boys. Now if we had been girls, it would have been different. The girls, for instance, were not allowed to read. Not that any of them wanted to read anyway, except for my own sister Pam. The girls were supposed to be doing jobs all the time. Washing up, doing the rooms, tidying away the clothes in bundles. Little housekeepers. But Pam was always being caught with a book. She got the names then. Dilly Dreams. Burrow-in-the-book. Bookworm. What, for God's sake, were Richie and me, if Pam was a bookworm? We, who were encouraged to read? And when Richie and me had to get out of the middle room because it was being done up for a visitor . . . even that did not stop the all-night reading: Blackie's Classics and *Newnes Pictorial Knowledge* were moved into the backroom where the rest of the boys slept. And then each night, when Richie eventually threw his book on the floor with a bang, one of the smaller ones had to get out and turn off the light. And I let it happen. Usually it was Jamesy.

'Jamesy, your turn,' says Richie.

Jamesy would be fast asleep. 'What, what?'

'Wakey wakey, Jamesy. Turn out the light.'

'No.'

He had to do it, though. Jamesy, one hand on the light switch, the other gathering his pyjama bottom in readiness, and then the instant the light went out the big leap into the safety of the bed. If I was fearful of the dark and the phantoms in the attic and so on – something I kept to myself – Jamesy was even more fearful. Richie knew that. Sometimes he caught Jamesy, threw him into the bathroom, held the door shut and turned out the light. The light switch was outside the door. The roars of Jamesy then. And the sudden appearance of Mam: 'I have never heard anything so ridiculous: afraid of the dark.' The night that Richie hid beneath his bed and stuck his cold hand out, catching Jamesy by the ankle as he made his leap in the dark . . . The house was nearly brought down that night. Up came Mam. I could hear the stairs groan like an earthquake. 'What's going on?' Sudden silence. Total silence. The fairy of instant slumber casting his silvery spell upon the room. Nobody dared tell on Richie.

In any case. This particular night in the bathroom, hot and steamy night, water all over the floor after the others, I am sharing the bath with Jamesy. Richie is not having a bath. He is out nursing a sow who is about to have her bonhams. He will stay up all night probably. He will tell us later how many bonhams he has saved from the jaws of the wicked sow. Strange that sows should wish to devour their young. So Jamesy and me are last in the bath and we are lingering. Maybe we have been forgotten . . . Something that quite easily happens in Ivyhall. People are often forgotten. Anyway, things are peaceful. It is comfortable in the bath. And what comes out, but the Lone Ranger.

I cannot avoid showing it to Jamesy – it seems to have grown since its last public appearance down at Glen. I quite enjoy showing it off to Jamesy, but rather than frighten him, I put one of Connaughton's empty Brylcreem jars over it. Glassed off like that, it is as safe as a tiger in its cage.

'Look, Jamesy.'

'I can make that happen too,' he says.

'Make it happen so,' I say.

'I have no jar.'

The medicine shelf is alongside the bath. I reach over and get Jamesy a jar with a narrow neck.

'Here, this is probably the right size.'

He makes it happen him all right. And there are our men for a few minutes in their jars, the Brylcreem jar with the wide neck and the Ponds Cold Cream jar with the narrow neck, bobbing up and down in the hair-oily water that the suds have gone out of, like two divers in their helmets. Then Jamesy's man gets stuck. Stuck within the jar. Jamesy is in terror. And the more terror-stricken he becomes the more he is stuck. I can see it through the glass. Blue, and all veins, like his face when he bawls. And now he is bawling. And what can I do, what can I do to make it go back to its right shape?

'Stop, stop crying,' I say. I stick the wash-towel over his mouth. 'Mam will hear you.'

'I'm tellin', I'm tellin'.' He tries to get away from me. He slips in the bath and goes under. I can hear his jar clunking against the sides. But when he comes up again it is still stuck on him. 'I'm tellin', I'm tellin'.' There seems no stopping him from telling now. He is spitting soap and reaching his hands out blindly.

When Mam comes in she sees it all. Not me, my Lone Ranger has shrunk back to normal. But Jamesy. She sees it all and with one whack of the flat of her hand she knocks him out of the bath. 'Dirty little maggot,' she says. One minute Jamesy is in the frying pan, the next, without having had time to notice the difference, he is in the fire.

That is the night when Jamesy's skin, from head to toe, goes red with the lashing he gets on the wet bathroom floor. I don't get a whack, just a lash of her tongue: 'Corrupting sneak'.

Jamesy was the one who went to Connaughton. He was the only one of us ever who would dare.

'I want to go away, Daddy,' he said.

And he did go too.

Jamesy thought he was going for good. We children all thought he was going for good. To America, to live with Mike and Ita. Why did we think that? Well, there was a party for Jamesy; first time ever in his whole life that he had been made the centre of attention. And – he blew out candles on a cake. Why did Jamesy blow out candles on a cake? Because he was going away to live in America, of course. And Mam bought him cotton clothes for the heat. And more than anything else: she kissed him goodbye. Jamesy closed his eyes for that kiss from Mam but she left hers open. It was a silent kiss and yet I could see a smacking movement of her lips. As if she couldn't stop those lips doing what they wanted to. Yeh, missing him already.

More than anything, it was that kiss which made me cry about Jamesy's departure. It was the first and only time any of us was allowed be singled out for a kiss. Then he and Connaughton went off in the car with Fern, who was to drive the car home because Connaughton, of course, was travelling to America with Jamesy to settle him in.

When Jamesy returned home, after only two weeks, he wore a cowboy hat down over his eyes. He wore it everywhere and would not take it off. And that was how he came to be known as the Little Yank. Mam continued to call him James the Less as she had always done. But James the Less or the Little Yank, he still looked the same. His hat could not shelter him for long. The name stayed but he continued to be picked on. In between times, when he was either running from those who were picking on him or out riding on his beloved ponies, I learned about his trip to America. He loved to talk of it. Yes, he may have come home from America, but he had gone there too: he was the only one we knew who had done it. Connaughton too spoke of it, but not much. Listening to what they both had to say, here is what I made of it.

In the aeroplane everybody was talking to Jamesy and giving him money to spend in New York. Everybody was even bigger than Daddy, he said. It was awful hot when the aeroplane door opened and they got off.

One day they went to the seaside. What happened at the seaside was that the grown-ups had drinks and lay down in the sun. At the beach everybody rubbed cream on their skin. At the beach this day Jamesy won stuffed rabbits. He won so many stuffed rabbits he couldn't hold on to them all. All the other boys there were winning rabbits also. You only had to knock them off a wall with a ball, it was easy. While they were winning rabbits the grown-ups were clapping them on and having more drinks. Connaughton did not drink and instead went down to the sea and swam, but Mike and Ita did, also lots of other people did with whom they were great friends. They went to the seaside again another day and did the very same thing. More rabbits and more drink. (When Jamesy arrived home in his cowboy hat he was actually clutching a rabbit. After a few days Mam took it from him and put it in the pram with the baby.)

According to Connaughton's story, what happened in New York was that everybody worked very hard. All of Mike and Ita's friends were like them, Irish, and they all worked in the government jobs, at offices, and lived in very tidy homes, up apartment blocks. But on Sundays they went to a place called Far Rockaway, where they lay in bathing togs and got burned to a cinder without noticing it until it was too late, drank lots to keep cool and fell asleep and let their children win rabbits all day long. There was no protection from the heat of that sun, Connaughton said, but to sit indoors, and they preferred to lie in the sand. The Yanks were very decent people, he said. He joked that Jamesy would have been altogether spoiled if they had stayed any longer in Stuyvesant Town. 'Isn't that right, Jamesy?'

If Jamesy was spoiled by his stay with Mike and Ita, it was all so quickly made up for when he came home.

'Look,' Richie said one day. He threw one of the black cats out the dairy door. Ivyhall cats were not like the lazy old hotel cats. They were all black, almost mad with wildness; you only managed to catch them when they went into the dairy in search of milk spillages. 'Did you see that,' said Richie. 'Cats always land on their paws.'

'They don't,' I said.

'Don't do that, it hurts,' Jamesy said.

'Doesn't hurt. They always land on their paws.'

I argued on Jamesy's behalf. I had seen Jamesy talk to the cats, and make little comments to himself about their small paw marks on the dirt. He liked cats. I argued that it did hurt a cat when it was thrown and that they didn't always land on their paws.

'What would you know about it, Blinky?' Richie said.

'Prove it,' I said. That was a mistake. I should not have asked him. Richie was a great man for proving things.

'OK,' he said and caught the cat again. And where did he go, where did we follow him? Up the castle. Yep, up the castle, the place he told me was out of bounds on the very first day I met him. Through a hole in the ivy we went. We climbed over the rubble in the ground floor. We smelled rusting tins. Light poured in through narrow slits. Norman windows, Richie said, for shooting out arrows. 'Come on.'

Richie went first. I don't know how he managed to hold the cat. It squealed with terror. It squirmed. I saw the white button of its butt like a lit cigarette under his arm. He tightened his clamp.

'Leave him go, leave him go,' Jamesy was calling. 'I'm not going up after you.' But Jamesy did go up. Like me, I suppose, curiosity was killing him.

Up we went, up a winding stairs with a smell of dampness, up through archways and shadows.

'Are you afraid?' Richie said.

'No.'

Such a matter-of-fact character Richie was in some ways, you had to hand it to him. Walking up that stairwell, he was able to give us a whole history of the castle. The shelves in the walls, the drops at either side of us. 'A priest was starved to death in there.' 'And there, see that hole, that was the torture chamber.' I was nearly taking an interest in spite of everything.

Then we were on the top. And for a moment I forgot what we had come up for. It was like a field up there, a little square field on a mountaintop. Grass and little shrubs and the sun shining on them and a crow flying off. Except that you dared not look directly down. You stood on dizzy heights. Which, of course, was the very thing Richie made you do.

'This used to be even higher; where we are standing was once the floor of the top room. Look down.'

I did, for one second. Lifting my head over the parapet of the castle, I caught the wind. And caught a glimpse of our yards and buildings, and couldn't believe how quiet it all was down there. The roof of Ivyhall asleep just below us. How calm. And where was Mam, and all the arguing hordes of children?

'Stand back out of the way,' Richie said. 'I want to throw it out as far as I can, so it clears the concrete path and lands in the lawn.'

'No, no, don't, don't. You can't.' Jamesy's wails flew like wisps of smoke off the top of the castle.

'Before you do it,' I said, 'you always think you're right, don't you?'

'Stop blinking, Blinky,' he said.

The next thing the cat was gone. In the mid-air, shooting straight forward, legs wide apart, a terrible screech coming out of it. But the screech was only for a second. Until it stopped flying and dropped out of sight. I don't know if I heard the thump or not, the guts hit the ground below. Richie was saying, 'Landed on his paws, he'll be all right. He won't be drinking cream for a while, that's all.' And I attacked him. Up there, on that high plateau of grass and scrub, I went straight for him. 'You stupid fucker. How can we know if it landed on its paws or not.' I threw blows at him. He wrestled me until I was pinned beneath him. The empty blue sky was spinning around above me. The smell of ivy was in my nose, my face bruised against it. He shook me. 'You can't fight up here, you lunatic, we'll both fall over. I'll have to kill you to stop you, if you fight up here.'

Murder was in my heart too, but he had me pinned with his strength and with his logic.

Jamesy, meanwhile, was gone. And the roars out of his wet throat were sliding up the stairwell, up the slimy walls: 'The cat is dead, he's dead, he's dead.'

And Richie, exasperated, shouting after him: 'How could he be dead. Didn't you never hear cats have nine lives?'

I don't know what took hold of me then. I just laughed and laughed like a maniac.

The cat. Had it landed on its paws? I was still wobbling with vertigo when I got down. The cat lay flat as a pudding, its legs and tail still in the outstretched positions as when it had taken to the air, bubbles coming out its nose, and a wheezy, oh awfully dying noise.

It lay there all evening. Nobody seemed to pay it any attention. Later on, somehow, inch by inch, it crawled into hiding. Some days later I saw a black cat slink across the yard, the slack pouch of its stomach dragging between its legs. Richie, once again, had been right.

Why did Mam never tell tales about us to Connaughton? I look back now to the flight of the black cat: in its sightless sail through the air I see things. I see the adult in me as it was emerging for the protection of Jamesy. I see the child in me, buried deep by that adult, but ever more a child for having being buried. Ever more buried and because of that, ever more eager to come forth. I see the children in all of us. Connaughton, who ran a farm and a business, I see the child in him. I see it come forth in him when things become too difficult. Mam, who had to run the family in order to let him do his work, she was the only adult.

10

The only other bad trouncing apart from the Little Yank's that I witnessed in Ivyhall was administered to . . . No, not to me, who was always afraid of it, ever since the time of the tanning from Fay. Not to me, but to who? You won't believe . . .

Richie's room was decorated for the visitor. It was now called the visitor's room. The visitor had duly arrived. Two visitors, in fact, around the same time. Granny, who was called Granny Power, and a baby, who was Mam's second baby with Connaughton. Granny was the visitor who got the room.

I might not have bargained for a new mother. I certainly hadn't bargained for a granny. This one was not the gentle soul sort of granny you read about. She was big and ferocious. She was a retired music teacher, even though she didn't resemble one. She resembled Aunt Leg, except she was Aunt Leg with a bad temper. Huge baggy eyelids covered her eyes most of the time but when you did see the big bloody violent eyes it was frightening. The good thing, the amazing thing, was that she hated her own grandchildren, hated them even more than us, the new brood. She didn't seem to have much time for her own daughters either. Mam, Auntie Tessa, her other daughters. They laughed at her in the kitchen behind her back. And she muttered. They threw up their eyes in mortification when they saw her hitch up her big knickers beneath her dress, or wash her false teeth at the sink. She told them they were no good for anything but smoking cigarettes and listening to the dirty smoocher, Frank Sinatra, on the radio. She said she'd had to go out and teach music all her life because of their father, a waster. Then Mam, the eldest of her daughters, got mad with Granny and put her in her place with a tongue lashing, saying she'd had enough from her when she had been a child and no, no sir, was she going to let her treat her like that now and Granny went off muttering and woe betide any of us children she caught laughing at her because she got the wooden clothes hanger to us. 'Déanta sa tSúalann.' Oh yes, made in Sweden. The strongest timber.

Strangely, as I have said, it was not the newcomers who got the hammerings. Richie got the worst ones. She couldn't stand him. You could say he deserved it from her, I suppose. He never let up baiting her. He pretended to hold a clothes peg in his nose and followed after her, sniffing as if he was taking in the most putrid air. During Granny's sojourns in Ivyhall she was put to knitting and darning. Whenever she got up from her chair – Granny's residence, as Mam called it – a sagging old armchair with bales of flattened cushions and lumps of wool and sock darnings, Richie caught one of us and shoved our noses into the chair until we almost passed away. Richie got beatings, but the worst beating Granny ever gave was to my stepsister Breda. Granny caught Breda in the mirror one day pulling faces at her. 'Dirty little scobber,' she said. She took a coat hanger to her and then was so exhausted herself she fell against Breda knocking all the wind out of her. She had to leave the house after that. Mam drove her away, bags, songbooks, knitting needles.

Granny had complicated lodging arrangements. She would spend three months at a time with each of her daughters. She had four daughters altogether. She didn't go full term with us that time.

She would return though. She didn't seem to go the full terms with her other daughters either. To tell the truth about Granny: I secretly liked having her around. As she said herself, when she was around there was never a dull moment. She could sing. That was a thing I liked about her. She had one of those wobbly, milk-curdling voices. '. . . Oh the days of the Kerry dances . . .' She encouraged those of us with voices, and lucky me, I had a voice. While Richie, she said, was only an old crow.

She had a smell, she was violent, she had a good voice. She came and went and broke clothes hangers. But a Granny-beating with a clothes hanger is not what I am about to talk of here. A Granny-beating was a tame and even laughable affair by comparison with the one that occurred on the night we had the babysitter, Miss Crippen.

It happened during one of Granny's exiles. Granny had been in residence when the baby arrived, the idea being she would help with the baby, but every time the baby cried Granny stuck her apron in its mouth to silence its bawling, because every time the baby cried was surely the time when the phone rang. And Granny was very inquisitive about phone conversations. So again it was danger to someone's life – this time the baby's – which forced Mam to get rid of Granny.

One day, after Granny had packed her bags and left, Mam announced that she and Connaughton were going to the pictures. It would be their first night out since they had got married, she said. So we were to behave. Mam said that while they were gone we were to have something called a babysitter. Strange title indeed. Her name was Miss Crippen, she was a friend of theirs, a schoolteacher, very strict. Very strict but very cultured too. Mam got the girls to put out the best books beside the lamp in the visitor's bedroom.

Dancie did not much like the idea of Miss Crippen. She thought she should have been entrusted to mind us. Mam said she would have enough to do with minding the baby and Dancie's blue eyes glared through her spectacles in disagreement. Maybe it was because she didn't approve of Miss Crippen that Dancie got the idea that she was a child murderer. In any case, long before the arrival of Miss Crippen, the song, mostly to scare Jamesy, had been composed: 'The teacher Miss Crippen is a murderess. Every child she murders is a schoolchild less.' Devilment was in the air.

Marguerite tried to give us some news. Because Marguerite was the eldest of the girls, she could overhear certain conversations between the grown-ups. Miss Crippen, she tried to tell us, was a spinstress and not a murderess. She had overheard Mam tell Aunt Tessa. Miss Crippen was someone who was looking for a husband, and Connaughton and Mam were helping her find one. So we shouldn't be singing songs about her like that. But Richie told Marguerite to shut up, Miss Bossyboots.

Oh there was devilment in the air all right.

It was in the air that evening as we did our homework in the backroom.

The backroom had once been a spare room full of rubbish. It was down three steep steps, away from the rest of the house. It had been done up when the Connaughtons arrived in Ivyhall. It was where we played cards; it was where we mostly lived. Because it had been built against the castle, its walls were uneven. Now we were all seated, doing homework, around the square table. The table had a slippery surface that was great for sliding books along, except only Richie was allowed slide them. 'Give it back to me,' he commanded my little sister, Noeline. He had just crashed a book into her ribs and she was bent over in a Z. It was the biggest book he had and he wanted it back so that he could thump the breath out of some more bodies; so that down the long swoop of table the book could go again, knocking papers and pencils out of its way. Yes, there was gaiety in the air. Richie had been expecting Noeline to get off her chair, walk round and hand him back his book; his submissive slave. Instead, it must have been a sudden moment of bravery, a moment in which she grew out of being the little child she had always been known as and became a girl – she sent it scattering back to him. Then we were all at it. Brown-paper-covered books crashing and flying in the air. It was like a startled hen-house.

'Stop or I'll tell Mam.' Marguerite was on her feet. Miss Bossyboots. Not that I disliked Marguerite. I liked her. She was Richie's real sister but they were mortal enemies, you had to like someone for that.

'Do your homework or I'll tell Mam.' Marguerite always said

this. She said it so many times we knew it would never come to anything more than a threat. Then Breda, almost the same age as me, started sniggering. Once Breda began the sniggering there was no stopping her. Breda could hold a snigger in for a few minutes – under pain of punishment – but it did not go away. I knew all about the snigger because I suffered from the same affliction. You could hold it in for a few minutes, until it began to pump up inside you. Then you had the big ball of snigger-wind within you and you had become so helpless, not being able to talk or move or respond to adults' commands: 'Stop that unbearable snigger,' they called. Until in the end you had to release it, like a fretting animal let out of a box it went – phwhooshh – bursting through your lips which had become limp as the neck of a balloon.

'Stop that giggling,' said Marguerite.

'Phwhooshh. I can't.'

Then Marguerite turned on the smaller ones. She always did that when control was slipping out of her hands.

The smaller ones – Murt, Noeline, Jamesy and Martin – had their seats down at the dark end of the table and most of the time lived an existence independent of the rest of the family. 'Stop talking you four,' Marguerite called. 'Do your homework.'

So there we were, Richie at one side of the table, Pam and me at another, Marguerite and Breda at another, the four small ones at the end, and the sniggering about to begin. A situation Richie absolutely loved. You were there, trying to hold your snigger in, bursting yourself, and Richie came along with those scobby faces he made to prise the snigger out of you.

A fountain pen dropped beneath the table. It happened during a moment of silence and you could hear the spraining sound as the nib of the pen hit the floorboards. A hand reached down to retrieve it. A foot drew it away from the outstretched hand. Two feet met in a tussle for the pen. Others joined. A tug-o'-war beneath the table. Then the table began to hop about. Richie all the time pretending to do his homework but hopping the table about hardest of any of us. Then, blue murder. Noeline got a kick on the ankle and the bawling began.

'Shut up, babby,' said Richie.

'Now look what's happened.' Marguerite jumped to her feet. 'I told you something would. Who kicked her?'

'Sit down, cow-bossyboots,' Richie said.

That was too much for Marguerite. The kick on Noeline's ankle hadn't the least offended her. That had.

'Now you're for it. I'm going straight up to the kitchen to tell Mammy.'

'Off you go,' said Richie. 'And bring me back a drink.'

'Funny, aren't you?'

Marguerite leaves the room and after a second or two all is in utter silence. After another second there is a clatter of noise down the hallway, hall stand quivering on its legs, door spinning open, door handle hitting the wall and Mam is on the step looking down at us. Marguerite slides in alongside Mam, looking pleased with herself: it is the first time she has got such a dramatic response out of Mam. Nobody knows what to expect.

'Sit down you.' Mam pushes her away.

Mam pushed Marguerite away as if she didn't know her. It was what Mam was so good at. That way she had of ignoring her own children, as though they mattered to her no more than we, the new lot. Mam had a saying. I often heard her say it to Aunt Tessa over cigarettes at the kitchen table: 'I won't make fish of one and flesh of another.' I knew what it meant and yet didn't know what it meant. It meant everybody would be treated the same. But who was fish and who was flesh? In the normal course of events, which was it, fish or flesh, that got the better treatment? Aunt Tessa said it was all wrong not to make fish of one and flesh of another. Everybody needed special treatment sometimes. Our house was like a school, she said. An army regiment. Aunt Tessa did make fish, or flesh, whichever it was. When I drove down the lane with her in the car, I always felt that fish – or was it flesh? – treatment. Soft words, licking of the lipstick as she passed the workmen if they were about, fixing the sunglasses, heaving with fish, or flesh, favouritism. I was often nearly asleep with pleasure by the time we got to the gate. 'Better close the gate after me or your father will blow a fuse.' And then I would have to get out and feel the cold wind.

'What's the matter?' Mam said.

'Noeline got a kick.'

'Who kicked her?'

Noeline's head was down on the table, covered by her arms. Apart from her muffled sobbing, there was silence. I could see Breda was struggling to keep in a snigger. Richie had his back turned to Mam. He was trying his best, turning his face into scobs, to get a response out of Breda. His life's vocation was to get people into trouble. Then he gave a little belch. My own snigger gave a violent push to get out of me. I concentrated with all my might on something to distract me. I couldn't think of anything. I caught a big chunk of cheek flesh between my teeth, biting it so hard I must have been bleeding inside. I saw Breda pinch herself on the arm. 'Stop it,' she said to Marquerite, as if the snigger that must have been just about to come was all the fault of Marguerite. Richie gave one more quick scob. Then the spray of spit exploded out of Breda.

It had an extraordinary effect. Mam actually smiled. A moment of indulgence. Nobody got into trouble. I knew immediately that I was seeing Mam in the best spirits she had ever been in. And it was because she and Connaughton were going to the pictures. I felt somehow pleased for her. I felt somehow pleased too that it was because of Connaughton she should be happy. Yet, at the same time, I felt sort of foolish. What was making me foolish? The idea that she and Connaughton should be going out together, watching the pictures and sitting alongside one another and everything, and a box of chocolates? Somehow the idea didn't seem right. I didn't know why. It was something like the feeling I felt on Christmas morning. When we all had to bring in our presents to the bedroom, following a tradition the Connells had before we Connaughtons arrived. And the sky outside was still black and the lino under our feet was still cold. And we had to say, look Mam, look Daddy, look what I got.

'Say thanks to Santa.'

'Thanks Santa for my new slippers.' And to myself, saying, And for not bringing me a new gun this year. Yes, thanks very much.

It was so strange to see them in bed together on those Christmas mornings: a table at his side with cigarettes on it. A table at her side with a brush and the plait of hair which she unrolled from her head each night. A part of her removed, like an amputation. The curtain half-drawn on the half-dark and me half-looking. At my father and at this woman in this big tangled bed. At a dressing table over in a corner that had a chair for her to sit in and do herself up in the mirror. Who for? For my father?

My mind was wandering away like that.

'That's enough,' Mam said. 'No more of this inane giggling.' An edge had returned to her voice.

There was silence again and then we heard a car in the yard and Dancie's voice come down the hall.

'That's her now, ma'am. Here she comes now.'

For Dancie the arrival of this strange creature called a babysitter was as momentous as it was for us. We listened for sounds of her on the hall but Mam closed the door against all sound; she had instructions to give out and she wanted us to know she meant business.

'None of this stupid sputtering while Miss Crippen is in charge. It's unbearable. One word of complaint from Miss Crippen and it's your father deals with you. Not I. And it will be the first and last time we ever step out of this house at night to go to anything.' She paused for a moment to let that sink in and continued: 'Four small ones, you go to the bathroom now. Wash. After that you go to Dancie for supper. When you've finished, you go into Miss Crippen in the sitting room with the five big ones for the rosary. You're all on trial.'

There was not a sound out of us until we heard the car go down the laneway on its way to the pictures. Then Richie pushed Marguerite off her chair.

Miss Crippen the babysitter sat in the armchair, hidden behind the high stack of Mam's and Granny's *Woman's Own* magazines that were resting on its arm. When we went in, Miss Crippen had the poker in her hand. She was holding it at arm's length to the fire, as if to see if she was seated in near enough to it for poking. She wore thick glasses with pink rims, orange hair, thick lipstick, a very thick covering of face powder.

'Hello everybody,' she said. We were trooping like soldiers into the sitting room. 'How many have we? One, two, three, four, five . . . Oh the babies are gone to bed, are they, Marguerite? Let me count again: A h'áon, dó, trí, ceathar, a chúig.' I think Miss Crippen liked the shapes her fat lips made when she counted, either in Irish or in English. They flapped and buckled like a sink plunger.

'Oh no they have not, Miss Crippen.' said Marguerite. She was supposed to be on special terms with Miss Crippen. Mam had told her that Miss Crippen had taught her once in her baby-infants school, but she couldn't remember that. However, she tried to give the impression that where Miss Crippen was concerned she stood on more intimate grounds than the rest of us. 'They are just slow-coaches putting on their pyjamas, Miss Crippen.'

'Children, isn't it nice for your Mammy and Daddy to be able to go out together tonight?' says Miss Crippen, in that way that schoolteachers have of turning even the most ordinary comment into a question.

'Yes, miss,' we all, except for Richie, had to reply together. Richie just smirked at our schoolchild responses.

'And children, do you know where they are going to?'

'Yes, miss. Thurles.'

'Yes, but what in Thurles?'

'The pictures, miss.'

'Oh no, indeed not. Nothing so common as the pictures. They are going to the opera. The Grand Thurles Operatic Society. And shall I tell you what opera they are going to?'

'Yes, miss.'

Miss Crippen was still being schoolteachery. Now she was on the giving-out-information-for-learning part. At least that wasn't as bad as question-time.

'It's called *The Pirates of . . . The Pirates of . . .* where? Can anybody tell me where the Pirates came from?' Back to question-time again.

'Of Penzance, miss.' It was Pam came up with the answer. That was the thing about Pam. Due to her wide reading when she was supposed to be making beds and so on, she carried all sorts of information. It just went into her head and then was never used. Here suddenly was a chance for her and she looked pleased with herself for having been given it.

'Oh the clever young lady, and where is Penzance?'

I think Pam was flushed with her success. 'In France,' she said.

'No, sorry, I'm afraid not in France. In Cornwall. England.'

'France, huhu.' Richie threw up his eyes to the ceiling in mockery.

In my disappointment for Pam, who so rarely got a chance to

show off, even be noticed, I still had time for wondering why Miss Crippen thought Mam and Connaughton could be gone to the opera. Had they not thought themselves that they were off to the pictures?

The small ones squirmed into the sitting room in their pyjamas.

'Ah, ah, six, seven, eight, nine. A full house.' The counting again. Then she had to get their names, and who was who and all the rest of it.

'Little Martin, and what are you going to be when you grow up?'

'The Pope, miss.'

'Very good. And Noeline, a little Christmas-born present called after our Saviour, am I right?' And so on.

From such unpromising beginnings the most memorable rosary of our lives began.

To our amazement, instead of kneeling on the floor and cocking her tail end towards the fire as everybody always did for the rosary, Miss Crippen climbed on her armchair and knelt up there. She was like one of those women you saw in comics, afraid of a mouse. But I suppose that was the way they did the rosary in her house.

'The First Glorious Mystery,' says Miss Crippen.

Richie took the first mystery: 'The First Glorious Mystery: The Resurrection.' Richie always took the first mystery. By the end of it all of us, except for the small ones, were perched on our chairs: what Miss Crippen did, so we had to.

'The Second Glorious Mystery: The Ascension.' It was Marguerite's turn. By the end of the second mystery, marvelling at one another on our novel vantage points, we were in titters. Only Marguerite still managed to hold a straight face.

I announced my mystery, me being four months older than Breda: 'The Third Glorious Mystery: The Descent of the Holy Ghost on the Apostles in the form of Tongues of Fire.'

A serious competition was now in session: who could climb highest. Cushions were used, books. Then Richie balanced a stool on his chair and rose upon it. I rose on the arm of my chair. Now even Marguerite was rising. With that careful way of hers, she had closed the lid of the piano and was kneeling on it. From the piano's cat-gut belly came little twangs. This was great. I was looking down on Miss Crippen's fervently bowed orange-haired head. But Richie was top man. Then Breda went top. Top perch, monarch over all. Breda had risen on the sideboard. Richie glared furiously at her for having ousted him.

For a few Hail Marys our praying family was like a heirarchy, as in those paintings of cathedral angels who hover on buttresses of varying heights. We perched on books, on stools, on firewood logs, the piano, the sideboard. Only the four little ones remained on the floor; the rest of us restraining them with fist-clenchings and finger-waggings: they were kneeling too close to Miss Crippen and we couldn't trust them not to destroy the fun. On the last Hail Mary of 'The Descent of the Holy Ghost', Breda came toppling down. It was Richie's doing; he gripped her ankle and yanked her off the sideboard. There was a rocking of the sideboard, and a twang of springs as she landed on Granny's armchair.

'The Fourth Glorious Mystery,' says Miss Crippen, never even looking around as she announces it.

It was Breda's decade of the rosary. But how could Breda take it? Richie had pinned her beneath the cushions of Granny's residence and he was kneeling on top of her. Breda was not available for her decade and Richie was furiously pointing at Pam to take her turn. There was a long pause and still Miss Crippen did not look around. The titters were now flying in every direction. What sort of teacher was this Miss Crippen? I wondered. I wouldn't have minded attending her school. Pam, whose turn it was next, did not take up the fourth mystery. She wanted to show support for Breda. She was probably the only one of us in the room with a sense of justice. The four little ones looked around expectantly. They wanted to take it. We waved our fists at them and frowned our disapproval. They never knew how many Hail Marys to recite. They could go on to twelve or thirteen and that would be a shocking disgrace in front of Miss Crippen. Then Richie took it up himself. And Miss Crippen didn't even notice!

'Hail Mary full of the grace,' he said on the second Hail Mary. 'The cat fell down and broke her face.'

'Holy Mary Mother of God,' we replied. 'I carried my mother across the bog.' This was unbelievable heresy we were indulging in. We'd never before had such freedom.

'Glory be to the Gander and to the Hen and to the Holy Goose.'
We were in knots.

It was the same moment that Father Glee chose to make his entry.
And then we each, apart from Miss Crippen, had to inch ourselves
slowly downwards until we were back on the floor.

Father Glee: he was a regular visitor. A fat man whose priest's
clothes still managed to look loose about him and he had a face as
soft as putty. Dancie hated him. He drove around in an aeroplane of
a car, she said. And never visited or talked to coal-miners or poor
people but was always coming around to the rich houses. Connaughton didn't have much time for him either. Personally, I had
nothing against him. He often picked me up and took me away for
whole days to college sports meetings in Cork and places. Mam
would dress me up in the tweed trousers that itched the insides of
my legs. 'You have to look smart for Father Glee.' We would have
set off early in the morning, driven as far as the high stretch beyond
Fermoy, where we could see the army rifle range in the distance,
and then he would stop the car, hand me the newspaper and ask
me to read the hurling and football reports. He enjoyed that, sitting
there, eyes closed in pensive mood. Artillery would pop. Bang
bang of empty air, somewhere across the moor. Then he would
get out of the car and walk along the road, reading the day's section
of his breviary. He would tack down that road like a schooner, his
trousers out full sail in the gusts of each passing lorry. On his return
to the car again, he would tell me what a great woman was Mam:
'Practical woman; the mind of an engineer. Oh what a great engineer was lost in her. Or an army officer. A great commander of
men.' These were the things he enjoyed: calling Mam a practical
woman and a commander of men, listening to my match reports,
and at sports meetings, stopping the pole-vault athletes in their run
up to the jump and giving them tips: 'Pick up your stride, young
man, and lift your head. And vault not over the bar but into the
heavens.' 'Thanks, Father.'

Dancie did not like him and that was why his arrival in the sitting
room went unannounced.

'Carry on with your rosary,' he said, and sat down and his eyes
drooped, as if he'd received an instant sleeping draught.

But once the fifth decade ended he was off: 'Hail Holy Queen,

Mother of mercy, hail our lives, our sweetness, and our hopes . . .' His arms outstretched, his eyes lifted in adoration at a spot on the wall. 'To thee do we cry, poor banished children of Eve . . .' It allowed Richie the opportunity to release Breda, and she slid out, lifeless as a calf in the moment of birth, from beneath Granny's cushions.

Then Miss Crippen, with a sort of end-of-ceremony finality, re-placed her beads in her handbag and got down off her high kneeler. But knowing Father Glee was far from finished, we children had to remain kneeling. Twisting ourselves into more comfortable posi-tions, we leaned our behinds against our chairs. We had been through what was to follow before. Only Miss Crippen's half of the rosary was over.

The first time I had beheld Father Glee's Enactment of the Mysteries of the Rosary was the day he came out to bless the farm. The day we walked the land. He'd given a few performances after that, end of the rosary was his favourite time but Connaughton had always told him he would have to stop because we children had to be got to bed. 'When they are a little older then, with God's grace,' says Father Glee.

Miss Crippen seated herself in her armchair but we remained kneeling. Father Glee liked you to be in the kneeling position for his Enactments.

'Did you see it?' He was wasting no time. His sticky eyelids snapped apart and then gelled together again as if he was contem-plating a ripe pear. And poor Miss Crippen, she had hoped to get back to reading her *Woman's Own*.

'See what, Father?' we asked. We weren't sure which mystery we were supposed to be seeing.

'On the wall?' He pointed to a spot above the piano, a spot on the wallpaper. We looked at the wallpaper: the ivy-patterned wall-paper, dark and light green leaves of ivy coiling on a grey back-ground.

'Did you see it?' He nodded down at Miss Crippen as if she was in school, and not a teacher but a pupil like the rest of us. When she said she hadn't, he shook his head in disappointment. He paid no more attention to her but concentrated on us children.

'Look, look now.' He started to present his Enactments: 'Oh, all the things I have been seeing on the wallpaper while you recited your holy rosary.'

He looked into our faces. What he had seen should also be reflected in our eyes, he said. He continued to ignore Miss Crippen.

'The Resurrection,' he said. 'You all saw him? In all his splendour. Rise again from the dead.' He pointed to a space between two ivy boughs on the wallpaper. 'He was there. The angels shrank back and then the women came and saw the stone had been moved. It all happened one heavenly Sunday morning.'

I was carried away for a few moments with Father Glee's Enactment. The others were also, all of us looking into the wallpaper.

'You saw the serpent cower away into that hole?' he asked. He pointed at a spot on the base of the wall where the plug socket was fixed.

'And then, the Ascension,' he shouted, rising out of his chair. He pulled a white handkerchief from his baggy trousers and fluttered it in the air. Then he went silent and pointed up at the ceiling. He stared. Something was happening up there. 'Sshh.' He pressed his waxy finger to his lips.

I don't know how long we remained silent. I had a pain in my neck from looking up. I could hear the glow of the coals in the fire; I could hear the clatter of cutlery in the kitchen and Dancie complaining to herself at having to make tea for Father Glee.

'He has ascended into heaven,' he said at last. A hinge of spittle snapped in the corner of his mouth. 'And where is the serpent now?' His eyes searched for where the serpent might have hidden itself. 'It has slunk into that coal scuttle, look.'

There was a knock at the door and a clink of china. Dancie, with the tray. She pushed the door in with her shoulder and walked, backwards, into the room. 'A cup of tea and a few biscuits, Miss Crippen.'

Dancie had suddenly become all sweetness and light towards the murderess Miss Crippen. 'You must be tired Miss Crippen.' It was her way of showing her displeasure towards Father Glee. She placed his cup on the table, without a word to him.

Father Glee wasn't finished with his Enactments. He drew a tin of saccharin tablets from a pocket in the shiny black vest that overhung his stomach and splashed some tablets in the tea. He waited then for Dancie to leave before continuing. But Dancie did not leave. It was then the fit of sniggering we had somehow managed to contain while looking into the wallpaper and the plug socket and the coal scuttle at last broke out. It was then there was spluttering from every corner of the room. Dancie glowered at us. Father Glee solemnly ate his biscuits as though nothing was happening other than an intermission in the unfolding of a movie picture. He started up again: 'And the Holy Ghost descended among them in the form of tongues of fire . . . Can you see them?' But the spell was broken; the tea and biscuits had broken it. Breda was bursting at the seams now. She ran from the room, a napkin stuffed in her mouth to hold back her laughter. Everybody was rising. And Father Glee was carrying on regardless with what was left of his audience. 'You saw them?' He still managed to capture the attention of the four small ones. 'Tongues of fire. Dripping from heaven?'

Dancie looked around, not sure what to make of the pandemonium. Miss Crippen sat there, looking even less sure and decided the best thing was to take up her *Woman's Own*. Where were Dancie's loyalties? With, much as she hated him, the pillar of the Church? Or with the blasphemers? 'Bed,' she said in the end. 'Your mother is going to hear all about this when she comes home.'

The last thing I heard as I went up the stairs was Father Glee telling Miss Crippen how he would have preferred to have enacted the Sorrowful Mysteries. 'The Crucifixion,' I heard him say. 'A more apt story for young minds. Oh, the taste of salt and vinegar in our Saviour's mouth as he hangs from his cross.' I could picture Father Glee, holding his teacup, the scowl on his lips as he enacted the taste of salt and vinegar.

Sleep came slowly to the boys' room that night. We watched the car lights swing around the walls of the room as they turned out on the lane. First went Miss Crippen's car. We knew it by the sound of its little engine. So she had decided not to stay the night. Father Glee must have driven her out of the house. Then he left, with an enormous clang as he crossed the cattle-grid. Ages later it seemed, with a cartwheel of lights across the ceiling, Mam and Connaughton returned. The gravel crunched in the yard.

I must have fallen asleep. Every now and then voices penetrated through my dreams and in the end they woke me. The three small boys were talking. They slept together in a big double bed in the corner of the room where the ceiling sloped. The talking got louder. Richie and me had a bed each. Richie must have been asleep in that dead way he had of falling asleep after he finished reading each night.

'What did the tongues of fire look like then, if you saw them?'

'Like hearts.'

'How many was there?'

'Ten, no five.'

'You didn't see any.'

'Shut up. I did.'

'Did you see them, Martin?'

'No, I'm going to sleep.'

'Then why did you tell Father Glee you did?'

'I don't know. His shoelaces was open. Did you see them?'

Then they were all laughing, in stitches laughing at the idea of Father Glee with his shoelaces open.

'Shut up,' I said, 'go to sleep.' Richie was asleep, so I, next eldest, could dish out the orders.

At that very moment the light came on and Mam was standing there, a thunder-cloud, looking down at us. I had never seen her look so deadly severe. Her solid black hair, beneath the shine of the light, seemed as though larded to her head. What is going on? I thought. Who told her? Did she meet Miss Crippen on her way home or what? Surely she should have been happy after the pictures, or the opera, or whatever it had been.

'What's going on?' she said.

'Nothing.'

Suddenly Mam had a clothes hanger in her hand. 'What's going on,' she roared. She looked around. There was a titter of laughter which was more like the sound of a frightened animal escaping.

'You, Mister Innocent.' She swiped down at the silent form of Richie. 'Stop that laughing.'

Richie, awakened by the whack from the clothes hanger, must have been astonished at her action. He jumped up in his bed, his eyes blazing: 'I won't stop laughing. Haw, haw, haw.'

She lashed at him. The clothes hanger came down on him. He tried to shield himself.

'Brazenness. I won't have it. Why did Miss Crippen go home?'

'I don't know.'

'Don't tell lies.'

She pulled away his bedclothes and brought the clothes hanger down on him again. He reached out for his trousers to protect himself. The clothes hanger cut across his arm and broke. One half hit the ceiling, with the other half she continued to lash. I couldn't believe what was going on. She had lost control. Like Granny but worse: Granny would have grown tired, Mam's heat burned without end. It was frightful.

Richie made another attempt to rise in the bed: 'Why did you tell Miss Crippen you went to the opera and not the pictures. You're the liar. You are.'

She beat him down until in the end he was pleading. 'Ah Mammy, no, no. Not me. Don't hit me.' I had never heard Richie plead before.

'Yes you. I will hit you, Mister Innocent. I will not make fish of one and flesh of another.'

I couldn't understand why each blow she landed just made her become more and more enraged. Then she stopped, out of breath. I had been afraid of the rest of us getting the same treatment as Richie but now she had no puff left in her. She was standing there, her hand on the light switch. And the next thing, Dancie was standing alongside her, in a pink gown, tiny alongside Mam, her false teeth missing.

'Ssh, ma'am,' she whistled through her collapsed lips. She took Mam's hand. 'Sssh, you'll wake the baby.'

Mam looked down at her. It seemed to be taking her a long time to recognise her. Then she said, 'God, Dancie, I have a headache.'

'Come on, ma'am, I'll give you something for it,' Dancie said.

Mam was shaking and she let Dancie lead her down the stairs and we were in the dark.

Richie lay there whimpering for a long time. When he had recovered a little, he cursed to himself. 'I didn't do anything. I didn't do anything.'

I felt sorry for him as I never had before. I felt he had been wronged. And somehow not just this once, but a lot of times. That was the worst trouncing I ever saw administered in Ivyhall.

But if Mam had trounced Richie just to show to the rest of us that it made no difference to her that he was her own eldest son and it did not mean she should make fish or flesh, whichever it was, of him because of that, why then had she veered so wildly in her treatment of him? Who did Mam favour anyway, if not Richie? Nobody? Those were the thoughts that remained with me.

Not until days later did anybody find out what Mam and Connaughton had seen at the pictures. Then the girls overheard her telling Aunt Tessa: she had gone to a film with Frank Sinatra in it. And Miss Crippen had not been told because she would only have disapproved.

Yes, Frank Sinatra was Mam's hero. Whenever he came on the radio her ears cocked. But most especially if Granny was around and said, Turn off that pagan. Then she only turned him up: 'Come fly with me, let's float down to Peru . . . In Llama Land there's a one man band and he'll toot his flute for you . . .'

Aunt Tessa said it to me on our way down the laneway, with a big laugh: 'When your Mam first saw your father he reminded her of Frank Sinatra. Ever hear anything like it! And they both at a cattle-mart up to their eyes in muck at the time.'

She was laughing and I saw my chance: 'Who does Mam like anyway?'

She said she couldn't give me an answer to that.

'Which would you prefer?' I said. 'To be made fish of or to be made flesh of?'

'Personally I'd prefer be made flesh of,' she said with a giggle.

No matter how much I thought about it, though, I could not figure out why Mam had trounced Richie so badly. A dissatis-faction with the world outside, having left that picture house? Was that it? No. Mam's world was never that unbearable. A lie told to Miss Crippen? Perhaps. In the end I came to consider that it was because of something deep that lay between Mam and Richie. It was all because they knew one another so well. Yes, that was it. A knowingness that lay between them. A bond. Yes. And that was a discovery which made me so lonely; myself not knowing her as intimately. Having no bond.

And there was something about that trouncing that affected Mam also. It seemed to change her: to make her lonely too. Or helpless. She never, all the rest of her life, trounced anyone again.

And on the very following night, Mam made us all write to the boy Christopher, who was lost in England. That's stupid, Richie said, you don't even know where he lives. That's a waste of time.

So you see, there was the proof of my theory about Richie and Mam. Mam could flake him and next day he was arguing again. If that had happened me, I'd have kept my mouth shut forever.

'Write your letter,' she said. She told him she wanted no lip and told us all that we should count ourselves very lucky people. We had a home and family, whereas Christopher had none. When we had finished – and even the little ones, with all their sucking of pencils, wrote something – she collected up our letters and said Christopher would be grateful. That was the first time we wrote to Christopher. What did I write? I told him the names of all the people in my family; I told him their ages. I thought it might help him in his confusion should he ever find our nine letters, or rather should our letters find him.

11

Things passed you by. You made head or tail of very little, you could hardly put two and two together, but sometimes you got a chance to think.

Fay, there was one who helped you work out things. A pity we did not have more of Fay. Once she came home and that time I worked out a lot.

Here is the day that Fay arrives home from America and we young people are eagerly seated around a table at the airport. It is ages since we have last seen her; she has been in America since we went to Ivyhall and hasn't been home until now.

'Oh, this is exciting,' she says and laughs. 'Oh I see changes, I see changes in you. Tell me, tell me, tell me. I want to hear all your news. I want to hear all the changes in your lives.

'Waiter, waiter,' she calls. We are at Shannon Airport and she buys a bottle of Blue Nun wine, which the waiter pours for her into a narrow glass and she gives him a tip. 'Hurry up,' she says to us, 'I'm only here on a visit and I want to hear everything.'

We don't know what news we have, what changes there have been in our lives. Any time we try to tell what news we think we have we only end up contradicting one another. Anyway, Fay is the exciting one.

For years Fay has been a memory. But as the years pass, the stories of her adventures have been adding to that memory, so that by now she has become a legend. Fay is somebody who knows all about the world. She has been out there on her travels. She has opinions about everything. She has been on a civil rights march in Washington. 'Alleluia, Martin Luther King,' she says. She wears striking clothes and scarves. Blue, yellow. She wears slacks. It is Fay's news we want. 'Come on,' she says. 'Start from the beginning.'

There was a time, a few years ago, when I would have regarded the return of Fay as that of a saviour. But that was then. Now here she is, with her American travel bags all unzipped, seated at the airport lounge, waiting for our story, her face sensitive as a bird, little puckers of sadness in it. But she is laughing all the time and the laughter is keeping her at bay from us. And the eyes are looking at us and devouring us. Fay, who minded us that time after our mother died when we were little, looking at the changes in us. And, no doubt, looking for the tracings in us of what in those times we had been.

But we are looking at Fay. No, we have no stories. We don't have beginnings, we don't have endings. All we have are middle bits. Here and now bits. How can you tell a story when it has only a middle? We are looking at Fay: Fay, please, you tell us the story of ourselves. We are dying to know about ourselves. Show us ourselves in the mirror; we haven't got any mirror. Have you?

Then we all went home to Ivyhall in the car. We didn't hear the story of ourselves. Fay was taken on visits; renewals with relatives, everywhere.

'Tell me all about yourselves,' Fay is saying again. This time she is returning to America. Another bottle of Blue Nun is on the table. It is raining outside where the aeroplanes are parked. Now there are only Pam, Jamesy, and me around the table with her. Not the gang there was the day she arrived. Not Richie, who called me Blinky when I got excited on the first day she came home. This day Connaughton has dropped us at the airport and driven on to Ennis to meet a butcher he wants to work for him at his butcher shop in Templemore. Fay's flight is delayed but he will get back before she takes off. Richie, who has come also, allowed to do some of the driving, has gone with him. There are only Connaughtons around the table.

'Lordie me, you were only that size when you were my little baby,' Fay says to Jamesy, holding her hands apart. Jamesy, probably more than any of us, has not been singled out for special attention in years. Not since the time he was the Little Yank. He is affected by Fay singling him out. Yes, she is still his saviour, I can see it in his eyes. She has returned to protect him from the indifference of Ivyhall. But he is wrong. It is painful to watch him. She did return; now she is abandoning him again.

Now, on the day of her departure, we are more inclined to tell her our story. Or to make up a story – of how we have lost the favours we once enjoyed. Maybe we are still making an appeal to her: Please stay. She has allowed me a glass of wine because, she says, it is educational. We feel free to talk.

We are talking about where you could go back to if you wanted to get to the start of the days she wants to know all about.

You could go back to the hitchhiker, Jamesy says, back to the hitchhiker that Connaughton picked up one night coming home a lonely road somewhere in the middle of Ireland.

'Why?' I say.

'Because you told me so, Lally.'

'I never told you any such thing,' I say.

'Well I don't know so,' he says.

I say, no, you could go back to long before the hitchhiker, to a time Jamesy was too young to remember. You could go back to our move to Ivyhall. And to Mam.

Pam says, no, she hates going back, you should only go forward. And anyway, if you had to go back, the start of it would be even before Ivyhall. You must go back to our own mother dying, she says. Nothing to do with Mam, but our own mother.

Our mother dying is a subject none of us knows how to talk

about, so I get out of it by going back even further again. I say the start of it was the day Connaughton, even before he was our father, went up to the west of Ireland to buy cattle. He saw a woman schooling a fancy little mare over poles in a field in the plains of Mayo. He liked the look of the mare and stopped and asked the woman was it for sale. And everything was fine until one day he had a row with the girl's father. And the sad thing about the row was that it could have been patched up. But when the girl married Connaughton she went down the country with him and never went home again. She was our mother. Husbands came first, that was our mother's motto.

'How do you know that was our mother's motto?' Pam bursts in, but I carry on.

'From then on all contact was broken off with our mother's people and that should not have happened because they might have taken us and looked after us when our mother died of a broken heart.'

'What is a broken heart?' Pam says. 'That's rubbish. Is a heart on a hinge, or something that goes rusty and snaps off? That's romantic mush. Our mother died of childbirth.'

I feel like telling her to shut up. I am only saying the bit about a broken heart for the sake of it. Taking a chance, I am. Thinking it might impress Fay. Not often does a fellow get a chance to say something dramatic such as, 'our mother died of a broken heart'. Anyway, I carry on, pretending to pay no heed to Pam's interruption.

That row was all because of the civil war, I say. Because Connaughton's family and our Mama's family had been on different sides. And a terrible pity the row was, because Connaughton had really liked this man who was our grandfather. And Connaughton needed friends; any friends he could get. Big Mooney, our grandfather was called; he had come home from America after making his fortune on the railroads and on the Klondyke. 'Did you know he had one shoulder which was stooped, the shoulder he carried the rails on in the making of the railroads?' I am enjoying myself as I tell the story. And why had he gone to America in the first place? Well, that was because of his father. His father went to America to escape the famine . . .

Then Pam butts in again and says, 'If you must insist upon going back, then it is back to the famine you must go. And anyhow, that's not how Connaughton met her. That's rubbish. More romantic notions. He met her at a hunt ball. The same way as anybody met anybody. She was the singer at the ball. She was a last minute replacement for her sister, our Auntie Delia. Daddy showed me the ballroom once when I was small. It was in the army barracks in Templemore. He showed me the piano. A small and dusty piano on the edge of a big wide stage. So there, if you want to know,' says Pam.

'Well that's what Connaughton told me,' I say, beginning to doubt myself because of the vivid way Pam is able to describe the piano.

'Don't mind Connaughton,' Pam says. 'He's just a romantic too.'

Fay is smoking a Winston cigarette during all this and she is thinking deeply.

'I will always remember that night,' she says, taking over from Pam.

'Your father came late home to Cranagh after that ball. I was still up.' Fay's eyes go dreamy in that dreamy way they have of going whenever she thinks back in the past. 'I remember well . . . at the time I was nursing your grandfather who was in his final illness and I used to stay up all night with him. Your father, oh your father, he swaggered in and sat on the bottom step of the big wide stairs in Cranagh and he laughed and laughed. I went down the stairs and he leaned his head back until he was looking up at me. I can still see his black hair falling back off his head. "And do you know who I'm going to marry?" he said. "Sit down until I tell you about the girl I met tonight. I'm going to marry her." I sat down on the step behind him and his hair fell on my lap.'

I am loving Fay's story. I have never heard stuff like this before. Fay stops for a moment. I can see in her eyes that she is looking back. Continue your story, I say to myself. She continues.

'Oh, I said to him, and after you marry her will you let her continue to sing in hunt balls all around Ireland?' Fay laughs thinking about that. Then she turns to me: 'You are also correct, Lally. He did go up to Mayo. A little later. He was intending to buy cattle from Mooney but bought a racehorse instead.'

That stops Pam and me arguing for a minute. But then Pam starts up again, telling me I am wrong about the civil war as well. The civil war had nothing to do with any row between Connaughton and Mooney, she says. They were great friends, especially when they had a drink. Mooney didn't give a continental damn about the civil war, Pam says. It was simply that our mother stopped Connaughton seeing Mooney because they had such a time of it drinking whenever they got together and our mother had got a promise from Connaughton that he would take the pledge and never drink again. So there was no row.

'There was a row over the civil war,' I say.

'Can I be of help here again?' Fay says in a little voice and the nerves around her eyes contract making her face go dreamy again and the cigarette smoke wafts around about her head. 'Children, children,' she says. 'I wish I were around more to inform you of your own history.'

Then Fay tells us that there never was a row, over the civil war, or over anything, between Mooney and Connaughton. 'There was a row over the civil war, all right,' she says. 'Oh boy, was there a row over the civil war. But it was between Connaughton's parents, my own parents, your grandparents. Neither your father, or Mooney, your other grandparent, had anything to do with it. Mooney was not at all interested in the civil war, or what came after it, but in showing off the farm he bought and restored with his hard-earned dollars. Your daddy's parents . . . they were the ones who fought, they never spoke, except in argument. It was their families who had taken separate sides in the civil war. Except the civil war your grandparents engaged in had nothing to do with what had happened in the country and everything to do with what was happening between your grandparents.' Fay shakes her head. 'Nothing at all to do with their families having taken different sides in the civil war, but because they two were completely incompatible.'

She laughs at that for a second and then her face becomes sadder: 'Your father didn't have a minute's peace growing up in his own house. He was the cockpit in which they had their rows. Both of them dragging at him for his loyalty. And he had the sort of nature which was easily affected by that sort of thing. It turned him into an impulsive man who never gave himself a chance to have a mind of his own. That is why he can never make decisions, even nowadays, but always jumping headlong into everything, never giving himself a chance to work things out for himself. And never, never, taking heed of advice from anybody.'

Pam becomes thoughtful then: 'So it's our father's nature that you should go back to?'

Then I butt in because I am getting really fed up with Pam and her superior way in an argument and how she can use words like 'continental damn', and 'romantic'. It's all the reading she does has made her like that. Reading when she should be making beds. I would prefer any day to listen to Fay talking about Connaughton and him being a cockpit and so on, rather than listen to old Pam. 'Shut up, Pam,' I say. 'So what about our father's nature? So what about going back? Who cares? You could go back to Adam if you wanted to. So what?'

Then Jamesy says again, 'You only have to go back to the hitch-hiker for the start of it.'

And then Pam says, 'For the start of what? I don't know of what, do you? Did some particular instance, at some point of our lives, radically change us?'

Then I lose my head completely and say: 'Yes something did but if you don't want to know then shut up. Because you are only pretending it didn't, Pam. It happened because Daddy jumped head-long into marriage without looking. Now, fuck it, just shut up.'

That brings the subject to a dead end. Nobody has an answer for that. I am left with a feeling of having disgraced myself totally in front of my Auntie Faith. But I have been driven to it. Something did happen.

I am not much use for anything after that. For talking, for telling the story of ourselves, I have no appetite. I am in a sulk. I am trapped in it. It is terrible. And what makes it even worse is that I want Fay to feel sorry for me. Sorry for me for what?

But Fay was the best storyteller going. In telling stories, she could shame the sulk out of you:

'You children and your civil war,' she laughs at us. 'You are closed in upon yourselves like sheep in a pen this rainy day in this airport lounge.' Fay was great at letting in the air. 'It's not as though our little civil war were the only one. There was more than one, you know. What about old Stonewall Jackson and General Grant? Why, if you want to go back, why not go back to Stonewall Jackson? Can't you just hear the sound of leather and the jingling of horses' bridles. The sound of the world's history-makers.' She gives a titter of laughter.

Then she launches off again: 'Did you know the history of the Powers of Mooncoin, your Mam's family? The Powers were of Norman stock, whose ancestry went right back to Strongbow. Did you know that? They probably went back before that even, to Hastings, to Normandy itself. Spoke the language of royalty. Did you know Mam's family had a fine farm in south Kilkenny along the River Suir? That was before old Master Power decided he was no longer a farmer. He had one son who was as little interested in farming as he and so his eldest daughter had to become the farmer. Did you know that Mam went and studied agriculture in a college in Herfordshire, England? And her brother stayed at home, learned songs from a gramophone his father had bought and then went away and joined a dance band in Northern Ireland. Lives now, it is said, somewhere in New York. 'Broke his own mother's, your Granny Power's, heart.'

And that was how Fay got launched into a subject: by just saying the word *history*. And you knew she was launched when she started to take tiny sips from her glass and to flicker her eyes in the way of posh people, she herself being one. You relaxed then and listened.

'Mr Power, who was a regular old toff by all accounts, saw himself as a gentleman about the town of Waterford and left your Mam to do the farming. She kept him in his finery. And then, in his latter days, had to nurse him. As well as run a farm. As well as keep her mother entertained. Now, there is important history that you really should know.'

I had finished my glass of Blue Nun. If Fay was sipping hers, nothing much was coming out of it. The bottle wasn't even half empty. It was not meant to be drunk, that was Fay's way. I would have liked to drink it. I liked what it was doing to me; how it was allowing my understanding to desert me and my mind to hover away and sit with the smoke from Fay's American cigarettes by the window of the viewing platform.

When Connaughton turned up I said I was not going home. Are you crazy? he said. He didn't know about my breakout of bad language, of course. I was still sulking. I hated sulking but sometimes what else can a fellow do? Using bad language, getting into a temper, knocks the good out of a fellow, wears a fellow out, puts him in a sulk. Leave him be, Fay said.

'That's the end of this year's history lesson, children,' she said to me as we walked along the departures corridor. I had made a slow recovery. She had caught my eye for one second as her head lifted back in laughter.

She knew she had impressed me. She knew that in my preoccupation with the Connaughtons I had never before considered the history of the Powers.

Then she went back to America. A great one for arrivals and departures, was Fay. And for half-finished stories. That was my conclusion about her. Why would she not finish them? She should have. She should have told us more. She should have told us about Connaughton's trip to New York. Because Jamesy, all the rest of us children also, had the wrong idea about why he had gone there that time. It was not to live there, no sir. A Yank for two weeks, he had only been taken to keep company for Connaughton who had gone over in search of Mam's missing brother, Dick Power. Now I remembered the present Jamesy had brought home to Mam. A wide LP record with the smiling face of Frank Sinatra on the sleeve. When Jamesy handed it to her, Mam sang from one of the songs: 'If you let me down once more I'll join the French Foreign Legion . . .' Then she put it away. She never played it.

A song could lie alongside the memories in your head and bed them down there forever. Like the visit of Fay. Like her story of Dick Power and his dance band in New York: 'If you let me down once more I'll join the French Foreign Legion. Bet you they would welcome me with open arms.' One evening I sang that to the cows in the cow-house and Richie overheard me. First he scorned me: 'Jaysus,' he said, 'the French Foreign Legion.' Then he asked me to sing it for him.

'Go away,' I said.

I would not repeat the song for Richie. He was always asking me to sing for him or to tell him stories. I would sing for the cows but not for him. There was this big woman, Richie's mother, who never spoke about the past. And there was Fay, and her half-finished stories. At least Fay, who told half-finished stories, was better than Mam who told no stories at all. Not even about a lost brother in Brooklyn who played with a dance band.

PART 3

1

People who Mam did favour, and whether they were fish or flesh did not seem to matter, were the workmen.

Workmen came and went in Ivyhall. All Mam's old lot were long gone. Not that they had anything much wrong with them. Like Ted Ruttle. He was a Protestant. A few Protestants lived around our parts. The Protestants were of two sorts: the miners, the farmers. The ancestors of the miners had come from England long ago to work down the mines. Most of them had other jobs now, or drew the dole; what anthracite remained, ran in deep seams and to go chipping down in those narrow roots of the world with your little pick was one dangerous occupation. The farmers had always been around. The Protestant farmers had a little church behind trees, at which on Sundays you heard them singing their heads off. Locals. The Ruttles, the Smyths, and from back Fethard way, the Ponsonbys and the Casenoves. Normally the quietest people you would ever see; they swelled out the walls behind the sycamore trees on Sundays with their evensong. The miners didn't go to church and didn't seem to care what religion they belonged to. Connaughton said they were very low church. But what a great fellow was our Ted. He didn't care about anything low or high. He had a motorbike he gave us all rides on. He cared about it. A bike as old as the hills. He was like the dusk itself in his black goggles and beret. He combed his hair before donning the beret and he kept our garage clean and everything there in its proper place. A pity he got the sack; Connaughton was in a mood for giving the sack, and Ted got it.

We now had the hitchhiker, Harry Crowe. Har the heart, Mam called him. He spent a lot of time sleeping. He slept on the trailer loads of hay coming down from Farpark to the hay barn. Once he fell off, but miraculously broke no bones. As he said himself, if you fall when you're sleeping, you have no bad thoughts and so you fall safe as a baby. He took naps in the hay barn. And even though the nap might last only ten minutes, he always tied binding twine round his trouser ends beforehand. To keep out rats, he said. He had seen rats do damage to men. When he woke he showed you tricks: how to touch your nose with your tongue, how to light a match off your teeth, how to scratch boys' cheeks with your stubble. (His stubble was every bit as rough as Scanlan's, the commercial traveller long ago in the hotel, except he had it only down one side. It didn't grow over the port-wine stain.) Then he fell asleep again. I think Tierra del Fuego knocked the good out of Harry Crowe. There was nowhere else for him to go and Connaughton knew it and for that reason, maybe, he was one man who would not be getting the sack.

And we had Witheroe. Thomas Witheroe had worked in the mines but due to ill health, brought on by the settling of coal dust on his lungs, he'd had to leave. He was with us over a year now and it didn't seem he would be getting the sack either. On his first day, he came in off the road to Connaughton with a story that Mam had met him in town and had told him there was work in Ivyhall. It was after the day Connaughton and me brought home the mare from County Wexford. I know that because my first memory of

Witheroe is of a small bald man standing at the mare's paddock and patting her and saying, 'Shush girl and what have they done to you?' Every time afterwards that Witheroe walked into her paddock she hobbled over to him and then he patted her, lifting her hooves for inspection and cleaning her shoes until the sunlight glinted from them. He had bright blue eyes that looked very clearly into everything. But there was anger in him. His eyebrows were crossed like barbed wire.

Connaughton had given him a chance that first day he appeared at the gate and after a few days had told him he was a topper to work. Witheroe's only problem was sometimes on Monday mornings. As he said himself, the only bad habit of the mines that he had not been able to break was the drink. Dancie and Witheroe were brother and sister. You would never know it to look at the way they carried on with one another. It was Dancie who had told Mam that Witheroe needed work. They were alike, had the same blue eyes, spoke in the same fiery way and if they didn't like someone, always said so. Their angriest words were directed against one another. Witheroe was always asking Dancie for cigarettes. Even though he was her brother, Dancie called him Witheroe. So we all called him Witheroe too. She seemed to think very poorly of him but at the same time looked after him. She gave him the cigarettes, money even at times. 'And don't spend it on drink but take it home to your wife Ettie and family.' During mealtimes, when we all sat together, they would throw insults at one another. As time went by their arguments became a source of amusement to us children, especially as we began to notice the great laugh that Mam was getting out of them. That gave us permission to laugh also and so the antics of Dancie and Witheroe became light relief at the dinner table.

Mam got on famously with Witheroe; he was her favourite of all the workmen. Witheroe had a large family, the same as ourselves. His son, Bunny from my school, began to come out to Ivyhall with him on Saturdays. Bunny was a good boxer. Even Witheroe said that of him. He had fists like needles, he said. What a wonderful way to talk about your son! A person might be forgiven for thinking everything about the Witheroes was great. But that would be a wrong impression. For there was a tragedy about Witheroe's family. That was the word Mam and Connaughton used when they spoke of it in private. Tragedy. It concerned Witheroe's eldest.

Witheroe was that very same man who Dancie had been cycling out to visit all those Sundays since she arrived in Ivyhall. Witheroe, and his wife Ettie. Now I knew. Their eldest son was called Christopher. And Christopher was the very same boy who Dancie had sent to Witheroe as a small boy that time she had lived with the publican in Wexford. But that was never mentioned nowadays. People only spoke of Christopher as though he had always been Witheroe's son, had never been the adopted son of Dancie. Or had never been the younger brother of Dancie and Witheroe, which was what the first story said he was, if you looked back far enough. In any case, it did not seem to matter whose son or brother he was because both of them claimed him as though he were theirs and theirs alone and blamed the other for the tragedy.

'Maybe your Christopher is suffering from amnesia,' Mam said one day.

'What's that, ma'am?' asked Witheroe.

'It's a loss of memory. A condition where a person can't remember who he is.'

'We shouldn't say things like that about Christopher,' Dancie said.

'Why not?' says Witheroe. 'Isn't amnesia better than that bad temper he has? That's only going to get him into rows.'

'My child has not a bad temper,' Dancie argued.

'He has. He got it from you.'

'He got it from you, sir.'

'He got it from you, and you spoiled him too.'

Dancie may not have thought too highly of Witheroe but she was crazy about Christopher. The tragedy was this: no sooner had Christopher reached fourteen years of age than he had gone to England. Wouldn't stay at home; wouldn't work in the mines. All Witheroe knew of Christopher's whereabouts was that he had started out from Birmingham; the first and only postcard he received had a Birmingham postmark on the stamp. Christopher had not once been heard of ever since. Presumed missing. His little man had walked out to see the world, Witheroe would say of him from time to time. The story that came back with fellows home on holidays was that Christopher had been involved in a knife fight.

Witheroe made a lot of investigations concerning Christopher. Mam wrote letters for him and sent them off. 'Any news, ma'am?' Dancie often said. Witheroe said it too, the same thing, to Mam, every time he got a letter back from priests in England in reply to his investigations. 'Any news, ma'am?' He gave Mam the letter to read because apart from comics which he swapped with us and with his own children, he never read anything. Letters came back from all parts of England. 'No news this time, I'm afraid,' Mam said. Witheroe always made a joke of it, 'Still no news from Christopher, the patron saint of travellers.' In addition to writing to the priests, Mam also wrote to Christopher. 'Don't be wasting your sweetness on the desert air,' Witheroe said. He joked, he laughed it off, but I knew there was more to Witheroe than jokes.

One day Connaughton asked Witheroe to patch up the crack on the castle wall. It was getting larger and something had to be done about it. Witheroe mixed his cement and got his trowel and ladder and stuck on his patch. Nobody noticed but myself: the patch on the castle wall was the shape of the map of England.

And on our castle wall the map remained. Often I stared at it, wondering whereabouts Christopher might be. What did Christopher look like? What age was he? Was he a young man now, was he becoming like an adult – or was he still like those half-adult fellows who stood outside the chip-shop in Wolfdyke after the cinema and fought fellows from other towns? What age was he? I was nine and a half years of age.

2

It was the end of my third summer in Ivyhall. I knew now what to expect of summers. Each one went much the same: long holidays of hay-making, silage-making, days of high skies, days for dreaming of distant futures, and then, in the evenings, our shouts of playtime which went on long beyond dusk. Summer, it seemed, was forever. Each day exactly like the day before, until suddenly it drew to a close.

Now it was September. It was a day I had gone gathering hazelnuts along the river in Glen, where once I had made the dam with Gananny and Meagher. The others gathered nuts too, but not with the same fervour as me. Closer in nature to squirrels, I must have been. I sat on the wall of the new silage pit with my bulging pocketfuls. With a small rock, I cracked the nuts and one by one laid the clean kernels along the wall. Then I ate them, blinking my eyes until my head was clear and the glare in the sky did not hurt.

Along came Richie. 'You're cracking the nuts wrong,' he said. 'You're hitting them too hard, they only need a gentle knock. Let me show you.'

'They're my nuts,' I said. 'Get your own.'

'I only want to show you how to crack them without mashing the shit out of them.'

Some seasons the kernels were hard, a brown skin forming on them – just like the hazelnuts you bought in the shop for Hallowe'en – some seasons they were pale and milky. It all depended on the kind of summer you had. This one had been hot; the nuts were hard. I had to hit them sharply to break them. But what did Richie know of these things? Anyway, he gave me a demonstration: 'Find me a flat stone.' And after a few minutes of cracking gently on one nut so that it came clean away and he was able to say, that's how you do it, he went away happy with himself. He didn't even eat the nut he had opened. And I was able to go on with my munching and with my deep reflections about this time of the year that gathered to itself all the scents of the warm days past, storing them within the hay and within the silage, leaving but a breath of itself, a pang of loss behind. 'Broken promises of summer,' I was able to say to myself, impressed at being able to make words sound so beautiful. I was able to go on with the sad and fruitful thoughts I had been thinking before Richie came along. What a nuisance was Richie.

Then another day came. Another of the hazy thoughtful days, Slievenamon a mirage in the distance. We were in the hay haggard this day, the workmen and me, all of us dreamy, all of us with our own thoughts. Richie was drawing up hay from Glen. In the intervals of rest, snatched following the stacking away of each load, we did our thinking. This was the first year ever that we had hay in Glen. And it was because the grass had grown so quickly this year even the bullocks couldn't keep it down. And then the weanlings were let in, and altogether they still could not keep it down.

'We'll have to cut it for hay,' said Connaughton.

'But that field is full of drains,' said Mam.

'No bother,' said Richie. 'I know where all the drains are.'

'Go careful cutting it,' said Mam.

'I will,' said Richie. He loved challenges, especially where machinery was involved.

Anyway, hay was saved in Glen. The field looked very strange when it was shorn. Bald and gleaming as a pin all along its newness. No shelter any longer for the weanlings. I loved how the weanlings sprang out of the flaggers in Glen, shot out with the speed of gunshot. Like little boys in short trousers on first holy communion day. Now there was nowhere for the weanlings to hide. Exposure didn't suit Glen. That was my thought. Indeed, that had been my thought since the day of the Lone Ranger. Maybe I was getting into the ways of Ivyhall myself: the hiddenness of the place. And just as the others, Connaughton and Richie, had begun to open everything up, knocking ditches, flattening fairy forts, cutting the flaggers in Glen, I was becoming more at home with things concealed. Richie had driven the mowing bar right up to the edges of the streams, right around the old mine shaft which once upon a time a cow had fallen into. Centuries of secrets exposed. The cutting of hay in Glen even drew upon us a visit from the Three Wise Men. They looked over bare Glen as though it was the moon and scratched their heads and said, 'Not if we had our way, he wouldn't cut hay in Glen . . .' But those Three Wise Men hadn't had their own way since the famous court case and they clicked their car doors closed and drove away again, still shaking their heads in disbelief.

About the cow that fell. One wet evening. I had driven the cows into Glen after milking. I was standing at the gate watching them fan out through the sodden field in their chosen directions. I looked down for a moment at the gate. The hasp was stiff and the evening all wet and cold and I did not have any desire for standing around. But when I looked up again I knew something had changed. A space had appeared between two of the cows; a space wider than had been there a moment before. It had happened as quickly as that, in the moment when I hadn't been looking. I immediately knew something was wrong. I did a quick count; yes, a cow was missing. I was in trouble. Cows can fly; it was my immediate reaction as I thought of the mythical minotaurs of Ancient Greece in my *Newnes Pictorial Knowledge*. What other explanation was there?

When I walked to the spot where I thought the cow had disappeared I found the hole. Clay was still trickling into it and the sod around it was bending inward. It was as if a meteor had plunged from the heavens and, clean as a whistle, left a neat tear in the earth in its wake. There was no sign of the cow down there, not even the shine of her eyes. I thought I heard the lowing of her once, way down, but I was not sure of that. I could not look right in because more of the sod might collapse and then I would be gone as well. She had disappeared. I had to go home and report. The men said it was a mine shaft; that it had opened because of all the rain that had been softening the ground. Richie wanted to go down on a rope to investigate. Mam wouldn't let him. Connaughton said he and Witheroe should go down, but Witheroe, having once been a miner, refused. 'That place nearly claimed me once. Sorry, boss, but it would be tempting fate to go down there again.' Witheroe always went all short of breath when he talked about the mines and then he had to get out a cigarette and have a smoke.

In the end they found an old butcher's block, cut it in half and wedged it into the mine shaft, blocking it so that it lay there forgotten, apart from when, every now and then, the poor cow was mentioned. She had been a roan cow, a good milker and almost about to calf. Witheroe said she still roamed the tunnels of the old mines, drinking from the streams, eating white weeds. She had given birth to a bull calf down there, he said. In time a herd of mad white-eyed roans would stomp around beneath the old shafts of Ivyhall. Some day they would find a way out. The thought terrified my younger brothers and sisters. It did not appeal to me either. And now, the day the hay was mown, the cut halves of the butcher's block were exposed again. And even though I had quite grown to like the hidden world, here I now was with an argument in my head saying it was better to be able to see things.

Glen being near the house, Richie had decided to carry up the hay on the back of the buck-rake, one cock of hay at a time. It would be quicker than forking the cocks onto the trailer and then forking them off again. So here he was – belting along at speed, down the laneway, along the road; wheeling into Glen; reversing with a roar of the tractor into the rump of a haycock; out again; hot licking it back to the hay barn with the haycock swinging behind and Connaughton complaining about spilled hay. Here was Richie, racing the guts out of the tractor, all because he wanted to prove his way was best.

Witheroe and the hitchhiker stood at the hay barn, their shirts off, throwing up Richie's haycocks to me. I was flattening it and building up the bale. That was one of the nice jobs in Ivyhall. It was nice because it never stayed the same. You started on the ground. You rose. After a while you had risen above the men; you saw only to the level of their open chests, then only their heads and then you were looking down on them as they squinted up at you and hay seed fell on their heads.

Richie was becoming angry this day because he was not getting the haycocks up from Glen fast enough to keep us working non-stop. We were snatching a five minute rest between each haycock delivered to us.

The men had their different ways of resting. The hitchhiker just lay down, licked his nose with his long tongue and was asleep, the port-wine stain on the side of his face reposed in the sun, the sound of the tractor lost to him somewhere a million miles away. Witheroe sat and slapped horseflies off his skin and flicked hay seeds off his beady nipples. Funny how the difference between the men was expressed in that way of their chests. The hitchhiker's chest was flat, with pancake circles around the nipples: Witheroe's was knotted, the skin in the circles curdling with anxiety. Witheroe would not sit still during the five minute intervals but got up to rake fallen hay or to examine broken machinery lying around the haggard. Or sing a snatch of song, his song, waddling his hips: 'One two and then rock, it's the funniest thing was ever told: the day that Mexico gave up the rumba to do-oo the rock 'n roll . . .' Or if he did doze, it would only be for seconds. Two men with different dreams.

So, while it was hard to get a word out of the hitchhiker, Witheroe was very lively. And I was very curious.

Witheroe had pure white skin. But just below the skin, along his arms and chest and even on his face, were these black remnants. Scars.

'What's all the black marks, Witheroe?'

'Bad blood, boy.'

'Where did you get it?'

'Down the mine. Your blood goes black down there.'

'Seriously, Witheroe?'

'How more fuckin' serious do you want me?'

'Tell me about it.'

Witheroe lit a cigarette. Witheroe always lit up – if he had a cigarette to light, that was – once a conversation got going and he got thinking about the past. But he had to sing a few words of a song first, another of his songs. 'The Pub with No Beer':

> It's lonesome away from your kindred and all,
> by the campfire at night when the wild dingoes call . . .

Then he took another pull of his cigarette: 'Yeh, you got a lot of knocks in the mines. Lot of dust. Every time the rock opened your skin you were left with a black scar. An inner fury, boy. Fucks up your insides.'

'Did you like it, working in the mines?'

'Wet and dirty, a bad job. I wasn't born to it and you had to be born to the mines. You were down there crawling in a three-foot shaft and the wooden props went *crack* and you didn't know whether it was the weight of the roof or the pressure coming up that was the cause. You fled along the dyke with the rats.'

'With the rats! Witheroe, there were rats down there!' I hated rats, those tails, so long and thick as they made their slow bumpy trail over the ground . . . Rats. They never seemed to flee fast enough as far as I was concerned, but always, whenever I came across them, to loiter. They were not afraid of me, rats.

'A bad job. That bad sometimes you felt like cryin' and goin' home.' Witheroe's barbed-wire eyebrows knitted as he thought about it. 'You went and drank beer, boy. It was the only grub that would clear your chest.'

'Did you hear that, Harry?'

'What's that?' The hitchhiker stirred himself. 'Is he back with a load already?'

'No. Did you ever get a bad accident in Tierra del Fuego?'

'No, I didn't,' he said lazily.

'Ah go on, did you?'

This time I got an answer out of him. My persistence must have awakened him, or else he was becoming irritated with me.

'No sir, I didn't. As long as you don't count being lucky to have escaped with my life from the grasp of a woman. See that mark' – he pointed at his port-wine stain – 'women take that to be a sign of great beauty.'

He and Witheroe laughed together when he said that. It was something he often said; a little joke between Witheroe and himself.

Stories about seas, cliffs and Indians, these were the things that interested me. He never wanted to talk about such things. The only thing he ever spoke of was a fellow Irishman for whom he worked in Tierra del Fuego. 'A mad dog of a man,' he would say. 'Treated his wife very badly.'

During those days in the hay barn, I was feeling good about myself. Grown-up, because for five minutes out of every fifteen, while Richie raced up and down to Glen, attempting to impress us but impressing nobody, I had the two men to myself, all three of us happy on our split-level world. I, happiest of all in the knowledge that in Ivyhall, most boring place on earth as it might be, two men had found asylum: Witheroe, from the mines, and the hitchhiker, Harry Crowe, from wild dreamings of Tierra del Fuego. And how did I know that about Harry Crowe? Because it was during one of those five minute intervals he told us that he had killed the man in Tierra del Fuego. Killed him because he had beaten his wife. And Witheroe said he had done the right thing. He too would kill any bad hoor that beat his wife. And I was of the same accord. The hitchhiker had done the right thing. We were all very happy about that.

'Jealous man, he was. Bad cess to him, I killed him. We men are jealous animals. Someday I think I'm goin' to throw myself into that river in Glen. A blessed refuge.'

'Make sure you're able to crawl out of it before you do,' says Witheroe. That was another great laugh between them, the hitchhiker having to smile from the side of his face which did not have the port-wine stain.

Briefly I wondered if his story was true. Here, at last, was a hint of the adventure I knew our hitchhiker had been keeping from us. And even if he had made it up, it still was just as good as true. What was the difference? It kept me going. If I was constructing any distinctions in my mind between truth and make-believe, they were very blurred.

Christopher. Where did he fit in my constructions? It was during another of those five minute snatches of words. While, from the corner of my eye, I saw Richie wing around Glen field like the devil on flying shirt-tails.

They had begun talking about Christopher. And, as always when the subject came up, the hitchhiker was feeling ill at ease. He straightened his back, lifted himself on his fork and looked down at the ground.

'Ever heard of Christopher Columbus?' said he.

'That lad, the saint, the patron saint of travellers?' Witheroe laughed. 'And isn't our own Christopher the great traveller, that can't even make his way home from Birmingham.'

'Don't talk to me about saints. I don't know any saints. I'm talkin' about that man, the explorer.'

'The Indians slaughtered that man, did they?'

'They did not. He was an explorer, and came home again.'

'Like yourself?'

'No, not like me. Like your Christopher will.'

'My son Christopher, the explorer,' said Witheroe. He shook his head. He rubbed the salty sweat off his forehead and raked the hay tossed about his feet as though he was astonished to find it there.

3

A new workman arrived: Sadlier from up Slievenamon. Things were hotting up in Ivyhall. Connaughton, in the course of less than three years – I would be eleven next birthday – had turned it into an industrious spot. Sadlier came with a suitcase so small he could put his hand around it. I didn't know how all his belongings fitted in there. You could hardly fit your socks in it. The loft above the garage was made up for Sadlier's sleeping accommodation. Mam gave him lots of books to read. These were books she would not give to us. He had simple tastes, she said. The books smelled of blotting paper. He was delighted with them. The loft smelled of old oats. That didn't worry him either.

From all of our workmen I learned a few things, but mostly I learned from Sadlier.

In Sadlier's case you never knew what to believe; I believed it anyway. After tea Witheroe got his gallon of milk to take home to his family. He went into the hitchhiker's room, where he sheltered his bike out of the sun and rain, and had a quiet cigarette there with the hitchhiker before cycling home with the gallon of milk on the handlebar. Sadlier, being a lot younger, about sixteen or seventeen, went walking down the lane to see if anything was passing on the road. Sometimes, like this evening, I went with him. It was a dry, dry evening, the lane was dry, a wind was blowing sand off its surface, and the setting sun was shining up from Glen. A bright evening, and yet a low band of cloud away on the horizon gave a reminder that darkness would fall. Our voices carried in the clear air. Sadlier was doing the talking. He was giving me some news, rather unappealing news it seemed to me, about things adults went in for with one another. We had let out the cows, they were ambling before us. I crooked my arm on the hip of the last cow in the herd, something I liked to do. Ramble, amble; cows had a hip motion that almost sent you to sleep. I liked cows. Wise old cows with the sadness in their eyes, younger ones with eyes full of fear, wary of the blow across the forehead. The same fright you sometimes saw in the eyes of women who lived off in the country, off in long lanes, and were never seen except on Sunday at mass.

Sadlier was talking. We walked past the diesel tank, its red-oxide paint deepening in the sunset. The tractor was parked alongside; parked by Richie since earlier. I could smell the diesel.

'Nobody does that,' I said. 'I don't believe that.'

'Everybody does that.' Sadlier whopped his cattle stick against a tractor wheel and it bounced away with a rubbery ping.

'I won't be doing that, you can be sure,' I said.

'You will, you can be sure,' he said. 'When you get a girlfriend. It's nice.'

'How could it be nice!'

'It's called love.'

To me it was called horror.

'Would you do it, Sadlier?'

'I would, and looking forward to it. When you get a girlfriend, so will you.'

It was hard to believe.

This revelation might not have been so shocking to me if it

hadn't been that shortly beforehand a girlfriend was exactly what I had got. My girlfriend was something that had happened slowly. It happened during breaktimes in our school yard. I was in my second year of school now in the town of Wolfdyke, three miles from Ivy-hall. A wall divided the yard of the girls' school from that of the boys'. Frieda was her name. One day, for no reason that I could figure out, the chants began to float across the wall from the girls': 'Frieda Ryan loves Lally Connaughton.' This sort of chant went on every day – the linking of one boy and one girl. It started up after the pissing competitions out the back, where a higher wall divided the girls' toilets from ours. The pissing competition entailed doing it over the wall into the girls'. There were really only two who could: Gussie Quirke who managed it through twisting the skin at the top of his laddie-boy into a nozzle and letting go in spurts. And Gananny, who being so tall, could do it unaided. He beaded his water over the wall, clear as tapwater in the sunlight, and you heard its empty flop onto the bed of the girls' toilets. And then the squealing began: 'Ailey Lynch loves Gananny,' and so on, until it eventually made its way around to the lower wall in the front. These chants floated over from the girls' school all the time. Except this time they were calling out my name. This was the first time of 'Frieda Ryan loves Lally Connaughton.' Then I began to notice among the faces of the chanting girls one face in particular. A very pale face, with dark hair. A face that said, pay attention. It stared across the wall at me, unblinking. Rain might be falling during breaktime, or the sun shining, but the face was always there. Within a day or two I was in love with it.

I was surprised at the nature of love. It was a sudden business; it kept a fellow on his toes. The notes began to come. Notes arranging meetings. Stack Straw lived on the same road as Frieda. His name was Stanisclaus, we called him Stack. 'Frieda says I'm your postman,' he said.

'I love you,' said the note. 'Meet me outside Costello's shop after school.'

The problem was that when she did meet me she didn't seem to love me at all.

On the first occasion we were supposed to meet, instead of standing so that I could say something, she ran round and round a car parked outside the shop. I felt I had to run after her. One time I got up quite close because she slowed down. I got so close I could see the colour of her eyes which were the deepest of blue, so deep they startled me, and a gap between her front teeth where they were broken. The broken teeth made her look wonderful. But then I slowed down so that she could get away from me again. This carry-on seemed to go on forever. Her friends tried to block her, so that I would have to catch up with her. Suddenly she stopped of her own accord. And while I kept running into her, not being able to stop, she said, 'How dare you,' and grabbed my schoolbag and ran off with it. My schoolbag was very heavy; it had all my scholarship books in it. She ran off, holding it in a lopsided manner, and then she hoisted it over the wall. That was the first time.

'I love you more each day. Meet me in the library,' her note said. Miss Pearl Tutty was the librarian. The library was upstairs over Austin Tutty's, the butcher's shop. They were brother and sister. Very strict people. From the moment you started up the shaky stairs, to the moment you got your books stamped at Pearl Tutty's busy desk, which was crammed with dried flowers and pictures and vases, you were supposed to keep silent. Thursday was library day for the boys and girls in the schools. It seemed ages before Thursday came around.

How could it possibly have happened that we both wanted the same book? She was standing in a group of girls and she broke free of them and ran for the book just as I lifted it. It was on the shelf beside the low window that looked down on the street. The window was half in the butcher's shop, half in the library. I think a floor must have been put in at one time so as to divide a single high-ceilinged room into two; the butcher's below, the library above. The same window served both upstairs and downstairs. And there was a gap in the floor where the window ran down so that you could see into the butcher's below. The smell of dry lard and carcases came up through the gap and lodged in all the books in that section. It was a smell that was supposed to be good for you. Witheroe, who knew Austin Tutty well, once explained to me about him. Tutty was like himself, having had to retire from the mines because of a poor stomach. (Even though Tutty had a good above-ground job, said Witheroe.) He had been advised to go into butchering by the doctor. The smell of butchery toughened the stomach wall, the doctor said. But I don't think it was because of the smell of butchery off it that Frieda grabbed the book I was now about to look through. It was a boy's book: *The Hardy Boys*.

I tried to grab the book back from her but it fell from our hands and right through the gap by the window.

'Now look what you did,' she whispered.

'I'll get it back for you,' I whispered.

That was the first time I was overcome with the idea of gifts. The first welling of my need to give. To shower gifts upon my sweetheart. For when I went downstairs to the butcher's I found our book embedded, edgeways on, in a stick of sausages. A plastic sign in the shape of a shamrock pinned into the pile, saying 'Quality Roscrea Sausages', had been toppled sideways. I righted the sign and pulled out the book but the sausages came also. It was then I thought of the gift, and a very obvious choice indeed it was. Austin Tutty was not at home. I could actually see him over on the corner, in his butcher's apron, talking to the Wolfdyke corner-boys. Austin had a strangely shaped head. Bulging out in front and behind and with only a thin neck, it was like the top of the Shell petrol pump down the town. All the corner-boys were ex-miners. Only Austin had a job. Every time Mam drove by that corner she said it was such a shame: able-bodied men wasting shoe leather. But I hadn't time to be thinking of things like that. The other thought had come to me and I had to act quickly. I had to get my gift of sausages for Frieda. And knowing the sort of stringy chains that sausages can be, I was not going to be fooled by them dragging endlessly after me up the stairs. I grabbed the thin-bladed knife that lay on Austin's block. Dangerous item to be leaving around. How many sausages? I lifted. Six? I lifted higher. Six more. And another one. A butcher's dozen, ha ha. I snipped.

'Your book, and would you like some sausages?' I said to Frieda, who was pretending not to notice my return. Ardently, I handed them to her.

'Sausages,' she screamed and slashed them away from her so swiftly that they flew off in the air.

The next moment there was a crash by Miss Tutty's table, the sound of something tinkling into small pieces, followed by a silence and then a piercing cry.

'My Belleek, my only bit of Belleek china I have in the world.'

Then there was another cry. Even more piercing this time. 'Austin Tutty, how did they get there?' She was pointing at the sausages. They were stuck to the wall behind her, fragments of Belleek china shrapnelled into them.

Austin was up the stairs in a second. When he saw the sausages he shook his petrol-pump head. 'Roscreas,' he said. I didn't how he was so sure they were Roscreas and not Donnellys, or Clover Meats. Stuck to the wall they were, bristling with Belleek china. I didn't know how he was so sure. He walked over to the gap in the floor and looked down and shook his head again. 'Roscreas, that's a good one. Didn't know Roscreas could fly.'

'It's Lally Connaughton and Frieda Ryan, Miss Tutty.' The chant went up from the girls. When I had got over my first sweet shock at hearing my name and Frieda Ryan's linked together in a public place I knew I was in trouble.

'What's going on? Show me that book, Miss Ryan.' Miss Tutty walked over to us in her tiny-stepped waddle. She always wore a long skirt down to her shoes. You were given the impression of legs that began from the ankles rather than from the hips, that short they were.

Well, my knees were buckling as the enquiry began. Austin and Pearl Tutty looking down on me, making me say outlandish things.

'Explain what's going on behind my back. Explain flying sausages.'

'I don't know. Maybe they blew up.'

It was an occurrence that defied logic.

'Why is there sausage on *The Hardy Boys*, Miss Ryan?'

'I don't know. Ask him.'

Back and forth the questions raged.

Miss Tutty might have accepted that there was no explanation, in the same way as she sometimes had to accept that there were no explanations for other occurrences such as sudden bangs or falling bookshelves or other things that happened behind her back, except that some of the girls kept insisting I had thrown sausages at Frieda Ryan and that I was getting married to her. My face was red.

'I'm holding you two responsible,' she said. 'You'll hear more of this.'

And that was really the start of things between Frieda Ryan and me. We might as well have gone down that stairs handcuffed together.

Mam was not pleased.

It was on Sunday after mass, just before dinner. We were all at the table.

'I hear you're getting married.'

'I am not.'

'Miss Tutty says you are. And what's for the wedding breakfast? Sausages and Chef sauce?'

'No.'

'And who's the lucky bride?'

There was no answering Mam when she spoke like this. She was furious, I knew that. Miss Tutty had spoken to her. She turned away from me then and laughed with Dancie. 'Oh I am so jealous,' she said. 'He'll have to introduce me to his bride-to-be so that I can give my approval.'

Was I too young at ten and a half to be getting married? I wondered. Was that what had her so worked up? Or because Pearl Tutty would now be announcing it to the whole street. A shame on Ivyhall?

I sat with my head down. Everybody was looking at me. There was no approval for marriage around that table. And I wanted more than ever to be handcuffed to Frieda Ryan. Frieda and me together against everybody. Oh handcuffing would have suited me.

It didn't seem to suit Frieda though. Why not? I thought all girls were supposed to want to get married. She ran around cars after school. She ran up to me and belted me with her schoolbag and ran away again.

'Ow. That hurts.'

'Good enough for you.'

The name Frieda, the sight of Frieda, it made me jump. I loved to repeat the name to myself. I tried to say the name to people. I wrote it down and then tore it up. I said it to Aunt Tessa once as I drove down the lane with her in the car to open and close the gate. 'Frieda,' I said, casually. 'Rita,' she said. 'Rita Hayworth.' She must have thought I said Rita but no I had not. She looked in her mirror and then down the front of her dress. Rita Hayworth, she repeated, and for a moment, because of the way she had said it, as if she was letting me in on something, I loved Aunt Tessa the same way as I loved Frieda. But the moment I got out of the car it all continued to be as lonely a business as ever.

It was just around that stage in relations with Frieda that Sadlier opened my eyes. And for a while then I it was who ran away from Frieda . . . Ten and a half . . . it was shocking. With all the mechanics it entailed, when I thought about it, it was too young to be getting married.

And yet, what else was there for me? In my anguish it was all I wanted: Frieda and me together; the heavy shadow of Mam would be swept away in the sunlight of our union.

4

Can you do the twist? Richie said one day. He was standing by the forage harvester. Bunny was standing with him. Bunny came to work in Ivyhall on Saturdays. He came and cut boughs off trees with his bushman-saw and carried them home for his mother's fire. Ettie loved our firewood. She said it to Mam any time she met her: 'Thanks, ma'am, and you'll go to heaven, for nothing beats the cold like Ivyhall firing.' I knew Bunny at school during the weekdays; but on Saturdays he seemed different. He seemed older. He had a deep voice and sharp fists. I knew that, because he showed me once how he could box and it stung when he hit me. He boxed in competitions. He was always talking about his brother Christopher who was in England and was a good boxer also. 'He's not your brother. He is your uncle,' I said once. I had been confused. I could never get out of my head the story of Dancie and the adopted boy, Christopher, her old parents' youngest son, and how for years she had brought him up before sending him home to Witheroe. So how could he be his brother? 'He is my fuckin' brother,' he said. He gave me a shot of his sharp fist into my arm. I didn't argue with him. Christopher was his big brother and that was all about it and he would soon be joining him over there in England.

'What about school, and the Master?' I said.

'Shag school,' he said, 'shag Gimp Flynn. I'm goin' to England.'

I was walking up the lane to the house this day. It was a quiet time. Richie had parked the forage harvester on the lane. He wanted to dismantle it, get inside it and understand how it worked. He loved to dismantle things. He was in the blue boiler suit that made him look like a man, even though he was only fourteen. The boiler suit meant business, its pockets flopping forward with spanners. Right now he had stopped dismantling and he was showing Bunny how to do the twist. He must have been showing him for quite a while because he was sweating. Hens had begun picking in underneath the forage harvester. 'Can you do it?' he said to me and he showed me too.

Richie was not thin and he looked a bit funny as he twisted, rubbing sounds coming out of his wellington boots and his clothes beneath the boiler suit. I said he didn't look right. I wouldn't say to him that he looked fat, which was what I meant, just that he didn't look right. But he knew what I meant. You should see Chubby Checker, he said. He had seen Chubby Checker on television once. All you had to be to do the twist was be fit, he said. Chubby Checker, even though he mightn't look it, was surprisingly fit. It goes like this, he said to Bunny, all earnest sounding. You swivel off the balls of your feet and you move with your arms. The swing of your arms is what gives you balance. He sang as he swivelled, 'Come on let's twist again like we did last summer.' Except he wasn't singing, but talking, in his croaky voice, because Richie couldn't sing for nuts.

Bunny looked on really seriously as Richie showed him how to do it. But then Bunny looked on really seriously as Richie showed him how to do anything. As if he was facing a boxing adversary. And afterwards he would say to me how Richie was a 'tub-of-guts' or an 'arse-in-pockets', and I would laugh. Which wasn't fair on Richie. He was fit: he could sprint fast over short distances – and that was not good if you wanted to get away from him after having risen his temper. And hurling. He could puck the hurley ball at such speed that it bent in flight and split you as you stood in the goal. He could ride the ponies too, gallop them better than ever I could. He was fit. But it gave me great joy that there were any weaknesses of Richie's that could be picked upon. And Bunny always did as soon as he got his back turned. 'Arse-in-pockets.'

I kept heading for the house. Come back and try the twist, Richie said. He was affable about it, not making me do it under pain of torture as he sometimes did. He wanted me for company. He wasn't sure of Bunny and wanted to have me to fall back on. Richie had strange ways of seeking companionship. But I didn't go back. I was too young for the twist. What would I, not yet twelve years of age, want with the old twist?

When I returned on the lane an hour later he was still there. Now he was on his own. I was headed for the field called Lisaneerin. One August in Ivyhall I had strayed upon the blackberry trees there. It was a great discovery; brambles that climbed high into the trees and then looped down again, blackberries hanging before your open mouth. You gathered the fruit in fistfuls and crammed it into you.

There must have been rain when I was in the house but now it was over. Everything was shining in the sun. I kicked a little puddle of water which always came in the lane after rain. Richie was hold-ing a spanner in one hand – Richie was always holding a spanner in one hand anyway – and with the other he was holding up the chute of the forage harvester. He had worked the nuts loose all round the neck of it and it looked to me ready to topple over.

'Hold that for me,' he said, pointing up at it. 'That other lousy clot, Bunny, went and left me when I had it half off.'

I pretended not to hear him but went on, kicking through the puddle. That was a new word he had, *lousy*. Where did he get that?

'Give me a hand. Are you deaf?'

'I can't.'

'It's fallin' on my head.'

'I have to go somewhere.'

'Where?'

'To pick blackberries.'

I kept going.

'You can't pick blackberries.'

I just kept going.

I wondered would he run after me.

The next thing I heard was the sound of the chute falling from the forage harvester, clunking down. It hit something hard. Richie shouted. He seemed in pain. 'Look what you've done, you blinky clot,' he said. I did not look around, but without seeming to, I quickened my step.

He was after me now. I could hear the wellington boots picking up speed on the gravel. But I couldn't hurry. A journey to eat blackberries was one you undertook in a casual manner. And my purpose was to eat blackberries and not to run away from him. To run away from him would be to indicate I had done something wrong.

But suddenly, all around me, everything had grown furiously active. The crows were rising over where the blackberries grew, cawing and criss-crossing in their flight. A hen ran off so fast that she lifted from the ground. Her clutch of chickens, attempting also to take off, made little *print* sounds across the runway of the sticky lane but they couldn't rise and just went bumpety-bump after her. The dog jumped up from his sleep by the gateway and barked. Everything was frantic. My shoulders hunched in readiness for the blow. I heard the spanner drop from Richie's hand. Thank God, at least when the blow would strike it would not be with the spanner. And it would be on soft ground, that was another bonus. The last time he had got me it was in the hard yard and when my head bounced off the concrete I heard a hollow sound just like an echo from the centre of the earth. Now I was running. I had to get to those blackberries before he got to me. I had to get a handful at least. I had to follow my purpose. Once I had begun to run, I flew. I pulled a clump from the first bramble I reached and casual as I could manage I put it in my mouth, berries, spriggets of thorn, raindrops and all.

But the scuffle of his boots was upon me. I had to jump a bit out of the way. Nobody wants the guts beaten out of them. But I got it anyway, fists and kicks. Then I was lying there, Richie on top of me; I was lying and crying and wondering what was so terrible about wanting to eat blackberries. I had a picture of myself, my mouth, teeth and lips, a big broken juice-blue hole.

'Now look what you've done to yourself, babby,' Richie said. 'You're dribbling all over your coat.'

I wasn't dribbling on my coat. How could I be when my mouth was stuck in the wet clay and the dribbles were flowing down the blades of grass? 'I'm not dribbling on my coat,' I tried to say, but my words were muffled in a bubble of spit.

He caught me by the arm and wrenched.

This was always Richie's way. Once he had administered the heavier punishment, he always stayed on. He prolonged the punishment, but it was only to get you talking again. So that he could be happy you were not dead, and, after that, happy you harboured no hard feelings. He wanted it both ways.

After five minutes or so of lying in a flattened position beneath him I tried to make myself more comfortable.

He knew now I wasn't dead. He gave my arm another wrench. 'Do the twist.'

'I don't want to do the twist. Let go.'

He twisted harder. 'Sing a song so.'

Here was where I came in handy for Richie. He loved songs, hit songs, but couldn't sing them. So out of my mouth would have to come his voice. I was his means of expression.

'I can't,' I said.

'You can.' This time he gave my arm a jolt that sent real pain shooting through it.

'Ow, that hurts, flip off. What will I sing?'

'Sing a hit song.'

'I can't think of one. Leave go.'

'No, I'll loosen you.' He loosened his hold on my arm. I was still bent like an S-hook on the broken roots of grass and bracken. I knew he had me. He had beaten me up and now he was going to get a song out of me also. I was supposed to feel grateful for that.

I had a selection of songs I sang to myself going about the fields of our farm. I had named them for my own amusement: the Ten All-Time Greatest Tipperary Hit Songs. I was compiling my own hit parade of songs I heard from the radio. I sang one of them for him:

> How would you like to be
> Down by the Seine with me?
> Oh what I'd give for a moment or two
> Under the bridges of Paris with you . . .

As I sang, his hold loosened. By the time I had finished he had let go altogether. I was able to lift my head. The thing about Richie was that no matter what you sang for him he loved it. He was easily pleased really. It was just that I would not please him. He got up off me with a grunt, half-happy. 'I'll show you how to do the twist,' he said. 'And this time, watch.' He made a silent twisting movement then, going down on his knees, and the sagging tail end of his boiler suit swished the heads of grass. 'You have to be very fit to dance the twist,' he said. 'You should learn it.' He looked at the patch of earth his twisting wellington boots had cut into the grass. 'I'm good at it.' He walked back to the forage harvester, still only half-happy. I felt sorry for him. And I felt sorry for my song. I should have put more heart into it. It was a good one, deserving of everything I had got. I hadn't done it justice.

To make up for it I sang my All-Time Number One on the Tipperary hit parade. I still wasn't feeling great but I sang it:

> Some enchanted evening
> You may see a stranger
> Oh you may see a stranger
> Across a crowded room . . .

Richie had returned to his work on the forage harvester. He had lifted the chute back on to its neck. It was standing erect again. I could hear his spanner tightening on the squeaky nuts.

'That's a good song.' he called across to where I lay. 'But you have to put a quiver in your voice. Like you hear with good singers on the radio.'

It was his way of trying to cheer me, improve my condition. Richie was a great improver of everything.

'Put the quiver in your voice.'

'OK,' I said, sitting up in the grass. I spat out a few blackberry seeds, stuck in my throat.

And somehow you know
You know even then
That someday you'll see her
Again and again . . .

I put the quiver in my voice. Maybe I was still crying, I don't know. Or maybe my voice was maturing. A natural development, maybe, was the quiver. I felt good about that. And bad and all as he was, there was something nice about singing for Richie; something nice about singing for somebody as hugely in need as he of a song well sung.

When did Mam begin to refer to Christopher as Patsy Fagan? I think she did it just to bother me. To remind me that she knew my Mama's songs. But of course she wouldn't say it right out. Hints and undercurrents, that was the way she worked. She got a letter from England. 'Hello Patsy Fagan, you can hear the girls all cry,' she said. She read the letter out to Dancie at the kitchen table. There was no news. No news of Patsy Fagan, she said. Patsy Fagan, she had given to Christopher his new nickname. Mam, the nickname specialist.

'Sing "Patsy Fagan" for us,' she said to me. Why did she ask me a thing like that? It was a shocking embarrassment. I might have sung for Mam if, like Richie, she needed it. But Mam did not need songs sung for her.

5

I was eleven and a half. The carnival came to Wolfdyke. McCormacks' Road Show. A troupe of the most handsome men and pretty ladies were those McCormacks. The most wonderful records they played, through loudspeakers above the stalls. Ruby Murray singing: 'Softy, softly, turn the key and open up my heart.' Oh how I wished I could say a thing like that to Frieda. Knowing of course there would be no point. 'Ugh, you make me laugh sick,' she would say. However, with the arrival of the McCormacks, my love letters to her showed a great improvement. Became more imaginative, more decorative; the borders became a mosaic of shattered hearts, riven with quivers of arrows, blood gushing everywhere. Stack Straw was the busy postman. And still the same note came back from Frieda. Naming the meeting place: 'Meet me at the shooting-gallery stall.'

I stood at one end of the stall; Frieda at the other. In a row, along the counter, the sharp-eyed men shot at the bull's-eye and the woman with the red headscarf bent the guns in the middle and reloaded them again and let the ash from her cigarette run down along the outside of the barrels. And the same mournful songs played over and over again, escaped into the starry night that peeped through the awning: 'Sailor, stop your roving. Sailor, leave the sea. Sailor, when the tide turns, come home safe to me.' All the places that sailor sailed to: 'Deep in the harbours of my heart, oh my love is there to guide you . . . In Capri or Amsterdam, Honolulu or Siam.' I knew those deep and hazardous harbours.

McCormacks, the Roadshow of Longing: Mam and Dancie gambling at the pongo; Frieda and me standing either end of the line of stooping men along the counter of the shooting gallery. Either end we stood, and would not draw any closer. The men concentrated. We watched. Darts with feathered tips shot from the guns. Paper targets hung from clothes pegs. Dunk, dunk dunk. Piece by piece, the paper shredded. And not a word from anybody, but songs, songs. A boy sometimes popped out of a tent and introduced the songs. He was about thirteen but looked like a grown-up film star. He wore a gold cravat, an open white shirt and, on his face, stuff that glistened of gold. All the girls knew his name. It was George McCormack. Frieda looked at George, dazzled. 'Appearing at the Grand Ole Opry tonight, ladies and gentlemen,' he shouted in a boy's voice. 'Give a big hand to Hank Williams.' And then the song came on: ' . . . There's a tear in my beer and I'm cryin' for you dear, you were on my lonesome mind . . .' Each new night of hope my heart was wrung out dry, while the shadow of Stack flitted somewhere close and plucked out of our hands, like leaves off trees, the messages Frieda and me scrawled to one another. Everything seemed to be about to happen, yet nothing did.

The McCormacks left town. Left the field bared behind them, even took the sawdust. Then a day came when Stack Straw was no longer our only sidekick. Gananny had become interested. It was because of Frieda's friend, Ailey Lynch. Their names were still being chanted together over the school wall and now Gananny decided it was time something was done about it. He started to make proposals: could he walk along with me after school and we could meet Frieda and Ailey? Ailey Lynch was not my idea of beauty. Not the real thing like Frieda. Ailey had red circles round her cheeks, pinches of white in their centres. One stocking was always lower than the other. The hem of her dress was always higher in the front than in the back. But laughter was always erupting out of her, careless and generous, and when she and Frieda were together the heat was off me a little.

It was around then that Sadlier left: my sisters liked to drive home the cows for Sadlier. They lingered with him in the cowhouse as he milked. To give him company because he was lonely, they said to Mam, when she called them to answer for themselves. Then one evening after milking he was gone. Slipped away in the night with his little suitcase. Left behind, in a neat pile in the loft, all the books Mam had loaned him, all the work clothes she had given him, and went back up the mountain. Got the sack. It was a pity, because right then I could have done with a little friendly advice concerning Frieda.

Sadlier went. Then came Bunny; he had come full-time now, not just the Saturday visitor who cycled in with Witheroe, and cut down old whitethorn boughs for firewood. He was left school now but he was not allowed go to England. Witheroe laid down the rule and Dancie backed him. Not allowed go to England until his brother Christopher could first be located. And certainly not allowed to work in the mines. Witheroe continued to think very highly of Bunny. 'He has a great pair of hands,' he said. 'If he goes over to England and catches up with any fellow who malusted his brother, he'll kill him.' Bunny hit Witheroe a few slaps every now and then. Witheroe told me: 'He hits me a few slaps if I get out of order with him. He has a sting in his fist.' He was proud of being hit by his son.

Bunny was very quiet when my father was around, but not so quiet with me. Once he was sure of me and knew there would be no tales going back from me to Connaughton or to Mam, he was able to swear and curse. I had always thought of him as being tall, he had a way of walking – nervy and muscular – but now he had stopped growing and had begun to look stout and squashed. He had funny words. *Browl*, *brellick* and *bollax* were his favourites. You browl, you brellick, you bollax, he would call me. Where did he

219

get such words? He sang: 'I was born on a morning when the sun didn't shine, I stood six foot six and weighed two forty-five.' He recited his song, striding along the centre channel of the cow-house behind the cows, his head hardly visible over their tail ends. 'Big John', the song was called. Big John was a story about a miner. 'He was a tough man, Big John,' Bunny said. 'But I bet he wasn't tough enough to work the mine where Witheroe worked above in Copper Cross.' Sometimes Bunny pucked cows, lifting them in the air as he practised his boxing moves. 'And everybody knew they didn't give no lip to Big John, Big Bad John.' He told me to put my fingers in his mouth so that I could feel his teeth; two of them at the back had come loose from boxing. 'In the red corner,' he would say, 'the champ, Bunny Boy Witheroe.'

Of Sadlier I might have expected advice, but of his replacement I could expect no such thing.

The wanderings began. After school. Gananny, Meagher and me out along the road with Frieda and Ailey. Yes, Meagher came too. He laughed and smirked all the time while Gananny and me ran away from the girls and back to them again. Picking blackberries, throwing them at one another. Faces smudged as Indians. The girls kicking up dust with their cloddy shoes. In the end the running stopped. One day we all went into a field. There was a tree in the centre. The girls said that hanging off this tree was the best idea going. They often did it. Meagher fell into the drain as we crossed the ditch. Gananny threw his schoolbag in after him. If it had been my schoolbag, it would have sunk. But Gananny and Meagher had only a jotter and a pencil rattling around in theirs and Meagher's schoolbag floated merrily down the river like a boot, with Meagher shouting after it, 'Come back you hoor.'

When Meagher went chasing his schoolbag it became much quieter. Then the girls climbed into the tree. They didn't seem to have much bother, considering their cloddy shoes. Frieda didn't anyhow. Ailey wiggled her bottom as she squeezed between the branches. 'Where do I put my foot now?' she said. Frieda told her to watch out for dead branches. 'Go slower, Frieda,' she called. There was this constant murmur going on between them. They were doing all this climbing without asking us anything. Then a branch broke with a loud crack and Ailey screamed. She grabbed another branch and stood for a while without moving. Then she followed Frieda again. Once they got up to a wide branch where they could stand safely, they started looking down on us and laughing. Gananny was looking up. 'Aw Jayz, look what I see,' he said. I did not look up to find out. 'What do you say about that?' he said to me. I felt I was disappointing everybody because I had nothing to say about anything. 'Look at the eejits down on the ground' – the girls were laughing at us like that for a while. I didn't know what to do, climb up or stay down, but I had a definite feeling that something was expected of me. The girls just stared down at us, their faces half-covered by leaves and their eyes peering through. The silence had come back again. Then the squealing began: 'Frieda, I'm stuck. Oh I can't get down. Help, help.' The more Ailey cried help, the more she spluttered with laughter.

But who was going to help? It took Gananny no time to find out that he was. Ailey was bigger than my girl Frieda. She had big legs but that didn't worry Gananny. He held his hands out beneath her. When she fell she landed sturdily on top of him, flattening him into her. I heard the gasp of his breath go out of him. Whatever happened, whether he was hurt or she was hurt, did not seem to worry them. Because she continued to lie on top of him. And after a while they rolled together away behind the tree without either of them seeming to have made the rolling occur.

That left me and Frieda. 'I'm stuck too,' she laughed. I wished she wouldn't laugh at it but would take being stuck more seriously. Then I could have said, Oh wait a minute, wait a minute, I'll get a ladder. Or have stood near and said, It's all right, I'll catch you. But I said nothing. I just kept wavering beneath the tree, my hands held vaguely aloft as though the moon were about to drop out of the sky. Then she lowered herself on the branch until she was hanging from her arms. Her legs out in midair, she was like that picture of Alice in Wonderland, as Alice is floating down the rabbit hole. 'Ha, ha, ha, catch me,' she said. Then she let go. I had a quick glimpse of a knickers. Oh come down on top of me, fill my arms tight with you, please, I said to myself. Celestial body. But she didn't. She missed me entirely and hit her head off the hard ground. It was a

221

most disappointing let down for her. And for me. And I thought she was finished with me forever.

Frieda began to come out our way on Saturdays, all on her own. So she wasn't, after all, finished with me. Indeed, it was all becoming a very serious business. Gananny and Ailey didn't need to carry on any more because they were together now, going to the pictures at the De Luxe in Wolfdyke and everything.

Once only, I was in the De Luxe at the same time as Frieda. We did a school play. 'The Croppy Boy'. I was the Croppy Boy because of having a good singing voice. Miss Pearl Tutty was called in by the Master to give advice on our costumes. They decided I should wear a kilt. What was it but a girl's dress, with a big safety pin down the front to stop it opening. The Croppy Boy – a girl. Everybody was laughing at me.

The night of the play the weather was fierce. A night of lashing rain, and lightning in the sky. My parents were there. The actors had to queue up out in the yard, waiting for their turns to come on. The gutters danced with the downpour. Rain hopped off the cement yard. During the flashes of lightning I could see Frieda's pale face, watching me. Then, when she had the support of all the girls around her, she said: 'I have something to cool down that thing under your kilt.' Everybody laughed: 'Frieda has something for cooling down the Croppy Boy.' I was very disappointed with her. Was she my girl at all? If she was, she would not have said a thing like that. The rain hammered on the tin roof of the De Luxe all through the performance. When it came to my turn I had to sing louder than ever to rise above it. You brought the house down, Mam said, going home in the car. I was too sick – I did not know whether with the passion of my performance or with the closeness of Frieda – to decide whether she was mocking or praising me.

'Meet me at the pictures,' said the notes that Stack Straw gave me now. But that was out of the question. I was not allowed go to Wolfdyke at night. Stack would tell me about all the pictures he saw in the De Luxe – Norman Wisdom, The Three Stooges. Stack was a sunny boy when laughter crossed his face. Over and over he would sketch the plots, laughing, while I did my best to put his snatches into one coherent story. But it was no good. I could never get the plots. And I was not allowed go to the pictures. So Frieda began to come out our way. Saturday, once a simple day of mucking out manury horse stalls and scoury calf sheds, was now a complicated misery. Waiting for Frieda: climbing the castle on the lookout. Timing her arrival. Watching her roll the high-wheeled pram off up the road by Mrs Gananny's low cottage. Hiding behind the ivy on the wall along the road; passing the time by counting the snails stuck on the mortar beneath the ivy roots, until I heard the click, click of the pram wheels. Sauntering across the road then, pretending to be going down to Glen.

There seemed to be always some bother with the baby the moment I appeared. 'Ssh, what's the matter, alanna.' Frieda stuck her head into the rubbery-smelling darkness beneath the hood and when it came out she seemed all grown-up and disinterested in me.

This day I set about attracting her full attention. I had gone on a shopping expedition to Woolworths.

'Aahm, I have presents for you.'

'It's not sausages?' she asked, looking in at the baby.

'No. It's jewellery.'

'Show me.'

'A rosary-beads.'

She grabbed the rosary-beads and threw it in the pram beneath the baby's fat little ankles. It didn't look a very religious gesture to me.

I showed her the rest of my jewellery.

'It's a ring.' The hard purple diamond on the ring lit up when the sunlight hit it, washing all the rich purple out of it until it was the colour of glass.

'It changes colours,' I said. 'Good, isn't it?'

'Oh lovely.' She snapped the box shut. 'Amethyst,' she said.

I could imagine it all purple again inside the box. Yes, she could appreciate things. But then I found myself too close to her and I went back behind the wall but followed her from inside, bursting over briars and fences all the way to the end of our farm.

'You're like a bull,' Bunny said when I got home. 'You'll tear your mickey on the barbed wire.'

How could I be like a bull? How could he say that? I was deeply hurt. I, who bought presents of rings, rosary beads, even earrings once, earrings that didn't need pierced ears.

'You won't tell on me, Bunny.'

'Fuck off. Go in and steal a fag out of Dancie's box for me.'

Oh Saturdays. And the Saturdays she did not come were even worse.

Bunny knew I was in love. 'Frieda Ryan from the cottages.' He clicked his lips in mock disappointment. I wondered would Bunny tell the grown-ups. I wondered would he tell Mam. He didn't have to in the end. Because I made a disgrace of myself. On a day that as well as being one of the worst days of my life was also one of the most exciting. It came about because of Frieda's great idea.

One of the Saturdays I walked along the road with Frieda, she asked me to wheel the pram a bit for her. It was misty. The wheels were humming on the wet tar, knocking up four little fountains of water behind them. We came up to the tinker camp on the hollow of the road; the camp of the Cartys, the horse-tanglers. The place was smoky with the dampness of a dead bonfire. The Cartys owned no caravans but hooped tents made out of tarpaulin. In the misty day it was easy to mistake the camp for the little hillocks of our field, Lisaneerin, that lay behind. A strange place, that field. A place, the hitchhiker said, where it wouldn't surprise him if fairies lived. It was made of hills and hollows of a long ago mining camp and old moss-covered trees grew in the hollows. Whitethorn trees. The hitchhiker said they could never be cut down because the place was a fairy fort. It was strange that the hitchhiker, who didn't go to mass or anything, should believe in the fairies. I agreed with him that the trees should not be cut down. I agreed with him only because Richie was keen to get rid of them.

The girls played house in Lisaneerin sometimes. I played with them if there were no jobs to be done, and so long as Richie or Bunny or any of the grown-ups were not about. The girls made imaginary tea and cakes and we lay on the dried leaves. 'That's your bed. You can be the daddy. You have to go out and get the cows.' 'Can I be the mammy instead?' I said. 'OK so.' But that was the only time, playing house with the girls or picking blackberries, that I felt happy with Lisaneerin. It scared me. If calves strayed in the crackling sticks beneath those whitethorns, I shouted at them until they came out. The hitchhiker said he saw a big hare in there one evening. He was in the feeding house, passing the time by looking out his window at the night coming on, and he saw it. The dogs chased after it but they returned yelping. The next thing, a white horse clattered right by him. I felt that if the hitchhiker was so confident our religion was all a cod, then surely there had to be something to those fairies.

No sound came from within Carty's tent. And not a dog, or pony outside. But I had a feeling about the tinker camp that was something like how I felt about Lisaneerin. Nothing might appear to be stirring . . . Currents were passing beneath the ground, however, or little swirly winds that you felt at the tips of your ears. And you braced yourself for the pounce, and the earth to bolt open before you.

'Would you like us to live in there?' Frieda said suddenly out of the blue.

Oh my heart soared. There was nothing I would like better than for us to live in there. Fairies or no fairies.

It was then she said she had the idea.

'Come here and we'll look,' she whispered.

'Could be someone in there.'

'Is there anybody there?' she called out.

'You're afraid,' she said to me.

'No I'm not.' I walked on the mossy floor that lay at the edge of the tents to show her I wasn't.

'Wonder what's it like inside?' she said. 'All you ever see is old rags.' She pointed at brown rags hanging from the tree behind the tents and all along the ditch. 'Wonder what's inside?'

I was very surprised with Frieda then. And not sure whether I should be disappointed. Because for the first time she wasn't talking about me and her, or she wasn't running away from me or I wasn't running away from her or anything like that. She was talking about something else entirely, curiosity about the tinker camp had overtaken her. She was taking me for granted.

'I'm going home now,' she said. 'I have a great idea.'

6

Frieda's idea was indeed great. The annual fancy-dress competition was coming to Wolfdyke. Frieda's idea was that we, she and me and Gananny and Ailey, should dress up for it.

'I'm going in the fancy-dress,' I told Mam one day, as she was talking to Aunt Tessa in the kitchen. The best time to tell Mam anything you didn't want to tell her was when she was smoking fags with Aunt Tessa.

She took a big draw from her cigarette and then opened her mouth wide to let the smoke out. That was the way Mam smoked. She did not inhale. The smoke drifted out of its own accord. Aunt Tessa was the same. When they were at it together they were the same as two smouldering bonfires, smoke signals slowly rising out of their wide opened mouths. They would be unable to talk while these smoke signals were rising, but would be allowing themselves time to think of the next thing to talk about.

'I have a great plan for you,' she said. Then she and Aunt Tessa started talking and laughing about the previous years' entries. There was a man, Bogan Haley, who won the fancy-dress every year. Last year Bogan had gone as Marilyn Monroe. He had gotten himself up on a tractor-trailer: '*Marilyn Monroe walking down Fifth Avenue with nothing on but the radio*'. They laughed remembering that. Then Mam said he had only won because of the novelty and it hadn't been very wholesome. 'I'll think up something more wholesome for you,' she said.

A thing about Mam nowadays was that she devoted more time to me than she had done before. All these things she would say: 'How is your homework coming on?' 'Would you like to be a priest?' 'You have lovely hair for combing.' 'You should put more feeling into your singing.' She would show me how to sing 'McNamara's Band'. 'Oh my name is McNamara, I'm the leader of a band . . .' I should stride out, she would say, as I sang it: 'Wave your baton,' she would say.

'I can't.'

'Give the song a bit of jizz. Don't be so dead and alive.'

I couldn't wave a baton. Everybody breaking their backsides laughing at me. And 'McNamara's Band' was just not one of my All-Time Greatest Tipperary Hit Songs. And I hated having to sing for Mam. Why should I have to sing her way? I didn't understand Mam. Would it not have been more satisfying for her if I sang badly? After all, I was not her son, so why did she wish to improve my singing?

Here was Mam's idea for the fancy dress: 'I want you to dress up as a cabbage.'

'A cabbage?'

'A cabbage. Cabbage leaves pinned to you, head to toe: *I'm not as green as I'm cabbage-looking*.'

'What does that mean?'

'It's an old saying.'

'Better dressed than Marilyn Monroe, Mam.'

I drew a laugh out of her for that. I could get a laugh now and again from her these days. I would have to draw my breath in case my joke was not going to work, but it always did. However, I had no intention of being a cabbage. Who would understand what 'I'm not as green as I'm cabbage-looking' meant?

The big day: I had my bundle of old clothes in a bag under my arm. 'Drop me into town, please.'

Richie drove me in: 'What are you dressing as? '

'Not telling you.'

Nowadays I could talk back like that to Richie. But he had changed too. Once he might have insisted on giving me hints on how to dress, his usual attempts at improving me. Saying: Blinky, you don't want to make a feckin' eejit of yourself. Let me show you. He would still have given me hints, but now he was becoming more involved with things other than me; he was growing more distant, and where before relations between us had been by way of shouts and fights, a self-consciousness had now come in the way. Anyway, how could I let him be involved in something as intimate as changing my whole personality? Because that was what my fancy dress amounted to: I was to be the tinker father of the Carty clan.

There was huge activity where the fancy-dress parade readied itself for take-off outside Burns's garage at the end of town. Contestants were nervous. Fellows who had dressed up as women were shouting and showing off their balloons under their cardigans: 'Here, pinch my bosoms!'

Bogan Haley was in a bed this year, on the back of a lorry. Covered in blankets, he shouted at the hairy fellow alongside him in the bed who was attempting to kick him out. 'Charlie Chaplin On Honeymoon', his placard said. In the shade of his lorry stood a group of angels, white-skinned and skimpy, their mothers busily pluming their wings.

I walked past revving lorries and prancing horses. I had reached almost to the end of the assembly. There I found the rest of the Cartys. Frieda had done great work: she had commandeered an ass and cart. A framework had been constructed on the cart, old sacks slung across it to give the impression of a tent. A painted sideboard stood on display, broken cups and jugs arranged on its shelves. 'The Cartys Go On Holidays', it said it in writing on a big banner above the tent.

But only Frieda seemed happy to be going on holidays. 'Go on, act your parts,' she was saying to the others. Gananny wore a huge plaster on his head with a placard above him saying: 'Beaten Up By The Guards'. The ass too wore a bandage, and a placard above his collar which said: 'Beaten up by Guard Heaslip, another ass if ever there was one'. He kept flicking his ears against the placard in an attempt to knock it off. Congo Hegney held the ass by its collar. Congo was a poor boy about the town. He ran errands for the corner-boys. He always had problems with his watering nose and ears; his torn clothes fell from him. He had a constant stye in one or other eye. The Master, in front of the class, would often attempt to pluck out of Congo's eyelash the rotting hair which he claimed was the cause of the stye. Congo, like Stack Straw, always hung around near Frieda and she gave him jobs to keep him happy. Stack would have been her first choice but Stack had work to do for his father. Congo's father was out with the Irish army in the Belgian Congo, keeping peace. Congo was to lead our donkey.

Gananny was to walk behind the cart, holding an accordion, which he was to squeeze from time to time. But he looked very glum. Ailey had a pillow under her cardigan. 'Child Number 12', her placard said. She was to walk alongside Gananny. It was a toss-up as to which of them looked the more unhappy about child number 12. All of us, apart from Congo, were disguised in old rags, hats or headscarves. I felt good about that and blackened my face with puddle water to further improve my chance of not being recognised. But Congo was himself. 'Congo, stay the same as you always are, pet,' Frieda said. It was very hot. No sun in the sky, but sweaty hot. I was to sit in the cart with Frieda, doing tinker jobs. My nerves were jumping.

Then, with a quick start all along its length, which I felt as a jolt in my neck, the fancy-dress parade took off. *Clippety-clop*, trots Neddy, our donkey, his hooves skimming the tarred road.

For a while there were no people along the roadside. Then we got up near the first onlookers. There was a man with a big black-board. He was Austin Tutty.

'Slow up, spread out the parade,' he ordered.

'Me fuckin' donkey is runnin' home on me,' said Congo.

'Mind your language before the judges,' Austin said. 'I'm the chief steward and I'll have you fucked out of the parade on your ear.' He told us to go slow and leave plenty of room after the previous contestants, who were the fairies, and not to be stampeding them because that would force them in under Charlie Chaplin's lorry, which was ahead of them.

Laughter from the onlookers was reaching back to us. It was hard to make out what they were saying. There were exclamations of admiration for the little children dressed as fairies. I wondered would there be the same admiration for 'The Carty Family Go On Holidays'. On a lorry behind us sat a big machine. It was sawing beams, and wood-chips were flying in every direction. The machine was an example of early industry in Wolfdyke. Timber-sawing: beams for the mines, for the bog. All the men working the machine wore beards. As they hauled on a wide fan belt, they sang a hearty song. They were like the seven dwarfs. Up the road from us was Charlie Chaplin on his honeymoon. Charlie was jumping out of bed and back in again. Every time he jumped back in, his hairy bed partner flung up his arms and roared. But to the crowd, he was still Bogan Haley. They were all shrieking: 'Ah you're a topper, Bogan Haley. Give us a laugh, you're a solid gallery.' So, Charlie Chaplin, cavorting ahead of us, and the seven dwarfs, chanting behind, ours became the very whisperful troupe in the centre of the huge space made by chief steward Austin Tutty.

I could feel the gaze of the people. They had found Chaplin on Honeymoon easier to understand. There they all were, holding before themselves ice creams and ice pops, their tongues halfway out of their mouths, stilled in amazement in the act of licking. Are we just making them think, I thought to myself, or are they gone into a state of shock? Then I could see the mouths begin to move as they read our placards and sometimes I could hear them: 'Beaten up by Guard Heaslip, another ass if ever there was one'. There were laughs for that: 'Ah, that's a good one.' And they said to one another, 'Hey lads, is Heaslip in the crowd, lads, the bollax, wait till he sees this.'

For a second I thought of Guard Heaslip and looked out for his uniform. Guard Heaslip beat up the miners whenever they got scuttered in the pubs. He beat up the tinkers too. On Congo Hegney's father's first night home, he beat him up, Congo already having beaten up his wife and the young Congos. Some thought he was right to beat up Old Congo, some thought he was not, but nobody seemed on friendly terms with him. Only Connaughton ever had a good word for him, saying it was not right that a garda should have to live in the same place where he worked.

Right now I could see miners inside the windows of pubs, looking out from the darkness. And there was no sign of Guard Heaslip.

Clippety-clip went the hooves of our little ass. Our iron-wheeled cart ground along the road. Oh, what a bumpy spin. Now the main part of town was coming up and I had no time to look out for Garda Heaslip or for anyone else because there were too many faces I knew anyway. Far too many, and the silence out of them as we passed was so deep that whenever someone spoke it rang out. People seemed mostly to want to know who we were: 'There's the Congo Hegney anyway. Know him anywhere out of his father. 'Would that be . . . ah no it wouldn't.' It was me they were trying to identify. Mouths going, heads nodding . . . 'That be young Connaughton above in Ivyhall, well I do declare. And that's young Frieda, Roundy Ryan's daughter from the cottages. Well I do declare indeed.' My mouth had gone dry, I felt a band of heat pressing into my forehead. All they wanted was to know who we were. All the enquiring faces, as we trotted by on our lonely little cart: Miss Pearl Tutty, tut-tutting like a hen; Gimp Flynn, fingering his moustache.

And then something caught the corner of my eye and sent me into a spin of terror. I had suddenly sensed the eyes of Mam bear down upon me and I felt burned to a cinder. I had spotted my sisters in the crowd, which meant that Mam was somewhere close, judging me. What could I do? Now Frieda was hitting me with a wooden spoon, the actions of a good tinker wife. 'Go out and do your day's work.'

I did. I rummaged for my hammer and horseshoe. I beat the horseshoe. I beat and beat. There was such confusion clanging in my head that I could hear no sound from the horseshoe and yet before my eyes it was turning silver. I could not look up; I was sure that if I did, Mam would be staring right at me. The same fellow who was supposed to be dead and alive, who would never make it in McNamara's Band, now he was working overtime as he passed her. Oh why had I not done what she had suggested? How I would have welcomed cabbage leaves. Cool green leaves all down my body. *I'm not as green as I'm cabbage-looking.* An old saying. What did it mean?

Then I saw her. Up the Cashel Road, I saw her, standing back a little from the crowd. Expressionless. Tessa alongside her, nudging her. The hitchhiker too. What was he doing there? He was standing some distance further behind, under a tree, a tall hat on his head. Not looking at the parade at all but instead at Mam. Whatever he was doing did not count. Mam was all that counted. I knew she had seen everything: she had uncovered the secret world of Lally Connaughton.

From that moment the parade became only some event unravelling outside of me. A play going on outside of another play. The parade carried on but now I was no longer part of it, I being an actor only within my own play. We passed the judges. They sat at a rostrum made up on the creamery platform: a priest in rolled up shirtsleeves and sunglasses, two white-haired women with pens and copybooks. The priest was still laughing after Charlie Chaplin. The women were looking sternly at him. They all ignored the Carty Family. I didn't care. I didn't care any longer who saw us, or didn't see us. Only for a moment did I suffer disappointment at the lack of interest shown us by the judges.

Then we were at the far end of town. Miners stood in the door of a pub and shouted at us. 'Go home the Carty tinkers. Your wheels are buckled and your ass is fucked.'

The end of it all was when young children from the school began singing taunts at Congo:

> Will you come to the Congo will you come
> Bring your own ammunition and your gun
> Congo Hegney will be there,
> Firing bullets in the air,
> Will you come to the Congo will you come?

I was still hammering, spitting on the silvery heat of my horseshoe. Congo looked around at us with his watery half-closed eyes and Frieda said, 'Don't mind them, Congo.'

But the children started up again:

Will you come to the Congo, will you come?
Bring your own ammunition and your gun
You'll be lying in the grass
With a bullet up your arse
Will you come with Congo Hegney, will you come?

'I'm goin' home,' Congo said, and suddenly he was leading the donkey and cart down the laneway where people came at night and stood and ate chips from the chip-shop next door. And that was it. We had left the fancy-dress parade to carry on without us. I took one look behind. Gananny and Ailey, whom I had completely forgotten, were turning in the laneway after us. And I could see all the rest of life streaming away from us, sidelining us into a pocket of disgrace.

'Congo, you eejit,' Frieda said. 'We won't win a prize now.'

Congo said nothing. Empty chip-shop bags rustled in the breeze of the lane. Stiffened by dried out salt and vinegar, the noise of them made the donkey sharpen his ears in fear. Congo took a firm hold of the reins, steering us carefully down the rocky lane. The sound of our cartwheels bounced off the walls on either side. The donkey picked its way over the ground and the cart shook so that our crockery came tumbling from the sideboard. Then Ailey said she was about to drop child number 12 anyway and Gananny let a quick squeeze out of his accordion, and we all laughed and laughed. I laughed until I thought it was possible that I might forget forever what had just taken place. I laughed until I became one with the others, until I had emptied my mind of the voices I had heard in the crowd, separating me from the rest of the Cartys because of where I came from – a Connell-Connaughton of Ivyhall Castle – and then we went to Frieda's to untackle the ass. And while the rest of the parade continued to the sports field for the prize-giving, we played House. 'Real House,' as Gananny said, when he and Ailey came out of the back room afterwards, all red and sleepy looking. Real house. Frieda and me had been playing it in the front room. Real house was putting real sugar in real sugar bowls, drinking real tea and looking at real ornaments on the tiny mantelpiece over the hearth of Frieda's tiny sitting room, real Mammy Frieda heating real buns in the oven for real Daddy me sitting on a little low armchair, and Congo doing gooseberry outside for the return of real, very real, Roundy and Mrs Roundy Ryan.

Once, Frieda came very close to me and I saw the white of her skin underneath her dress. Her breath was warm. I smelled face powder. The world went silent. The clock, standing on its three fat legs on the mantelpiece overhead, so merrily ticking its little heart out until that moment, seemed to stop and go dumb, all other sound too fading into nothingness.

It was a cosy little house, much cosier than Ivyhall.

Two things ended House. On the day after the fancy-dress parade, Mam drove me to Frieda's house. She stopped outside her door. 'Shall we say hello to your future family now?' she said. Then, as if contemplating something really tragic, she sighed. 'Because soon we'll be gone to boarding-school and we'll have to kiss them good-bye.' I said nothing. Then she drove on.

The other thing that ended House was the loss of my postman, Stack Straw.

That really was the goodbye kiss to the Carty family.

7

School at Wolfdyke had seemed to go along without change for years. For months anyway. Uneventful . . . All Wolfdyke's classes stuffed into two rooms: the Master's, the Mistress's. All its features permanent; same walls, same desks. And same faces; Stack Straw's was one of them. Life had taken on a sameness.

Of course, with Frieda around, danger was never far away. Yet even the danger had about it a smell that was always the same. Life was about Frieda and me and our sidekick, Stanisclaus Straw and that smell of danger and nothing else. And then Mam stopped the car outside Frieda's door that day and said, 'Shall we say hello to your future family?' That was the beginning of the big change, the big change in everything. The loss of Stack made the change complete. The last day of my postman.

Stack Straw was not very good at school. He certainly was not stupid, but he was so rarely in school that he didn't have much chance of improvement. He lived in the miners' homes. His father, Pop Straw, was someone everybody wagged fingers at. He was never seen sober. Owing to an illness from his days working in the mines, he was not seen much at all. But whenever he did get up the town, ten minutes in a pub was enough to make him drunk. A small man, with flapping coats, then he stomped about town like an angry little bull.

Stack had to work for his mother and father. He also did jobs for farmers. Every Sunday he walked out to Ivyhall. He had a grinning face which gave the impression that everything he saw was funny, he had black teeth that had never been brushed and he always had a letter in his pocket from Frieda to me. I greeted his Sunday arrivals with a great whoosh of pleasure.

Everybody liked Stack. Even Gimp Flynn liked him. The Master did not like me. He made it a policy not to like the children whose parents had money; my brothers and me must have looked as if ours had more than their share. He made it a policy to like Stack.

Then I got Frieda, and Stack became my postman and my most important friend.

After I had spent a few months in seventh class, doing business sums and writing job applications alongside the boys with big Adam's apples, the Master decided to put me into fifth. This was not demotion. The scholarship class, he called it. From fifth you went to sixth and then you did the scholarship. The fellows in seventh stayed in seventh and never did anything. Even though the Master never tired of telling them that he would get them somewhere, that in spite of themselves, whether it would be in the *gardaí* or whatever, that he would get them jobs, very few of them ever seemed to leave. Gananny, Meagher, big Lawlor, big Considine and so on, they just stayed there, doing jobs for the Master and learning, over and over, multiplication tables. The sort of jobs they did for the Master were such as cleaning out and lighting the fire. Or getting rid of fart smells. Or F smells, as the Master called them. This was done by heating the coffee lid at the fire. A boy would heap a spoon of Maxwell House on the lid and heat it, then he would walk round the room, the heated coffee lid held in the claws of the tongs, a mound of burning Maxwell House on it to kill the bad smells. And all this time the Master would be loudly complaining: 'Pigs, there are dirty pigs in this room, control your innards.' And the boy would be swaying that coffee lid, the black smoke that rose from it exorcising the place every bit as efficiently as a priest and his thurible in the act of Benediction.

A day arrived when Stack, who had been in fourth, went straight into seventh. Skipped fifth and sixth, the scholarship class, entirely.

'Take a bow, Sir Stanisclaus,' the Master said, 'you have been elevated to the upper echelons.'

This was the sort of treatment Stack received all of the time from the Master. Stack never knew whether to take it seriously or not. We all laughed, relieved to see old Gimp in a good mood. Patch-in-the-trousers Competition, the Master announced every now and again on a Friday. 'Take a bow, Sir Stanisclaus, you have won again, sir.' And Stack had to bow and show off his patch, never sure whether Gimp was serious or laughing at him.

The Master was serious of course. Stack always received ten boiled sweets for his prize. It was a competition I could never win. It was the Master's way of balancing things. But it was a pity Stack had to sing so for his money.

A day arrived, though, when Stack did not sing. It was an important day for Stack because that day he left school never to return. And an important day for me because I lost my postman.

Connaughton drove my brothers and me to school that day. I remember that because we were early, very early. We were always early when he drove us because he had a million places to travel off to and we had to be got out of the way first. Driving us to school was Mam's regular job, but this morning Connaughton had said no to her. She was suffering with her knee. It was the complaint that first made itself noticed that day she limped from the car in Limerick and from time to time ever after returned to bother her.

There was not a sound in the yard when we arrived. Then a few fellows stirred themselves in corners of the shed, fellows from out the bog direction; it was like they were waking themselves from a night spent in the yard. A few crows in the elm tree above us were stirring themselves in the same way. It was wintry, still dark in the sky. Then Teddy Holland walked across the yard with the electric heater under his arm to plug into the Mistress's room. The Mistress was his mother. He did this job every morning, walking up the street with the bars of the heater still glowing from having made the toast in his own kitchen. Holland was the brightest boy in the school. He was not liked by most people – too smart for his own good, they said – but I liked him. He made me laugh. He always had something to say.

On this particular day, Teddy Holland announced the end of the world.

'It's dark,' he said to me. 'This is the third day's darkness now. This is the end of the world.'

'What are you talking about?' said I. Anything Holland said was interesting and I wanted to know more.

'My mother has this notion that three days' darkness is a sure sign the end of the world is nigh.'

Holland was a strange mixture: cynical of everything, and yet he came out with these old stories of his mother's. In fact, to see him walk down the street with his mother after school was a comical sight. She, as wide as a barrel, weighted down with bags of copy-books for corrections; he, sharp as a flint, having to walk alongside her with the electric heater. His father, a teacher also, had left his mother. Now he taught in some other part of the country. By all accounts he was an unusual man. His name was Ted Ash. His mother did not want young Teddy to become like his father, so she changed his name from Ash to Holland, her own name.

Then he told me about the American presidential election. It was being run that very day: according to Saint Somebody or other, his mother had said, American election day always ran a good chance of being Doomsday.

It was then that, between the two of us, we hatched up the idea that it was the end of the world. It was not, as it turned out, but it was the end of Stack Straw's school days.

The end of the world was not something new to us. Every now and then the scare of it ran through the school. There needed only to be the whiff of a rumour of it and it was off like wildfire. And Holland was the one who fanned the flames. I had only to keep my nerve and agree with what he said. End of the world, he said. Twelve noon, today.

238

'End of the world,' Holland said, and, in a flash, fellows walking their dozy ways to school were wide awake.

'Did you hear that?' the shouts ran across the yard from one pupil to another: 'The prophecy of Saint Malachy. The sun dancing in the sky.'

In no time, boys were coming into the yard having already heard the rumour before they had even got there. 'Heard it up the town. End of the world. Twelve o'clock today.'

Gussie Quirke came in; an excitable fellow was Gussie, who sweated all the time, and who did jobs for the Master, but mostly got slaps for his troubles. 'Mullally's cows is up on the top of Mullally's Hill. A sure sign. Out of the way of the flood.'

Another story beat Gussie's: 'All the French people is driving up Mont Blanc out of the tidal wave, did you hear that!'

Fellows were swearing our time was up. It sounded so true I had to remind myself where the rumour had sprung from. When big Lawlor and big Considine turned up in the yard they went around pucking fellows, saying: 'Who the fuck told you 'twas the end of the world? I'll bet a pound with you that it's not.'

'Huhu, get lost, Lawlor,' Meagher said. 'And how is a fellow to collect his winnings from you if it is the end of the world?'

Lawlor pucked him.

'Get lost, here's Gimp,' Meagher said.

Then the Master, pinching his moustache, turned up. Everything went quiet, we all filed into class and once the door was closed lessons proceeded as hushed as normal.

Tiny Gimp Flynn, for he was tiny, had a way of puffing his cheeks as if he suffered from some internal freeze-up. He was always cold. It was that constant coldness about him that ensured the hush in his room. Even Lawlor and Considine, who towered above him, would not utter a peep out of turn. Only Holland was disrespectful of the Master.

Everybody said the Master was a great teacher. Holland and myself were his star pupils. We sat together in the scholarship desk. Those two will get schols, everybody said. But Holland did not give a damn for him and laughed behind his back.

'Go out to Cleary and get the ten'clock news. See would he have results of the election.' The Master leaned over me to get at

Holland. Holland ran Gimp's important errands.

Every half hour Holland had to run out to Cleary's the news-agent. And every time he returned he whispered, 'No news yet, sir.' Then, as soon as the Master was not looking, he pointed at his watch. It was to indicate to the class the passage of time and the hastening of the world to its end at twelve o'clock.

'Fuck off, Brains,' Lawlor mouthed each time he pointed at the watch. A strange thing that – big Lawlor, the man who was dying to be off to England, was afraid.

At eleven on our loud clock above the wall map, the door opened and Stack Straw slapped in on his floppy wellingtons. Stack always wore wellingtons. They made his thin legs look even thinner.

'What kept you, Stack?' the Master said.

'Ah, ah.' Stack always suffered a stutter when he spoke to the Master. 'Isn't it the La-La-La-Last Day, sir?'

Stack took everybody's breath away: here was the concern which had been occupying all our minds, and Stack had brought it out in the open. And we all knew it was not the sort of stuff the Master warmed to.

He pinched his moustache. 'And why should the last day hold you up from school?'

'Hadn't I to collect Mrs Cantwell's eggs, sir.'

'Mrs Cantwell's eggs or her hens' eggs?' We all laughed. It was best to laugh at the Master's jokes.

'Ha, ha, her hens' eggs,' Stack says earnestly. 'Didn't they lay them in the river.'

'Mrs Cantwell's hens, are they water hens? Would that be why they lay them in the river?'

We all waited for Stack to say something else the Master might be amused by. Gimp knocked out a lot of fun at Stack's expense, which was strange, considering he liked him.

Stack looked around the class, fear showing on his face. 'Di-di-didn't they lay them down by the river on account of it being the Last Day, sir? Mrs Cantwell toe-toe-told me it was.'

'The last day, Stack?'

'The La-La-La-Last Day, sir. The Mistress got her class out to confessions on account of it. Didn't I see them goin' up to the church and I comin' in. Are we goin' to confessions, sir?'

Everybody quaked; the Master hated us wasting time on confessions.

'Come up here, Stack. I'll give you confession now.'

And that was it. Stack gets two slaps and sits huddled at his desk, and nurses his bruised hands between his bony knees while the rest of us do lessons and await the end of the world at twelve o'clock.

During morning break we went out in the yard and looked up at the grey sky. The omens were not good. Lawlor and Considine trapped Gussie Quirke in a corner and beat him up for saying that the Antichrist was on the way. 'You don't know what you're fuckin' sayin',' Lawlor said. 'Antichrist is a deadly word and your arse will be hot in hell for sayin' it.' Then we trooped back in.

At twenty-five minutes to twelve a tremor was heard somewhere outside. It rippled through the classroom and the windowpanes rattled. I was frightened.

'What's that? Is that it?' I whispered to Holland, taken in by my own rumour.

But he was sagely shaking his head, nodding up at the clock for the benefit of whoever was watching him. And one of those watching was Stack, whose face had gone even whiter than usual.

Then the Master sent out Holland for the twelve o'clock news.

Thirteen minutes to go. The tremor was felt again. The windowpanes shivered. Somebody explained what the noise was: 'Blasting in the colliery'. The whisper went round the classroom. 'Blasting'.

Yet a strange feeling had taken hold of the room, and it would not go away.

We listened for more blasting. Everything sounded normal. The creamery lorry passed up, jingling a little with the noise of empty churns. A sound of sticks came from outside. Sticks breaking and falling through branches; the crows at work on the elm tree.

Then the clock wound up for its twelve o'clock chimes. Then: *dong, dong, dong* . . . The clock was tolling the knell of our parting lives. Louder fell each dong upon our bowed heads. And then it stopped. And all went into suspension. *Tick tock.* Nobody looked up. Was this how the world stopped? One eternal silence? Then came the loud noise.

It clanged right across above our heads. The rattle of the world breaking at its seams. The heavens renting open. Everybody startled.

But it was not the noise of the end of the world. Almost immediately I knew that. It was something rolling across the corrugated roof. However he had done it, Holland was behind it. It was not an end-of-the-world noise.

But Stack thought it was. He jumped from his desk and coming down again he missed his seat and fell on the floor.

The Master stood up from where he had been seated with his back to the fire. He gave a few sniffs of his nose. 'Coffee and coffee lid,' he said to Gussie Quirke. 'Heat it up.' Surely he didn't think the noise on the roof was the sound of someone letting off Fs. There was shaking going on now in the desks. Suppressed laughter. The Master looked at Stack in a heap on the floor. Then Holland walked in. Innocence itself, but with a little smirky grin he could not manage to hide. And he whispered the twelve o'clock news to the Master. And the faltering world steadied itself and continued on its merry round.

I saw the look of triumph. I saw it slowly grow across the Master's face. He smoothed his moustache.

'Yes sir, yes sir, more coffee, sir, for the Fs.' Gussie was waving the coffee incense above Stack's head, swaying it above him until it seemed he was smouldering. 'Pigs in the room, sir' – like a parrot, Gussie always repeated the Master's words.

Whatever Holland had told the Master, he still bore the triumphant grin on his face. 'Sit down, Gussie Quirke,' he said. He looked at us all then for some time, studying our faces in a strange way. I wondered what he could be up to.

'Stand up, Gananny.' he said in the end.

Gananny stood up.

'Up straight, Gananny.'

Lanky Gananny tried to stand straight, but couldn't manage to get the kinks out of himself and became stuck in his desk.

'Sit down, Gananny, you won't amount to much in life. I'll make something out of you. A Garda Síochána maybe, God help us, but you'll never do in the White House.' He shook his head in disappointment. 'Stand up, Gussie Quirke.'

Gussie shot up. He was sweating all over his face.

But the Master shook his head again. 'Won't do either, I'm afraid. What about a waterworks officer?' The Master was slyly reminding us of a day he had caught Gussie pissing over the wall of the girls' school. 'Would you like a job on the waterworks?'

'Yes, sir.'

'Sit down.'

What was the Master up to? He was looking all round the class. He even looked at me, but I looked away. As I always did. While wondering what it could be he was thinking he might make of me.

Finally his gaze fell on Stack where he lay, still spread out on the floor.

He stood above him. 'Arise, Sir Stanisclaus,' he said. 'Take your place at the head of the class so we can have a good look at you.'

This wasn't fair. He was picking on Stack again. Stack's face was set in puzzled concentration. I felt sorry for him. I thought he'd taken enough for one day.

Stack wouldn't rise. 'I didn't do it, sir. I didn't.'

'Do what, Sir Stanisclaus?'

'Do nothin', sir, do the Last Day.'

'You do not stand accused, Stack. "Take your rightful place among the nations of the Earth." Who was it said that?'

'The F sir, I didn't do it.'

'There are plenty of pigs in this room, Sir Stanisclaus. But you are not one of them. Do you think President–elect John F. Kennedy would have wasted his time making a pig of himself when he was in school? He would not. Up to the top of the class.'

Stack rose then. The Master caught his arm. This time, instead of slapping it, he rose it above his head. I heard it creak in its socket. 'Salute the champ,' he said, as if he was hailing a victorious boxer.

Stack was not sure what to do, so he gave that puzzled smile of his. He could never be sure of whether or not the Master was making fun of him. His wellingtons squeaked together.

'Behold, gentlemen, an honest man. Today, gentlemen, while we may have pigs in our schoolhouse, we have had an Irishman elected to the White House. Can we believe it? And now I ask you to behold a future Irishman in the White House. A future President of the United States of America.' He stood proudly alongside Stack.

Gimp was not making fun of Stack. I knew it. Holland was shaking his head as if he had gone mad. But I knew he was serious.

Stack did not see it that way. 'I'm not listening to ya. Ya, ya needn't think you're makin' a foo-fool of me,' he said.

In the hushed gasp that followed I was amazed to hear my own voice. Maybe it was because I felt what was happening was my fault. I was responsible for the Last Day. 'Listen to him, Stack,' I said. 'He's not making a fool of you.'

'I won't. 'Cause he won't lave me alone. I'm goin' home and not comin' back.' He pulled his arm out of the Master's hand and as he ran by me to get his bag I felt the snot-weighted sleeve of his pullover brush against my ear.

The Master did nothing. He just stood there as Stack, suddenly in tears, passed before him again.

'May-may-makin' a fuckin' eejit outa me, Gimp,' he said. He fumbled at the door handle but the door wouldn't open and his schoolbag fell. 'You can't do that to no-no one.' Once he had got the door opened he ran out sobbing. 'Foolin' with me all the time. And all the rest of ye too. La-la-laughin' at me all the time. Ye needn't laugh. I'll get ye.' His words wailed back as he passed through the Infants classroom. 'It wasn't me made the fu-fuckin' fart.'

The Master puffed his cold cheeks. They looked more wizened than ever. Then he fumbled beneath his desk and pulled out the boiled sweets. 'Straw, Straw, come back.' He held the sweets foolishly before him. Stack was gone.

He sat down then until lunchtime.

That was why he blamed himself for what happened next.

All of them, Witheroe, my father, Mam, Dancie, were in the kitchen, smoking and looking distracted.

'Gimp Flynn looked very shook too,' Witheroe was saying. 'Blames himself for it all.'

They had just returned from a funeral and it sounded like it had been a very sad occasion. Mam had been talking about the boy's father, who had also looked very shook. About the piteous sight he was, as he had tried to throw himself on the grave.

Then Witheroe had said that the same man was mad with drink all his lifetime anyway and that losing his son like that would only drive him over the top altogether. 'He can go bury himself now too,' he said.

'Why Mr Flynn?' Mam returned to Witheroe's earlier comment. 'Why should he put the blame on himself?'

Nobody seemed to know the answer to that. Connaughton just said if anyone was to be blamed it was a system that let a young lad leave school to straightaway go to work down a mine. Or else to go to England, where people only got lost like young Christopher. I think Connaughton said that without giving himself time to consider Witheroe's feelings. It was the sort of thing he would be sorry for having said afterwards. Witheroe, because of the funeral, only nodded in agreement.

They all thought privately for a few seconds. Maybe they were thinking about how our schoolmaster could be to blame, and then Mam came up with this question for me and I could see she had come the nearest to the answer.

'Did the Master hunt Stack out of that schoolhouse?' she asked, amazing me once again at how quickly she got to the root of things.

I didn't know whether or not she was expecting an answer from me, but she didn't get one.

This sad day had come shortly after the time the hitchhiker had left. Nobody knew why Harry left. His room had become the feeding house again. Two days previous to the funeral, Witheroe had walked into the feeding house and told me about the accident that caused Stack's death. 'Oh,' I had said. Just 'Oh.'

It had been six months or so since Stack's last day of school, six months since I'd spoken to him. Once, as the miners' bus passed by I had seen him looking out its grimy window. He had waved at me and I had waved back. His smile shone right through the window. The first shock that now came to my mind was not of Stack's death but of how in such a short period away from him he had already become a distant figure in my life.

Witheroe told me about the trolley car in the mine shaft. How Stack didn't have a chance, hit by a runaway. He told me about runaway trolley cars, how he was nearly killed by one himself.

They rolled along underground rails, loaded with coal, and sometimes they ran out of control. 'Ugly-looking fuckers. Made of solid
cast iron.' I had a picture of a runaway train. Then Witheroe
became suddenly mad and kicked a bag of beet pulp to the feeding
house floor, one of those big loose bags from the sugar company,
and when it only flopped to the floor and did not spill he kicked it
again. 'Young lads should never be let down that pit. That he may
shiver and fuckin' quake, that bastard Donoghue, and starve and
die.' Donoghue was the mine foreman. I had never seen Witheroe
mad like this before but I didn't think about that. I just looked at the
writing on the bag of beet pulp that Witheroe had kicked. I was
absently reading it, 'Cowhlucht Siúicre Éireann'. *Siúicre*, that means
'sugar'. A song was running in my head:

> Hello Pasty Fagan, you can hear the girls all cry,
> Hello Patsy Fagan, you're the apple of my eye . . .
> You're a decent boy from Ireland, there's no one can deny
> You're a harum scarum devil may carum decent Irish boy . . .

I was making promises to myself, all sorts of promises: promising
myself to learn the rest of that song; promising myself to remember
Stack, never again to lose him from before me. Promising myself all
sorts of things . . . to remember the two 'i's in the word *siúicre* if I
had to spell it in the scholarship exam for boarding-school.

8

Sometimes you got a chance to think. I had a bad dose of Frieda-itis – that was what Bunny called it. I hadn't seen her for weeks. I had no way of contacting her. The other girls said she was kept at home to study. Frieda, where are you? Where are your letters? Stack is gone. I am up in Farpark.

If ever there was a place for thinking, it was up on the back of Ivyhall. You were on the high moor then, overlooking all the countryside. You could burn your heart away thinking about Frieda and when that was done you could think of other things. Sound carried up there. The sunshine was sharper, picking up everything in its light. Any tractor or jeep climbing over the fields, you could see approaching for miles. Even the sound of horses carried up there. You could hear the snorts of a chain of cantering horses, hear the bridles jangle, the reins come unstuck from sweaty necks. Every now and again a sound clattered up from below – an empty milk churn hitting a cement yard; a dog's yelp. The activity of the floor of the world, with people's little helpless shouts coming from various corners of it. It reached you up there, but yet you were cut off from it. You had become absorbed within the sound of constantly springing water as it soaked back into the earth. You could be feeling sorry for yourself, enjoying, at the same time, how alone you felt.

Those were the thoughts passing through my mind up in Farpark. When I stood up to go my trousers were all wet behind from the soft ground I had been sitting on. I sauntered at first on my way homeward, and then I found myself quickening, my feet carried from under me by the downhill flow, quickening. Stop it, I said. Go back to the top of Ivyhall. Something was rushing me, panicking me downward. Was that the day, just as I had begun to recognise something I loved, the solitude at the core of its being, that I had already begun to say goodbye to Ivyhall?

I sang to slow myself down.

I sang my Ten All-time Greatest Tipperary Hit Songs.

I had other thoughts: I had done badly in all my exams. The sums were too hard; I couldn't write the essays. Would I fail? How could I have done so hopelessly? Words rang in my ears. 'Boarding-school for you, boy. Away from the distractions in the cottages.'

By the time I reached the wicket gate at the Deerpark, I was galloping. My songs had lifted my spirits, I bounded over heather banks, breathed musky gorse; I felt the earthy thump of the sod beneath me. I was dancing across the high roof of all beginnings. Boarding-school was for me and I was willing.

Bunny stood at the wicket gate, waiting for milking time. 'Woah, horse,' he said. 'What's your sweat?'

'I'm Ronnie Delaney,' I said. 'In the Olympics.'

'Yeh. And I'm Jack Dempsey the boxer. Take this.'

He knocked the wind out of me with a puck in the solar plexus.

PART 4

1

‘Hanging, sir?’ I said.
‘Yes, hanging.’

It was my first day of boarding-school. The teacher had a gruff voice and a long, hooked nose. He had caught me loitering out by the door.

‘Don’t ever let me catch anybody hanging out of this door,’ the gruff voice said.

‘Hanging?’ I made a noose of my hands around my neck and let my tongue hang out.

‘Yes, hanging. What’s your name, funny man?’

‘Lally Connaughton.’

‘You have made an immediate impression on me, Connaughton. Make one further impression on me over the course of the next five years and I will make a lasting one on you.’

I sat down. I had made a good start to my boarding-school career. The halls were huge, the corridors were long, hordes of boys bashed about in queues, in the junior dormitory lay rows of beds, silent as gravestones. But I had made an immediate impression.

I got myself out of Woody's class as quick as I could. The 1A class. Woody, that was hook-nose's name. We knew already that first day. I knew he meant what he said. I said I didn't have enough brains for the class I had been put into and I got into an easier one. 1B. Then I was able to settle down. I didn't have to work hard to keep up and that suited me fine.

I was delighted with the place. Sometimes I got lonely but there were so many fellows like myself and it was such a new life and there were no more calves to feed, no more squealing mealy-faced pigs. Instead there were handball alleys and soccer. Yes, soccer, which I only read about in comics or when I read the sports results in the newspaper: Spurs, Wolves, Arsenal and Everton. Those fantastic names wherein dwelt a world of heroes: especially Everton. I had come across Everton one day in Ivyhall. Behind the castle, on the dump, where newspapers, tin cans, eggshells lay strewn beneath the cinders. A newspaper headline. It caught my eye. I went down on my knees to read it: 'Everton Tame Wolves'. What a headline! And now here I was, playing this game. Every moment I could. Out on the frosty tarmac before breakfast, soles of our shoes slapping off the ground; out again after tea, our shouts ringing in the dusk: 'Keep the ball on the ground. Don't handle it, you bogman. Pass. Pass, you prick. Slide it across the box, lad. Goal. Everton one up!'

To think I had been threatened with this place.

I had homework. I got into all sorts of trouble. I had hours and hours in the study hall. But in between it would always be Everton. Everton one up.

It had been a trying old summer.

'Your father and me are very disappointed with you,' Mam said. At least it was Mam had said it. I would die if it was he had said it. But he never said things like that. Oh he would shout, but that was OK. You got over that. He didn't give personal instructions. Not since the old days of the pony in the gardens behind the hotel and then the reading lessons had I any instruction from Connaughton. 'Your father and me know you can do better in school. We thought you would win a scholarship.'

Oh how could I have won a scholarship, Mam? When every scholarship exam I sat, there was Frieda sitting just a few rows away from me. As lively as that last day I had spoken to her, the day of the fancy dress. And every time I looked up to think out answers, where should my eyes wander? And I was unable, in the frantic sound of scribbling pens, to utter a word. And no postman Stack to run messages, to mend the breakdown. Once at a schol' exam in Clonmel, Frieda sat and wrote for the whole three hours. And I felt neglected as could be. And I failed. Holy God, I even failed the Primary Cert! How could I have achieved such failure. Frieda was giggling into her exam paper all through the Primary Cert. She had got her hair done in special curls which I hated. Even some of the fellows in seventh got that exam. Now they could become shop assistants in Thurles. Holland got the scholarship. Frieda got the scholarship. But not me.

'You'd better improve in boarding-school, my man. We are paying for it! No distractions in boarding-school,' Mam said. 'No holidays for the Cartys in boarding-school.'

I burned up when she said that. She was a bitch. How could she bring up the Cartys' summer holidays now. She came out with things when you were at your weakest.

That day driving off to boarding-school: I had a suitcase of new clothes. New smelling. Football boots. Jerseys. A pair of long trousers – Mam had put that in the case too. I said nothing about it, deciding to myself that I would not wear them. I would continue to wear short trousers. I was not about to become a little man like Richie. Everybody stood at the door and looked at me as I left. A tinge of something passed through me all right. Especially when I saw my old dogs as we drove down the lane. All faithful-looking and sad-faced. Goodbye Ivyhall. Hello Waterford. Hello a place called Mont La Salle. A college. What is it like there? I was a new man and I was speechless. Not the lad who twittered to Auntie Tessa and made her laugh when he went down to close the gate after her. Not the skylark in the air. Not the lad who made anybody laugh. Only Mam and me in the car. Very serious business.

Somewhere along the road Mam made a swerve. I still remember exactly where it was. We had been driving alongside the river. It was wide and brown and I was imagining myself sailing on it. It was the Huckleberry Finn river. The old Mississippi. I was rafting along with faithful Jim to some unknown destination. Then the river took a turn. The road took a turn too. And the car was swerving round it and something flashed open. I felt a wind and saw the roadway jump up to say hello to me. God, it was travelling. Hello road, I said in resignation. But something was pulling me back. And I was upright in the car again, the scalp lifting off me and Mam holding lumps of my hair in her fist.

When she steadied the car out of the crazy road-staggers it had gone into when she'd had to let go the wheel, she stopped. She leaned across me and pulled shut my door. Her arm was shaking. 'Were you trying to escape on me?' she said.

'Thanks,' I said.

At Mooncoin Mam said, 'There's a song Granny sings. It's called "The Rose of Mooncoin". I'd love you to learn it off for me.' We had gone through the place before I even noticed it. There had been a tall church I imagined the Rose of Mooncoin might have gone to. But that seemed to be all there was. 'The Rose of Mooncoin,' I said.

She was pointing out all sorts of places for me now. There was a small house with a square porch. On top of the porch was a statue of a man's head. He wore a riding cap, or coachman's cap. 'A murderer once lived in that house,' she said. Since she had hauled me back in the car somewhere beyond the merchant houses of Carrick-on-Suir, she was becoming a regular chatterbox. I, a very good talker, was even finding it hard to keep up with her. So I listened, and then, all of a sudden, she comes out with this one: 'My old home where I grew up is near these parts, Lally.' She had straightened her back, lifting herself at the wheel as she said it, at the same time making it seem casual. And because she had made it seem casual like that I pretended not to be surprised. But I was. Very. Why was I so surprised? Why should it never have occurred to me that Mam had once upon a time grown up; once upon a time known another home? I looked at her: Well, what a friendly soul, I suddenly thought. And I thought something nice was about to happen and I wanted her to tell me all about where she came from.

She didn't. Instead, she went in another direction entirely. She brought up the 'Rose of Mooncoin' again.

'Your mother sang it. That was her special song. I often heard her sing it on the radio.' Mam had never mentioned my mother before in all her life, and now she comes out with this. What had taken hold of her?

My heart leaped. 'Who?' I said vaguely, as though I did not know the person she was talking about. It was easiest if I were to give her the impression that this person was somebody so distant, so far away, of such insignificance to me, that she was not worth talking about. And I must have succeeded because she said no more on the subject.

Then the river became very wide. Our road, alongside it, widened also. Sunlight was falling on it, all the way. My new home lay along that road. There was no topic now that would come into our heads, nothing that would fill the wide spaces that appeared before us. We were going down a hill. The city was coming up and I was suffering from butterflies in the belly. It was too late to jump out of the car. I felt like leaning in close to Mam. It was too late for that also. Anyhow, she was too big, too powerful, for that kind of thing.

Helter-skelter, up and down the five flights of stairs. A Brother went up before me the first time. He hitched up his soutane. He wore rubber-soled sandals that made no noise on the stairs. 'I'll show you our grade A hotel.' He swung his legs, two steps at a time, his soutane catching at his knees. My suitcase swung in his hand. 'Where are you from? Tipperary. Ah the Cork lads will show ye how to hurl.'

After each landing I looked back and saw the houses of the city getting smaller below me. So he was from Cork. Cork didn't seem that bad after all. What could I say to him? Was he a teacher or what did he do? 'Tipperary are the best,' I said, standing on the dizzy heights of the top landing and it sounded like a whisper.

Boys were folding clothes on top of beds. One boy was crying and the others were ignoring him. Fellows wanted to show me different places.

'Come on. What's your locker number? We'll show you your

desk in the study hall. Show you where your locker is. There's a church. It's all part of the one big house, imagine. Dining room. It's called the refectory. Show you everything.'

A tall fellow said: 'You, squirt with the short trousers, you can come with us.'

I looked around. I was the only one, apart from the boy who was crying, in short trousers. I joined the helter-skelter of boys: we started off as two or three.

'One hundred and one beds in this dorm, I counted them,' somebody shouted with amazing confidence.

We skidded along the centre aisle of the dormitory. Up and down the stairs; a flight at either end of the dormitory. Long silent corridors on each floor. By nightfall we were hunting in a pack of ten. The tall fellow seemed to be in charge. His name was Kelly-Jackson. In time I would get to know him well.

'Anybody see Snowflake?' he asked every now and then. Once he spotted a little fellow. This little fellow had white hair and white eyelashes. 'There he is, the little rat, kill him,' he said.

'His name is Chalky and not Snowflake,' somebody else said.

'No, he's Snowflake,' said Kelly-Jackson. 'After him.' He ran after Chalky. Chalky was terrified and ran into the church.

'Leave him alone,' somebody said, 'he's an albino.'

We continued our hunt about the building. It was late at night before the whistles started to blow and the Brothers to clap hands. They sorted us in rows, and quick march, led us off in procession. Up the stairs again, this time to bed. It was the end of freedom. But by then I knew where every place was. Wash before bed: I had a quick glimpse of a face in the line of mirrors at the wash-hand basins; one among the white-faced row, with toothbrushes sticking from mouths. I hardly recognised myself. I found the long trousers in my case. I took them out and laid them at the end of my bed for wear next morning. Mam, I had to concede, had her good points. She had saved my life on the road and now she had saved it again.

The fellow who had been crying was called Chesty. (Richard Duff, actually, but after one day it had already become Chesty.) He was little, with blotched skin, crinkly hair and a wheezy chest. His bed was alongside mine and every night he whimpered with homesickness. He gave me the idea that maybe I should get homesickness also. And so I lay there in my bed with the lamps of the city lightening the dark, the rubber soles of the Brother pad-padding as he patrolled up and down the aisle behind my head, and I thought of Ivyhall. I succeeded in making myself unimaginably miserable. I started by thinking of Ivyhall, but somehow that did not do the trick. Mam somehow did not fit the bill either. Now if I was Richie, I thought. Maybe then I might cry for her. But what is a stepmother? What are you supposed to feel for a stepmother? It was the first time ever, I think, that I truly pondered the stepmother idea. Then I thought of my mother. I'd had a mother. I had not thought of her in a long time. Once upon a time, back in the hotel, and then for a while in the secret parts of Ivyhall, my mother haunted me. Out of nowhere, I would suddenly feel her presence. She would begin to take form, right before my eyes. Ready to start telling me things. Poor Mama, she could never get enough of me. But I never gave her time to reappear, I ran away in terror. Now was a good time to think of her and before I knew it she had returned to me with feeling. My guardian angel. I brought myself to tears. For a few nights she came to me like that. It was very lonely for both of us. In the end I had to stop it. I began to get letters from home. Each week a letter from Mam, and surprisingly, sometimes with the orangy glow of a ten shilling note in it.

A man with thick black-rimmed glasses and Brylcreemed hair sat on a high rostrum at the top of the refectory. For dessert every day he ate prunes and we counted them, twenty-eight, twenty-nine, thirty prunes, our heads lowered to our tables, pretending not to look, as he spooned them into his mouth and then slipped out the stones onto his spoon like brown spits. He banged on a bell when he wanted attention. He told us he was the Dean of Discipline. His nickname was Discharge. Fellows said he would let off thirty discharges if he had thirty prunes for dinner.

One afternoon in first term I had a visit. I was out on the playing fields among the horde of footballers that followed every puck of the ball up and down on its travels through the field. The playing fields were down by the river. Those boys who were uninterested in the game looked over the river, and in parts where it was a mud-flat they plonked rocks, laughing at the slapping sounds the rocks made. 'Sunk it,' they shouted at the echoes of emptiness left behind when rocks were sucked beneath. Or they tried to skim stones across to Clover Meats, the factory on the far side. The smell of the factory blew across our low lying playing fields.

I was interested in the river but even more interested in the game. This afternoon I was one of the swarm of boys surrounding the ball. I think Discharge had been calling me for a while but I hadn't heard. Maybe it was because he hadn't been getting my attention that he joined in the game. He never needed much excuse anyway. This is Discharge and football: one second he's on the sideline, the next he's letting a roar: 'My ball, my ball,' he calls, his arms high in the air, his hands clapping for the ball, the gold watchstrap wobbling on his wrist. 'Give it to me.' He pulls off the thick specs, yanks up the soutane and then, like a bulldozer, he is in among us, knocking boys to left and right, his bib crackling with starch as it crumples against us. 'And that Kerry great, Joe Keohane, gets his first touch of the ball. Will he go for a goal?' The bib jerks against his bulging neck. After a moment or two, in which he plays first for one team and then for the other, he shouts that he has been fouled. 'Who fouled me?' Now who could possibly foul Discharge? Who would foul a big Kerry Dean of Discipline?

Discharge looks all around him. 'Fouled by Kelly-Jackson,' he announces. Kelly-Jackson was the tallest boy in first year. And the best-looking, his hair combed back in a way that I was attempting to copy. KJ had already been marked out by Discharge as number one trouble-maker in first year.

'I didn't foul you, Brother,' says Kelly-Jackson.

'Less lip out of you when you're talking to the ref,' Discharge says.

He takes his free. 'Inches wide,' he says as it cracks into the trees surrounding the private garden of one of the big houses along the river. It was miles wide.

Then he remembered me: 'Lally Connaughton, a visitor for you in the visiting room. Take off you football boots before you go in.'

There was a hush for a moment as everybody considered the idea of a visitor for me. Every now and then boys received visits. Each time a visitor arrived everybody knew about it. The school term had been only two weeks old when, one evening that we were in the study hall, Discharge walked up behind the white-haired boy called Declan Skelly – Chalky – and whispered that he had a visitor. Then, when Chalky had walked down the study hall, everybody looking at him, and walked through the swing door at the end, Discharge cleared his throat and boomed out, 'Let us kneel and say a decade of the rosary for the repose of the soul of Declan Skelly's mother who died today.'

Chalky came from County Donegal, far away as could be. His walk down the study hall that day was to create an aura of loneliness around him which was never to leave him. Not even when he was in fifth year and was larrupping the Brylcreem on his white hair, slicking it back lardy and yellowed.

Now here was I, drawn from the hub of activity, the eyes of everybody following me as I left the field, wondering was something like that about to happen to me.

But it was Mam. She kissed me. It happened so quickly and then it was done. I was amazed she was so pleased to see me. Not since the day she kissed the Little Yank on his way to America had I seen her kiss anybody. I had given a little jump towards her. I was amazed that I was so pleased to see her also and at the flow of warmth that came over me. Just goes to show you, I said to myself, how naturally things can happen once you let yourself go. She stayed ages talking to me, laughing as she related the antics of Connaughton. I laughed too, not the slightest worried about being disloyal to my father. As she was leaving, I walked down the steps alongside her. I felt a wind blow up from the city, the cold of it, through the mesh of my football socks without boots. Mam had made a favourite of me. Fellows saw us.

'That your mother?' they said afterwards.

'Yes,' I mumbled. To explain to them about a stepmother would have been far too complicated.

Brother Robert was the president of the college. We didn't see or hear much of him. That created about him a sense of pomp. The night Declan Skelly went home, we heard him. It was after the rosary. His voice came from the back of the chapel and told us that today there had occurred a contingency but it was something that should not alarm us. Contingencies such as these occurred from time to time and would occur to each and every one of us. They were God's doing and it was best that we not be put off our studies by them. 'Three Hail Marys for the repose of the soul of Declan Skelly's mother,' his voice rose. It sounded as if dust was stuck in his throat.

2

It was strange that: when you went home on holidays you felt that in the eyes of the others you had changed while you were away. And when you went back after the holidays Discharge told you that you had changed while you were at home. 'You're slouching about. Hands in the pockets, thinking you're a big fellow. What bad company have you been in? I'll get you back to shape before many days are out!' It seemed that everybody else could see you changing before their eyes and yet, look in the mirror as you might, even measure yourself on the ruler in the physics lab, you had nothing to show for it. Five foot three inches. A year after, five foot three and a quarter inches. You didn't notice changes in yourself. Oh you noticed changes in others: our baby girl growing bigger and dressed in more grown-up clothes every time you went home, our second baby growing fatter and learning to laugh. The only change you noticed in yourself was when you were on the stairs. In school, and at home. When you went home you sprang up the stairs, two steps at a time, so accustomed you had become to the college's five flights of steep, iron-tipped steps, and when you returned to school you found it hard work all over again. No, you weren't changing. You never changed. It was everybody else that was changing. And oh, particularly Frieda Ryan, who nowadays you only caught glimpses of at Sunday mass. Or did she go at all?

Growing. Now the Christmas trees, they really did grow. One day, on my first Christmas holidays, I was up on the top of Ivyhall. I was with Murt; we were cutting down the Christmas tree. The trees in the little plantation grew taller each year, making you feel you really were getting left behind. There were now five stumps in the tree grove, one for each of the years that Murt and me had cut down a tree and then dragged it all the way home along the bumpy fields. The sky was clouded over. I was hot from my sawing exertions and the smell of pine in the little grove overpowered me. It was slow cutting. The tree resin stuck to the saw-blade and the cut closed in on it. But at last the tree was toppling.

'Timber,' I shouted to Murt to humour him. The tree slumped down on its pine needles. Then, once the sawing had stopped, the silence took over.

'Come on, we'll go,' said Murt. That was the difference between Murt and me. He was unnerved by the silence up there. I loved it.

So we were on top of Ivyhall this day, in the silence you got after the tree had been cut, when a sudden whistle of wind passed over my head. I looked up and saw a wheeling flock of birds. I didn't know what sort of bird they were. They kept going at a fantastic speed. They had come from across the plain below. They had risen to take the hill and now they whooshed away due north, leaving me behind. They were caught in a flash of light as they soared on and the sky behind them brightened before dimming again to its normal colour.

On such moments I left my stuntedness behind: when I stood above the fallen Christmas tree and the light poured in and my soul peeled away with the birds.

I was not one bit grown-up. I certainly didn't feel so in school. Yet on every holiday return to Ivyhall I had to act as though I were a new person. My brothers and sisters expected it of me. They expected me to be turning into some brainy genius. And I obliged by putting on an act. Maybe it was due to putting on the act that in the end I did begin to change. But it was in everything outside me, the changes were most marked.

On my first Christmas home I heard the news that Gananny and Ailey had married. It was hard to believe but I understood what had happened. It had happened on the day we all played House in Frieda's after the fancy-dress. Gananny's marriage to Ailey made me realise how the courses of people's lives can change. Gananny and me, we had sprung from the same watershed – Glen river to be precise; we had quickly flown in different directions.

I saw them once. He had bought a tiny car. An Austin Seven. With the two of them inside, they almost filled it. What space there was left in it was filled by the accordion which he played with the dance band he drove off to join every night. Out of his accordion he was already making a living, while I couldn't see myself ever doing anything but going to school.

I found out that Frieda went to last mass. I had always gone to the early mass with Connaughton but on my first Easter holidays from boarding-school I made excuses to go to the last one. Connaughton looked at me with a pained expression as if I were a lapsed Catholic. Last mass was for those whose souls the Holy Spirit barely kindled. But I saw Frieda. She was with her mother and younger brothers and sisters, a few pews ahead of me. She wore her boarding-school blazer. My heart jumped: Frieda, standing alongside her mother for the Gospel. Her mother was looking across her shoulders at her and then down at the long string of children stretched along the pew. Her eyes roamed over their heads and back to Frieda and finally settled on her own shoulder, at her coat and how it looked on her. She flicked a speck of dust from it. It was Easter Sunday morning.

Alleluia, said Father Glee in a sleepy half-song, and the last mass crowd responded with deep snores. Frieda was the only one there to greet the risen Christ, though he was well risen by now. The sun from the high window shone down upon her. I saw the side of her face, her throat moving in praise. But her mother's eyes were roaming again, roaming over Frieda, over her children and back to the specks of dust on her shoulder. Suddenly I was deeply unhappy. Frieda was not mine. Frieda, along with the rest of the chicken clutch, was sheltering beneath the wing of the mother hen. That, I did not mind so much. What I minded was Frieda's pretence. Frieda had strayed. Frieda no longer belonged within the clutch, so why did she pretend she enjoyed its continued safe keeping? That made her seem as far away from me as could be.

When the organ pealed through the rafters after mass my heart jumped in my mouth at the thought of walking close to her. But the crowd coming out of the church got in my path.

Second year in Mont La Salle boarding-school was when I reached scholastic heights I was never again to achieve. Second year, 2B; I always came first in the class. I even got sent a pound note from home once, just for having done so well. It was a time when I felt very bright and so I decided I should have a nickname to go with my brightness.

I'd had that nickname at home which was not at all a reflection on my new-found standing. Blinky. That terrible name Richie called me. Then after a while my sisters began calling me also. But they called me Double-Blinky. I hadn't known about the double-blinking until they pointed it out to me, but according to them, I was a real blinker. Real fast, I blinked. Double-blink. So fast, they said, that I was lucky to be able to see at all. 'Look, he's double-blinking,' they said. 'He's in a bad temper.' Apparently being in a temper and double blinking went hand in hand. The girls noticed all these things. Then I began to notice the double blinking myself. It was true. When I got in a bad mood the double blinking fits came on. The only thing to do, then, was go away from everybody and blink to my heart's content. I quite enjoyed a blinking session once I could be on my own doing it. Mam did not mention the blinking, but one day in Mont La Salle Discharge told me I was having an appointment with an eye specialist. 'Your mother's orders,' Discharge said.

Whenever the blinking came on bad in Mont La Salle, I asked for permission to go to the jacks. Nobody in Mont La Salle ever called me Blinky and that made me confident that nobody noticed it. But now here was Discharge talking about an eye specialist and so I began to worry that someone might.

The eye specialist asked me to read letters and when they got so small I couldn't see them and started making them up, he told me I was anxious. Anxiety is your problem, he said. Relax. Was it any wonder I was anxious? I'd had to read off a board that was placed miles away from me these letters that made me blink so much they disappeared altogether. He gave me eye drops, which I lost even before Connaughton wrote to tell me how important it was to take them. He had been surprised, he said, that eye specialist fees were so high. In any case, it was after the eye specialist I decided I should give myself the nickname. In that way, I figured, I would already have one before some smart snotface, one day out of the blue, shouted: Blinky.

The name I decided on was Dixie. After Dixie Dean, who had once upon a time been the great goal-scoring hero of Everton. It was the sort of name that suited a bright fellow with an active intelligence like mine. I shouted it out in the play yard when I scored goals or played well. 'Dixie Dean on the ball. Dixie scores again. Two-nil to Everton.' I hoped it would catch on. But nobody ever said: Aye, Dixie, pass. Or anything like that. They ignored Dixie entirely. I got another nickname instead. It wasn't great, but at least it wasn't Blinky.

It happened in The Gent's class. He was our English teacher. A lay-teacher, with steel-hard hair combed back in waves like corrugated iron, a blue suit, white shirt tightly collared and a small mouth. The very first day he came into our class he sat down and said, '2B or not 2B, gents, that is the question.' We didn't know what he was talking about. But he said it in such a sneering, menacing way that we knew that any reply, either by way of smart remark or otherwise, would be out of the question. Shakespeare, he said. Hamlet.

I was good at English. A fellow in my class, Keeffe, a day-boy from out the country, Ferrybank way, was not. There was this poem, called 'The Wild Swans of Coole', which The Gent never tired of asking Keeffe to recite:

> The trees are in their autumn beauty
> The woodland paths are dry

> Under the October twilight
> The water mirrors a still sky . . .

Now, no matter how many times Keeffe attempted to recite this poem he could not get any further than the word 'water' on the fourth line. Then he would have another stab at it: 'De turees are in dere autumn beauty . . .' In his country accent, which was even stronger than mine, he would take run after run at it, only to get stuck once he reached 'water'. 'Under de October twilight the water . . .' Then he would stand, getting redder and redder in the face, until he was sweating. The Gent, who was really no gent at all but a bastard, seemed to love watching Keeffe in torture.

In the end I began to understand Keeffe's problem with 'The Wild Swans of Coole' and why no matter how many shots he took at it he could never get past 'water'. The problem was the metre. That line of the poem, 'The water mirrors a still sky', was too long for the metre. You were lead to believe that line was supposed to be the same length as the second line. But as soon as you came up to the word 'water', you knew it was going to be too long. It was the same as a pony galloping up to a jump and then stopping dead because he was all out of step for it. Keeffe was placing the word 'water' at the end of the third line – where maybe it should have been anyway – and after that the beat in his head got entirely knocked out of rhythm and he could go no further. And then his forehead furrowed up in distress. It hadn't been very thoughtful of the poet, and that was my opinion. Not very thoughtful of the poet writing a line like that, considering every day that Keeffe had a shot at it he got stuck on 'water' and then got six slogs off The Gent for his troubles.

Then when The Gent had delivered the medicine he pursed up his little mouth, 'Gents, gents, do we ever learn?' And he settled his collar after his exertions and turned to me: 'Recite it for Keeffe, Connaughton.' Which I had to.

Here was a poem The Gent had a real go at one day:

> In Xanadu did Kubla Khan
> A stately pleasure-dome decree . . .

He wrote it on the blackboard.

'Alliteration, alliteration, gents,' he said. 'A poet who was never afraid to alliterate was Coleridge. The intoxication, gents, of assonance and alliteration. Oh poetry, the opium of the ear.'

The Gent looked at us, pleased with himself, while outside in the yard a shower of rain suddenly stopped and the sun burst out and shone with a dazzling glare on the puddles.

'But does Coleridge overdo it in these lines?' He paused for an answer. Not that there was any point in pausing for one, because he wasn't going to get one anyway. And when he didn't he carried on.

'Does Coleridge overdo it, gents? Or, can we not alternately say that in these lines the sparkle of his genius produces the wittiest example there is of alliteration in the whole of the English language?' The Gent looked around the class as though he were inspecting prize cabbage plants. 'Hhhm? I want you to find it for me, gents. I shall leave you a few moments to your own excellent devices so that you may peruse the examples of alliteration on show here.' He looked so smugly pleased with himself then. The cat licking its little lips after the cream: 'By the way, I might issue a warning: come up with any other than the correct example and you pay for it.'

In the moments in which The Gent left us to our own devices and looked in admiration at the lines on the board, it became so quiet I could hear fellows trying to think. I heard a door bang way down the corridor. The sun outside shone its heat into the classroom until it was baking.

'Well, gents,' he suddenly turned to us. 'Why do I hear a silence?'

Naturally The Gent heard a silence. Nododdy was going to take chances, given the examples of alliteration on show.

' Tell you what, gents . . . How many examples of alliteration do you hear in this passage?'

Fellows felt put under pressure now. The replies began to come: fellows were trying it on their lips without actually committing themselves:

'Tt, tt, tt, tt, oo examples.'

The Gent sucked breath between his teeth. A warning lest some misguided clown put the whole word together and say, two.

He looked around. No offers.

'Fair enough, gents, two you imply. If there are but two

examples of alliteration, it should be easy to tell me which is the masterpiece and which the dud.'

Still no offers.

'Keeffe?'

'De turees are in dere autumn beauty, sir. The woodland paths are dury . . .'

'Sit down, Keeffe. I may not slap you on the grounds that you have not provided the wrong example. I may only marvel at your density.'

'Kelly-Jackson?'

Kelly-Jackson, tall as he was, had a way of slowly putting his feet beneath him and then standing by a series of coiling movements, so that his ears, moving in a circle towards every corner of the room, had a fair chance of plucking out of the air whatever hints might somehow be floated on it.

Unfortunately this time there were two hints doing the rounds. If Kelly-Jackson were smarter, he would have chosen neither of them and then he would have stood a good chance of getting off scot-free, as Keeffe had done. But Kelly-Jackson did not know what alliteration was anyway, and so didn't know what it wasn't either. He picked up the hint being whispered loudest.

'Kubla Khan, sir.'

'Kubla Khan, no sir. Rather obvious example of alliteration, don't you think?' The Gent looked wearily down at the class as he directed Kelly-Jackson's hand from above his desk so as to get a good skelp at it and not hit the fellow alongside him: 'But I suppose in Kelly-Jackson's case, gents, we must not assume anything to be obvious.' There was a swish as the first skelp skimmed Kelly-Jackson's fingertips. 'Because alliteration would not be obvious to Kelly-Jackson, not even if it got up and bit him on his assonance.'

While Kelly-Jackson lay bent over his desk with his big hands slogged and sore in his armpits, the rest of us quaked.

Who was he going to ask next? Who was going to sign his death knell by saying 'dome decree'? Because as sure as I knew The Gent, 'dome decree' would be wrong also.

'Am I in a good humour today or what?' he said. 'Because I think I shall tell you.'

He must have been in a good humour. Here he was with a

perfect opportunity to inflict more punishment and he was going to waste it by letting us off the hook.

'I'll say it once and you'd better listen. The two sounds that demonstrate Coleridge's alliterative wit.' Then he said them, 'do did.' Or that was what we thought he said.

'Everybody, write down what I have said. Those two sounds. And those two sounds exactly and only as they appear in the poem, "Kubla Khan".'

Well hell's bells, I thought. It suddenly leaped to me what he was at. The sadist.

He looked at our copybooks. 'Do did. Do did. Do did. Where do you see "do did" written in those lines on the board?' he shouted. Whorls of his steel-wool hair, tamed down by about a jar of hair oil, were beginning to sit upright.

Every person in the class, bar one, got four slogs. And Kelly-Jackson got another four. The Gent was puffed, sweating, even though he still did not loosen his collar. Four of the best to everybody but me. 'Now, look at the blackboard.' The class of 2B, sprawling all over their desks and clutching their burst palms, squinted up at the lines on the board.

I alone had not written 'do did'; 'du did,' I had written. The wittiest alliteration in the English language.

'Shout it out for those doleful duffers,' The Gent said to me.

He wrote quickly on the board, making a clattering sound with the chalk. 'In Xana du did Kubla Khan . . .'

'New combination, gentlemen. Du did, Du did.' He twice underlined the new combination. 'Internal alliteration, gentlemen. We make the mistake of listening for sounds with our eyes. We should employ our ears. The sounds, gentlemen, are there for our ears if only we were not afraid to hear them.'

When we went out in the yard I felt a wide space all around me. As though I were some freak alien that could hear sounds others could not. The sun was soaking up the puddles of water. Suddenly another shower of rain swooped down.

Then Kelly-Jackson walked over to me. 'Dudid,' he said, and gave me the full of his fist into my forehead.

Oh that one-night crash course long ago on the sounds and spellings of English with Connaughton. Hadn't it stood to me well?

And the next day, when Keeffe failed again on 'The Wild Swans' and The Gent nodded to me: 'Connaughton, recite it for Keeffe', Kelly-Jackson shouted up from the back of the class: 'His name, sir, is Dudid.' And everybody laughed and The Gent licked his lips, letting them enjoy their laughter for a moment, before doling out to Kelly-Jackson the four slogs that would quell it.

That was how I came to be nicknamed Dudid and not Dixie, my Everton Dixie hero.

And how I wrote home to Mam about Kelly-Jackson's knuckles on my conk and got two ten shilling notes by reply.

'Dixie would have been delightful; Dudid will have to do,' says I to myself out in the jacks, manufacturing alliterations to beat the band as I pocketed the two ten shilling notes and blinked away to my heart's content.

It was my first time ever looking for sympathy from Mam. What an old babby I was – writing home to tell on the big boy for being a bully. What a sap. Or maybe not. Maybe that was the right thing to do. It was what other fellows did. I had taken a chance on it. She could have told me to stop my snivelling and dry up. I didn't want to accept her sympathies, but she was proving to be a softer touch than Connaughton. I had to concede that.

3

'Frieda has a new boyfriend,' Bunny said, when I went home on holidays. He drove me into clouds of jealousy. 'Frieda has a fellow now and he has a car that he takes her off in.' Bunny, you cruel bastard.

Bunny did all of his baiting down in the feeding house. Frieda was floating away from me. What way was there now of contacting her? Who was there to talk to? I spent a lot of my time in the feeding house. The hitchhiker no longer lived there, but was gone, gone to God-knows-where. The mirror he had used to shave himself had been left on the windowshelf and every day I rubbed the barley dust off it, trying to see myself clearly.

One thing I did see. I was growing away from Ivyhall. Every time I came home I was growing further away. Or else it was shutting me out. The hectic noise of Ivyhall continued to be all about me. My younger brothers fought and argued. They rode the ponies. I heard them clatter on the yard. But I didn't fight with them now. Neither did I fight with Richie. He was a big man now. He didn't just act like one any more. He looked like one. He drove the car everywhere. Even the shortest distance. He would drive the car just to do his shit, Bunny said. He persuaded Connaughton into buying modern farm machinery. He went to dances. I hated modern machinery. I wouldn't go to dances. And walking was much better than driving the car. Better for you. Like eating marmalade.

'Can you do the twist?' Richie still asked. He asked it now because he wanted me to know where his life was taking him. In that one way he had not changed. He might be going to dances, but he wanted me, at least in my imagination, to go with him. He still wanted company.

'Can you do the hucklebuck? You have to when you go dancing.'

'No.'

'Do the twist. Go on, do it.'

'I can't. I told you before, I can't.'

'Try it. Women won't dance any more with a fellow who doesn't know the twist.'

I had to try for him.

'No, you're not fit. You go like this. Sing it for me and I'll show you.'

I had to sing it for him. He swish-swished, making the same old wind sounds with his arms as he had done the day of the blackberries, his bum so low it was hitting the mucky floor of the cowhouse. He was fit. 'That's how you do the twist.'

Christmas was a good time for stealing bottles of ale. On my Christmas holidays of second year in Mont La Salle, Connaughton bought lots of bottles and put them in the dining room. Nobody seemed to drink them, so once it got dark in the afternoons I helped myself. Then Bunny and me drank them down in the cow-house. The ale was freezing when you drank it. But after a while, in the warmth of the cow-house, with the cows contentedly chewing their cud and belching up huge draughts of warm wind, you got sleepy and talked drowzily away to Bunny and belched up wind yourself.

He would have just a few cows to snig, as most of them would be dry, their fat bellies touching as they stood in their bays, awaiting the drop of the spring calves. 'Ever spot the ould hitchhiker on your travels?' he would say. 'The rumour is he went down Waterford way.'

'No I never saw him.'

'Fuckin' eejit. He had it handy here. The last I saw of him he tould me he was afraid that time was beatin' him and he'd have to move on or old age would catch him.'

'What age is he?'

'Isn't that it? He tould me he was turned fifty. Time to stay put, I said to him.'

Then I would tell Bunny all about school and the Brothers and heading goals at soccer and mitching out about the city and he would be silent, happy for a little while not to make fun of me but to listen. And he would tell me about his life and the amounts of large bottles he could drink in different places, and dance halls and women that would go for him and that would go for me too, if I wanted it. He would tell me about the nights he got into fights at the dances. And he would look at his clenched fist and then let the knuckles relax and say, 'Maybe I'm gettin' a bit too old for fightin'.' He would tell me about visits to Ivyhall of the Three Wise Men; about rows they had with Connaughton. Bunny, leaning against the belly of a cow; having it handy in Ivyhall, handy to remain there the rest of his days. Telling me about whiffs of the where-abouts of Christopher, no firm news yet but whiffs. Me then looking out at Witheroe's map of England on the castle wall. Low murmurings in the cow-house. Bunny and me keeping abreast of things.

Who should arrive in Mont La Salle in the middle of second year? Kicked out of the school he had originally gone to? I saw him on the driveway one afternoon in March. I was in the dormitory, the only one there, looking out the window. Though the novelty of it should by now have worn off, I still sometimes wandered about the big draughty building on my own, enjoying the atmosphere when the other students were elsewhere and it was empty and it was against the regulations to be there. I knew as I looked out the window that I was the only one watching him. He was all on his own, struggling with a big suitcase. Then he stopped and kicked the pebbles on the driveway and looked up at the college. There was something comical in the way he squinted up. I wondered what was going on in his mind. He looked isolated.

It was Holland.

Except he was no longer Holland, but Ash. He was Teddy Ash now. He had reclaimed his father's name. He tagged along with me on his first few days and when sometimes by mistake I called him Holland he told me to stuff it. And he laughed when others called me Dudid.

'Dudid,' he said, 'that name is cat, boy. What tool gave you that name?'

He had been kicked out of the school he had gone to and he had also left his mother and now lived with his father in Ennis. His father was cool, he said.

He told me all these things over those first few days of his arrival to Mont La Salle. He asked me about Frieda. 'Does she write to you?' he asked. 'I have a biddy myself. How does a fellow get a letter from a biddy into this place?' I told him to shut up about Frieda. His utterance of her name had given me a tingle I could not bear.

He stuck close to me those days. I was pleased to have him and to introduce him to the others. He was quite a catch. Fellows were impressed when he told why he had got kicked out of his previous school. 'Drink.' As he said it he wiped imaginary suds of beer off his mouth. The priests in his last school were tools, he said. He knew all about pop music. In a very short time he became an important member of the Kelly-Jackson gang.

One day we visited Reginald's Tower. 'Come on, Dudid,' Ash said. We had done a bunk over the wall. 'Let's check out this tool Strongbow.'

The tower was a squat building, not anything like the size of Ivyhall Castle. It was a museum now. There were pike staffs along the wall. Ash and me didn't much like the look of Strongbow, so after a while we took target practice at him with the pikes. When the news of the damage got back to the college, Discharge isolated the 'huns who disgrace Mont La Salle'. He gave us six of the best each on both hands, refused us permission to go downtown for the rest of that term and told us that we were lucky he was not reporting us to our parents. Lucky, I did indeed feel then. Being reported to my parents would have been death to me. Connaughton's face, I could picture it, crumpled like a paper bag; Mam's worse, set and grim, no give in it at all. Ash said he didn't care. His father wouldn't give a damn.

Some fellows said he was sneaky. I knew him better. Those were the times I felt like putting my arms around him. For a while we were best friends. We would line up together during Sunday walks to Ballygunner and all those other small roads beyond the city. We would throw arms across each other's shoulders.

'Cigarettes make you look good.' Ash told me that one day. We were down at the back, skimming stones over the mudflat on the estuary. And we went in behind the tidal wall. A long ship was out on the river when I lit up for my first drag with Ash. Leaning heavily in the water, the ship was chugging downriver. We could hear the racket of the engine. 'The Irish Ash', we saw the words, in big letters, written along the side of its deck. A sailor up there was looking down at us. All those ships sailed past Mont La Salle. The fleet of Irish Shipping. Names like: *Irish Pine, Irish Poplar, Irish Oak*.

'*Irish Ash*. There's my ship,' Ash calls out. 'Get to work, sailor.'

I collapsed in laughing, cigarette-coughing admiration. If your mother could see you now, Ash said.

Honeymoon. Those were our honeymoon days. However, as time went on we drew away from one another, embarrassed. He changed. He walked with Kelly-Jackson's crowd. Like a small bulldog, his tie loose and his shirt opened around a thick neck. Kelly-Jackson's adviser.

4

Now every time I went home on holidays the changes just jumped at me. It was not only me who was changing; Ivyhall itself was taking on a new complexion. More modern every time. Connaughton put in a new milking parlour with money from the sale of his butcher's shop in Templemore. Now there was nothing left of Templemore but his undertaker business. People, like Aunt Tessa, said he was a foolish man to be investing all his future in a farm that wasn't his.

'Tell me if it's none of my affair but suppose, God forbid, something happened,' said Tessa.

'My future is with Kit,' said Connaughton.

Kit, that was Mam's name. Connaughton very rarely used it. Among grown-ups maybe, sometimes, he would use it. An adult name for adult company. Only once I heard him say 'Kit' in front of us children. That was after an argument. He must have forgotten himself altogether that time because not only did he call her Kit, upset that he had hurt her feelings, he even called her Kitten. In my books, Mam was no kitten.

So instead of a twelve bay cow-house and a calf shed alongside, there was now one long cool house with bays for twenty-four cows. And a milking parlour that hummed at milking time. A sparkling clean new floor had been laid in the cow-house. A power hose to flush it down. And though the cow shit still flowed out the same old hole in the wall it had always gone through, things had changed from the days when the dung rose up to the ceiling and the dead calf had been found in it.

The first I knew of the new dairy was one day a row broke out between Mam and Aunt Tessa. It was on an end-of-term day and I had just returned from Mont La Salle. I walked in the door with my case, driven home from Waterford by Fern, who loved doing favours for Mam. She and Tessa were seated at the kitchen table and the cigarette smoke was fogging to the high heavens. Connaughton was standing at the kitchen sink and two of the girls, Marguerite and Breda, were at the table listening for all they were worth. Tessa was saying this thing to Connaughton I had heard her say before – about it being none of her affair that he should plough his own business into Ivyhall but that in her opinion he was a fool-ish man. Seeing me, Connaughton said, welcome home, and then made his reply to Aunt Tessa.

'Tessa dear, you know my future is with Kit.' He did not look at Mam. I think he may have wished to but could not. Then he walked out of the kitchen. I could see the hairs on his bare arms flattened from dried milk and I could smell the milk's sweetness from him as he walked past me.

'You,' Aunt Tessa accused Mam, once Connaughton had shut the door behind him, 'you shouldn't have let him do it.'

I noticed Mam's neck go all red. She hunted Marguerite and Breda from the table. They were reluctant to get up. 'Nosy parkers,' she called them. 'Don't be listening to adult conversation.' She said nothing to me, maybe because I had just returned from college, and so I stayed, making myself invisible.

'You are letting him spend on Ivyhall what should be for your future. His and yours. You are letting him hopelessly sink it in this dump. What happens if it all goes wrong?'

'If what all goes wrong?' Mam said.

'If this place goes wallop. You know from our own father that farming is most uncertain . . . Or if one of you should die . . . Jesus Christ, forgive me tempting fate, but if one of you should die . . .'

'Am I hearing this?' Mam said. 'I don't have to listen to this.'

'You do have to,' Aunt Tessa said. She was surprising me. Ever before, I had only heard her make gossip and criticism, stuff at which she and Mam would laugh. I didn't know she could grasp anything deeper than that. And this was deep.

'That man gone out the door' – she nodded towards where Connaughton had stood sad-faced at the sink – 'all that man has left now is his undertaker's business in Templemore. Everything else is gone. You seem to forget that you and he do not own this farm. You may have got the High Court to rule in your favour but that is only a temporary arrangement because control still rests in the hands of the three Executors. And when the day comes that the estate passes back to the children of your late husband, as it clearly says in his will, that is the day the Executors will waltz back in here and leave you and that man high and dry.' It was an awful long speech Aunt Tessa was making and it nearly winded her but still she was able to finish off: 'Kit, beware the Three Wise Men. Connaughton will be left holding a greasy pole. And it is you who will have been responsible.'

'Are you finished?' Mam said.

'Yes.'

'Get out of my house and don't come back.' The redness had gone from Mam's neck. Now she was white. 'And you can mind your own business in future, and your own little husband's.'

Tessa jumped from the table. She knocked over her chair in her hurry. It bounced off the floor. It was the first time Tessa left the house without taking one of us children to open the gates for her.

'None of her business,' Mam said, hearing Tessa slam the door of her car outside. I was still standing there. Dancie had come to see what the commotion was about. Mam was not talking to either of us, but to herself: 'None of her business. Or mine either. As if I could ever tell the boss what to do.'

'Calm yourself, ma'am,' said Dancie and held Mam's hand.

The floor of the cow-house had circular designs cut into the concrete. I thought it looked lovely. I asked Witheroe about the circles, he being the main builder.

'The circles in the floor is not for ornament but to stop the cows slipping,' he said. 'I made them by pressing the neck of a jam jar into the setting cement.'

A very handy man, Witheroe, a master builder. He liked working for Mam; she admired his skills. He did not like working for Connaughton, who always worked too fast and never took breaks. He did defend him, though, against the Three Wise Men.

'They should fuck off and let the boss alone. It's his money he's spending and not theirs.'

He liked the changes the boss was making about the place. Yet the map of England on the castle had not changed, not one peninsula knocked off it, but like a cobweb, still binding together the crack in the wall. It had been given a jersey, that was all. A new coat of cement slapped over its slim English shoulders and down as far as its bellybutton at Birmingham. A jersey with a design of jam-jar circles, made from cement left over from the building of Witheroe's cow-house.

Witheroe and Mam would gang up on Connaughton. What could I do about it? What was I doing the day in the calf-house when Connaughton's finger was stuck in the jaw of the squeezer, the Burdizzo, and he was roaring and Mam was saying, 'God, control yourself!' That was the day Witheroe, Connaughton, Mam and me did the castration job on the spring calves. It was dark in the shed, only a slit of light coming in over the door. The calves bunched tightly together for security. One by one, Witheroe and me caught them. Mam held the blunt-jawed squeezer while Connaughton located with his fingers the vessel in the calf's testicle bag and then told Mam to squeeze.

'Stop, you're crunching me!' he squealed.

'You told me to squeeze,' she shouted back.

I was holding tight the head of a bull-calf, looking into its wide forehead, into its brown eyes in their white circles of fear. 'I'll hold on to you old son, don't mind the pain,' I was whispering in its ear, not knowing it was my father's finger was caught in the clamp of the squeezer, the muscles of my mother's arms seized by panic locking it tight, Witheroe's body slumped against the wall in helpless silent laughter. Oh if only my father's bawling would stop. I held tight to the white-headed bull-calf to give myself comfort.

That's what I was doing that day in the darkness of the calf-house. Every time I went home on holiday it was not just me had changed. My parents had changed too. In a world, grown shadowy and intimate, in which, increasingly, they alone inhabited. In which they damaged fingers and damaged pride. In which I no longer recognised my place.

When Aunt Tessa was allowed to return, she did not mention the new dairy. Nor the herd of Friesians Connaughton had bought to go with it. She just smoked her cigarettes and talked about the rich people of Thurles, the 'Johnny-jump-ups'.

So now we had twenty-four cows. Connaughton bought the additional twelve down in the Golden Vale. Lovely light young Friesians. 'To grade up the herd,' he said.

One summer evening he came home from a race-meeting. He was in a state of panic. Glen gate was open and the Golden Vale cows were gone. We were back down to our original twelve again.

'Who left the gate open! Ring the guards!'

'Would it have been the Three Wise Men?' I said to Bunny.

I knew it hadn't been, of course. It was myself had left the gate open. Forgotten to close it when I had driven out the cows. Thinking of Frieda probably. I still had hopes of seeing her during my school holidays. I had taken to making lots of mistakes and that was only one of them. I had left a dairy can of milk in the yard one day. A piglet had dived into it and become stuck within, drowning itself in the pinky pond, its legs kicking up in the air, its neck purple against the narrow rim of the can. Another day I had not put the brake on the tractor when I got off it and it rolled down the lane and smashed into a pier, only seconds before Auntie Tessa drove in, looking at her cleavage in the rear-view mirror.

'You're a loose cannon,' Connaughton said to me.

The cows were located. Many miles away; the far side of the colliery, still hot-footing it along the road when Connaughton, Murt, the Little Yank and me got to them.

'There's a night's milk gone down the drain,' Connaughton complained.

I volunteered to hunt them home, there and then. That way I wouldn't feel so bad about what I had done. Connaughton said it was a good idea and so he and Jamesy drove along behind the cows while Murt and me stayed ahead of them to steer them along the roads.

It was the night Murt got the pains.

It grew very warm that night, then it grew dark. Everything was going quite well. Connaughton shouted at us every time a cow darted out of line but once darkness had fallen the herd settled down, except for when they lowed into the silent fields which would then briefly waken up with the cries of cattle. All would then return to quietness again, the sound of the cows hooves slicking along the roads, hind legs rubbing swollen udders, sending us into a dream. We were going like this for a while when suddenly we came around a corner and standing high on a ditch before us was a huge beast with puffs of fog coming out its nostrils. Murt was very frightened. 'A bull,' said he. I could feel the tremor in his voice.

'It's not,' I said.

'It is. I'm not passing. It's the white bull that fell into our coal shaft.' He was wailing now.

'It's not.' I hated people getting worked up. 'Give me those glasses. You can't see. It wasn't a bull that fell into the mine, you fool. It was a cow.' I took off Murt's glasses and wiped the spatters of mud off them. 'And it was a roan cow. This is a black bull. Don't be so stupid. He can't get out at us.'

We passed the bull. It pawed at the bank. I could smell the fresh turf. Murt said it was looking very wildly at us and was about to jump on us. I knew it was not taking the slightest interest in us. The hoof-taps of our dainty heifers was all that interested the bull but I didn't feel like telling Murt that. 'Shut up,' I said. We were silent then for a while until Murt began his bitter complaints about the pains.

'Where?' I said.

'In me chest.'

'Where in your chest?'

'In me tits. Where me clothes rub off them, it's real sore.'

'Hold your clothes out from them.'

After a while he began to whimper. 'I'm afraid.'

'Why?'

'Me tits are getting real big like a woman's.'

'You're turning into a woman,' I said. 'You'll have to wear a bra, Murtie. You'll be called Titsy.' I was being cruel. I knew that and didn't care. Until I remembered something that stopped me. I remembered my own chest pains.

I too once had that problem. It had been like my tits were filling with milk. Painfully swelling with it. Like the tight tits of the heifers we were now herding behind us. Dimly then, I understood what was happening Murt. And what had happened me that time. There had been nobody I had been able to tell about it. But now I felt sorry for Murt. Suddenly, walking along the road, hedges bending in towards us, I felt sorry for all of us and our growing up. I even felt sorry for Richie, wondering if he too once suffered the tit pains. What could I say to Murt? I said: 'Don't cry, Murtie. Tell Mam when you go home. She'll rub ointment on for you.' I felt a pang of love for Murt. For a whole moment I felt happy for a situation where a trusting boy could tell his Mam and where she could treat tenderly with him.

Yes. When it came to boys smaller than me, I was no angel. Take in Mont La Salle: take Chesty, for instance, my next-door bed-mate. Not only did I beat him, but once I was started I couldn't stop it. And why was that? Even as I was thudding him, I was saying to myself: What am I doing, beating the shit out of this poor geezer? Not that I didn't get plenty of hidings myself. I'd got them in Ivyhall from Richie. And in Mont La Salle, where Kelly-Jackson was my tormentor. But Chesty? It was like Chesty was a scab on your knee, or on your face, that you just kept picking. I just kept picking on Chesty. Kelly-Jackson would hammer me, all knuckles and bones. Even though sometimes I managed to upend him. But I hammered Chesty whenever I got the chance. Thudded him until sounds came out of him like the voice box in the belly of a teddy-bear.

No, there was no excuse for me.

When did I give up beating Chesty? The time I got my worst

ever beating from Kelly-Jackson? The time everybody turned on Kelly-Jackson and called him a bully, and fellows in fifth year pulled him off me? Did it occur to me then that I too was a bully? Did it stop me? No. It did not. Hammering the stuffing out of Chesty was just something I would grow out of it. Things yet to happen in my life would make me grow out of. In the same way, probably, things yet to happen in Chesty's life would make him grow out of allowing himself to be hammered by me.

My worst ever beating from Kelly-Jackson came about because of the tablecloth. Each week Discharge ran a tablecloth competition. I am in third year. It is Saturday in the refectory, we are finishing dinner and the noise is reaching the rafters. After a good dinner the noise is even greater. A good dinner is when the potatoes are not soapy. Discharge is eating his prunes at his table, on the podium, above everybody. Twenty-four tables awash in a sea of light below him, like boats in a harbour. All with their new tablecloths. Tablecloths are changed each Saturday before dinner. He rings the bell for silence as soon as he has piled his prune stones on his plate. The silence comes slowly. He rings again. 'The results of last week's tablecloth competition,' he announces. There is a great wave of laughter, of anticipation, but it is dispelled by another tinkle of the gong.

Discharge reads out the prize-giving: 'For the winning table, the table which has maintained the cleanest tablecloth over the course of the week, there is permission to go to the movies this afternoon.'

That is Discharge's prize for the winner, but for the losers, and almost all the other tables are losers, there are fines. The fines go to the Missions. The boys cheer at the announcements of the losers. Two shillings fine for this table; five shillings fine for that . . . Discharge tries to stop the cheers but as the fines increase the cheers grow louder. He doesn't make a great attempt to quell the noise; he is making money for the Missions, and that pleases him. Who will get the biggest fine this week? It is usually a table of fifth years. They are the messiest. But this week everybody is staring at our table, the Kelly-Jackson table, and we are only in third year . . . An auspicious prize-giving is about to enfold.

During that fateful week an accident happened on our table. An incident with the gravy boat. It overturned on the tablecloth.

Kelly-Jackson said it was my fault. Yes, I had been holding it, but others had too; everybody grabbing it at the same moment. There was a pool of gravy. But then Jonah Whaley, big buckteeth Jonah, who sat between me and KJ, sprinkled salt on it. 'Get rid of the stain,' he said.

'Jonah, you lousy tool,' Kelly-Jackson said. But he thought it was funny. 'Will we add to the recipe, Ash?' he asked Ash.

Then everybody at the table, on Ash's advice, added to the recipe: pepper, milk, sugar, and KJ topped it off with the marmalade. 'A Dudid cake,' he said.

And that was only the first layer. Ash glugged the bottle of tomato sauce all over it.

'More salt,' KJ said. 'And lash on more pepper there, Dudid.'

It was hilarious. The cake looked like a jellyfish beached on the sand. We were laughing: 'Jonah, you lousy tool.' Distracted by our antics, a hush began to spread through the refectory. In the moment of silence, as all heads sought out the source of the commotion, the event was marked in Discharge's memory. Filed away for table-cloth competition day.

'Top fine this week: Kelly-Jackson's table. And in addition you are not allowed to the cinema for the remainder of this term. Fine: for the Missions in the Philippines: five pounds. Each.'

The refectory broke down in chaos. Those on the fifth year tables who usually got the top fines were looking down at us. Five pounds each? Who could these pretenders be who had received such a penalty? For one moment my heart swelled with pride. It was by far the biggest penalty in the history of fines.

That was the day I got the thrashing from Kelly-Jackson. 'All your fault, Dudid,' he told me. 'You small prick. Where do I get five pound to pay that lousy bastard for his lousy Missions. You can pay it for me.'

It was not a very pleasant fight. Up in the handball alley, a ring of fellows around us, our feet scuffing around on the tarmac. Knees and elbows, into my forehead, into my thighs. The breath was heaving out of my chest so bad I had a pain right across it. I was crying when the fifth years pulled him off me and thumped him and said, 'Pick someone your own size Kelly-Jackson, you bully.'

Did it make me give up beating Chesty? No. I didn't give up

beating Chesty until the time Mam, then me, went into hospital. But this was before Mam went into hospital. This was before I went into hospital myself. These events would not be for a while yet. I wrote to her after the tablecloth episode. I had to. I had no money to pay the fine. In my letter I explained all about tablecloth fines. The whole business. It was the longest letter I ever wrote her.

I often pictured Mam at home reading my letters. They would come in the bunch with Connaughton's business mail and with the letters from England from the agency concerning the whereabouts of Christopher Witheroe and she would sit at the table eating monkey nuts with Aunt Tessa as she read them. Nothing about Christopher, she would say. Did she look forward to my letters, I wondered? She must have been furious when she received that letter from me.

'I am coming to pay a visit,' she wrote back. 'Never heard anything so ridiculous.'

What was so ridiculous? Me, for messing?

I cannot forget that day. We were on retreat. Our first 'senior' retreat. Fellows were having vocations wholesale and I was one of them. I was up on a tree. We were allowed recreation during retreat. Periods of walking through the grounds for contemplation. Well, I was contemplating in my tree. I was also keeping nix for Kelly-Jackson and Ash, who were smoking a cigarette on the ground below me. I was like the man in the burning bush. It was then that Mam drove up the drive.

I found the whole thing very embarrassing. I heard the crunch of the gravel beneath her feet when she got out of the car. She climbed up the stairs, didn't look left or right at bells or statues, but rang the door buzzer. She sought out Discharge and asked him had he ever heard of plastic tablecloths. Then she handed him one she had bought in Shaw's and said it was to be put over our table. 'Thank you, Mrs Connaughton,' says he, all bent and pinched, as if he was addressing the Queen of England. He always bore that look when he had to deal with women.

After the plastic cloth, Discharge had it in for me: our cloth was the envy of the refectory. In no time at all every other table had one. I was popular with everybody. Discharge's source of funding for the Missions was cut off. And always it provided a great excuse for fellows to go downtown: 'Brother, Brother, can I go down to Shaw's to buy a new plastic tablecloth, ours is torn?' Now when you entered the refectory you got the smell of plastic: hot teapots on sweaty plastic. I was popular, but my popularity led me into ever more trouble. With a profile like I now held, I had to keep myself in the news. I had to be daring. Result: I got slogged; I had to pay many visits to the handball alley to warm up the hands in readiness. I was not allowed to read the newspapers. I missed one whole year's visits to the cinema and was consequently left behind in the matters of film stars and fashion. The only fashion education I received was from Ash, as he showed the Kelly-Jackson gang what he considered to be his most enjoyable pastime and that was to light up a cigarette by the mirror and study himself as he smoked it, making big luscious caresses of his lips and turning up the collar of his shirt like Adam Faith.

So I made my own freedom. I got over the walls and wandered the streets of Waterford. I was caught out of bounds. Major topic of conversation: 'Did you hear about Dudid; hear what he's done this time?' A candidate for corruption, I was, according to Discharge. And to think that rather than taking off on the road of the rebel, I might instead have been wafted up the hushed pathways of the vocation vibrating before me that day Mam arrived up the driveway with the tablecloth.

5

Then Mam too became a boarder in Waterford. It happened in March of that year, my Inter Cert year. Before the trees down at the river had come into leaf. Every afternoon for weeks, instead of first study, I went to visit Mam in Ardkeen Hospital.

Ardkeen was on a wide bend of the river. Discharge said I was to go along the road, but that was not the way for me. Our sports field ran by the river. It was very flat there, so that sometimes, when there was flooding, the place silted over and then for days the pong became unbearable. The gurgitations of the city on our playing fields. The smell of the gasworks and Clover Meats factory. However, if you walked further on, you came across the gardens of the big houses. Down to the river they swept, orchards, croquet lawns, tennis courts. It became a different river altogether, secluded, shaded riverbank, children's swings beneath the apple trees, ships passing way out on its widest reaches. Smooth as cardboard. It became my Mississippi again, my Swanee river, and I of course was its Huck Finn. Great heroes of mine, the outcasts Huck and Jim had always been. I skirted gardens with low shrubs not yet come into growth; I looked into gardeners' huts where garden tools lay neatly arranged; I ran down banks of laurel, chased by my own imagination and by the frosted smells of last year's apples; I became entangled in undergrowth. There was one garden I passed which had this sign: 'Dogs on duty'. I never saw dogs. I wondered should a sign, 'Dogs off duty', be put up sometimes. That gave me a titter. Anyway, if they were on duty, I was ready to run.

By the time I reached Ardkeen each day I was in a muddy sweat of excitement. Mam sat in the bed. She did not criticise my appearance. She noticed, though. She had a private room. We watched television each afternoon. It was the week of Cheltenham races. The television was not at the end of the bed but at the side. She would not have been able to see it had it been at the end because there was a big hump of a cage holding the bedclothes off her legs. She was in hospital for special x-rays. Her knee had been bothering her for years and something had to be done about it.

'Are you all right, Mam?' I said each day, remembering to ask.

'Sit down,' she said, patting the chair alongside me. 'You're looking well.' It was not the sort of thing Mam usually said. I think she was pleased to see me.

Mam would never have said she was pleased to see me. But yes, she was a different Mam those weeks. I pulled up my chair and drank the milk and two biscuits she got the nurses to bring in to me. I roared on Arkle and Flying Bolt, and Fort Leney on the television. The ground in Cheltenham was mucky, I could see clods rise behind the horses as they galloped. The Irish horses were winning all the races.

'The Irish horses are great, aren't they, Mam?' I said.

'Are they? I don't know,' she said.

Mam had often told me I was an untidy boy. 'God help the woman that gets you.' Now, though my appearance had not grown any tidier, she did not criticise. One day my shoes were sopping; I had slipped in the river. My socks were a mess. She handed me six pairs of white socks and told me to take them away with me. She leaned over in her locker and pulled them out.

It's funny. There are certain images I have of Mam. Most of them have to do with skin. The white skin of her knee that time I first saw her on the tractor when she pulled out the dead calf and her coat came undone. The white of her breasts beneath the nightgown on Christmas mornings when we showed our presents in her bedroom. Now again, the white breasts as she let her nightgown slip when she leaned over to get the socks.

'Do you not need socks yourself?' I said.

No, she said. She did not need socks any more. 'Make sure you keep them clean.'

When Discharge saw my white socks he said they were for Nancy boys. Everybody laughed. But the laugh was on Discharge rather than on me. For a while he had a new name – Nancy-boy – until after a while it was forgotten and he became Discharge again. No nickname could ever replace Discharge. It was nice to have clean white socks. In the eyes of Kelly-Jackson, Ash and company, I was, for a while, the height of fashion.

One day, just as I arrived on my visit to see Mam, a nurse left the room. Mam liked all the nurses and the nurses liked her. I thought she would be happy after the nurse's visit but she wasn't. 'Come here,' she said. 'I'm fed up. I'm so fed up and useless lying in this place.'

'You're not useless, Mam.'

' I am. I'm going to have an operation soon and then I'll be more useless than ever.' She did not look at me. She was staring out the window at the empty lawn.

'Don't, Mam,' I said.

'It's true.'

Something started up inside me, in my throat or my chest. Like bubbles breaking. I had to stop it.

'I love you,' I said.

'Don't be silly, you do not,' she said. 'How could you?' Then she bucked up and lifted herself in the bed.

The things that cross a fellow's mind when he is walking down a riverbank on his own, his thoughts distracted only by passing ships. One day I lay under a beech tree. There was beech mast on the ground. It was like a rough mattress beneath me and the smell of bluebells and other flowers, the buttercup, the garlic in its sheath of green leaves, was going to my head. I think I went to sleep. Was the monastic life of early rising catching up on me at last? And who should pop up before my eyes but the Three Wise Men. That woke me.

The Three Wise Men had been around at Ivyhall again recently. A long time since last they were around. How long? They've been around a few times, Bunny says. While you were at boarding-school. When have I last seen them? Not since that day we walked the farm with them. That baby, whose imminent arrival at that time I was unaware of, who turned up dressed all in blue, what age was she now? She was seven.

Mam is ill. She is in Ardkeen Hospital.

I slept and woke, slept and woke, that day on the river and the air breezed above my head.

In my dream Granny is singing. She is up out of Granny's chair and she is singing. 'Come back to Erin, Mavourneen, Mavourneen.' Singing for Mam. Then she is holding Mam's head in her lap. The Three Wise Men have come around. Why have they come around? Who do I speak to about it? Richie? Richie's head pops up. No, I cannot speak to Richie. Richie lives in another world now. He is away at dance halls all the time. Bunny? Should I mention it to Bunny. Bunny's face pops up and tells me this: 'Watch out,' he says. 'Those fellows could give us all the sack . . . Your father and all could get the sack . . .'

Am I awake or am I asleep? I am thinking about the day we went to Dublin. Connaughton went to Dublin one day during my school holidays and took Murt and me along for company. In Parliament Street he showed us a door. He was meeting auctioneers in there, he said. The door was so studded with letter box flaps it was the colour of brass. He told us to call for him there after we had seen the sights. What a day! And wherever I went, Murt had to follow me. Parliament Street with the tall houses, Dame Street, where we looked at dinner menus in windows, Grafton Street, where we saw teddy boys in pointy shoes and slicked back hair. Up to St Stephen's Green. I just had to see what that place looked like. It was only a park; we didn't bother going in. We studied the menus in more windows. They were all too dear.

I went into a shop. All grown-up looking, so that I would be served. A thin man in a nylon shirt stood high behind the counter. And flopping off the shirt, a label with a name on it. Keith. 'Ten Carroll's No 1, Keith,' says I, nonchalantly. 'Thanks, pal.' He handed them over and took my money. Thanks, pal. It sounded great the way he said it. It was the salute that went with the city transaction. 'See him?' I said to Murt. 'Thanks, pal. That's the way you have to talk up here.'

Murt looks in the window of the amusements arcade and I smoke cigarettes. I watch the teddy boys at the door of the arcade. Teddy Ash says he likes the clothes they wear. He says they are called after him, ha ha.

When Connaughton has finished his business he takes us to a chip-shop. What, not a hotel, as we have been used to? Oh but things have disimproved. I can see it in his face. I know. Murt doesn't. Murt loves the chips. I don't. Daddy is looking for a job, I tell Murt.

'Why does he want a job when he has one at home?'

'He wants a job in Dublin.'

'How could he come up here to work in Dublin?'

'An auctioneer's office in Parliament Street, Murt. Up on the second floor, looking down on the street. You'll like it.'

'I'm not coming to live in Dublin, Lally.'

'Why, Murt?'

'I'd be afraid.'

But what is going on at home? Executors coming around again. The Three Wise Men. Walking the farm. With questions: where is this tractor? where is that baler? When was the pier of the gate broken? Why didn't you mend it with the same stones? Where are the stones gone? Three Wise Men.

In my dream again: Granny is singing. 'Come back to Erin, Mavourneen, Mavourneen.' Holding Mam's head in her lap and singing.

I see my Dada. He is driving around in the car, looking for a job. He has a worried expression. Never fear, my Dada. He opens the window when he sees me, he throws out a smoking cigarette and he smiles at me so that his face is like sunshine.

How tranquil one's mind when in dream along a riverbank.

6

I was already home on summer holidays the day Mam came out of hospital after the operation: all Ivyhall stood still that day and was in the kitchen awaiting her return. I thought I was prepared, but I wasn't. The front door was thrown open wide. Then she was standing there on the step and we were looking up. Her face was pale. She was struggling with crutches. One leg was all that held her up. Where the other should have been there was a space. I was looking far beyond, looking through the space. I could see the yard, and beyond the yard, the Hill field. Strung across the field was the clothesline. A white shirt, flying in the wind, was filling all the sky.

'Ye'll get used to me,' she said.

Mam's one leg was bare. I thought of the six pairs of socks she had given me. Why had she not kept some them to wear on her leg? Poor Mam, I said to myself, looking at the bare leg. Blaming her, feeling sorry for her. Poor Mam, I said to myself.

Then Dancie came to the door, fumbling for her cigarettes in her pinafore and said, What are you all gaping at, will some of you get a chair and let the missus sit down?

7

On a warm afternoon in Mont La Salle, the sun heavy behind a blanket of cloud, I began my own stay in hospital. I was near the end of my fourth year of schooling. My second last year of Mont La Salle. We were standing at the side of the college, the Kelly-Jackson gang, playing cards. Building work was going on; a scaffolding clung around the top floor of the college and a bucket and winch was set up to take cement up to it. But this was Saturday and the builders were not around.

It was all Kelly-Jackson's idea. He had noticed that when the bucket was hauled up it passed by the window of the college president's office. Brother Robert, Bobbio, was somebody we rarely saw. It was rumoured that he appeared at the end of the church during mass and devotions but that was something we were not sure of as we were not allowed look around. We saw him only on prize-giving day. We didn't know much about him, but one thing we did know was that examination papers were kept in his office. It was the weekend before the beginning of exams. These were important examination papers; the summer exams before the Leaving Cert itself. You were expected to do well in them.

'We'll get in his window and we'll get the papers,' said Kelly-Jackson, and his face lit up with delight. 'Dudid, you're small, I'll pull you up on the bucket.'

'Not doing it,' I said.

'Ah do it for us,' Kelly-Jackson pleaded. 'If I was small like you, I'd go up myself.'

What could I say? That I hadn't a head for heights?

'No.'

'Ah do.'

I suppose I must have been pleased he should have asked me to get in the bucket when he could have asked one of the henchmen closest to him – Ash, or one of the others. And I was impressed with the look of desperation on his face.

'OK, OK, but nobody squeals on me,' I said, once I had been given a firm commitment from the gathering crowd standing around looking in at me in the bucket that they would keep nix for me and not let me down or go and tell Discharge.

Kelly-Jackson posted the gang on watch duty. 'No squealin' on Dudid,' he warned them.

Ash said he was having nothing to do with it. 'I'm shagging off outa here,' he said. He looked at me as though I should do the same. Ash didn't need stolen exam papers in order to pass exams.

It was too late now for me to turn away.

KJ was a good strategist. He placed his men so that they could spot Discharge long before he spotted them. Then he spat on his hands and splayed his feet against the concrete ground. 'Shout down when you're getting outa the bucket at the window. Shout so I stop pulling and the bucket won't go shooting up with no one in it.' The office was on the third floor.

'Oh those magnificent men in their flying machines . . .' Somebody sang. It was not a smooth ride. I was rising up in starts. With each haul from Kelly-Jackson, I seemed to take a leap into the air. After only four or five hauls I was already alarmingly high. I decided not to look and closed my eyes, but that made the sensation of rising even worse.

Then I heard KJ laughing. I couldn't believe he could be laughing. How could I have any faith in a person who could laugh while holding my life in his hands?

'Stop,' I said. 'Let me down.' An empty feeling had spread through my tummy.

'No, you're not there yet,' he said.

'Well, stop laughing, can't you? You're shaking the bucket.'

But he wouldn't stop laughing. He called the others. 'Hey lads, there's a hole in Dudid's bucket. Hey Dudid, is it cold up there?'

Then my shoulder hit something and I had to open my eyes to see what it was. It was a windowsill and I was stuck beneath it. I closed my eyes again quickly because I could see the roofs of the houses in Roches Street outside the wall of the college. The sun glinted off them with a sharpness that seemed especially meant for me.

'I'm there now,' I called down. 'Stop.'

But there was no reply from below.

'I'm there,' I called again.

There was still no reply. I suddenly had a feeling of being very alone. There was nothing for it but to open my eyes and look down. I could see nobody down there. Who was holding the rope? It was tightly stretched. It was disappearing into the boiler room way below. How could that be? 'Oh let me down,' I called. I shouted. I don't know how many times. It occurred to me how stupid it was to shout when nobody was there but still I did.

Then, just as a calm began to take me over, the calm that comes before a fall, Kelly-Jackson's voice returned. 'Sssh, you were heard all over the place. Do you want us all caught?' His voice came up in a strained whisper. 'There was a nix. I had to go into the boiler room. Jesus, I was lucky I wasn't caught.'

'Well, let me down.'

'It's OK. It's OK. He's gone now.'

'I'm fuckin' squealin' on you, KJ.'

'Stay up there, you dizzy prick.'

Oh dear, it is only when you are on a bucket on a winch, three flights above the world, that you realise how helpless you can be. I was not going down and would not be. No matter how I protested: Kelly-Jackson was still pulling.

But I was not going up either: my shoulder was wedged against the window-sill above me. Which left me with no alternative, sick and dizzy as I was, but to unwedge myself. With a twist of my body, I freed myself. Then vertigo finally took me in the palm of its empty grasp, because with one sickening surge I was dangling outside the window of Bobbio's office.

Except that it wasn't Bobbio's office, after all.

Oh the stupid tools, the Kelly-Jackson gang. How could I have depended on them to know the whereabouts of Bobbio's office? Men were staring out the window at me. Ashen-faced men in ashen soutanes with ash-drooping cigarettes in their hands. It was a smoking-room for the Brothers. How could nobody have known there was a smoking-room there? Was it a secret annexe behind Bobbio's office or what?

Well, now I knew.

'Nix.' I called down. 'Nix, nix, nix, nix. They're all there.'

'Who is? Is Bobbio? Is Bobbio there?'

Of course he was there. He was rapping the window at me. Telling me to move on, by the looks of things.

'Yeah. He is.'

Horror had begun to dawn across the face of Bobbio in the window.

'Oh fuck, lads, it's big nix. Run.' The command reached up to me.

'I can't, KJ.'

But Kelly-Jackson could. And he did. I heard the clatter of his shoes. And suddenly I was free as a bird. There was a moment while the force of gravity was weighing me up, figuring what to do with me. Then it let me go. Lets you down sooner or later does the old force of gravity. And with a little farewell gesture of my hands, I was plummeting. I had a last glimpse of the dismayed faces in the window. Time-warped they were, horribly bent, by the speed of my gallant descent. Oh Jesus.

I remember the thought that passed through my mind. It was of surprise at the speed with which things can happen and of how, when they do, there is no reversing them. I will be dead in a moment, I thought, and there is nothing I can do to stop it. My helplessness shocked me.

I did try to do one thing. I grabbed at the rope. But it burned, in an instant, such a hole in my hand that the pain of it was even worse than the fear of death and so I let go. I flashed past the second floor window. It was the window of the study hall, and looking in, I saw a figure sit at a desk. It was my desk and the figure was me. Strange things happen when you are about to die – it was the very last thought I remember having – how it is a fellow can be seated at his desk in the study hall, writing a letter home to his mother, and at the same time sliding down the world on a bucket?

The next thing I remember after seeing the bucket rope jumping before my eyes was hearing the voices of men. They seemed to be very old men and they were away in the distance somewhere. At a crossroads, somewhere like that. Complaining old fellows. Complaining to one another about not getting something in time. What were they not getting on time? Injections. 'Nurse, where's me injection?' Imagine complaining about not getting an injection. I hated injections more than anything. Always had done; needle with the boiling eye coming at me. 'Nurse, you're late for my injection.' Daft old eejits.

There was another problem I had to sort out. I could not figure out for a long time what it was. It drifted away and then came back to me. Then I knew what it was: one of the voices was familiar. It belonged to someone I knew. From somewhere. From sometime. I knew one of those corner-boys at that crossroad.

Lying back on what I decided must be a bed (some things were beginning to compose around me: that I was in a bed, that I was indoors not out at a crossroad, as I had thought) the idea came to me that I should go back over all the faces of my long life in an attempt to put one to the voice. But I failed. I might have gone back too far in my life or I mightn't even have begun. I was falling again.

The next time I awoke faces were staring in at me. They were far away. They frightened me; their shiny eyes and beaky noses, they were like birds. Some of them had masks. I thought they were going to throw stones at me, down, down the cliff to where I was at the bottom. Then there was a white sky overhead swirling with threatening clouds – I was outdoors again – and there was no escaping their onslaught because they had surrounded me from every side of the crossroad. 'Call the guards,' I shouted. My voice was inside my head as if I was asleep, but it made them run away with a squeak of bare feet like the squeak of the boys' bare feet in my dormitory in Mont La Salle.

The next time they looked into my bed – it might have been hours or it might have been days later – I was not frightened of them and it was only their curiosity I had to deal with. I let them look, wondering when they would have seen enough. I scrutinised them in turn. They were all so old. I thought I was in the County Home. When I was young, I used go there with Connaughton to deliver meat from our butcher's shop in Templemore. Mama used to tell me to be careful of those old people because some of them were crackers. Now I was a patient there myself. I wondered what had happened to all my life that it had whizzed by so quickly.

Then up along the road came a starchy swish and the road was not a road but a corridor between beds and the men were running again because a voice was saying, 'Don't let me catch you. Why are you not wearing your slippers?' And a face that was bright as a skylight looked in at me. A face just bursting with laughter. She was a nurse and I was not in the County Home but the City Infirmary.

It took but one second for it to sink in with disappointment that the laughter on the nurse's face was not for me but for another nurse. It took but a few more to figure out everything else.

Nurse Hoyne – that was the name on her brooch – was talking, at the cheerful top of her voice, to another nurse behind her: 'Oho, the Archangel Gabriel has decided to wake up and join us.'

The other nurse, whose brooch said, Nurse Dalton, looked in at me. 'Did he leave his wings at home when he dropped out of the sky?' she said. They both laughed. 'I'd advise him to strap on his wings the next time he goes trapezing in a bucket.'

'Did he not know that there was a hole in his bucket?' Nurse Hoyne said.

They straightened up my bedclothes, laughing away to one another as they did so. Laughing and swishing going on above my head and I incidental to it all.

Then the voice of one of the men was calling: 'How is the trapeze artist from Duffy's Circus, hah? Duffy's Circus, hah? Down off the operating table, hah? Is he alive?'

And another voice was hollering, over and over again: 'Duffy's Circus, folks. Come see Duffy's Circus, one night and one night only.' They all sounded completely mad.

'Be quiet, Jack,' Nurse Hoyne said.

So I was Gabriel the Archangel and I was a trapeze artist in Duffy's Circus. And I was back from the operating theatre. And I was alive. I gave a little inward chuckle at that but the pain it caused down deep inside me was hardly worth it. It was one thing to worry about staying alive when I had thought I was going to die. Now I didn't care.

These were the things that slowly dawned on me: my leg was strapped up but it may as well not have been there at all because I couldn't feel it. My head was bandaged. I didn't know how much of it was bandaged. From neck to tip, I had to suppose. With only holes for my eyes and mouth and nose. And my ears, I had to suppose, there must have been holes for my ears also, because I could hear. There was a bandage on my hand. The pain in my hand was bad. It was funny that it was the only pain, in any part of me, that I could feel. The burn from the rope. I remembered the rope. How far had the rope burned in? I wondered. Had it cut my hand right off at the palm? Because that was how it felt.

I went to sleep; I woke up; I learned a little more each time. Hazy learning, coming through miles of drowsy pain. I had to make a huge effort to keep attention, otherwise I slipped away; sometimes I even fell again, the windows of the college whizzing past my eyes. But to make the effort was worth it. It seemed all so vitally interesting. Hospital was, in fact, I decided, the most interesting place in the world.

And who was in the bed across the ward from me? The one whose voice puzzled me during my nightmares? It took a while to work it out. In the end it was not the voice, but what the voice was saying, that solved the puzzle for me.

'Ruby Red-face', the others called him. I could tell from the way they talked that they didn't take him seriously. That surprised me. I had always taken him very seriously.

'Hey, Ruby. Tell us your story again.' They were younger voices.

'What story?' Wearily the older one answered.

'About where you went. The time of all them sheep you were riding.'

'She'll be ridin' round the mountain,' another voice sang, and there was a smirky laugh.

'You're some tulip, Ruby, tell us where you went again.'

'In Tipperary?'

'Jesus, Ruby, not in Tipperary. Before that, in what do you call it?'

Ruby, they called him. It was a good name. But not as good as the name I knew him by. Harry Crowe, that was his name. That was who was in the bed opposite me. Our old hitchhiker, that Mam called Har the Heart. I was so amazed, I tried to look across at him but the weight on my head was so great I couldn't. And now he was called Ruby Red-face.

'No, not in bloody Tipperary,' they shouted at him.

'Where?'

'In what do you call it? In bloody Tierra FanDango. Told us the night you came in, you were raving. You're some tulip.'

The first person who jumped to my mind once I realised I was in the City Infirmary was my old friend, Ash. I had been in the infirmary before. I visited Ash when he was here with appendicitis. In third year, that was. Now he would be calling to visit me.

Ash: third year was the year Ash changed. When he was in second he had eyes soft as a calf's and was so lovely and simple to look at. I could look at him forever. Ash was different now. It happened after he got the appendix out. Big he was now. The appendix kept a fellow small. Food got stuck in there and didn't get used up. I still had mine in. I always noticed that about the fellows. When a fellow left school for a while – got his appendix out or broke a leg or something – left school and then returned, he always returned completely different. With a moustache and a deep voice, long legs in long trousers, and an embarrassment about playing the games he would have played before. That happened Ash. Talked about clothes, Ash did now. Fashion. All the time. We no longer went together now, not on walks to the pictures, with Discharge going *lickety-lick* on his sandals alongside us, we did not sit side by side in the refectory, or anything. A pity about that. But he would be coming up to see me in the infirmary. Fellows took any chance of getting out for a few hours. All the fellows, including Ash, would be coming up to visit me soon. I wouldn't know what to say to him. That was why he was the first person who had jumped into my mind.

And the hitchhiker was here. How could that have happened? I didn't even know why he left Ivyhall. Why did the others say he was 'some tulip'?

I was learning things, though. As I lay and listened. As I fell in love with the nurses. Oh with all of them. With their warmth. Their very presence itself was warmth.

I didn't know what to do about the love. Was I supposed to tell the nurses? They didn't seem interested in talking to me. Maybe in hospitals it was like that. I had already fallen in love with two of them outright, though I wasn't sure from one moment to the next which they were because they came and went with such puzzling rapidity. Was it the way in hospitals that you fell in love with the nurses and they knew that and purposely ignored it? Anyway, they were too busy to be bothered about me and about whether I loved them. So I didn't tell them. They would be far more interested in knowing if one of the other patients loved them, I reckoned. They being more the age for it. So I consoled myself with having been in love before. Though it had been years back. In fact, it was when I fell in love with the nurses that my love for Frieda returned. Bursting out of my heart like birds out of ivy. Only, now was the first time I learned that love caused such real pain. Love pouring out of me like a stream, and going nowhere near those capable hands with those goddess bodies, except back into me, drowning me.

Yes, and I learned why Ruby was some tulip.

Here is the conversation. The patients had eaten dinner. I knew they had eaten by the clatter of trays and trolleys, then the silence while they ate and then the conversation that always came after it, slowly at first, until after about ten minutes it was going full pelt. I was looking up at the ceiling.

It was the two young fellows talking. I had now decided, from the sounds of the voices, unable as I was to raise my head, that there were four patients in the ward; that two of them were older, Ruby and the one called Jack, and that the others were younger, about nineteen or twenty or so.

'You're some tulip, Ruby. Didn't you not know the tide was out when you tried to drown yourself in the river?'

'No.'

'Didn't you not see the gap of daylight under the bridge? Didn't you not see the mud, you ould shagger? How can a fella drown in mud?'

'It was night-time.'

'You're some tulip all the same. All night up to your belly in mud until an ould woman saw you on her way to mass. Why didn't you fill your pockets with stones?'

'What makes you think I was trying to drown myself?'

That was why they said our hitchhiker was some tulip.

Later that same evening they talked about what it meant to be in love.

I was all attention.

'How do you know when you're in love?'

'Were you ever in love, Ruby? Tell us about the time of the sheep.'

The hitchhiker groaned and said they did not know what they were talking about.

'I know when a fellow is in love with the nurse,' one of the men said. 'It's when he's dying to get her into the bed alongside his laddie-boy.'

'No, it's not.'

'What is it then?'

'It's the other way around, it's when she's dying to get into the bed alongside his laddie-boy. That's when he knows he's in love.'

They hadn't heard her, but Nurse Hoyne was in the little caboose getting the injections ready all the time they were talking about love. She put her head out and said she would have to stick suppositories up their bottoms if they didn't shut up.

Love? Which of those two had the correct version? I thought about it a long time and found that having to decide on either one or the other version was making me unhappy. My own idea of love was totally different. I was burning inside, a slow tender burn. My feeling for the nurses was the sort of thing you felt for a woman who cared for you . . . A mother? No, she was not so much a mother, but a sister. She was a sister, a big sister, who was always on the verge of letting you into a big secret. Whisper in the ear big secret. Dangerous and tantalising. And if she would just tell it to you, flutter it into your ear . . . oh even more than a big sister would she be then. You and she, all in one. But my ears . . . as far as I knew they may as well have been covered with the plaster of Paris.

8

The nurses swished in, all business, and pulled the curtains around me. 'Now sir.' They sat me up and unfurled the bandage from my head. It came down in coils on the bed. I felt like a tree whose branches had been got at by a slash hook, a cold wind was swirling all about me. Then, when I was feeling my most naked, the curtain was pulled back again and about ten doctors marched in, all clipboards and stethoscopes. The nurse stood behind them, I wanted her to hold my hand but she only stood at the curtain, closing it again, and one doctor, who had about twenty Biros stuck into the top pocket of his white coat, bent over me and looked very closely into my eyes and then along both sides of my head. He nodded to the other doctors. 'He'll live,' he said. They nodded back. Then they all slid out through a slit in the curtain, leaving me marvelling at how crowded my quarters had been.

On the same day I had my first visit. I was propped up in the bed, gingerly manoeuvring my head inside my fresh bandages when they appeared around the corner of the ward. Through the slit in my cordon of curtains I saw them. The two Brothers. Oh holy God, dressed as though they were attending a synod or something – the solemn outdoor clothes, hats, topcoats and black gloves. My eyes slammed shut. They stayed shut, they had been open for long enough. They had seen whose faces the white collars and black hats belonged to. One of them was old beef-face himself: Discharge. The other was a face I had very recently been staring at through a third floor window. Yes, the president. Brother Robert. Bobbio. I pretended I was asleep.

'Sit down,' Bobbio ordered Discharge, in a voice loud with authority. It surprised me. I had to suppose that was the way of it back in the Brothers' living quarters in the college. The president doing all the ordering. I could imagine Discharge's meek consent; none of the fury we beheld everyday in the corridors. I heard the cane chairs squirm beneath the weight of the two fat bottoms. 'He sleepeth,' Bobbio said. 'He is not dead but sleepeth.'

That drew a laugh, or a cough that was an excuse for a laugh, from Discharge. 'This'll put a stop to his gallop,' he said.

I could feel a pull on my bedclothes. I knew instantly what it was: Discharge cleaning his glasses. He was always cleaning his glasses, talking at you as he did through eyes rimed with frustration. I tried to let my muscles relax. You could not pretend to be asleep when you were seated rigid as I was. I began slowly to slide down the bed.

After a spell of silence, while I wondered if either of them was going to say anything more or if I was going to have to wake up and say something myself, I suddenly detected a familiar aroma. I guessed what it was. It was right beneath my nose. I was so surprised I had to chink my eyes open to see if I was correct in my guess. I was right, cigarettes. A packet of Aftons, opened before me. Same cigarettes as Connaughton smoked. Bobbio was holding them out. Ordering again. 'Have one.' They fogged away then to their hearts' content. It was that quiet time of afternoon before you heard the shimmer of the tea tray and the tea girl came in with the tea. All the patients must have been asleep and the only sounds were the sounds of contented puffing.

'But wasn't the chapel freezing this morning at mass,' said Bobbio suddenly, out of the blue. 'I'll have to talk to Bursar about the boilers.'

The Brothers must have felt very relaxed inside my little haven, cut off from the whole world. Bobbio sniffed, he was always a sniffler; after a while he began to speak again. With a different voice, grown friendly.

'Con,' he said, calling Discharge by the short version of his name, Constantine.

'What, Robbie?'

'You remember that concern we had from the Provincial?'

'When? During his last visit?'

'No. That letter he wrote.'

'Remind me.'

Bobbio gave one of his sniffs. 'Don't disappoint me now, Con. The toilet paper, remember?'

Discharge took a while to remember. He must have been thinking hard, trying not disappoint Bobbio. Fellows in the college said about Discharge that he had a creaky brain. That his parents stuck him in the Brothers after primary school because it was the only place where he would get steady fodder. Sometimes I could almost feel a pity for him. Like now. He had a willingness. Behind the cunning in his face, which was not cunning at all but fear of being exposed by quicker-witted people, he had a willingness. I could almost hear it now in his slow thinking.

'Oh yes, you were telling me. He had a complaint about the waste of toilet paper. He asked you to explain to him how come the boarders used so many rolls of toilet paper in one term.'

'That's it, Con. Good man.'

'Did you work it out, Robbie? Did you explain it for him?'

'Yes, I gave him his figures.'

Robbie and Con. It was strange hearing them talk like this. But I had heard Brothers at this stuff before, this first-name stuff when they thought they were in private.

'I gave him his figures, Con. Wrote them off to him by reply. "A multiplication sum: boarders in the college multiplied by days in the term multiplied by three. Do your sums, Provincial, and you'll get your answer".'

'You gave him his figures,' Discharge said.

'Yes, boarders by days by three, except he's written back again since, querying what the three stands for.'

'That's no business of the Provincial's anyway. That's the bursar's job.'

'I agree.'

Now I wanted to know what the three stood for. I was disappointed that Discharge had not asked. Probably pretending he knew all along. But Bobbio let it out anyway.

'God protect me, Con, and if I didn't write back with the answer he deserved: three for three rubs of paper. One up, one down and one for polishing off. The boarder's handshake.'

There was a muffled strangulation for ages after that. I could feel my bed jolting on Bobbio's side of me. Laughter, he must have been doubling up, doing his best to contain it. Every now and then a wheezy escape: 'The boarder's handshake, Con.' Then jolts from Discharge's side, 'The boarder's handshake, Robbie, you have me crying laughing.'

I felt like crying laughing myself, or crying at least. I was remembering what the Provincial looked like. He visited, in turn, all the schools in the country. He wafted ghostily around the corridors of Mont La Salle and if you ran into him, he stared you up and down as if you were an abstraction. If the Brothers passed him, they dropped their eyes and made a polite sound in their throats. Especially Discharge. Bobbio gave out the prayers with special fervour the week the Provincial was around. Now here they were, in stitches of laughter. I desperately wanted to open my eyes and see them. What did Brothers look like when they carried on like this. The President and the Dean of Discipline. What was the world coming to or had it always been this way. Was I forever being hoodwinked. But could I take a peep to find out? No, I could not, because now they were off on a conversation that insisted my eyes remain clamped even tighter. Rip Van Winkle was going to be nothing to me if they didn't stop talking. The conversation had turned to me, to my very own self. And I was feeling guilty with what my ears were receiving, like a thief that is half-hearted about his work.

'How do you find him?' Bobbio was asking. 'Not a bad lad?'

'Not a bad lad,' Discharge warbled back. 'But easily led.'

'He'll get a decent Leaving Cert?'

'If he works . . . If he can be kept away from Kelly-Jackson and company . . . There are lots of ifs in it. Lots of ifs. He has the brains, though.' Discharge really was discharging now. Full throttle. The same slobbery sound that pontificated out of him on dirty table-cloth day.

'Kelly-Jackson and company,' Bobbio sighed. 'As though he won't have distraction enough on the home front this coming year.'

'What's that?'

'His mother. I rang the father to tell him about the young lad going into hospital. He was furious. Furious. Wanted to know how could we let something like that happen? Said he would be taking his son out of the college. Then when I calmed him down and pointed out that moving the lad in Leaving Cert year might be destabilising, he agreed. Said he was a bit worried about the mother and Mont La Salle might be the best place for him.'

'He's worried about her?'

'She has to go back to hospital for tests. Kilkenny.'

'Secondaries?'

'He hopes not, but maybe. You know what secondaries are like, Con.'

'God help them.'

After that they started on about the Brother-Provincial again. Discharge told Bobbio he would be in line for the job when it came up again. Bobbio said it was coming up shortly but he had no interest in it himself. Why wouldn't you? Discharge said. You should.

'I have enough responsibility as it without taking on any more,' Bobbio said. 'I don't want an early grave.' And on and on they droned, Discharge arse-licking and Bobbio loving it, except I wasn't listening any more.

Secondaries. What were secondaries anyway? The Brothers eventually got up and went. My eyes, by that time, had become so used to being shut that it was a pain to open them. A bunch of grapes sat on the locker alongside me.

My mind was shrinking to the size of a pea with the current of thoughts going through it. I tried a grape. It hurt my jaws and it tasted of Aftons.

My father's cigarettes, Aftons. My mother's, Craven A. The ditty that the hitchhiker had liked to repeat whenever he saw her smoke one: 'Craven A today, cravin' butts tomorrow, ma'am.'

What were secondaries? The electric current was rushing through my mind. I remembered the last time I had been driven back to college. Fern drove me. Mam, I didn't remember why, couldn't do it. Good old Fern, do anything for Mam. Loved any excuse to drive Mam's car. Tessa passed by as we drove off and he got out and spoke to her for ages. She was shaking her head as though she couldn't believe something and then she was crying. A great crier, Tessa. That was the big thing about Mam; never once a cry from her.

The same fellow who said 'Craven A today', now he was in a bed across the ward. Lying there tangled in his knot of sheets. Suddenly, I don't know how it hit me, I knew he loved my mother. I wanted to talk to him but couldn't. What was there to say: Remember Ivyhall, remember my mother? He would be lying over there, staring at the ceiling. Eyes that the light had gone out of. Yes, that was it. The light had gone out of Harry Crowe's eyes. Mam had done something good for the hitchhiker. But then, what happened? Had she disappointed him? Had he disappointed her? Had he lost nerve and walked away from Ivyhall? Could I remind him of why he had walked away from Ivyhall? Because now I was sure he had.

Then I was not thinking about Harry Crowe but about myself. My mind had run away with me, and with me alone. Up and down labyrinths where the light was vanishing. There was I, in the middle of the world, nobody else was there. Deciding the fates. The sweetest, at the same time the most forbidding of thoughts, was passing before me. A petrified conversation going on in my mind. Let her die, the voice in my mind was saying. And let my freedom come, my release. And then, Let people feel sorry for me. All over again. As once they must have done when my own mother died. I have been hoarding up this opportunity. Nobody has felt sorry for me for a long long time. I have had to indulge in bouts of feeling sorry for myself because nobody else has felt sorry for me. Let me into this easy world where no effort can ever be expected of me, where it would be just too cruel for anybody to ask anything of me. Where I do not have to disappoint anybody. That includes, especially, Mam. Where I can do as I wish. Where, at last, I can be me.

Then I was in a panic. My mind shrivelled at the treachery of its own designs. Mam would never die. People as real as Mam did not die. Mam was a person, not an event about to happen. There was too much of Mam. Death could never take her.

I tried another grape. My jaws still wouldn't close on it. My head wasn't right yet, no matter what the doctors said. Then Nurse Hoyne came along with the evening bowl of goodie. 'Open wide.'

9

More grapes. I couldn't eat them either. It was Connaughton. I saw him before he saw me. Oh Good Jesus, there he stood, hesitating, at the door to the ward. It was mid-morning. Silent in the ward. The men were all asleep, or dead, or what. Worn out from having been woken so early. My heart gave a leap when I saw him but at the same time, poor Daddy, I nearly cried. He looked so small. He was from the normal world, the world out there, the world I had forgotten and that seemed suddenly so small and dear to me and far away and strange. He had such a smile on his face but it was breaking down at the corners with worry at what he might see as he scanned the bodies in the beds. Then he walked towards me, a brown parcel in his hand. The smile had grown even wider, lighting all his face, lighting the edges of his eyes. The children straggled behind. The three little ones: Noeline with the bunch of grapes, Jamesy with an apple, and Martin with a banana. They were unsure of themselves and did not look at me but in embarassment heaped the fruit on my bed.

'Hello, brave man,' Connaugton said. Then he saw the grapes left behind by Discharge. 'I see you've already had visitors. Glory be, but you will be like a prince of Arabia now with your fruit piled about you and your head turbanned with bandages.' In the parcel, he said, was a cooked chicken. And it was Mam's idea, because she knew how much I liked chicken. 'How are you?'

'I'm all right.'

'Could you not have been more careful?'

'What?'

'Falling like that.'

'Sorry.'

The story I had made up was that the jaunt in the bucket had all been my doing. I could not have squealed on KJ for he would have been expelled.

'Oh well, the Just Man fell three times. Ever heard that phrase?'

He looked around him then at the forms of the other patients lying in the beds and he sang to himself a little snatch of a song, his usual trick when he was happy or relieved or didn't know what to say next.

Suddenly it was me who was filled with anxiety. I remembered the hitchhiker. Harry, in the bed opposite. Connaughton was going to spot him, or Harry was going to lift his sleepy head and spot Connaughton. I did not want that to happen. I did not want them seeing one another. I had my ideas why the hitchhiker had left Ivyhall, but did Connaughton? I only knew he had liked Harry, and I did not want any awkward moments now. I wanted to protect them from one another and from any difficult moment that might arise. Or I just wanted to protect myself. But the hitchhiker was sound asleep. Then a terrible desire came upon me to tell Connaughton anyway. It was only right he should know. Only right. Something was nagging at me. Is this the first time I have hidden something from my father? I was thinking. Hidden something about the world, not just about myself, not just about keeping myself out of some trouble, but about important things of the world? It made me feel years older, for a few moments even older than he. As though it were I, not he, who was the father. Then he got up and with his happy silly face went looking for the nurse. He would have to demonstrate to her, he said, how the chicken should be minced small so that I could eat it. Mam's instructions, he said. As soon as he had gone, the little ones began to fight. They wanted to eat the grapes. Jamesy and Martin did, but Noeline would not let them. 'They are for Lally,' she said. 'Grapes are only for sick people.'

They looked at me as though I were a different species. The species of sick people. They grew more chatty. 'Daddy is real cross with you for falling,' Martin said.

'Shut up,' Jamesy said. 'He's not.'

When Connaughton came back he said we should say a decade of the rosary. It was for a special intention. I knew it was not for me. It was for a more important intention then me. Except, why did he have to say it here? In a ward of diehards. Including a hitchhiker who had never been a lover of prayers. Sleep on, I prayed, sleep deeply, men. Then, suddenly tired out by everything – my un-yielding bed, the smells of hospital medicines, the glint of hospital utensils – I gave up to some sort of peace and I mumbled the responses. It was his way of including me in what was going on at home; I let it happen.

During the decade of the rosary, 'First Joyful Mystery: The Annunciation by the Angel Gabriel', the stricken look came upon him but as soon as it was over he jumped up all happy and light again and kissed his crucifix: 'Lally, as soon as your Mam is better we'll both come and see you. I will be visiting her every day in Kilkenny Hospital and then we'll get her home and you'll be next on our list. We'll get you home soon too, for summer. And Cork beat and the hay saved. Have you ever heard that phrase?'

Daddy, you and your phrases. Yes, I have heard it. You've said it a thousand times.

Then they were gone. After a while I felt a warmth go out of the ward. Like an apparition had visited.

Kelly-Jackson visited and ate all my grapes. 'Howya. Discharge said I wasn't to visit, he's a tool, but here I am anyway.'

'Thanks for visitin', KJ. Yeh, he's a tool.'

Ash came a few times but never on his own. He was more inter-ested in the nurses than in me, winking to the other fellows every time Nurse Hoyne came around. I was mad with him for that; he was not up to Nurse Hoyne's standards and how dare he presume otherwise.

'Leave it,' I said.

'Dudid is on a horn beneath his blankets,' he said.

Hospital days passed quickly. I dreaded getting better and going back to school. The bandages got lighter. More than goodie was passing through my lips. More than goodie was passing out of them. I was learning dirty jokes from the other patients, the two young ones, Shortall and Foskin. The old one, Cantwell. I was telling them jokes in return. Shortall and Foskin were roadwork men, who had spilled a barrel of boiling tar over themselves. They were bandaged from the waist down. For days they cried when the bandages were changed. Then they began to get better.

'Come here, nurse, until I show you under my bandage.' They had found out Nurse Hoyne's name. It was Rena. 'Come here, Rena, until I show you.'

'You disgusting creatures,' Nurse Hoyne would skelp at them, her breasts rubbing beautifully beneath her uniform. Beautiful, beautiful Rena Hoyne. And you know what? I forgot all about what I had overheard regarding Mam. For ages I did.

Then one day the hitchhiker cleared his throat and spoke. It was a day the Vincent de Paul man visited. He was a thin man with a crown topper, the hair more like feathers than hair, feathers brushed flat, like a contented hen. 'Would ye like fruit pastilles, boys?' he said. The men said they would like fruit pastilles. Yes they would, thanks. All the men, except for the hitchhiker, said they would. They were given fruit pastilles, loose from a bag. Me too, I got them. And with every fruit pastille we got, we had to take a holy picture. That was the bargain. He was a busy Vincent de Paul man that day, doing the rounds of the beds. Penny pictures, he said, but works of art. And God loves you for taking them.

The pictures came in two colours: pale blue and pale green. There were three pictures: Our Lady being assumed into heaven; Saint Patrick trodding down serpents; the Baby Jesus, an enormous hood, like the hair dryer in a ladies' hairdresser's, over his head.

The hitchhiker would not take any sweets or any pictures.

'They're only playing cards,' he said to the man. 'For playing Beggar my Neighbour, you fool.'

'God loves you too,' the Vincent de Paul man said. 'You too will get better. The love of your Saviour will soon have you on your feet again.'

'I will not be on my feet again,' the hitchiker roared. 'How dare you presume?'

'I'll pray for you,' the Vincent de Paul man said.

When he said that, the hitchhiker cleared him from the ward. 'How dare you tell me I'll get better?' he shouted. 'What do you know about love, you fraud.'

The Vincent de Paul man could only smile and the others smiled back at him as he hurriedly left the ward.

When he had gone a few moments and silence had been restored, the men began to grumble, old Cantwell saying, 'Ruby, it wouldn't have killed you to take a few oul' holy pictures.' That was when the hitchhiker, with a special effort, cleared his throat. It was the prelude to the story he had already told the others prior to my arrival. Now I was to hear it.

'I've been listening too long to you lot and your talk about love. Pulling nurses into beds, is that what love is? And now this beats everything: a fool with playing cards telling me God loves me.'

'He's a harmless ould Christian, that's all he is.'

'Nothing harmless about love.'

'What's love, Ruby?' Foskin sang out, as though he was asking the simplest of questions.

'Love is a traveller's itch. Not being travellers, you lot don't know what it is, and neither does that fool.'

'Whisht, whisht,' Foskin and Shortall both called. 'Words of wisdom from Ruby. He's going to tell us about that place. Tell us again.'

'I learned love when I was a shepherd once. I learned it from a madman who owned five hundred sheep in Argentina.'

'Why was he a madman, Ruby?'

'He had two wives who spent their lives in the house looking after him.'

'Two wives, Ruby?'

'He had a moat built around the house, like an Englishman.'

'To keep in the women?'

'Naw, there was no water in it. He just liked the look of it.'

'And was he an Englishman?'

'No, bad cess to him, he was Irish, worse again. But he was the boss man. He had big notions.'

'Tell us about the day, Ruby.'

'A day came, a bright sunny day you would sometimes get in those parts. The sheep were grazing the lawn and the women were darning his lordship's socks at the kitchen table inside, when a ram walks up to the big bay window and sees his reflection within.'

'And what did he do?'

The men were already laughing in anticipation. I could see they had enjoyed the story before and now were relishing it again. The hitchhiker too rose in his bed to make a special effort to tell it.

'Oh a big bucko, this ram was, with upright horns. Didn't he think he saw another ram inside; he lowered the horns and charged at himself, across the moat, full pelt, making smithereens of the bow window. And you know sheep: just like humans, where one goes they all have to follow. Five hundred sheep jumped that moat and followed him through the window and then around the kitchen table, on which the two women were now standing for safety, shouting their poor heads off. Away up the stairs with them then, the whole flock, bleating for their lives, tramping through all the rooms, looking for a way out, grinding sheep marbles into all the floorboards until they found the back door and their escape. And ever after they could not be caught, but ran wild around that farm, never to be rounded up again. Oh mad as bloody hatters.'

'And how did you catch them?'

'The bossman gave me a shotgun and I had to creep up as near as I could and shoot the sheep. One by one I shot them, one a day. And one by one I carried them on the handlebars of a bike to a knacker's shop in the town. And he sold them as the best of mutton.'

'And the women?'

'The women lost their reason from it all. Every now and then he threatened them with the sheep. He was a laughing jackass. And every time a shot went off they leaped out of their skin.'

As the hitchhiker spoke I watched him closely. He had become more intense than ever I had seen him. The port-wine stain on his face seemed to have grown darker.

'Two lovely women,' he said. 'And I didn't know which of them I was fondest of. You couldn't say boo to them after that but they would run for their lives. I couldn't watch them. I gave him my notice in the end and I walked away. It was that or kill him.'

'You're some tulip, Ruby.'

'Now get out your holy pictures and play your Snap.'

Days in hospital when the white sky shone in upon your face and dazzled you so that you had to close your eyes . . . A little lip of sweat settled upon you and you felt yourself go clammy, though the sheets had just been changed. Sounds came in from the distant street below, barely reminding you there was a world beyond the hospital. As you sat there, your eyes vibrating in the light, you thought about things that had happened in your life. You relived an empty feeling. What prompted that feeling you did not know. You did not know, but you decided it could only be something called love. You felt love but didn't quite know what had started it off in the first place. You were thinking of the hitchhiker's words. Love is a traveller's itch. You wondered did he kill that man, as one hot summer in the haybarn of Ivyhall he told us he had. You wondered how some people could contain such things, taking up their bags again and moving on. Not me. I wanted to shout it out: love is a traveller's itch. Love is loneliness.

10

And then there were nights when you lay in the bed and listened to all the clatter and commotion going on downstairs. Trays banging, doors slamming. Were there secret midnight feasts going on down there? Your mind became very active. You slipped out of bed and looked over the city of Waterford. At the line of the river. The lights of Ferrybank on the far side. The lights of Mont La Salle up on the hill. You marvelled at yourself each night. And why? The convent was over in Ferrybank. The boys were in Mont La Salle. A fevered spate of love-letter writing had started up between them. Why? Because you, that is, I, Dudid Connaughton, had become a postman. Rather, I had become the post office. Love letters were being posted in to me from every side, c/o Dudid Connaughton, St Patrick's Men's Ward, the City Infirmary. (No censorship.)

And that was how I wrote to Frieda again. And the long days of my eunuch's apprenticeship came to an end. Boarding-school boy; I had been leading the life of a dreamer, washing my teeth each night at the line of basins, sending my barely yellowed underpants to the laundry each week, walking around in a dream of boys, pranks and football; rules of a celibate. I had forgotten Frieda. Now, like the men in the beds opposite, I sweated beneath my blankets. I plucked, out of the long folds of my foreskin, curds that had been sacredly fermenting in there for years, sacramental offerings. I got in touch with Frieda.

Here is how I became a post office. One day two boys from second year arrived up on a visit. Two little squirts. I had never even spoken to them before, just about noticed them around the college. These two were always combing the hair, always admiring their own clothes – shoes pointy, trousers tight, to the very limit of what Discharge would allow. They even wore waistcoats, the little dandies. 'Hello, Connaughton, what happened you?' And I recited off the whole story all over again, showing off once more. So anxious to make an impression, I was even willing to accept an audience from second year. But what did they want? What they wanted was: had I received love letters posted for them?

I had. Two. C/o Lally Connaughton, postmarked Muineachán. Nurse Dalton had given them to me one morning, saying I had a fan club. These midgets had girlfriends who were boarders in Monaghan and they had come to collect their mail. Monaghan!

Frieda's school. The very same. That was how I wrote to her. These two little geniuses had a contact there. Frieda's school. I joined up. I was on the mailing list again. Five years after Stack Straw delivered my first letter. In no time my bed had become the central sorting office. And all the letters from boys in Mont La Salle to girls in boarding-schools all over Ireland came through my post office.

It wasn't true about no censorship. I read all the letters, steamed the envelopes on Nurse Rena Hoyne's kettle in the caboose when she was not about. And in my own correspondence to Frieda, I included the choicest bits from the letters I had opened.

All that. And marriage was on my mind again. My letter to Frieda said I wanted to marry her.

And did that, in time, cause me bother, oh boy!

Those clattering nights, when the trays and the cutlery drawers and the doors played slamming games down in the bowels of the hospital, when business hours in my post office were over and the mail, stacked and arranged for collection, lay shining in the light from the city below . . . Mine was the occupied mind those nights. I didn't have time to wonder about Harry Crowe or about Mam. And in the days, I was busy also. I was learning to walk again. I was walking about with the help of a crutch, I was getting up to use the toilet, as big a nuisance to Nurse Hoyne as any of the others. I would not touch her, though. I was not like the others. They attempted to drop the hand, as I had done with Una back in the days of the hotel. Those things had come naturally to me then. Now, and increasingly with the passage of time, while my ideas of what I wanted to do with girls were becoming more purposeful, I was also becoming less daring. I wondered what indeed I would do when the time would come for me to do something with a girl. With Frieda.

Then the pain came back in my leg. Every night it came. Deep throb somewhere in the ball of my knee. I began to have an awful thought. It concerned the conversation about Mam and her 'secondaries' that I had overheard from the Brothers. But it was not Mam I was worried about; it was myself. Fear for my life; fear for my leg. Then, suddenly, Harry Crowe became very important to me again. Our hitchhiker. He became like Our Father Who art in Heaven. I decided I had to tell him a few things about Mam. I was keen to hear what he would have to say; it would give me an indication of the fates in store for me. First of all, though, I would have to introduce myself to him. Because this is the strange thing. Not once since I had come into the ward did he give an indication that he recognised me. Not even when my head bandage was taken off did he recognise me; my head being no different then to what it had been in Ivyhall, apart from the Indian-like shave of it and the war-paint of Elastoplast and iodine.

This was the story I wanted to tell the hitchhiker. It was not about Mam's secondaries. As I had lain in my bed of sweat, my knee going throb throb, I had worked out what Mam's secondaries were all about, what her primaries had been all about too. I wanted to tell the hitchhiker about Mam's primaries.

Mam's primaries had been in her knee. I thought back now of when she had been in hospital. Most of the days I had visited her in there she had been very unhappy, until suddenly one day she told me she was in great form. She had made a decision, she said, that was why. 'Here's a good song for you,' she said, and she sang:

> That's life
> That's what the people say
> You're flying high in April
> Shot down in May.

'That's your man, Frank Sinatra,' I said. (God, didn't me and Mam get on great when she was in hospital.)

'Too true, Lally,' she said. 'Too true, it is Frank.'

Now I was in hospital and I was in mortal dread that I had primaries myself. The treatment Mam had on hers was the same I would have on mine. I wanted to fill in the hitchhiker on a few things I had worked out. I had to talk to somebody and it had to be him. I could not talk to the nurses about it, and especially not to the doctor. I had visions of the operating theatre, the knife in the doctor's hand and myself counting the Biros in his pocket to distract me from my leg on the chopping block. If the hitchhiker agreed with me on my analysis of Mam's medical history well then I too was for the chopper.

It was my belief Mam's problems all sprang from the kick she got from a cow that night down in the dairy; that night she and the hitchhiker had been doing the milking and I met them at the wicket gate on the slope up from the yard. She was moaning with pain, hanging on to his shoulder, her foot all loose along the ground and when we got her into the kitchen and Dancie sat her down with a cup of tea she was white as death. It was the only time ever I heard Mam cry out in pain, even though it was only the beginning of a pain, which, I am sure, in time, got worse. I had worked a lot of things out: that day of the Munster final when she had gone limping off to the hotel, the car horn pinging away in her wake . . . She had her primaries then, of course she had . . . Another day when Connaughton told her she had a limp and she told him he was trying to make out she was an old woman . . . How many years had she known about it before she was found out? How many years could I expect before I would be found out myself?

I never did have my talk with the hitchhiker. You would not believe this, but there never was time. Always somebody was calling, or Shortall and Foskin were going on about something. It was impossible to get an audience with that hitchhiker. Or maybe I didn't want to; didn't want the bad news.

One day, as I made my painful way to the toilet, I stumbled.

'Why is that fella limping? He shouldn't be limping like that,' Nurse Hoyne said. 'Show me that knee.' She put me on the bed. 'Nurse Dalton, Nurse Dalton, did you see this fella's knee? It's out like a balloon.'

I got my audience – with the one I least wanted – the doctor. 'Fluid on the knee.' The big knife did not materialise, but the long needle. Oh how I welcomed, for the first time in my life, a needle. They drained the fluid out of the knee.

Oh how I worried over what had been done to Mam's knee on those nights I lay in the infirmary while I still was not sure if my own knee was on the mend. And how I thought I should have to seek the hitchhiker's knowledge! That inscrutable man who wandered our farm with his wide-brimmed hat shadowing his portwine stain, I felt he owed me something. I wanted to wake him up out of his walking dream. Wake up! How could he have scraped his beard against me in the hay barn and not know me now? How could he have shown me how to tip my nose with my tongue?

It would be all wrong if I were not to tell him I knew him. It would be ignoring our past.

You would hardly know the hitchhiker was in the bed. Flat out he lay, most of the time. The last day he had spoken was when he told us about the ram jumping the moat. That must have done him in. Then he got pleurisy. Then he got pneumonia. It had been sitting there, Nurse Hoyne said, since the day he jumped in the river. For four days he gasped for air; he was weaker than a stick. There wasn't a pick of flesh on him when he came out of it. Then he could only eat chicken broth. The long thin beak of him opening for the wobbly spoon.

I never got to tell the hitchhiker about Mam, about her amputation and my own fears of the same. The need left me. My leg had got better. Also, the day came when the hitchhiker's bed lay empty.

He left the infirmary before me. He would have shuffled out of the ward without a goodbye had the others not called him and forced out of him his going away speech.

'Bye, Ruby,' Foskin and Shortall called. 'No more swimming in shallow water now, you hear.'

He laughed. A laugh from the hitchhiker was a rarity, even in his Ivyhall days you didn't catch much laughter from him. I noticed, as I had not before, that his mouth was grown gummy, the teeth that remained, crooked and gapped. He made his speech.

'When you get to my age you swim closer to the shore,' he said. 'I'll tell you one thing, mates. The reason I came down to Waterford was to go to sea again. I thought of taking a berth on an old rock-dodger sailing up to Arklow. I sat on a hill overlooking the sea one day out at Dunmore East and I looked down over the grey skin of it and it frightened me. A ship lay out there, anchored, safe. I looked at that ship and knew its sailors had some knowledge we on shore did not. It was lying out, away from rocky dangers. Away from us. And it knew something . . . Knew something about that grey cold old sea . . . There wasn't even a wave moving on the sea that day. But I knew something too. I knew that sea was waiting for me and waiting to drag me down to its salty bottom. I knew. 'Take me,' I said one night I lost my patience and that's why I jumped in the river at John's Bridge. No, this old man won't go to sea no more. This man is beat.'

Old Cantwell seemed sadder than his mates: 'Ruby, you have many years in you yet, many years in you, boy. Don't say that.'

'Why?' said the hitchiker. 'Am I Methuselah, do you think?' A smile cut a crack in the port-wine map on his face.

He slipped away then. Not really looking as if he had many years in him. And he left behind not even one special word for me. Not even a look in my direction. A week later I limped out myself.

I left that infirmary feeling empty. And it was not just because of the hitchhiker. Not just because the man I had felt so warm towards once upon a time had failed to acknowledge me. Failed to reinforce a bond I had always felt had lain between us. Failed to tell me why he had left Ivyhall and where his travels were now leading him. Failed to tell me stories, in the way I wanted them told, in the

Huckleberry Finn way I knew them to be, stories about a land called Tierra del Fuego. Yes, because of him I felt empty, but also because I missed the company of the others – Shortall, Foskin and old Cantwell, with their coarse sayings. And the nurses, Nurse Dalton and Nurse Rena Hoyne, so casual, who yet had reduced my heart to love-torn shreds by the intimacy of their nearness.

I left the infirmary empty as an eggshell. I had discovered a thing called a broken heart. It was my first time finding out that sometimes hearts yearned for recognition from other hearts and got in return only emptiness. And that sometimes it was the opposite: sometimes hearts received the recognition but could give in return only emptiness. I thought first it was my own heart had been broken. But it was not my heart; it was the hitchhiker's, Harry Crowe's heart that had been broken. Mam had been good to him. That had been his problem. He had not known what to do for her in return. It broke his heart. That was why he had never acknowledged me. He did not want to be reminded.

But why should I have felt I knew the hitchhiker's problem? With whom did I have the problem of being unable to empty my own heart? Where did Mam figure in my life? Powerful and aloof that she was. Oh Jesus, was I crazy? Had hospital softened me? Like the soft boiled eggs I watched Nurse Hoyne spoon through the hitchhiker's lips. It all bothered me fearfully. I had a sudden fear my own life too would be one of empty wanderings.

And I may not have decided on it as I stumbled back to the world beyond the hospital door, the towering sun on my head, but I never again belted Chesty.

11

Shortly after Mam had come out of hospital following her 'small op', as she called it, she had got an automatic clutch installed in the car. Then she was on the road again, able to operate the pedals with the one leg. This was before my accident. One day she and I went to visit Witheroe, who had himself gone into hospital with a stomach problem. He had been there a long time, all through Mam's hospitalisation, and he looked melted down to nothing inside a pair of thick cotton pyjamas. She gave him cigarettes and they smoked and laughed. Such laughter there had always been between those two. Such teasers, when they were together.

'Tell me, ma'am,' says he, 'where's the leg gone?'

'Buried,' says she. 'Stuck in the ground. Ate by maggots and gone, isn't that funny, and the rest of me still standing?' They laughed their heads off at that.

Witheroe had recovered and come back to Ivyhall. No longer did he cycle home after his day's work but instead took the tractor. Mam ordered it. He balanced the gallon of milk so that it did not spill on the bumpy road home and on wintry nights he slung a sack over his shoulders. It was cold on the open-topped tractor.

One day Mam had to read him a letter from England. It had come from a priest at the centre that traced missing Irish persons, the place to which Mam had written off many letters to Christopher and to which she had once sent the batch from us children. Dancie said she had a bad feeling about the letter and she went out in the field to hang out clothes so she wouldn't have to listen. This day was like all the other days that letters had been read out around the table: Tessa smoking; an air of expectation. But this day Mam did not read out the letter. Her eyes skimmed over the page and then she said she would just give out the gist of it. The gist of it was that they still had not found Christopher. They were suggesting, because such a long time had passed since his disappearance, that it might be serving no purpose to write any further letters and that we might prepare ourselves for the idea that he had passed away.

'Yes, maybe we should,' Witheroe said.

Mam thought for a minute as if she was weighing up something and then she looked at the letter and said: 'He signs himself, "Yours in the Lord". Well now, Mr Yours in the Lord, we will not prepare ourselves for that. And you needn't think this is the last letter we'll write you.'

'You are worked up, ma'am,' Witheroe said. 'Calm down, please.'

I didn't think Mam was worked up. I thought she was feeling sorry for the idea that Witheroe should accept things.

'It is not the last letter we'll write, Mr Yours in the Lord,' she repeated. 'I am now going to write to Mr Yours in The Lord and tell him that he had better keep the letters we have written, and will continue to write. If he doesn't, I'll haunt him. Because a day will come when Christopher will turn up, and then, if he wants to, he can read our letters. And now, what I am going to do is write a long letter to Christopher, full of news.' She called the little ones from where they were, upstairs. 'Out with your pens,' she ordered.

That first time, years ago, we had all written to Christopher.

Only the little children wrote this time. They got their pens from their schoolbags and made a few scrawls.

Aunt Tessa had said nothing while all this was going on; she just puffed out haloes of cigarette smoke – a trick she had newly acquired from Witheroe, who nowadays spent a lot of his time in the kitchen rather than on the farm. She stabbed her tongue in the smoke and let the haloes rise around her head and kept her thoughts to herself. Witheroe shook his shoulders and said Mam was great to bother any more. He said that Christopher had probably made his own life now anyway, wherever he was. He said he would not be telling Ettie any news like what he had just heard from Mr Yours in the Lord and he certainly would not be telling any clergyman. Certainly not Father Glee. He made Mam promise to tell Dancie if it ever came around to that. But to be very careful when telling her. She would take it hard, he said.

Then Witheroe began to talk about the hitchhiker. You'd miss Harry sometimes, he said. He would have had something to say about this.

And what would Harry Crowe have said to make Witheroe feel better? He always did have something to say when Mam sat down at the kitchen table and read out those letters that had no news. Much as he hated to talk about anything under the sun, for he was no talker, he would always muster up words for Witheroe's Christopher. 'Where there's hope, there's life,' he would say. 'The wanderer always returns,' he would say. 'For what reason the wanderer always returns, I am beat if I can find an answer. But the wanderer always returns.' Harry Crowe would not be saying anything now. Because Tierra del Fuego and all those other worlds he had wandered in were well knocked out of him now. And because Witheroe was dead.

Yes, before Witheroe had even gone into hospital for the first time, the hitchhiker had already left Ivyhall. And when Witheroe went back to hospital for the second time it was just after I had returned to school. It was the beginning of a new school year – the first of my two Leaving Cert years. Then I had come home again, for Christmas. That was when Bunny told me. Told me over our usual bottles of ale in the cow-house. He was quiet about it.

'Cancer in the stomach, that's what killed my father. Not the lungs in the end. The mines did it.'

'Why did nobody write and tell me?'

'You had your studies, I suppose. Or your rambles around Waterford!'

'Sorry for your troubles, Bunny. And what about Dancie?'

'Dancie only talks about Christopher. She promised my father before he died that she and your mother would find him.'

'Poor old Dancie.'

'Scabby ould badger is what Dancie is.' Bunny became suddenly agitated.

'Why, Bunny?' I was surprised. The occasion on which a person told another of the death of his father was supposed to be solemn. Why should Bunny now talk like this about Dancie?

'Doesn't matter.'

'Tell me.'

Bunny looked at me as if he was deciding something. He seemed suddenly to have aged.

'All right so. Go up and rob a fag from her and I'll tell you.'

I returned with one of Dancie's cigarettes for Bunny. He kept his word.

'My brother didn't have two parents but three. They were my father, my mother and Dancie. But especially Dancie.'

'What do you mean?'

'They ruined him. They spoiled him. Each of the three of them wanted him for themselves. You've always wanted to know where Christopher fitted in, well I'll tell you. He was my aunt's son. She was in an accident; it killed her but first she lived a few weeks and she had a baby and he was safe. Then Dancie took him to Wexford with her and then my father and mother got him and between all of them they never stopped rowing about what was right for him and blamed one another for anything wrong he did or any trouble he got into. He had three chastisers instead of two. He got fed up with the lot of them and fucked off to England.'

It looked to me then as if Bunny was about to slam his fist into something – a cow's belly or a bale of hay. He didn't. Instead he grew small and slumped; the Bunny of old knocked out of him. That was when I knew he had not meant what he was saying about Dancie. And knew he too was just as protective of Christopher as any of them. I could see, at long last, why the argument had gone on between Dancie and Witheroe: a desire to protect their dead sister's son. What could I say?

'Will they find him ever?' I asked.

'Your mother says they will.'

Bunny did not look too sure. And I knew one thing. Bunny would not be going to England in search of his brother, as he had once promised. Bunny had changed. Some people travelled; some people remained. Bunny was the workman now. He no longer sized up his wrists like a boxer. Now he was sizing up the notion that he was head of a family. He would always remain at Ivyhall.

PART 5

1

I was on my last summer holidays from boarding-school. One year left to go. Mam gave me ten cigarettes to have at the dance. 'Don't drink, but smoke,' she said. 'A person who neither drinks nor smokes is mean. Don't drink.' She appraised me. 'Close the middle button of your jacket,' she said. I did. 'No, that's not right. Close the lower button instead. Don't look so miserable. Smile. Ah, that's better. He looks like Frank Sinatra, doesn't he?'

Connaughton laughed and said he didn't know what Frank Sinatra looked like. Mam made to do a little jig on the floor with her good leg but she stumbled and had to regain her balance. She sighed. It was the nicest sigh I heard ever.

I was relieved also at her turn of good humour. After Mam got the artificial limb she had been in very poor form for a while, irritable with everybody. Then she mastered it, and she became the opposite, very cheerful. Now she was becoming so used to it, driving the car and everything, that she just took it for granted. The problem now was that everything else also reverted to how it had been before. She got the pain in the throat sometimes too and that didn't help. Mam could be very sarcastic. The girls bore the brunt of this – because of having all the housework to do, they could not escape her tongue by getting out of the house, whereas the boys could make themselves scarce. One hot Sunday we were at dinner. Connaughton started it: 'Would you not eat a bit of roast beef and potato instead of those awful crispbreads?'

'I'm on a diet and I'll eat what I like to eat.'

'That's sawdust. Bad for your throat. Can I cut a thin slice of meat for you?'

Mam said nothing. She scraped butter over one crispbread and then over another, making a grating sound. My teeth were on edge. There was a starchy smell of peas and roast beef. It was too hot in the kitchen. Connaughton should have shut up, but he couldn't.

'You'll turn into a skeleton.'

'He wants me to turn into a lump,' Mam said to nobody in particular. 'Here, load up the plate for Two-ton Tessie. That's right, Two-ton Tessie. Anyone fancy going around on one leg carrying the weight of a lopsided Two-ton Tessie?'

That was too much for Connaughton. He bolted for the door, screaming. 'Sorry, sorry, sorry.'

'Where are you off to?' Mam shouted.

'I'm going for a Sunday drive,' he shouted back. He took off in the car, ninety miles an hour, leaving a scurt of dust behind him as he tore down the lane.

'Let him be off,' Mam said.

He was gone a long time. I don't know how far he drove. In my mind I followed him: Murphy's Cross, Crohane Cross, turns, twists, humps and hollows, Mullinahone. And I followed all the thoughts going on in his head. It wasn't the first time he'd done this. When he returned he was humming a little tune to himself, good as Punch. His Sunday drive, however, had brought about no improvement in Mam's humour.

'Why don't you go off and have a drink while you're at it?' she said. 'Why don't you go off and become a hopeless drinker, because

I'm useless anyway? A hopeless drinker is better than a dry drinker, what you are at the moment.'

Mam, it was, who couldn't keep her mouth shut this time. It was not fair. Considering the many times they both went off together to homes of hopeless drinkers, trying to do something to get them off the drink and taking chocolates and cigarettes and making a good night out of it, this was not fair. Connaughton was not a dry drinker, never that I knew of.

He took off again, this time loading up the car with the younger children. He put them on it, not in it. He sat them on the hood, on the bonnet, on the boot. They screamed with delight as he bounced down the lane and they slid off and climbed on again.

That was Connaughton's way of dealing with his temper.

'Madman,' Mam said, calming down herself.

During the period while Mam first came out of hospital, Ivyhall had become a gentler place. But now, apart from occasions such as when Connaughton took off with seven kids on top of the car and Mam had to shake her head in wonderment, that mood had all gone away. Mam had reverted to her distant determined self. Sometimes Connaughton suggested she should have the condition in her throat seen to, but she said, no thanks, no more hospital.

When she said that about Frank Sinatra as I headed off to the dance it was like a breaking of the new ice that was forming.

Richie jingled the keys of the car all the time Mam was fixing me for the dance. 'Hurry on,' he said. I didn't know if he liked the look of me. It would have been a help if I had known he did. He didn't say. He picked up Thos and Fern at the Cross. Nobody said a word to me, so I still didn't know if I looked all right. They looked OK, even if their suits were a bit old-fashioned. Then he picked up another fellow. Vere Hunt. He was standing by the piers at the end of his avenue and I got in the back, letting him in my seat.

'Cashel or Thurles,' he said, 'or Las Vegas?' He brushed a fleck off his light blue suit and thumped out a dance with his feet against the floor of the car. Vere Hunt. He was the son of old Kimberley Hunt. I had heard of him but I had never met him before. 'Hello,' he said to me. 'Do you know me?'

I said I didn't.

'I met you when you were four and I was six. You came to our house with your mother, God rest her. And all you wanted to do was play cowboys.'

I was impressed at Vere Hunt's assurance. Nobody in our house ever said things like: 'your mother, God rest her'. He had a light way with words; they somersaulted out of him, carefree as air. And I was impressed with his memory. I had thought I was the only one with a memory. His was even better than mine. All I could remember of that house I had visited was paintings – paintings of horses stacked everywhere – and a woman who wore trousers and spoke with a deep voice just like a man. Ducksy. I could not remember him. Indeed, I could only marvel now at how this daring man could have arrived out of that house of my dust-laden memories. Yes, it was nice to be remembered by Vere Hunt. Even though nowadays he might be Richie's friend.

He laughed then. 'A wee minnow you were. So now you're grown-up. So now we have another lady chaser.'

'Hands up for Cashel,' said Richie. He was driving in that direction anyway, flying it.

Thos and Fern discussed Cashel.

'Still the best place,' Thos said.

'For what?' laughed Fern. He poked Thos with his elbow, and jostling one another, they went into a cuddle.

Vere Hunt laughed at them. 'Two old goats,' he called them. With a flick of his fingers he spun a cigarette butt out the open window. Good shot, I thought.

'Hands up for where, young Connaughton?' he said to me.

'Cashel,' I said.

'Hah, who has a date tonight?' Fern said. Now they were laughing at me.

I did not have a date tonight.

I did not have a date tonight; next week was my date. A date next week with Frieda. I wasn't telling the others, though. I wouldn't tell them. I didn't like the word *date*. The word sounded wrong, inappropriate. Wrong for us, me and my one and only love, Frieda.

You watched the dancers from the balcony. That was how you learned. Watching fellows like Vere Hunt; he was the best jiver in the hall. Slow numbers were easy. You just sort of stuck to your partner and went into the middle of the dancers. Then you were moved round and round under the crystal ball. Jiving was not easy. I could have watched Vere Hunt jive all night. From watching him, I knew one thing: I wasn't ready to take the floor yet.

I practised a descent of the wide, shallow-stepped stairs. I did it slowly. The carpet was plush beneath my feet. It felt good. If any girls happened to be looking up, they could appraise me. They mightn't yet have the pleasure of dancing with me but at least they could get a foretaste of my Frank Sinatra-like movements. But Dickie Rock was singing, one hand over his heart and the other wavering before him, as if he was divining water or something, and even in the dim light of the hall I could see all the faces looking up towards him and every now and then, little whoops of admiration. Dickie grabbed his microphone and shook the flex like he was cracking a whip. A layer of dust the colour of face-compact rippled above the swaying crowd. Nobody was noticing Frank Sinatra on the stairs.

I went into the gents. There was not a soul in there. It must have been because everybody, even the learners, had taken the floor for the slow number. I was able to look at myself in the mirror. Normally you couldn't get near the mirror because of the queue of fellows combing their hair before it. Fellows had to stoop or bend sideways or rise on tippy-toes to get a glimpse at themselves. There could be ten faces all crowded into the little mirror at the same time. Now there was only me. Maybe it was because I was receiving the mirror's undivided attention, but my face was thin, and all the colour was withdrawn from it and the hair was weak as paper. No girl would ever even look at such a child's face. Then somebody came in and I had to look away and I went over to the urinals.

The fellow was Vere Hunt. I knew the light blue suit. He stood at the urinal right beside mine. He was making a very loud splash and I hoped he wasn't listening to me because I was barely managing to make any sound. He took the cigarette he was smoking out of his mouth and kept splashing. I was finishing now so I had to slow it. It was that or leave, and be thought little of by Vere Hunt. Then he pulled out his comb. Both hands were in use now. One holding a cigarette, the other combing the hair and the splashing going on louder than ever. I didn't know how he was managing to point his laddie-boy out without any hands. Nonchalance, I had to suppose, that was what was doing it. Then he put his comb away, put his cigarette back in his mouth and with both hands furiously shook himself.

'Hardy night,' he said to me, 'and how's young Connaughton?' His shoes clapped on the tiles as he walked out. 'Watch out ladies, Vere Hunt is coming to get you,' he sang, the smoke going into his eyes and deliciously blinding him.

Clapping came from outside, then Dickie Rock was on the microphone: 'Thank you, ladies and gentlemen, and take your partners for the next dance.'

Supposing Frieda had another boyfriend, supposing he was somebody like Vere Hunt – well then I was sunk.

That was the first time I went dancing.

2

And now had arrived, a week later, the second night of the dance: Donie Collins and his showband. In silver suits. Donie sang:

> Come on, Donie, and be my guest.
> Come to the party, stick out your chest.
> Everything is gonna be all right.
> So be my guest tonight.

I had gone for the practice the first time. It was too late this time for practice; this time was it. Life had suddenly moved me into a faster gear and I had to try and keep up with it. The hospital correspondence. That's what brought about the change of pace. The sudden impulse to write to Frieda. The bulging twelve-page letter, written on both sides. I got one page back in return:

Thank you for your letter. Everybody in our dormitory says you have lovely handwriting. Re. your marriage proposal. Should the bride wear white? Ha ha! I will be going dancing every Sunday during the summer, viz, Cashel ballroom.

NB I have to make the best of this summer because next summer I am becoming a nun. Joke.

PS Can you drive? I remain your sugarlumps, Frieda.

PPS Not the first Sunday in the hols. The second one.

Frieda's letter depressed me. I hated the tone. All this grown-up style of vizes, NBs and jokes. She sounded far too sophisticated for me. And so casual: 'Not the first Sunday'. Well, where was she going to be on the first Sunday then?

But anyway, here we were on the second Sunday: 'One for the money, two for the show, three get ready and go go go.' Donie Collins was sweating.

The girls lined up along one side of the floor and the men, as they pushed past, reviewed them. I got myself into the middle of the crush of men. There was no sign of Frieda. I recognised a girl from Thurles who was holding hands with another girl. She worked in Woolworths. She wore banana-coloured lipstick and had tight blond hair and blackened eyelashes. She stood with one foot curled up against the other. I had a sudden impulse to ask her out. She looked like the real thing, and if I could dance with her, I could dance with anybody.

'Will you dance, miss?'

She just shrugged, not at me but at the girl standing beside her, and then she stood down off the step that ran the ring of the dance floor. Her arm went up on my shoulder. Did that mean yes? It did. Could I believe myself? For my first dance ever, the girl from behind the sweets counter in Woolworths was leading me around the floor.

'North to Alaska. The gold rush is on,' went the singer. Not Donie, but the bass guitarist.

'Do you like the words?' I said.

'No.'

'We crossed the Yukon River in search of bonanza-gold,' went the singer.

'My grandfather crossed the Yukon River,' I said.

She was looking over my shoulder at the band and made no answer.

'He was a prospector for gold. He met his wife out there.' He did too. I'd had the whole story once from Fay.

She just looked up at the band all the time, at Donie Collins. 'See him,' she said once. 'He's Satan the Devil in a dance suit, that fellow.' That was all she said.

Donie sang a second song, then another one.

At the end of the dance I said, thank you.

Thos and Fern were by my side, looking her up and down as she went to join her friend. 'Did you see that?' Thos said. They told me that after a dance with a woman like that you asked for a second dance, but I thought I had done very well. I made a quick decision never again to discuss my grandparents out on the dance floor. That was the way you learned. Then, with my heart jumping, I began looking for Frieda.

We were dancing very slowly, in short steps. 'You can dance every dance with the guy that gives you the eye, let him hold you tight . . .' She smelled different. Not like in the old days in the lanes: fresh-airy and cowslippy, she smelled then. Now she smelled like a woman. It took a while getting used to. And lipstick, and mascara . . . The brown dress clung to her. And the hand over my shoulder was holding a packet of cigarettes. Oh, Frieda, Frieda, I wanted to say, you are the same to me as ever. Your two front teeth that long ago you once chipped when you had a fall are still as chipped, as lovely. The openness those broken teeth bestow upon your face was what first arrested me and still it does. You have no idea how much I love you. It is not fair how much I love you. But did I say all that?

No. I was too intent on keeping in step. A one two, a one two three . . . And on keeping a distance of at least arm's length between us. And on not staring directly at her. Because some things about her were different. Her sky blue eyes, which in the past had made her seem wild as a hare about to burst away in fields, were now grown more serious. Her hair, unrecognisable from the days when it had been straight and unkept, was arranged in ringlets that fell

341

forward and bobbed upon her breasts. And had I been drawn to that part of her before? She was like a pony. I was paralysed with the strange new beauty of her.

Up behind me came Thos. He was steering a very large woman around the floor. He was almost buried beneath her grasp but yet he managed to pull his head away from its nesting place between her breasts. He pinched my behind. It knocked me out of my rhythm. I saw his face, like a small animal's that has been in hiding. He made a grin and winked. The wink was to indicate that we were both progressing. Then he closed his hand and made a fisted motion in the direction of his partner. He nodded at me. 'Get dug in!' The dance tempo slowed. He guided his partner over alongside me like they were ballroom dancers. 'Slow foxtrot,' he whispered in my ear.

Thos was my teacher. They were all my teachers: Thos, Fern, Richie and Vere Hunt. Thos and Fern, I accepted as teachers on the grounds that between them they would have had, in their quest for women, at least thirty years' dancing experience put behind them. Richie, of course, had always been a teacher, but one I had tried not to heed.

We danced three dances, Frieda and me. What did that mean? What was I supposed to do now? She was looking up at me with a sort of openness, or of trust, that suggested her compliance in whatever I decided to do. That worried me a little. She didn't seem at all the same person who had written me the flippant note. Once, when Vere Hunt was dancing nearby, he winked at her and, though more modest about it, she winked back. But my confidence was growing. Our third dance had been a fast one: Donie, doing Chubby Checker, putting on that lovely dusty distant desire of Chubby's voice. 'Come on let's twist again like we did last summer, let's twist again like we did last year . . .' I had found myself surprisingly adept. In an unstructured way I could move around to the beat. The lessons in twisting that I had learned from Richie must have come back to me. But I still could not jive like Vere Hunt. He kept his dancing tight and controlled, his partner and he always surrounded by a circle of empty floor. Like a spotlight was on him; making him, in his blue suit and coifed hair, the main attraction on the floor. However, in a fashion that was loose and easy, I could master the twist. I could move. That was why, when Richie walked over to me and whispered instructions, I did not panic. I, for once, heeded him.

'Shift her now before the dance is over.'

'ok'

'Here's the keys of the car.'

'No, I don't want them.' I didn't want the car, didn't want everybody looking in the window at me and Frieda. Privacy, I wanted. Privacy, I judged, was the essential ingredient of love.

'ok with me,' Richie said. 'If you don't want them, I'll use the car myself; you take her for a walk.'

'ok, thanks.'

I sang to myself: 'But don't forget who's taking you home and in whose arms you're gonna be . . . so darling, save the last dance for me.' What a sad and lonely song, but what a happy ending.

I took Frieda for a very long walk. Privacy was hard to come by in Cashel that night. There were couples in every doorway, in every lane. Undignified sights, I thought. Sometimes huddled darkly, sometimes smirking out at me, cigarette glows shining out of the night like cats' eyes. Were we to be as undignified as that? No thanks. I kept walking us at a steady trot up the hill to the Rock of Cashel, the music from the dance hall following behind us. Where better place, I was thinking to myself, than the Rock for privacy? Long ago castle of Ireland's High Kings and bishops – nowadays the quietest spot you could find. Frieda wore a bright yellow coat with shaggy nylon tufts and every time we walked beneath a street light it shone. It was a startling coat, but it was lovely. We looked lovely together, I thought. She in her coat, me in my suit.

'How far have we to walk?'

'Just a little further.'

'It's an awful climb.' She was running out of breath. 'Can we stop?'

'Just a little further.' I still felt the prying eyes. They were behind the trees lining the road; they were in the grounds of the Bishop's Palace alongside us.

We had to climb a high wall with stone steps built into it.

'What are you taking me in there for?' she said from the top of the wall.

'I want to show you something.'

'What?'

'Cormac's chapel.'

'Oh Jesus.'

But she came. Frieda, to her eternal credit, had not lost her old spirit of adventure. There were no steps on the inside of the wall.

'Can you get down?' I asked.

'Can you help me?' she said.

I had to hold her legs, guide her feet into crevices of the wall. My hands nearly fell off me with the feel of her nylons. I had to look up as she descended. 'Put your foot there, now there.' Up her coat I saw, it couldn't be helped. White knickers, beautiful, sailing past me; beautiful as the moon sailing through the clouds. Then we were both on the ground and I was holding her hand and a thought was going through my mind that we would not be able to climb out. It was a high climb without any steps. We would be on the Rock for the night. I wondered would she mind. I wouldn't. She clattered across the stones in her high heels, gawky as a foal. Maybe it was getting her away from the dance hall and the lights that had done it. We were not meant for restrictive places like that, the high outdoors was for us. Higher and higher we climbed, flitting beneath archways, the yellow coat illuminated, then cast in shadow.

Cormac's chapel was locked. Or blocked up, or broken down. Anyway, I couldn't find it.

'Come on,' I said. I slipped through the bars of a gate and I was climbing a flight of stairs in the wall.

Frieda called after me: 'And who do you think I am? Think I'm skinny as you? You won't get me through there.'

I was embarrassed. It seemed our ascent was to be called off because of the size of Frieda's breasts but she sized up the bars in the gate, opened back her coat, and then she slid through, one side of her in and then the other. Lithe, like the flipping over of fried eggs. A free spirit. I dithered. 'Up here,' she said as she passed me out. And suddenly she was my old Frieda of our frisky, road-rambling childhood. She led me along a wall which dropped on one side so that with a flop of your stomach you could only barely look on the slope of the Rock below. We went into a sort of room. We could look out over the country and the town.

And there we kissed and I felt the nylon of her coat against my face. Me, in the Rock of Cashel, and I feeling the safest I had ever been in my life.

I loved the kissing. I found it the most silent and sweetest of occupations. How I wished it could have gone on forever. But of course nothing is forever. For I'd had suddenly to get into a talking mood. I'd had to. A problem had arisen: the laddie-boy, it was misbehaving. Stumbling forward on a journey of its own. An embarrassing situation. Something I'd never before had to cope with. To be true it had stirred itself before, often. But not in actual company. I tried to distract her attention from me.

'Thank you for coming up here,' I was going on. 'Here is where Saint Patrick converted the High King. Patrick's staff pierced into his foot and he thought it was part of the ceremony, imagine that!'

'The poor eejit,' Frieda said.

I was talking on and on. Meanwhile my body and mind were working in different directions. While my kisses were telling their own sweet story, I was having at the same time to stand edgeways to Frieda. I bulwarked my hip against her, my front faced away and out towards the drop at the window. My kisses were sweet; I could not let her know about the not so sweet state of the rest of me. I knew it looked stupid. I felt like I was the gable end of a house or something. But what could I do?

'You're hip, it's hurting me.'

'Sorry.'

I did a partial pirouette towards her but not completely. We kissed.

'Sorry, is my hip still hurting you?'

'Yes.'

'Sorry.'

'What was it you said you wanted to show me anyway?'

It wasn't what I wanted to show her, but I did.

We lay down – whose idea, I didn't know. 'Twelve o'clock Rock.' I could hear the song from below, clear as day, coming up the hill and over the wall. Donie Collins: 'A one two three o'clock, four o'clock rock.' All the lights of Cashel were down there. You could see them reflected in the sky. All the plain of Tipperary lying around the Rock of Cashel in semi-light. And beyond, heading for Devil's Bit Mountain, the darkness. That was the last dance. A silence fell. Frieda's dress had a slit down the side. It was like a tulip opening. Why had I not noticed it during the dancing? She put my hand in. Then the national anthem got going. 'Laa la la la la,' the tenor sax. And for Frieda, sweet Frieda, I rose stiffly to attention. Then it happened inside me. One light touch of Frieda's fingers. That did it. A touch, up along the back of the stiff soldier, and inside in me, deep inside, there came an explosion. Like a tree it shook, lifted from its roots, shattered in a lightning storm. And then everything that for years had been trying to fall out of me was falling, first shooting off and then falling, windfalls onto mossy ground. Then I was crying, tears and wet everywhere, and Frieda was telling me it was all right.

'I love you more than the world,' I said. 'Do you know that?'

Frieda was telling me it was all right, pet.

Then she was wiping me with her fingers, down there where the shaking had subsided, putting her fingers in her mouth and licking the wet off.

'What are you doing?' I said.

'You're nice, you're salty and nice.'

I was having to look away. The storm had calmed but not the tears tilting down my face.

'No, it's you who are nice, not me. '

'Pet,' she was still saying. 'It's all right.'

I could hear the doors of cars banging shut and engines starting down below. I was saying, It's not all right. We won't be able to climb out of here. We're stuck.

Frieda found a way out, a gap where the wall had collapsed at its base, so that only the top part remained. She laughed going under the arch of it, uncrumpling her coat and dress, saying, if anyone asked what we were doing, we would say we were doing the twist. I followed, thinking of the taste of salt and feeling all the wind of Tipperary blow at me through the gap broken in the rocks and freeze me where I was still wet.

3

But that was the beginning of a glorious few weeks. Every evening Richie drove me to the top of Knockanure Hill. Frieda walked up from the town side of the hill to meet me. We walked along an overgrown laneway, ending in a barbed wire gap with an open field beyond. We stood by the gap, looking out. Every evening Richie did this for me. Why did Richie do this? Vere Hunt always came along with him. They took a great interest in the love between Frieda and me. The general idea of love, I suppose, was on their minds.

'Hello, Fred,' Vere Hunt said out the window to her when they were letting me off. He was smoking a cigarette and he blew out the smoke so that it went upwards and lifted his hair off his forehead.

'Hello, Vere.'

Vere Hunt had two crooked teeth in the front of his mouth, a slight bulge of his lower lip, which gave to him an air of joy, a face that was gifted with a most reckless expression. And he had a way, always, of leaning. Or hanging. If he was in the car, he leaned against the window. If he was outside, he leaned against the car, the door, anything. He always leaned, or hung. Where had solid Richie come across him? I had to wonder how he was coming across such cool company while I was away in college. I was jealous. Vere would sing out words of some song every time just before they stopped to let me off: 'There are some folks who say that I'm a dreamer. And sure, no doubt, there's truth in what they say . . .' He would put the quiver in his voice, just as Richie had once instructed me. Vere's songs were always full of meaning.

Those were the weeks when I felt Frieda was more than ever mine. Some evenings the sun shone on our faces, some evenings it rained and it was cool; it was June and changeable, but something very unchanging was going on between us. I sang songs for her. I had built on the little repertoire from which sometimes I had to perform as party pieces in Ivyhall. I sang because she told me she had loved my voice ever since back that time of the play at Wolfdyke. 'Sing for me.' For Frieda, I sang like a skylark.

I could sing for Frieda, whereas I never could for Mam. Now, there was an issue that needed working out: I could always sing for a person who I thought needed a song, like Richie the time of the blackberries. But not for Mam. Mam always wanted me to sing with all the expressions and hand movements. 'Don't stand there like a stick.' She had wanted me to sing like Mama? Had that been her thinking? Mama's voice was a legend and it was to be born again in me? Was that it? What tricky, tortuous thinking went on in Mam's head. Why should my stepmother have wanted me to sing like my mother? Why should a stepmother have wanted anything to do with a mother? I didn't know. And I was not about to ask.

And yet sometimes, vaguely, I did know. Mam was secretly proud of my mother, proud to be married to the man who had once been the husband of a legendary singer, even though her voice was now buried in stacks of old unplayed records . . . Was that it? Was Mam hoping that, through my singing, my father should be reminded of my mother? What, and why, would she want to allow him have such dangerous memories? Was she being generous to him or what? But to have me stand up and sing and remind my father of my mother . . . That was something I would never have the nerve to do.

Whereas Frieda had no motives whatsoever.

Things, however, could not go on so beautifully.

'How did you find this lane?' I said to her one evening we were looking down over the darkening bog.

'I've been saving this little place for you for years,' she said.

Suddenly, for the first time since the resumption of our relationship, I felt a little sting. It was as if some cog had slipped out of gear, and I was freewheeling along on my own. She had made a joke, but it was at my expense. She had sensed suspicion in my question, that was why. Suspicion was something that did not appeal to her. For an awful moment I felt Frieda had abandoned me. That evening my kisses burned with an insistence. And I knew that in my suspicion I was justified.

The very next evening she told me she might go to England.

'England?'

'Will you come?'

'I will.'

England! England was miles away. Why would I go there! England was for fellows who went for jobs on the buildings, for girls who went into factories. They left school at fourteen, got the permission from Father Glee and went. Then many of them, like Christopher, were never seen again. I was already almost seventeen. But I did not feel old enough. England was out of the question.

'You will?'

'I will.'

We kissed. It gave me a chance to think.

'Ah no, I can't.'

'You won't?'

'And you can't go either.'

'Why not?'

'The Leaving Cert. We both have to do the Leaving.'

But the wildest thoughts were going on in my head. England. Yes, I would go. I had only to scratch through the shallow surface of myself; beneath, there lay a total lack of restraint. Maybe it was because Mam had gone back to hospital. And because Connaughton was preoccupied. A sort of unshackling had come over me that I hadn't felt in years; not since the year my mother left my life and I had roamed the streets of Templemore unattended. My mind was cavorting through its second summer of freedom.

And there was more to it than that: if I didn't go to England with Frieda, then somebody else would. I was afraid of that. She had told me what Vere Hunt had told her. That England was much better than at home for dancing the rock 'n' roll. Great jivers in London, they did the splits and all. Frieda had stood on the roadway and shown me how to do the splits. I felt very awkward having to do it with her, with no music or anything. And I knew she was telling the truth. London was better. Vere Hunt had told us one night coming home from Cashel: 'When they do rock 'n' roll over there, they don't just stand around like the wallflowers you see on this side of the pool.' Vere could do the splits. Vere could go to England with Frieda. 'The day that Mexico gave up the rumba to do-oo the rock 'n' roll.'

'Or we might just go to Dublin,' she said the next time we met. It was a Sunday and it was in the middle of the day.

That Sunday was the last time. She was edgy. Was it because we were meeting in the day rather than beneath the easy cloak of twilight? But things did seem different. We seemed less familiar to one another. She was edgy and what was I?

I was desperate.

I was desperate with a fear of my own jealousy and suspicion. I knew those emotions were the very things that, if they hadn't done so already, would break our love apart. But what could I do to stop those wreckers? They were running away with me.

What can one do in such circumstances? Nothing. I had no hand in the matter. But a lucky thing happened that delayed the wreckage. In the form of a voice in my ear the bad moment, when things might have broken up forever between us, was held at bay. A voice that reached out of the distance at me until all the dusty desire of it was singing in my head. It was Chubby. Old Chubby Checker to the rescue. He blew away the clouds of destruction.

'Let's twist again,' he called to me.

'Let's twist again,' I said to Frieda. I laughed. I could hardly hear myself whisper it. We hadn't done it since the Rock of Cashel.

'What?' Frieda said. Her face looked happy. That was the lucky thing that happened. We were both laughing again.

> Do you remember when we used to sing last summer?
> Do you remember when we used to sing last year . . .
> Round and round and up and down we go again.
> Darling can't you see I love you so again . . .

We slid under the barbed wire and in the corner of the field we lay on Frieda's cardigan. Grass seeds on long stalks tickled my ears. Why did I cry again when it was over? When I had wet myself all over again at the behest of my own urgent need? And was left with the feeling of being a horse that has bolted its stable, having hardly entered, having had only a glimpse of the new straw on the floor within, the soft hay ready to be kicked up . . . Once, you could understand. Not the second time. I cried because now I knew my suspicions were real: my suspicions of myself. I wanted Frieda more than it was good for anybody to want anybody. She was not a wanter like me. And I knew I could never hold her to be mine and mine alone. I cried and I laughed. I was looking at her broken front tooth, at her white face and at her hair in the sun of summer. Crying or laughing, I did not know. I was looking beyond her. My eye was following the line of the country: I saw the brown bog, I saw Thurles, its windows reflecting like a lake of glass, I saw the hump of lonely Killough in the middle of a plain. I saw further beyond again: the Devil's Bit, the Keeper Hills, the blue of the Galtees, the run of the distant Knockmealdowns and Comeraghs, until I travelled on to Slievenamon, the Mountain of the Women, and then back to Frieda as she kneeled in the meadow, picking seeds out of her cardigan. I was lost in Tipperary, lost in Frieda.

Then I went away to army camp for a month. My life caved in when I returned.

4

A rmy camp. Fay had come home on holiday from America. Mam was still in hospital for tests. We Connaughtons wondered if Fay had come home for good. Had returned to assist Connaughton as once before. She had not. She said that Mam would shortly be out of hospital and that then she would only be in her way. But that, meanwhile, certain aspects of our developments which dismayed her had to be dealt with.

I saddened her most. I, after all, had been her special protégé all those years ago when, beginning with the counties of Munster, we had embarked on a study of the world. What are you doing with your life? she said. Have you any hobbies? What do you propose to do with this summer? It's your summer. Your life is running by. Her desperation at the ebbing of my life filled me with the same despair. Boys your age in the United States, she said, they go snorkelling . . . They go in the Peace Corps . . .

I thought about my empty life. Where would I snorkel? Where would I find a river? Even a puddle? Down in Glen? Where would I find a Peace Corps? Then I suggested the FCA, summer camp with the auxiliary army. She said it was not exactly what she had in mind, not like John F. Kennedy's Peace Corps back in the US but that it would keep me out of harm's way. Then she returned to America.

So I went to camp. To keep out of harm's way. Couldn't think of anything better to do. The FCA. The Free Clothes Association, as some of the soldiers themselves called it. Four weeks bivouacked in the Glen of Imaal. Four weeks in an army that robbed figrolls from all the shops of Baltinglass town. I learned to drink tea with powdered milk. I learned to wash up a thousand plates at a standing, to dump a thousand pink inedible sausages into a barrel. Gunner Connaughton, Private, second class.

I came home in my FCA uniform. A hero. Dropped off at the gate by Commandant O'Neill.

First day home I was told she was going out with Vere Hunt. Bunny Witheroe told me, down in the cow-house: 'Every evening you can spot them up in Knockanure, her yellow coat shining in the sun going down. Hammer and tongs at it.'

'You liar, Bunny.'

I didn't see her after that. Not for ages.

I don't want to see her, I was saying to myself.

Mam came home again from hospital. She had made a decision when she was in hospital, she said. She told Dancie to sit down at the kitchen table and ordered everybody else to get out. Afterwards she asked Connaughton, who still had his undertaker business, to make a special mortuary card from a copy of the old photo of Christopher sitting on the fridge. It was not to be called a mortuary card but a remembrance card, she said, because Christopher was not dead. She would continue to write. Nothing was changed . . . She had got a letter back from England. A box was stamped across the letter and in the box was the word: UNKNOWN. But nothing was changed. She put the remembrance card in a gold gilt frame. She asked Dancie if she would like to call on Christopher's mother and say prayers with her. She wouldn't, she said. She didn't believe in prayers. Connaughton and Mam went to see Ettie on their own. Dancie gave even greater care to her two small charges, the Connell-Connaughtons.

I paid little attention to this news. Nothing was changed with Christopher . . . Or was it? It didn't really concern me. Lovesickness was my problem. I hardly thought of Christopher. I hardly noticed Mam around the house; Mam, whose presence everywhere had once so obstructed me. Was it that her influence had diminished? Or that all the space around me had diminished, swollen as I was with my heartbreak? She noticed it. She said I was moping. She encouraged me to go dancing. 'I hear you are great at the twist,' she said. 'You must teach me to do the twist someday.' She was sitting in the kitchen. She sat most of the time now at one of the high chairs, the problem with the low chairs being that she could not get out of them. She was scrubbing the kitchen table, leaning into the same old scrubbing brush that had been there when first I came to Ivyhall, except it wasn't the sour caustic she used any more but something that was kinder to the hands. 'Let's twist again,' she said, making a swivel of her arms and laughing. I frowned at her. 'Have a laugh,' she said. 'Don't grow up yet. I can see you growing up and becoming a misery.'

Trying to jolly my spirits, she was, I knew that. I would not acknowledge her offer. It should have been me trying to jolly her. How dare she turn the tables? That was how I felt. Then it was the end of the holidays and I returned to Mont La Salle.

And I was growing up. And I was becoming a misery. And for my first few days back in school I thought of the moment when I should have told her. For there had been a moment: I had been at the kitchen table, over a last cup of tea before returning to boarding-school, thinking of a way to ask for extra money for term time. But suddenly, knowing money was not enough, it had rushed to my head to tell her life indeed was a misery. To tell her that ever since the end of Frieda, life was a misery. After all, what else was a stepmother for, if not to discuss the misery of a broken love life?

But that day in the kitchen, just as I had been about to speak my desolation, she had ripped my words out of my mouth. 'I saw Miss

Frieda Ryan the other morning,' she said, breezy as though she was talking about any old person at all. 'Miss-Nose-in-the-air,' she said. 'Does she not want to fraternise with us any more?' She discarded Frieda as she would any old rubbish. Tore me in two like a mildewed sheet, those words did. It was obvious Frieda had no further need of me and Mam was letting me know it and would not pity me for it. And I knew that never, never, would I discuss the subject of misery with Mam. Our ways of approaching such subjects were far too opposing.

What sort of slobby prick had I become anyway? That I should be growing homesick in final year instead of when I was in first year, when homesickness would have been the normal thing? Doing everything arseways, I was. Back in the study hall again, seated at my desk, I was able to picture how it should have happened: how her white arms, leaving down the scrubbing brush, might have come to me. Naked as love. She would have been capable of doing it. Capable of comforting my heartbreak. I had only to say the words.

But a week or two after my return to Mont La Salle, among boys again, I could surprise myself at how close I had come to disclosing myself to Mam. What a mistake that would have been. Now I was listening to Ash and company talk about their uncomplicated girlfriends during their uncomplicated summer holidays: girls, girls. Not an involvement of a mother, or of a stepmother, anywhere. No need.

5

Discharge leans over and whispers in my ear. I am studying for the Leaving Cert. *Discharge, discharge, discharge,* he goes in my ear. By whispering he is intending to indicate how he regrets this disturbance to my studies, but he might as well be shouting it out anyway. Everybody in the study hall looks at me. I can smell the cigarettes on his breath. His mouth is a quarry of rough teeth. 'Brother Robert wants to see you in his office,' he blares.

Bobbio's office was at the end of the long corridor. The brown lino of the corridor gleamed in the places where there were light bulbs overhead; in between was in shadow, as if the floor polish needed buffing. Just to see if it did, I tried sliding along a shadowy part. It was just as polished and slippery as under the lights; I floated like a swan.

I was feeling better about Discharge: I got on OK with him these days, he treated me like a grown-up, almost. Once you got into fifth year, senior year, Discharge treated you like that. You were a man; or supposed to be. If you were not, you were letting him down. Amazing how much a fellow was supposed to have matured over the course of one summer holiday. Nights spent on the Rock of Cashel, was that what did it? On account of the illness in my home, he was particularly nice to me; letting me off being completely a man. I was nearly one; one with diminished responsibilities, as attested by odd lapses in behaviour. It was my second trip to Bobbio's office in a week. In a few moments I would be on my second trip home.

On the door of Bobbio's office, in gold print, it says: PRESIDENT. I knock. 'Come in.' I delay a second before turning the handle. I know about that place. The Brothers' smoking room at the back. That place cost me a month in hospital. I still was not sure how they got in there. Since I had learned about the place, I had been on the watch for movements: the give-away skulk of a Brother going in the door, a hand releasing the box of fags from the folds of the soutane. But I still had not seen one Brother, not even one, go into Bobbio's office. I had to assume there was some way in through the back. A trapdoor, a secret passage. The Brothers' smoking room was behind that wall; a place that might have been the other side of the Iron Curtain for all we knew of what went on there. Any time I went into Bobbio's office now I would make sure to wait a second before going in; allow time for the smokers to get out and get the trapdoor shut behind them.

But inside there was no one but Bobbio, seated in the brown silence of the polished desks and wardrobes that stood all about the walls, in a room without a whiff of cigarettes, of any life at all, the very same as it had been when I'd been summoned there a week ago.

I was growing to dislike Bobbio. 'So we have another emergency?' he was saying, looking up at the ceiling. He didn't talk to you, Bobbio. And if you answered his questions, he didn't listen to them but talked over your head, while at the same time picking little hard balls out of his nose and then absentmindedly chewing them, as he appeared to ponder some issue far loftier than the one he was asking you to consider. Bobbio's nose was pointy. His eyebrows curled quizzically into the distance, like a cocker spaniel setting a distant quarry. Bobbio sensed foreboding all the time. And he sniffed.

'So we have another emergency?'

'I don't know. '

'Well we have. And how many more emergencies should you think we can expect?'

We sat in silence. I tried to think of a number but could not think of one. He sniffed.

'Have we a Leaving Cert to do? I expect a first-class honours from you in Latin.' He paused for a silence. 'Or have we not a Leaving Cert to do?' He took a ball from his nose and sucked it in his mouth.

We sat in a longer silence then, longer than it would have taken to do a whole Latin unseen.

'We have,' I said in the end.

'We have what?'

'A Leaving Cert to do.'

'But now we have to go home.'

'Sorry, Brother.'

'We don't want any further emergencies. Skip tea. Pack a laundry bag like the last time and go to the waiting room.'

'Thanks, Brother.'

There weren't any further emergencies, as it turned out.

But what does Discharge do as I walk down the steps where Aunt Tessa is waiting for me? Slips four pound notes into my hand. 'Here, you might need it. You can't be bothering your father for money when you get home. Don't tell anyone I gave it to you.' Old Discharge, perplexed by what he was doing, he handed me the money as though he was handing out punishment. I felt as perplexed taking it.

Aunt Tessa was dressed to the heels, just as she had been the week before. Same journey home, same talk, same Tessa. She wore a different coloured gansy, that was all, but tight-fitting as ever. The heater was full belt on, baking the car, and so the coat was off. The necklace glinted in the lights of the quays as we passed through Waterford. It looked very empty and miserable on the quay that evening. Early darkening of the January evening and nobody about. Then we were out on the black road. Tessa was a fast driver like Connaughton, only difference being he sped out of haste, she because it gave her pleasure. Bulrushes on the marshy ground beyond the paper factory raced backwards along the river like rats as we swished by. It was nice in the car with Tessa, cosy, an uneasy but at the same time willing comradeship of unlikely souls; she with her large breasty laughs, me with my long-faced ceremoniousness.

We shared a few jokes about Connaughton, a familiar subject between us.

'Does your father ever take a rest?'

'No, he doesn't know how to.' (I hadn't thought this one up for myself. It was something I had heard from Tessa on an earlier occasion. I was only repeating it. I liked her to have her enjoyment.)

Tessa's bracelets clinkered on her wrists. The gear stick was high up on the steering column. That made gear-changing into an operation full of dash and flourish.

'Light a cigarette for me,' she said.

I did.

'Have one, yourself.' She looked across at me. 'Any girlfriends nowadays?'

I was getting hot and bothered and did not reply.

She laughed. 'Lots of girls would still love to have you for a boy-friend,' she said.

Still. She used the word *still.* I didn't know what to say.

'Of course the first is always the best,' she said. Then she told me what a boyfriend had done for her once. She was on holiday in Tramore. He was a friend of Dick Power, her brother. One morning he took her out on the beach and showed her something. He had written her name, Tessa Power, in the hugest letters across the strand. 'I nearly died when I saw it,' Tessa said. 'It was marvellous. It took up the whole beach.' He had been her very first boyfriend, she said, and there had never been, or never would be, another like him.

I pictured the sand. Clean and flat after a night of wind. The name written on it. How it must have shone out its welcome in the morning sun. And Tessa never had another boy quite like that first one. The sadness of it, the empty beach all around the name, it made me swoon with ecstasy. I felt full of purity as I thought about it. I saw the name Frieda written on the sand. Would I ever find a beach big enough to write it on? I felt a moment of gratitude towards Tessa, of closeness. Brother and sister, we were. In bondage to the art of hopelessly lost love.

'Will Mam be all right?' I asked after ages.

'Of course she will.' Tessa was racing through the darkness. She did not slow down until we were going through Wolfdyke. Then, to use Connaughton's word for her driving through the town, she cruised. On the lookout. What there was to look out for in Wolfdyke, though, I could not see. A town of pub windows, densely curtained, day or night.

Just within sight of the light in the gable of Ivyhall she said. 'Your father was a great man to marry my sister, and not leave her live out her end a widow woman.' Then she added: 'Of course, it suited him every bit as well.'

When we got home that night there was heavy frost on the fields around the house. The children were in the kitchen, all of them very quiet. Connaughton, Richie and Marguerite had gone to visit Mam in the cottage hospital at Clonmel. Dancie was looking through the hot-press for shirts. The missis, she said, had made her promise that she would keep everybody in clean linen, and she was going to keep her promise. I helped Dancie take clothes down off the high shelves, vests, underpants, shirts, pullovers. It was reassuring how dry and warm it felt up in the presses, with its smells of shirts slightly scorched by the hot iron. But then I discovered that on the very highest presses no clothes lay, just the bare latting boards, and the emptiness of those presses bothered me. Something struck me: Ivyhall had always been regimental; the domestic world of home every bit as regimented as the locker-room world of college. I had always felt that and disliked it. Now, in these moments I burrowed in the hot-press, I felt a grip loosen. I felt how nice it was to be home. I enjoyed taking down the soft clothes and laying them out on the kitchen table for Dancie: Murt's pile, Jamesy's pile, and so on. Yet I could not help feeling some unease; the draughtiness up in the highest presses bothered me. Taking the linen down had always been Mam's job.

That was a Friday. I will always remember, that was a Friday. Late in the night when Marguerite came home she took down a plate for her supper and saw streaks of egg on it. 'Who fried those eggs?' She pointed at the plate. 'Breda, you did.' Breda got a lash of Marguerite's tongue. 'You have to fry them hard,' she said. 'The red of runny eggs only sticks to the plate so you can't wash it off. Next Friday I'll do them myself.' Breda cried. In Ivyhall there were always eggs on Fridays.

Next day I had to feed the cows. Connaughton's job usually on Saturdays, he had already gone to Clonmel. The yard of the hay haggard was frozen and the hay so hard it hurt my hands pulling the bales apart. The cows at Ivyhall never changed. They gave a sidelong look at you when you passed between them with your wedge of bale; they looped the hay around their tongues, and with a shake of the head, loosened it from the bale. The elder ones, old faithfuls, treated you the same whether you had been away in school five years or had never left them. Others, the new ones, you had to watch out for. You had to take courage: stand away from them and they would let fly at you for your lack of nerve; stand up close and then they did not kick. The cows at Ivyhall, their soft belchy smells and jaws stuffed as women's handbags. There was something eternal about how they bore the weight of the whole old world on their hips.

When Connaughton returned he told Dancie. 'She left us at tea-time,' he said. 'I was out having a quick cup of tea. We don't know God's will.'

Dancie whimpered, as a bird in winter, curled into her pinafores like they were feathers.

Connaughton left very early next morning and so Aunt Tessa collected us for Clonmel. Fern came along, scrubbed and raw, a tie peeping over the neck of his jumper. 'Big crowd,' he said. We could see the crowd as we drove up the street to the West Gate. The rosary-sayers. They stretched right down the street, from the cottage hospital as far as under the Arch. They huddled against house walls in the shadow of the black frost that was falling all day. You felt their coldness.

We went in. I could hear Connaughton's voice. 'Hail Mary, full of grace.' He was leading the prayers. I tried to slip through the kneeling crowd; they knelt by the door, up along the stairs. The window was open. I got to the landing; people tried to let me by, but then I too knelt down. 'Three Hail Marys in thanks for an end of suffering,' Father Glee prayed. The crowd rose after that, kissing crosses of rosary beads then pursing them.

A woman was standing beside Father Glee, nodding: 'Isn't it very cold weather for people, Father?'

He told her we would all be shortly warmed in God's mercy and could she not already feel it? Then, as mourners moved aside, talking and shaking hands, I saw Mam. Her black hair was combed back and gathered within her crown of plaits. Thick and hard, like iron, the plaits lay on the pillow. I wanted to pull my eyes away; it was indecent to be looking at Mam like this, but my eyes would not obey. Something emphatic was written on her forehead below the sprout of her hair, and on her set lips. It was that look of hers, that always I had feared in her. Now it was more marked than ever. Sternness. It was the most noticeable presence in the room. Mam was dead, the sweet smell that lay about dead people was in the room, yet I could not help thinking she was still alive. Stern, and alive. I prayed. I didn't know what I said. It is hard to pray to a person who is not dead nor not alive. I prayed with emotion. But I was not sure if I felt any emotion. Could I, for instance, say to her, I love you? Because, did I? If I told her I did, would that be just throwing in my lot with everybody else? Just because, right now, everybody else felt that way, did it mean that so should I? For she would know. Oh yes, as soon as I uttered my prayer, she would sniff out any falsehood. Could I say I loved her now? Once before I told her I loved her. The time she was in hospital scared about her leg. Had I meant it? Easy, it had been, to think you loved Mam when she lay helpless in a hospital. But then she got her health back, her power, the grey eyes saw through you again and it wasn't easy any more.

She certainly didn't have her health now. And I was swooning with love for her. Or drowned. Drowned in an adult passion of loss and fear that was passing through the room and in which my own thoughts were immaterial. In sudden surprise, I found I was still looking at Mam's plaits. So glossy, they were. Then Father Glee was before me, the soutane curving over his round shoulders. 'When shall we go again to the College Sports?' he said. He held his glasses in his hand. He was wiping specks of dust off them, doing a thorough job.

There was talk of a thaw the next day. Going into Wolfdyke for the funeral, the sun shone so weakly it could hardly melt the muddy icicles hanging from the floor of the car. And yet it did, because by the time we got to the crossroads and picked up Fern again and he squeezed in among us, the drips of water were already running like a river off everything.

'Is there a thaw out?' he said, looking into the dazzling liquid of fields and hedges. 'Or is there more frost?'

'More frost, maybe,' Connaughton said.

'Dangerous roads so, tonight,' Fern said.

The church at Wolfdyke sat high and mighty above the town. When you were the centre of attention there, as that day I felt myself almost to be, it was like entering a theatre where you were to perform. It was this January morning, the windows were high above, the light poured palely but dramatically down, the crowd was stirred up all about.

And yet I knew I was not the centre of attention. It was not my mother's funeral. I did feel myself at the centre then, that time my mother died. Or I felt myself, at the very least, a little satellite spinning within the centre. Always, since that time, I had wanted to get back to that centre. Feeling I still deserved to belong there, but knowing I had had my time and now that time was long over. And so, in my attempts to return, I travelled in disguise. I wore a cloak of independence. A cloak of falsehood. Support from others, shows of solidarity, I craved, and spurned. Now here there seemed to be the chance of returning to that centre once again, of being one of the whirring satellites again. But to milk it, I knew, was to be an imposter. This time it was the turn of Mam's own children, the Connells.

Was that why I found myself, not on the top pew with Connaughton and the rest of my family, but ten pews back, ten pews – I counted them – seated alongside Tessa; a restless pool of people separating us from the others? I don't know how I got separated from them, except that, as my sisters and I walked up to the church, Tessa whispered out the window of her car which was parked beyond ours and asked Marguerite to wait while she sorted out a problem. The problem was, the strap had broken on one of her high heel shoes. I was the one who waited. It was all Uncle Gregory's fault, she said. He was a callous dog sometimes, she said, couldn't even take a day off for her own sister's funeral. She had to get his breakfast and drive him to work and he would not hurry up and then she broke her shoe banging it against the foot-panels of the car in her rush to the church. I got her out of the car and secured her strap by tying it with her handkerchief and climbed slowly with her up the steps to the church.

'Don't I look a proper tramp?' she laughed. She had on all her make-up, powder and lipstick.

When we walked along the aisle all the places were taken up. Ten pews back. Here was one occasion far too big for me to go drawing attention on myself by barging in among the others. And Tessa, even behind those Queen of Thurles sunglasses, must have felt the same.

The moment was coming – my heart jumped a million times during the mass at the thought of it – when it would all be over. And Mam, in the coffin, would have to be wheeled down. I would have to watch.

Then it happened. The coffin turned around. Slowly it wheeled, silent on its rubbers. Then Connaughton was rising. Richie, Marguerite, Breda, Pam, Murt. Then all the little ones, half rising from the kneelers, their heads looking up, waiting for a prompt, a sign to go.

It was all right. I could look. Connaughton was staring into the ground. Richie was telling Marguerite to walk ahead of him, alongside Connaughton.

'No, you,' she nodded. She indicated that she has to keep an eye on the little ones. All the big ones were keeping an eye on the little ones. Concerned that nobody should step out of line. I too was concerned. I wanted them to walk properly, not to bolt off, not to be afraid.

Pam seemed removed from it all; in a world of her own. Pam, the great reader of books. Mam and Pam, what had gone on there? Was Mam afraid of the books Pam read? Why was Mam so afraid of some things, such as Pam reading books? Pam knew the answer. Her eyes stared right through you, but in a soft, unfocused way. They were staring now, but deep into the distance, not at what was happening around her, large brown eyes that seemed to think rather than to look. I wondered what they were thinking now. Probably nothing. Pam had her way of dealing with things. She could see a way. It would be a very simple way, not complicated like my ways, it would be simple and daring. Such as when she had asked Dada for a Walnut Whip that very first day we went to Ivyhall.

These thoughts kept coming in my mind: what had Mam meant to Pam? What had Mam meant to me? But had I not pored over that thought so many times before? This was not the moment for such a thought; I felt ashamed. The little ones were tagging along, their eyes wide open, the better to see what direction they should be headed. Murt, Jamesy, Martin. Little Noeline, who had never given Mam any bother, had always kept quiet, had followed Mam every-where like a devoted dog. She was falling behind the others. Marguerite hauled her along. The whole church was heaving a sigh as it followed their progress down the aisle. The coffin gave a little rumble over a bump.

It was at that moment Tessa put her arm around my shoulder. And I recoiled. Pulled away as though I'd been damaged. Why did I throw off Tessa's support? Why should I have needed support, that was the question? Tessa's arm on my shoulder. It was pathetic. What was my involvement in all this?

The lid of the coffin, flat and smooth, was gliding past us when Tessa broke. 'Oh poor, poor Kit Power,' she said. I heard a noise, like something cracking, deep inside her.

What things change a person? I looked across at Tessa. Not up at her. That was the first thing I noticed. I had not noticed it before: that now I was the same height as Tessa and soon I would pass her out. Streams ran down both her cheeks. A sort of cruelty I had always perceived in the set of Tessa's lips, a hunter closing on its quarry, had melted away. There was mascara and bubbles all over her face. And she had no handkerchief to mop her tears because it was being used to strap her shoe. Tessa was helpless and suddenly so was I. The thing that changes a person is the helplessness of another. For suddenly I was comforting Tessa. 'It is all right, Mam is all right. Look.' I showed her my watch. 'At about this very minute she is hitting heaven.' Tessa was crying and I found myself with my arm around her, the fat of her ample waist closing around my arm like a hot-water bottle as she slumped into me. I was leading her down the aisle.

In no time at all I found myself become an expert comforter. Granny was standing at the end of the church with another of Mam's sisters. They hadn't allowed her near the top pew. She would only have made a show of herself, they said. Now she was calling up through the church. Accusing the Almighty.

'You are hard. I asked you not to let this happen, that you would let one of mine go before me.'

'Oh don't say that, Granny,' I said to her.

'I'll say my mind,' she said.

'We don't know God's will,' I said, repeating the words Connaughton had spoken to Dancie a day or two ago, even though it seemed like a year.

'He wasn't listening to my prayers,' Granny said, but she stopped her shouting. 'Aren't I to be pitied?' she muttered to herself. 'The Almighty, and he could not even find my own son for his sister's funeral. He may as well have taken him away from me too.'

Briefly a thought flashed through my mind. A nice thought: a picture: of Mam, when she was a young woman, hearing the songs of Frank Sinatra from her brother, Dick Power.

Once we got outside I was all over the graveyard, comforting all. Comforting Fern.

'Our ends come to all of us, isn't that right?' he was saying, trying to convince himself, his head shaking as if about to topple off.

'They do, Fern,' I said. 'Our ends come to all of us.'

I saw Meagher and Gananny sidle towards me. Not in years had I seen them. Their hands were unassuredly extended. 'Sorry for your troubles lads,' I said, taking their hands in mine. Somebody had to say it. I'd have to wait forever for them to say it. I had a picture of myself as I hurried about my duties. Big teeth, long face, a smile in it for all. 'Sorry for your troubles. I have to go now to see somebody else.'

Then I was at the graveside, where my little sister Noeline was hysterically crying and wrenching away from everybody's grasp; the tighter their grasps, the more hysterical she became. I grabbed her by the hands, swinging her away in the air in order to distract her. 'Whoopsy, whoopsy and away we go.' As we swung round and round, pictures flashed past my eyes: the gravedigger resting on his shovel; bowed mourners holding caps; the Three Wise Men in an anxious huddle; the priest, the petalling of altar boys about him; Connaughton; the gravedigger again. Faster, I swung my sister, beginning to lose my balance, the trees, the sky, the dark grass.

A few things happened back at the house. There were cousins and uncles I had never seen before. People who had never visited during the days of Mam and Connaughton's marriage. Mostly the Kilkenny brigade from over the coal hills of Slieveardagh, where began that secret county. They were tracing their relations. I loved tracing. I loved the pleasure people derived, carried away with no care for any other business, once they got on that subject. I had never properly learned Mam's connections. I had lots of questions. Avid Mooncoin Connells tried to fill me in, all of them suddenly overwhelmed with a fervent need to puzzle out the jigsaw of their's and Mam's associations, her death having given even greater urgency to the exercise. Others had to be called upon to help. They had become like a team of hurlers, shouted-out connections flying in the air. I was receiving a good grounding on the connections of Mam's side of the family.

A man spotted Richie and called him over. This man was from Mam's first husband's side of the family. His huge hand went out to Richie. 'She's in the one grave with your father now, back together again,' he said. 'And how many years ago is it now since your father died?'

'Thanks for being sorry for my troubles,' Richie said, looking away from him. He gave a look in my direction. He fumbled over his cousin's question, not answering it. I knew what was going through his mind: he did not want me excluded. It was as good as he could do for me and I was grateful to him.

I answered for Richie. Family histories may have lain untended in Ivyhall, buried since the time the Connaughtons arrived there, but I secretly cultivated them. 'It would be thirteen years ago since Richie's father died,' I said. I had been rushing around all day, comforter-in-chief, and still I had not comforted Richie. That was as near as I got to it. As good, in return, as I could do for earnest Richie.

Maybe I should have become an undertaker. The Three Wise Men, even they came in for my salving unctions. So sad they looked, standing at the window of the sitting room in the fading light. They seemed to be finding it hard to get their sandwiches down, yet they strove on, manfully forcing lumps along the pained lengths of their throats. I remembered Mam's words once as she looked at the empty plates she had been carrying out from the sitting room where they had been eating: 'Badness is the best sauce.'

'Mam thought very highly of you,' I said.

They had to make a few throat bulges disappear to reply to that: 'Good lad, good lad.'

Yeh, I felt sorry for them. But only for a moment. Connaughton passed by us pouring out drinks and they looked away. I knew something was going on, and whatever it was, I was on Connaughton's side.

'They were there from Murroe, Ballina, Killaloe . . .' somebody sang. 'I wished I knew the rest of that song,' he said and stopped.

They were there from my father's side of the family as well. Some of them I did not know. Connaughton's brother, my good Uncle Pearse, always concerned, pointed some of them out to me. There were two cousins of his from Wexford. Fintan and Francis Doran. One of these I had noticed in the church. He was so like my father. He had the same black hair, parted the same way in the centre, same craggy black eyebrows. Same wide mouth. Everybody else noticed him as well. 'Image of your father,' they said.

Uncle Pearse was concerned about the Dorans. 'Out of touch with the family,' he explained to me out of the corner of his mouth. 'Ne'er-do-wells.'

It was a great name, and I loved the way he said it. 'Ne'er-do-wells.' I kept an interested eye on them.

The Dorans wanted Granny to get up and sing. They had been saying for ages that they had to get home because they had a long journey. But they wanted first to hear Granny sing. Yes, they had a long journey ahead of them, Uncle Pearse said, encouraging them to make a start. I remembered for a moment my own journey of long ago to Wexford. Over the snowy hills and far away, where we had found Dancie. The Dorans kept making a start and then returning, the faces more receptive, the swagger in the shoulders more pronounced each time they returned. They lifted Granny out of Granny's chair. She was delighted. Granny always had been a singer. 'My poor voice,' she said. 'Let me see.' And straightening her back, away she soared.

It was amazing how Granny could command attention once she began to sing and yet how, for the rest of the time, she could be ignored. 'I'll take you home again, Kathleen.' There was a sweet, arresting quality in her voice. It came from somewhere deep inside her. It wasn't at all Granny. The room went quiet while she sang. 'Count John McCormack, you can't beat him,' she said when she finished.

Suddenly Connaughton was talking. His voice had crept into the moment's silence there was before the clap began for Granny. 'Panis Angelicus,' he said. He was telling us about the Eucharistic Congress in the Phoenix Park in Dublin. He named the year, nineteen thirty-two. He had been there, he was seventeen years old, and he remembered the voice of the tenor, John McCormack, ringing out over the crowd. 'Panis Angelicus'.

We had all been preparing to join in the clap for Granny but once Connaughton began to talk nobody would make a sound. 'I'll never forget as we were walking up to the park that day,' he said. 'The tallest man you ever saw in your life was in the crowd. A giant, a freak man, he swayed head and shoulders above us. Carried along, I suppose, by faith and by hope. I'll remember him more than anything else.'

Connaughton's eyes had gone all wistful in the deepness of his memories. I could see in them, as he spoke, the giant freak man who had swayed above everybody else, full of faith and hope, on the way to the Eucharistic Congress. Then Granny was away on another song: 'The Rose of Mooncoin'. It was for Mam she was singing now. I knew that. She was hunched now. Her back had become rounded as a ball. Granny, who never sang for any reason other than to attract attention, had briefly forgotten herself.

Flow on lovely river, flow gently along,
By your waters so clear, sounds the lark's merry song,

On your green banks I'll wander where first I did join
With you, lovely Molly, the rose of Mooncoin.

'Ah, lovely song,' somebody said halfway through it.

'Life in the old girl yet,' she said, recovering, when she finished. It broke the thoughtful mood that had taken over the room.

'Yeh, you still have the legs of a lark, Granny,' Aunt Tessa said, and everybody laughed.

Granny's moments of glory. They had quickly been taken from her. I saw her muttering to herself, slumped in her chair again. A thought flitted through my mind: Mam too had needed to take Granny's moments of glory away from her. Mam had needed to chastise Granny for wronging her in the past. Granny, somehow, had been responsible for the departure of her brother, Dick. I had always suspected it, and now, watching Granny sit there on her own, muttering her innocence, I knew it.

But everybody had been a little overcome by her singing. Especially Fintan Doran, Connaughton's lookalike cousin. Over he sauntered to the Three Wise Men. 'The Rose of Mooncoin,' he called out, boxing John Clancy, the tallest of them, in the side of the head. Whiskey, leaping out of a glass, was caught and held in the light of fading sunset. Like time held in a hand.

Then Connaugton shouted. I think there would have been more fighting if he had not. 'For Kit's sake,' he said, 'stop this fight.'

It ended with the Dorans leaving. They apologised to everybody. Connaughton went out to their car with them and told them they were great to have come such a distance and that he and they would have to meet up sometime other than for a funeral. It had become one of those cold evenings with a sharp tang that ran up your nose, cleaning a passage right through to your brain.

I don't think the Dorans noticed it. They cried and cried on Connaughton's shoulder. 'Lally, Lally, you know we would do anything for you.' Fintan was pushing his clenched hands against the side of their car with a force lifting it off its wheels.

The birds had taken up song. From various parts of the yard it came, in low long notes that seemed to be dropping off in sleep and yet was somehow mocking. Teasing the Dorans, teasing us all maybe, or maybe just murmuring for the parting day.

'Lally, you know we would do anything for you,' Fintan was saying. 'You know we're no trouble. Just give us one crack at Clancy.'

I felt my heart heave. The Dorans would do anything for my father. And I would as well.

It was late that night when the police in Wolfdyke rang up and asked would somebody in the house please go and collect Mr Connaughton because he had been fighting in every pub in the town all night, wrecking the place. They were mistaken of course. It was not Connaughton who had been wrecking Wolf-dyke, but his spitting-image cousin and his brother, the Dorans. Connaughton drove in and rescued them. Next morning, opening the wicket gate on his way to feed the cows, he had his first heart attack. The Dorans fed the cows, then they cleaned out all the yards, the old-fashioned way – fork, shovel, yard brush, dribbly slow watering hose still half-frozen – and then we never saw them again.

6

I returned to Mont La Salle for the final time, for the long run-in to the Leaving Cert exam. An impatience with the place had begun to grow within me. For a few days after Mam's funeral, fellows said, Sorry about your trouble. But in a very short time that was forgotten and I too put it aside. My impatience with Mont La Salle grew daily, I wanted to be gone from there. I studied, but not very diligently. I worried. I awoke before dawn each morning, awakened by the songbirds in the grounds of the college, a shrill alarm in my ears. It was cramming time for exams, planning time for future careers – of my own career, I did not have a clue. It was time for perfecting systems of cogging exam papers. Long evenings were spent smoking and recklessly cycling day-boys' bikes around the grounds, so that come bedtime the blood would be pumping with energy. Other fellows seemed to have lashings of money at this time. Lashings of money for fags and clothes. I had now to depend solely on Connaughton for mine. He had recovered from the heart attack. But he had never been good at thinking of money and I didn't like asking him.

Then it was over. It was Midsummer's Day, longest, brightest day of the year. I was on my way home on the bus, me and Teddy Ash. I was headed first for Clonmel town.

Now the breezes of freedom blew through the open window of the bus, tugging one moment at the collar of my shirt, and the next at the corners of my mind. Freedom may not yet be yours, it told me. Not unless you find those little slips of paper, out of which you copied your Leaving Cert examination. Your masterfully written cogs. You have cheated. What happens to you if you are caught?

The bus dropped me in Clonmel and through its rear window, as it drove off along a narrow street, I had a last look of Teddy Ash's head. He was talking to the girls in the back seat. I can still see him now. Ash combing his hair with that habitual combing motion of his, his head getting smaller, receding until it was no more than the width of a bean pole.

Good luck, Ashy, I said. See you some time. The bus sluiced away between the rows of high houses. My feet were wobbly with uncertainty; the effects of last year's accident returned to weaken me. My suitcase clattered against my ankles. I was exactly halfway between home and Mont La Salle.

Halfway Town. That had a nice ring to it. Previously I'd gone home from school in our car, and along a different route. They had always come down to collect me, my father, or Mam, or Fern, and we had taken the shorter route home over the hills. This day I was travelling under my own steam: I was a big boy.

Halfway Town, it was also the busy halfway town along the length of the Suir, on a point where it often overflowed its banks. I knew the river there. I headed on my wobbly legs in its direction. I needed to change out of my 'going home' clothes. Then there was the river, suddenly dancing into view, open and bright. From the Mall a little further upriver came the sound of beer barrels clanging off a stone pavement. The reflection of the sun on the water rippled across the surface of my suitcase.

I was wearing my Mod clothes. Teddy Ash's word. I had worn

them on the bus, my travelling outfit, but that was as far as I would wear them. Though I didn't look as Mod as some of the other fellows leaving Mont La Salle, I could not go home in this get-up. I would be ridiculed in Ivyhall. It was time to change. And so, once I had found a private place, I laid my suitcase down.

Forty miles downriver now was Mont La Salle, on its hill overlooking the city spanned by the drawbridge. It was because of that drawbridge, because it was being raised as Mam and me drove up to it on that day I was to be dropped in the new world of boarding-school, that I could still recall my first feelings for the city. I had never seen a drawbridge before. On the other bank, streets of a city glimmered in the sun. Then the high wall of a ship's hull passed before my eyes. Five years I lived overlooking that city below the school. I had come to know an old Norman river-town. Insular and aloof. Yet my first impression of it never quite lost its glow. And so maybe I felt just a tinge of loss.

We had walked through the same city just a few hours ago, Ash and me, headed for the bus station, swinging our suitcases: they had never before seemed so light. We'd had to take home everything, even the school books that on previous summers had got left behind.

'Let me find no reminder of you next September. The only reminder of you I shall expect is your Leaving Cert results and they better be good.' Discharge's parting words to us.

Ash made a joke of it: 'Discharged by Discharge.'

Our baggage was heavy, and yet we swung it out the gate like it was fresh air.

'We'll get a bag of chips,' Ash said. We stopped at Friar Tuck's, the Italian on John's Hill, for chips. I was starving. We had just finished the Greek paper. Ash and me were the only two who took Greek. It was the second last paper and so all the others, apart from the few staying on for art, had already left. We had skipped dinner, which had been terrible all through the Leaving. Worse than ever.

The jukebox in Friar Tuck's was playing Cliff Richard, 'Summer Holiday'. I imagined blue skies and myself lying on a beach.

'This place never fuckin' changes,' Ash said, '"Summer Holiday" is fuckin' ancient, boy.'

Behind the counter stood the Friar, dusting our chips with salt. 'To have here or to take away?' he said. The salt was falling on the chips with a sound like sand, the sound that you never got off anything but chip-shop salt.

'To take away,' Ash called over.

We sprinkled extra vinegar on because they never gave you enough at Friar Tuck's and then we went over to the jukebox. Ash wanted to select something better than Cliff Richard but he couldn't talk or do anything until he had swallowed the handful of roasting hot chips he had stuffed into his mouth. He was standing on one leg, his head going round in a circle to try and cool it down, a little gap in his mouth to suck in air but not let out chips.

'What'll we play?' he managed to say out of the corner of his mouth.

'The Rolling Stones,' I said. Everybody in the Kelly-Jackson gang liked the Rolling Stones.

Ash searched the labels. 'Naw, this jukebox is cat useless, boy,' he said, when he couldn't find what he was looking for. 'Which Rolling Stones one so, Dudid?' He selected a number himself and we waited for the end of 'Summer Holiday'. But then 'Lucky Lips' came on, another Cliff number, and we had to wait through that. The friar was singing along in a sleepy voice: 'And with lucky lips you'll always find the baby in your arms.'

'Hurry on, hurry on,' Ash said, pushing the jukebox, even though the Friar was watching him. I knew we were asking for trouble, there had been trouble from these quarters before.

'Hey you, you wait your turn, I like the Cliff Richard,' he roused himself to call out over the noise of his frying pans. His face was sad-looking and wide, wide as his counter.

'We don't have time to wait. We have to catch a bus,' Ash called back. He looked at his reflection in the case of the jukebox and combed his hair.

The Friar was getting roused now and eating stray chips from the counter: 'You, godda' you, I give you the takeaway chips and you don't take away but stay.'

Ash gave the jukebox another shake.

'What's you godda' name. I tell Discharge on you.'

Ash gave me a wink.

The Friar ran a cloth across his counter. 'Hey, you look around when you spoke to by the Friar. You behave in Friar Tuck's.'

Ash did not look round. He looked into his almost empty bag. 'You behave in Friar Fuck's,' he said softly. 'You wait your turn in Friar Fuck's.' He licked the sprinkle of hard dry chips gathered in the corners of the bag. The Friar did not hear.

We waited as long as we could, but just as the arm was swinging the record out of the pack we had to go. We could hear the low groan of Mick Jagger following us onto the pavement. 'I can't get no-oh satisfaction.'

Bus travel. It was the only way to travel – so much better than by car – you were so much higher up. We settled for the front seat. I had always enjoyed the front seat; so nice it was when the bus swung around how you felt all the length of its swing behind you. Well, we were swinging around Reginald's Tower and Ash was combing his hair and I was being cool because I was leaving school forever.

But then I pointed at the tower: 'Remember the day we got out to visit the museum?' I said. Ash didn't remember. And I knew I had said something that was not cool at all.

'See that deadly coat?' The bus stopped outside Shaw's and he showed me a white trench coat hanging in the window. He was breathing in quickly. The one thing about Ash that never changed was his way of taking in quick breaths when he got excited.

'KJ doesn't like those coats,' I said.

'Fuck KJ He hasn't a clue about clothes. That's the first thing I save up for when I go to England to work for the summer is a coat like that.'

We crossed the river and Ash was still telling me about all the other clothes he would buy – a light blue shirt with button-down collar, a corduroy waistcoat – and I was realising that some important event, the crossing of the river, had passed me by. Life was like this; you thought the passage of important events should be marked by ceremony, but you were always too immersed in other things to mark them. And right now, was I immersed!

Immersed, that was hardly the word. I was drowned, buried. Right now I had a problem and it was bigger than crossing rivers, bigger than shopping.

'I'm really worried,' I said to Ash.

'Forget it,' he said. 'It'll go away. No more problems. Aren't we finished school? Look, there's one thing that better occur to you quick, because it just now occurs to me. Fuck them all, is what occurs to me. Fuck KJ. Fuck them all. And that's what should occur to you too. Look at me: made a proper bags of my Leaving Cert. Probably failed every subject. And so what? Because what occurs to me is, I'm all on my own now. And you are too, Dudid. And always will be. All on your owneo, little Dudid. Remember that.' Then he got out his comb and combed back the hair falling on his forehead.

So Ash starts combing his hair and talking about more clothes he is going to buy when he goes to England and I can see the clothes – polo-neck shirts and jeans – and I can smell their crispness and at the same time I am thinking of my problem. And I feel like saying: It's all right for you to talk, Ash. You, no matter what you may say, will not be on your own. I will, with my problem.

The bus stopped and an old man and woman stepped down. They looked grumpy. Ash and me were by the front door, so we could see the tall grass on the side of the road waving quietly in the breeze. I made a mental note about being back in the country again. Whether I was happy or not with that, I didn't know. Ash said, 'The slow boat to China, this bus is.'

'I left my cogs in my Greek paper,' I said.

He looked at me so seriously that I thought I must be in deepest trouble and I wished I hadn't told him.

'How do you know you did?'

'I didn't have them when I left the study hall. I sealed them in the envelope with the Greek answer sheet.'

I told Ash about the shock I got when I came out of the hall. When we had finished our papers, McGrath had been waiting just outside the door. McGrath was our Greek teacher; he always lurked outside the door during exams, and milled around us when we got out, grabbing us by hands grown limp from writing. 'How did you do, how did you do, how did you do?'

McGrath was a farmer as well as a teacher. There was always a smell of farm off him. Being from a farm myself, I didn't mind that, but the day-boys from the city did. Manure McGrath, they called him. That morning there was a stronger than normal smell off McGrath, he must have been silage-making, and the silage, mingled with the smell of the floor polish outside the study hall, seemed to produce in me a very heady effect. Or maybe it was the relief at having finished the Leaving, I didn't know, but when I walked out the study hall door some sensation arose in me and all my concentration went suddenly out the window.

'Oh great, great, I answered all the questions,' I said in my light-headedness. I was feeling in my trousers pocket, feeling in my blazer pockets, feeling for the cogs to stuff them out of the way. Because suddenly I had forgotten what I had done with them. And everything about the exam and about my cogs had become a blank. And then I felt my pockets empty and I panicked. 'Oh yes, Mr McGrath, great, I did great in the exam. Thanks you for all your help during the year.' I was saying all this stuff to McGrath. And I was picturing my cogs – so neat, so tiny, so masterful, so helpful. So gone. Only one way of knowing Greek grammar, and that was, cog it. I was picturing my cogs, folded in my answer sheet.

Ash took Greek in the Leaving because he wanted to go to university and become a dentist. 'Easier than Latin.' His father had studied it. 'Loads of money in dentistry,' Ash told me. I don't know why I took Greek. Because I wanted to go to university too, maybe. Because I hadn't a notion what I wanted to do. Because Ash said Greek was easy. But it wasn't. So I cogged it.

And chemistry.

Cogged chemistry too. I had to. I could not possibly have remembered all those formulas. I cogged all those formulas, the neatest little writing, packed onto matchbox ends. Slip in, slip out, as instructed by Kelly-Jackson, slip in, slip out, under the sleeve. Where were all my cogs now? My summer was ruined.

'What'll happen when they open my paper?' I asked Ash.

The bus was letting loose at last along the flat stretch by the river, the bullrushy grass giving a swampy feel to everything. I was having visions of a man calling to our house and telling my father what he had found in my exam paper. Was I going to have to carry that vision with me through the whole summer long? I was in big trouble. My summer was in ruins.

Ash had lost the serious look from his face. That pleased me, but I wasn't much helped by his thoughts of what would happen when they opened my paper.

'Was it a small cog? Look, fellows are always leaving things in exam papers. My old fellow is a teacher and he marks papers and he says he's always finding things. Comics and sweet papers and supplications to Saint Jude, patron saint of lost causes. Once, he couldn't mark a paper because the pages were stuck with chewing gum. He found a brown scapular another time and whatever relic was in it had melted and stained all the paper. Anything he finds, apart from the answer paper, he just throws it out. It's all rubbish to him. He couldn't be bothered handing up cogs. Other examiners, though, my father says, are bastards. Always on the watch.' Ash stopped to catch his breath and then continued. 'So was it a small cog? Anyway, what proof have they that it was you put the cog in?' He got his mirror out then and attempted to squeeze a blackhead on his forehead because, as far as he was concerned, the matter was closed.

I reminded him that he and I had been seated next to one another in the study hall, that we were the only ones taking Greek, and that could make him a serious suspect.

'If you get me in fuckin' trouble, Connaughton, you're fuckin' dead,' he laughed, and pucked me in the shoulder and people in the bus looked at us. I pucked him back on his shoulder, pleased with the unexpected contact between us – the first time since the old days. And he pucked me again. 'Dudid, you're in dead trouble. And I flunked the Leaving. So what?'

After about a minute, a silence came between us. Then he began to sing the jingle for an advertisement on the television. People got on the bus, mostly old people, who, with their baskets of shopping, were having trouble getting up the narrow steps. The driver was annoyed, slapping his brakes on and off impatiently. Then they only went short distances, and when they got off they had the same problems all over again. And as each passenger got on or off, Ash and me seemed to move further and further away from one another. 'Boom, boom, boom, boom, Esso Blue,' he sang. I could feel space and time drifting between us.

We passed the little villages. Mooncoin, where Mam came from.

Fiddown, where once I had nearly fallen out of the car. I dreamed a bit.

At Carrick-on-Suir two girls in candy-striped school uniforms got on. They pushed their cases into the luggage compartment alongside ours, and without looking at us, walked down the bus and sat near the end. I could see their bottoms move beneath their skirts.

Ash began to take an interest in me again.

He was talking again. His breathing became excited. He was doing all the talking, saying things that didn't require any talking back from me.

'Talk,' he said, 'talk, can't you?' He indicated behind him. 'Those pyjama uniforms really turn me on.'

'They can't hear us anyway, they're too far back.'

'Come on, we'll go back to them.' He loosened his narrow tie until he had it looking cool, with the knot dawdling about three inches below the collar.

'I'm not going back,' I said. But I loosened my tie too, two inches, just in case.

'I'm on a horn, Dudid,' Ash said.

We both sunk into our separate worlds after that.

'I'm looking forward to getting home,' I said after ages.

'I'm not. I'm getting drunk with my old fella,' Ash said. 'Then I'm shagging off to England after I tell him I screwed up the Leaving.'

There was a time when Ash had never said things like that. In the early years of Mont La Salle when we had been best friends. When what he said was not a demonstration of how far behind him I lagged. Suddenly a fury rose within me. I would have hit him. I was not looking forward to going home either. Why had I not been able to say that? Why had he, so cockily, known it? Did I not even know my own mind? Fuck you, Ashy, I wanted to say. I don't lag behind you. I am not as green and cabbage-looking as you think.

'See you around, Ashy,' was all I said.

'See you, Dudid.'

Then I got off outside the bus depot, thinking about Ash getting drunk with his father as soon as he got home. I could just imagine it.

Ash's schoolteacher father, relaxed in his holiday sports coat. Ash seated alongside him, breathing excitedly, the sun coming in the window and landing on the round table and lighting up their brown drinks. The father shaking his head in admiration at Ash telling the story about the jukebox: 'You behave in Friar Fuck's.' Could I imagine doing that with my father?

I got off the bus and stepped into a summer's afternoon. Its warmth had taken over the world. It was then that the sudden feeling of freedom overcame me. The street was bound up in its own headlong rush. Nobody, nobody, watching me. Mam dead – she would not be there when the bad news came – no more school, no more Leaving. I decided not to phone for Marguerite to come and take me home. Not just yet.

I felt the summer wind. There was nobody on the riverside but me. I read the poem on my cigarette packet: 'Flow gently Sweet Afton among thy green braes. Flow gently, I'll sing thee a song in thy praise . . .' Connaughton used to smoke Afton until Mam made him give them up and smoke Craven A, her own cigarette. Craven A, the tipped cigarette. Now I had my packet of Afton. Nine in the box, one in my mouth. And I was chewing the sweet little crumbs of tobacco where the tip should be. And as always, it was giving me, as the French nuns who were our nurses in Monte La Salle used say, 'le loose bowel'.

The nuns: the day Ash and me ran up and down the five flights of stairs, blotting paper layered in the soles of our shoes, so that we could get a temperature and get into sickbay. An infallible method, according to Ash. One of the nuns took our temperatures.

'You not sick.'

'But me have le loose bowel,' says Ash.

Then she went to attend to somebody else, leaving us with our thermometers stuck in our mouths for a second reading. Ash took out his thermometer and lit his cigarette lighter beneath it while she was not looking. And she came back and he handed it to her and she looked at it and nearly fainted and was about to send him off to the infirmary until the thermometer broke in her hand and the mercury rolled all over the floor like silver-lice.

I sat beside my case and let the thought pass. I looked in my case, picking and arranging my linen: underpants, vests, long black socks, white bobby socks that once had been Mam's, all jumbled together. The houses of the Mall were behind me, the windows staring blindly into the sun. In places where the river was shallow, the stones had dried out. Where the current was swift, the stones fell against each other with a gravelly sound. Where there were pools, I saw the bottom. I smelled the dried riverweed and all those drying surfaces.

If she were still around, what would I do? I would let her force the truth from me? Would I? No I would not: 'You look glum, mister. What's the matter?' 'Nothing.' And why would I not tell her – and let her have her way; let her get out pen and paper and write to the Education authorities? Because she would. Yes, she would. She would proclaim my innocence in the matter of an accusation of cheating at exams. I can see her do it: same way as she writes to lost Christopher in England; to lost Dick Power, the dance-band leader, in Brooklyn. I can see the flourish of her moving pen above the kitchen table at Ivyhall as she writes, those grim lines on her face, as she places the last cross on a *t*, the last defiant dot on an *i*. Lally, post these letters for me. And then I would have got away with it. And Connaughton would never have had to know. Yes she would do it. Why would I not tell her?

Suddenly I was angry. More than that, I was furious. I grabbed at Mam's white socks in my suitcase. They were nesting there, clean pairs, soiled pairs, like eggs, and I disturbed them. Another barrel clanged onto a pavement on the Mall. I grabbed the nearest pair to my hands. I was about to pelt them all, one after another, in the river. But I didn't. I only threw one pair and it didn't go in the river anyway; it overreached and landed on the bank on the far side. I stopped and I was whimpering and on the far bank lay the pair of socks, like a reminder, like a mushroom left not picked. Like a missing link. Like some unfinished business.

7

There was only one other man in the pub. 'You're too young to be drinking whiskey,' he says to me. He was drinking pints himself.

Curtains hung from a wire stretched across the window so that only a chink at the top was exposed to the outside. It was like we were in a wigwam, the way the light seeped down the little room. It reached right into my glass of whiskey.

The barman didn't seem happy with me drinking whiskey either. Without speaking, he served what I ordered, then he stared out at what he could see of the house opposite. Suited me. I had chosen the little pub in the side street because it looked so quiet. The tightly pulled curtain across the window was like a woman's dress, tied up to her throat.

The barman spoke to the other drinker. 'Well, put on the news,

Bobby, in the name of God,' he said.

He clicked a knob on the radio above his head. A song filled the low-ceilinged bar. 'My thoughts today though I'm far away dwell on Tir Chonaill's shores . . .'

'News is running late, Michael,' Bobby said.

The barman looked across the surface of the pint he was pulling for the pint-drinker, leaning back slightly so his eyes were lowered to the level of the glass.

'You're travelling far?' Bobby said to me.

'Not too far,' I said.

I was driving the car, driving home. Mam's car, which had the automatic clutch installed so she could drive with her one leg. Taking corners and wide bends, I was totally out of control, praying nothing was coming round the far side. Only with Marguerite could I have got away with it.

'Look at the cut of you,' were her words when she pulled up and leaned out the window to where I sat at the side of the street on my suitcase. The children in the back, who had come along for the drive, looked out at me.

'What do you mean?' I said.

'Drink taken, that's what I mean. I don't believe it.'

'Indeed I have not. How could I?'

'Teddy boy then,' she said, smirking to Breda and the others in the back of the car. 'Are you getting in or what?'

I didn't feel like telling her that while in Wolfdyke a few teddy boys might still be hanging out, too behind the times to know better, elsewhere they were long gone. I got in the car. 'Can I drive?' I said.

Now I was driving, scrambling over little hills, Tipperary rolling out before me. Roads I had always thought familiar were seeming suddenly strange to me. I was all questions. And Marguerite was very tentative with the information she was letting out.

'When is he going?'

'Soon.'

Three kids were in the back seat with Breda: Noeleen, Martin and little Rena, the elder of the two CCs. They looked shyly at me at first but soon they were chatting excitedly.

'Daddy had a heart attack,' little Rena announced.

'Shut up you in the back,' Marguerite said.

'But he did, Marguerite. What's a heart attack, Lally?' they asked 'Did he, Marguerite?'

'Yes.'

'I didn't know.'

'We couldn't tell you. You were doing your exams.'

'What's a heart attack, Lally?'

A picture was passing before my mind: Connaughton was staggering across a field. At the same time I was stuffing cogs down my trousers.

'Is he getting better?'

'He'll soon be out of hospital. Like the first time, he recovers quickly.'

'Why did he get it?'

'Tessa says it's because of all that has happened. And now him having to leave the house.'

'Oh yeh, because of all that has happened. I suppose. Why has he to leave the house?'

'The Executors of the will. They are hounding him.'

'God forgive me, but they'll pay for it,' Breda broke in, half laughing.

'Why?'

Marguerite again: 'Did you not know that the day of Mam's funeral they told him he'd have to get out of the house? That's what brought on the first heart attack.'

'No. I didn't know.'

I still had important questions.

'Who's going with Connaughton?'

'Who do you think? You are. All the Connaughtons are.'

'Oh.' My heart gave a sudden skip. A skip of freedom.

And there was yet another question: Why are the Connells not going? But I didn't ask it. Ivyhall was theirs; they were staying. My mind was bounding on in a fever of expectation in which the severance of the family seemed of no more consequence than the opening of a zip that has been binding the two sides of a coat together. The whole world to be mine, and Dublin, the faraway sounds of streets and traffic calling.

'When?'

'I don't know. People are talking about it. You've missed a lot since you've been away. And go easy. You are driving that car too fast.'

'What are people saying?'

The children in the back were making noise and Marguerite turned round to them.

'Shut up back there,' she said. 'We can't hear our ears with you. No ice-pops at Nellie's if you don't shut up.'

She turned to me again: 'I wish Daddy wasn't so impatient. He doesn't have to leave so quickly. Something could be worked out.' Then she turned to the children again: 'I thought I told you shut up. You're for it when we get home.'

Suddenly I was struck by how like Mam our Marguerite had become. How the replies to certain questions had to be given during the process of carrying out other dealings. And the harsher the voice in carrying out those other dealings, the easier it became to answer the questions. They slipped out.

Then Marguerite was talking again: 'What people are saying is ye'll be missed. They're asking what they'll do without the noise and shouting around Ivyhall. The place will be dead.'

I drove slowly for a while. I found that if you drove slowly the car did not go out of control on you. But then I was speeding again, losing control every time I went around a corner. The others did not appear to know it. I did. I was swerving around wide bends on a wing, hoping the car would take the right direction because I was not willing it anywhere.

See that jet? I said to myself. A jet was dipping down into the furthest rim of the sky. That's where we're going. Dublin.

And we did. But first I met Frieda again. One more time. In Thurles. The yellow coat was gone. Now she wore a red coat, very shapely. I wore my school blazer. 'Can you wear that blazer out?' Connaughton had asked me – no Mam around now to give the orders – 'get the full value out of it.' I was walking across the bridge where the Suir flows through Thurles, looking down at the little island belonging to the Ursuline convent. Ducks lived there and other wildfowl, making quacky noises against the swift current, bringing up their young, below the traffic noise. A bird sanctuary. When along comes Frieda. My heart nearly leaped out on the footpath. Should I keep walking, I wondered, pretend I hadn't seen her? Don't be a coward, I said to myself. Would she talk to me at all? I wondered next. Would she ignore me as she had done after mass? But she stopped on her dizzy high heels and, bright and airy, she said: 'How do you think you did in the Leaving?'

How do I think I did in the Leaving, Frieda . . . I felt a huge compulsion. I felt it rise all through me. Huge and fierce. I felt it cry from my mouth. I wanted to tell her she was still my pony. I wanted to nibble her hard as ponies do. I wanted to tell her everything, the cogging, my fears, my future. But where should I start? Suddenly I was steering her to a doorway in the lea of the old castle alongside the bridge. I was leaning against her. Traffic slicked by behind us.

'We must be serious about this,' she said. 'We can't do this.'

I put my lips in position for a kiss but when she opened her mouth and pulled away I noticed the broken teeth were changed. A gold crown gleamed there. Frieda was different and very grown-up.

'I'm going out with Vere,' she said.

'I know,' I said in shock and the world went into motion all around me, like I was on the helter-skelter.

Then, suddenly, I really did want to tell her. I had to tell her. I wanted to cling to her. But I didn't. I wanted to shake her. There was nobody else and in a moment she too would be gone. I didn't do that either. Instead, I just said I had my problems and I would probably fail the Leaving Cert.

'Don't be foolish,' she said. 'You have no problems. You'll get your Leaving Cert. You'll see. If Mrs Connaughton was alive, you wouldn't be thinking like that. You should say a prayer to her.'

'What?' I said.

And then she told me about Vere and Mam. She told it just the same as if she was telling about people in a storybook; as if it had nothing to do with her. 'Kimberley Hunt didn't want Vere going to dances,' she said. 'He was afraid of his son meeting Catholic girls, can you believe that! Didn't want him marrying a Catholic and having to bring up his grandchildren Catholics. Of course, Ducksy never gives a care for who Vere marries, as long as she can continue to paint her horses. So every evening before a dance your mother used to ring up the Hunts' house and leave a message that Vere would be picked up by Richie to go to the pictures. Your mother never saw problems and neither should you.'

Then she smoothed her coat and walked across the bridge, her hand on her head to keep her hair from blowing. I didn't see her again.

And I stayed standing there, a thought of a vague ironic nature fluttering in my head: that I should be standing by the Ursuline convent, that the cathedral should be next door and the Presentation convent, the Bishop's Palace, the seminary; that Kimberley Hunt should be a Catholic-fearing Protestant. Maybe he was right. The thought wisped away downriver on stronger currents. I stood there, conscious of my misery but at the same time conscious of the dejected figure I was sure I was presenting to passers-by and I dug my hands in my blazer pockets, through the torn lining of my pockets, so as to look cool. And it was on that instant I felt them – that instant after Frieda left never to return and it had begun to flow in upon me how much I was, at last, on my own. I felt them in the folds of my blazer's torn lining. The little papers, the cogs I had replaced in the pockets during the exams. I delved them out of their depths and threw them in the river. Bye bye, paper sailors.

8

'You take the high road and I'll take the low road.' Fern and Thos and me sang that day we moved the furniture to Dublin in the horsebox. We drove into the city and down the quays. Then we turned, drove over the bridge and were swallowed up in the city-centre traffic.

'Are we on the right road?' the men said.

We had come to a quiet part where the sun shone on tall houses with gardens. We couldn't find the house at first. We drove along a high road and suddenly there below us was the sea and a tower and in through our open windows came the screams of swimmers splashing in the water. The shallow water by the shore was dotted with the colours of bathing caps that swayed over and back. Choppy little waves slapped with the sound of hot-water bottles against one another. Beyond the shore, the sea stretched away out to where there was nothing but blue. I was not prepared for the great heave that emptied out of me; my soul or something, expanding into all that new space. It was hard to believe that in addition to getting a new house, we would be living so near the sea. Connaughton had never thought of mentioning that to us.

The men were in a hurry to find the house but they had to stop at the view.

'How would anyone get into that water?' our driver said with a shiver. 'It'd freeze you just looking at it.'

'Look, a ship,' Fern said

It was heading out from a jut in the land further on.

'It's only a boat,' the driver said.

'Ah lads, it's bigger than a boat, it's a ship,' Fern said.

We drove up a side road. Then we found the house, tall as a castle.

'There's the boss's car,' Fern said.

We looked up at the tall house where the car was parked. The road rose up a steep hill that went over a crest so that you did not see all the way to its end. The silence of the road was a bit surprising. It was as though it was holding its breath for the arrival of its newest occupants. I could hear the little shiver of wind which came up from the sea every now and then and shook the shrubs and palms growing along that road. Something seemed missing. My brothers and sisters looked out the windows at us, high up they seemed. They called me into the house.

Sometimes I can see her. She is at the kitchen table, seated in a pool of silence and light that is coming in the window. She is writing those long distance letters.

And I have in my mind a picture of a ship. It is of a ship out on a horizon. A man on shore watches the ship. The ship is out yonder and there is a story it would tell. He knows that. It would tell him about all that is to befall those on land. But it keeps its silence. The ship is sealed in the bubble of its own story. Messages it posts, but posts to the unknown.